Praise for *New York Times* bestselling author

MARIA V
SNYD

'*Inside Out* surprised and touched me on so many levels. It's a
wonderful, thoughtful book full of vivid characters…
Maria V. Snyder is one of my favourite authors,
and she's done it again!'
—**Rachel Caine**

'A compelling new fantasy series.'
—*SFX* **magazine on** *Sea Glass*

'An intense, excellent read.'
—*Locus* **on** *Magic Study*

'There is a lovely light touch to this series reminiscent
of early Anne McCaffrey, so it's gratifying to see that
Snyder has managed to deliver the old one–two
fantasy-literature punch.'
—**Rhianna Pratchett,** *SFX* **on the** *Study* **series**

'*Storm Glass* is accessible, unusual and most of all fun.
If you're looking for a quick, entertaining summer
read, you couldn't do much better.'
—*Deathray*

MARIA V.
SNYDER

TOUCH OF
POWER

Published in Great Britain 2012
MIRA Books, an imprint of Harlequin (UK) Limited,
Eton House, 18-24 Paradise Road, Richmond, Surrey, TW9 1SR

© Maria V. Snyder 2012

ISBN 978 1 848 45065 3

58-0112

MIRA's policy is to use papers that are natural, renewable and recyclable products and made from wood grown in sustainable forests. The logging and manufacturing processes conform to the legal environmental regulations of the country of origin.

Printed and bound by
CPI Group (UK) Ltd, Croydon, CR0 4YY

TOUCH OF
POWER

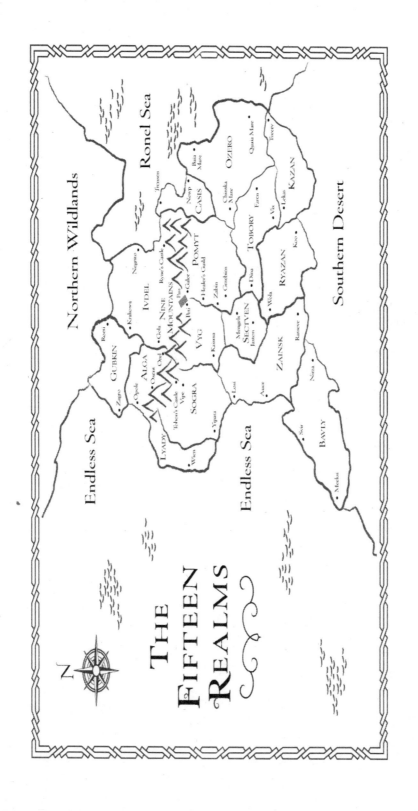

For Jenna.
I hope you enjoy your story!

CHAPTER 1

The little girl wouldn't stop crying. I didn't blame her. She was dying, after all. Her lungs were so full of fluid she'd drown in another few hours. Tossing and turning on my thin mattress, I listened to her cries as they sawed through the floorboards and through my heart, cutting it in two.

One piece pleaded for me to save her, urging me to heal the girl with the bright smile and ginger curls. The other side pulsed a warning beat. Her family would thank me by turning me in to the town watch. I'd be hanged as a war criminal. No trial needed.

The horrors from the dark years of the plague were still fresh in the survivors' minds. They considered those times a war. A war that had been started by healers, who then spread the deadly disease, and refused to heal it.

Of course it was utter nonsense. We couldn't heal the plague. And we didn't start it. But in the midst of the chaos, no one listened to reason. Someone had to be blamed. Right?

The girl's screams pierced my heart. I couldn't stand it any longer. Three years on the run. Three years of hiding. Three terrible years full of fear and loneliness. For what? My life? Yes, I live and breathe and exist. Nothing else.

Flinging my blankets off, I hurried downstairs. I didn't need to change since I would never sleep in nightclothes or without my boots on. When you were on the run, the possibility of being surprised in the middle of the night was high. There was no time to waste when escaping, so I wore my black travel pants and black shirt to bed every night. The dark color ideal for blending into shadows.

Another trick of being on the run involved finding a second-floor room with both front and back doors and no skeletons. They were hard to find as most towns had burned the plague victims' homes in the misguided attempt to destroy the disease. And many victims died alone. My current hideout was above the family with the dying child.

I knocked on my downstairs neighbors' door loud enough for the sound to be heard over the child's wet wails. When it opened, her mother, Mavis, stared wordlessly at me. She held the two-year-old girl in her strong arms, and the knowledge that her child was dying shone in her brown eyes. Her pale skin clung to her gaunt face. She swayed with pure exhaustion.

Underneath the sheen of tears and red flush of fever, the little girl's skin had death's pale hue. In a few moments, she wouldn't have the breath to scream.

I held out my arms. "Mavis, go to sleep. I'll watch… Fawn." Finally, I remembered her name. Another rule to being on the run was to avoid getting close to anyone. No friends. But I needed to earn money, and I had to make a few acquaintances in order to keep up with the gossip. I'd stayed with Mavis's children on occasion, which helped with both.

Panicked, Mavis pulled Fawn closer to her.

"The rest of your family needs you, as well. You should rest before you collapse or get sick."

She hesitated.

"I will wake you if anything changes. I promise."

Mavis's resistance crumpled and she handed me Fawn. Well beyond lucidity, the little girl didn't notice the change in the arms around her, but my magic sprang to life at the touch, pushing to be released from my core. Fawn's skin burned and her clothes were damp with sweat. I cradled Fawn as I sat in the big wooden rocking chair in the living room. The lantern burned low, casting a weak yellow light over the threadbare furniture. This family hadn't looted from their neighbors, which said much about them.

Next to the window I had a clear view of the street. A half-moon illuminated the burned ruins of buildings huddled along a dirt road. Rainwater had filled the holes and ruts. The plague had killed roughly six million people—two-thirds of the population—so there was no one left to attend to minor tasks like fixing the roads or clearing away the debris. The fact that this town…Jaxton? Or was it Wola? They all blurred together. Either way, having a local government town watch, basic commerce, no piles of skeletons and a tiny—a few hundred at most—populace was more than many other towns could claim.

I rocked Fawn, humming a tune my mother had sung to me years ago. Tendrils of my magic seeped into Fawn's body. Her cries lost the hysterical edge.

Mavis watched us for a few minutes. Did she suspect? Would she take her child back? Instead, she heeded my advice and went to bed. Waiting for Mavis to fall into a deep sleep, I rocked and hummed. Once I was certain enough time had passed, I stopped the chair. Concentrating on the girl in my arms, I allowed my full power to flow into Fawn until she was saturated with it. The release of magic sent a ripple of contentment through me. This was my area of expertise. What I should be doing.

Then I drew it back into me, cleaning out the sickness inside Fawn. My lungs filled with fluid as hers drained. I broke into a fever as hers cooled.

She hiccupped a few times, then breathed in deep. Her body relaxed and she fell into an exhausted sleep.

The sickness nestled in my chest, causing me to suck in noisy wet breaths. I couldn't pull enough air into my lungs. Goose bumps raced across my skin as a sliver of fear touched my heart. I hadn't healed anyone this sick before. Would I be strong enough? Had I waited too long to help Fawn? My own cowardice would kill me. Fitting.

The effort to breathe consumed my energy. Black and white spots swirled in my vision as I fought to stay conscious. Even though my body healed ten times faster than a regular person's, I was quite aware that it might not be fast enough.

Luckily, this wasn't that time. The crushing tightness around my ribs eased a fraction. I concentrated on the simple act of breathing.

Mavis woke me in the morning. I had fallen asleep with Fawn still in my arms.

"How did you get her to sleep? She hasn't stopped crying in days," Mavis said.

Still groggy, I searched for a good explanation. "My tuneless humming must have bored her." My voice rasped with phlegm and set off a coughing fit.

"Uh-huh." She peered at me with a contemplative purse on her lips.

"Her fever broke last night," I tried between coughs.

Unconvinced, Mavis gently lifted Fawn and transferred the girl to her crib. "You should rest, as well. You look…"

I waved off her concern. "Nothing a couple of hours of sleep won't cure." But my legs betrayed me as I staggered to my feet. Moving with care, I headed toward the door.

When I reached for the knob, Mavis said, "Avry."

I froze and glanced over my shoulder, waiting for the accusation.

"Thank you."

Nodding, I hurried from the room. The climb to my place drained all my strength. I hacked up blood as the sweat poured from my body. I needed to grab my escape bag and leave town. Now. But when I bent to retrieve the knapsack from under the bed, a wave of dizziness overwhelmed me. Instead of fleeing, I collapsed on the floor.

A part of my mind knew I only required a few hours of sleep to recover, while another part planned the quickest route out of town. A third part still worried. With good reason.

A fist pounded on the door hard enough that I felt the vibrations through my cheek. Waking with a jolt, I scrambled to my feet. A male voice ordered me to surrender. Darkness filled the room and pressed against the windowpane. I had slept all day.

Unfortunately, this situation wasn't new to me. I scooped up my escape bag and exited through the back door. Pausing on the landing, I scanned the area. Moonlight lit the wooden steps. No one blocked them. Hurrying down, I shouldered my pack and ran through the empty alley that reeked of cat urine.

A figure stood at the alley's southern exit so I turned around. Except the northern route was also blocked. The only way out was through the tight space between buildings to the street where there would no doubt be more town watchmen.

The crash of a door echoed off the bricks. Upon my landing, a man called, "Do you have her?"

The two in the alley closed in. Guess I would take my chances. I darted through the narrow opening and right into a waiting town watchman's arms.

Voices yelled, "Don't touch her skin."

"Take her pack."

"Cuff her quick."

The drowning sickness had rendered me too weak to put up much of a fight. In mere seconds, my hands were manacled behind my back. My three years on the run had ended. It was hard to tell if fear or relief dominated. At this point, both had equal sway.

The captain of the watchmen yanked my shirt off my right shoulder, exposing my healer tattoo to the crowd. It appeared as if the entire town had gathered to witness my arrest. As expected, they gasped at the proof of the monster in their midst. And to think, I had once been proud of the symbol of my profession—a simple circle of hands. From a few feet away, it resembled a daisy with hand-shaped petals.

I scanned faces as the watchmen congratulated themselves on their *catch*. Mavis and her husband stood among the gawkers. He glared and approached me, dragging Mavis along. She wouldn't meet my gaze. Little Fawn clung to her mother's leg.

"It doesn't matter that you saved my girl's life," the husband said. "Your kind is responsible for millions of deaths. And the gold your execution will bring this town is sorely needed."

True. Tohon of Sogra placed a bounty of twenty golds

for every healer caught and executed. I suspect the plague killed one or more of his loved ones. Otherwise, why would a powerful life magician care? The disease certainly didn't care, eliminating people without rhyme or reason.

Right before I was escorted to the jail, Fawn waved bye-bye to me. I smiled. My empty, pointless life for hers. Not bad.

Inside the town watch's station house I endured endless rounds of questions. They wanted me to turn over my healer cohorts. I almost laughed at that. I hadn't encountered another healer in three years. In fact, I'd guessed they had been smarter than me and had found a nice refuge to hide in while they waited for this current madness to pass.

I refused to answer their ridiculous queries, letting their voices flow past me as I concentrated on Fawn's healthy face. Eventually they removed the manacles, measured me for my coffin and locked me in a cell below ground level, promising tomorrow would be my last day. I had an appointment with the guillotine. Lovely.

At least the guards left a lantern hanging on the stone wall opposite my cell—a basic cube with iron bars on three sides and one stone wall. Equipped with a slop pot and metal bed, I had the space to myself. And no neighbors in the adjoining cells. The bedsprings squealed under my weight. My lungs wheezed in the damp air thanks to Fawn's stubborn sickness.

I wasn't as terrified as I had imagined. In fact, I was looking forward to my first solid night's sleep in three years. Ah, the little things in life.

Too bad, I didn't even get my last wish.

CHAPTER 2

A low cough woke me from a sound sleep. Instincts kicked in and I jumped to my feet before I realized where I was. In jail, awaiting execution.

"Easy," a man said. He stood near the door to my cell. Although armed with a sword, he wasn't wearing the town watch's uniform. Instead, he wore a short black cape, black pants and boots. The lantern's glow lit the strong and familiar features of his face. I remembered him from the crowd that gawked at my arrest.

I waited.

"Are you truly a healer?" he asked.

"You saw the tattoo."

"For a town on the edge of survival, twenty golds is a considerable sum. I've learned that desperate people do desperate things, like tattoo an innocent person. Is that what happened to you?" He leaned forward as if my answer was critical.

"Who wants to know?" I asked.

"Kerrick of Alga."

I'd thought he was a town official, but the Realm of Alga was north of the Nine Mountains. If he wasn't lying, then he had traveled far from his home. "Well, Kerrick of Alga, you can go back to your bed and rest easy. The watchmen caught the right girl...and by tomorrow this town will be safe once again." Which wasn't entirely true. At twenty years of age, I wouldn't call myself a girl, but *woman* sounded too...formal.

"What is your name?" he asked.

"Why do you care?"

"It's important." He sounded so sincere and he stared at me as if I held *his* fate in my hands.

I huffed. What did it matter now? "Avry."

"Of?"

"Nowhere. It doesn't matter. Not anymore."

"It does."

"Of Kazan. Happy?"

Instead of answering, Kerrick clutched the bars with both his hands and leaned his forehead against them for a moment. I had thought he felt guilty about my impending execution, but his recent behavior failed to match.

When he knelt on one knee, worry replaced curiosity. He withdrew long metal picks from a pocket. I backed away as fear swirled. Should I yell for the guards? What if he already had knocked them out?

He unlocked the cell. The door swung open. By this time, I had reached the back wall.

Straightening, he gestured. "Come on."

I didn't move.

"Do you want to be executed?"

"Some things are worse than death," I said.

"What... Oh. I won't hurt you. I promise. I've been searching for a healer for two years."

Now I understood. "You want the bounty for yourself."

"No. You're worth more alive than dead." He paused, knowing he had said the *wrong* thing. "I meant, I need you to heal someone for me. Once he's better, you can go back into hiding or do whatever you'd like." Although muffled, raised voices and the sounds of a commotion reached us. Kerrick glanced to his left. "But if you don't come right now, there won't be another chance." He held out his hand.

I hesitated. Trust a complete stranger or remain in jail and be executed in the morning? If he was sincere, Kerrick's offer meant I would have my life back. My life on the run. Not appealing, but that survival instinct, which had spurred me on these past three years, once again flared to life. What if he was lying? I'd deal with it later. Right now, it didn't matter; living suddenly took precedence over dying.

I grabbed his hand. Warm calloused fingers surrounded mine. He tugged me down the corridor. I hadn't been paying close attention when I had arrived, but I knew this way led to more cells. There was one door into the jail. And loud noises emanated from that direction. Fear twisted. Crazy how a few hours ago I hadn't cared if I lived or died, but now a desperate need to live consumed me.

Our way dead-ended, but Kerrick pushed open the last cell's door. Moonlight and cold air streamed from a small window high on the stone wall.

Kerrick whistled like a night robin. A young man poked his head though the opening. "What took you so long?" he asked, but didn't wait for an answer as he reached both hands out.

"Grab his wrists," Kerrick said as he boosted me up.

I clasped wrists with him. He pulled me through the window with surprising speed and strength for a skinny kid. His feat was due to the two men holding his legs. He reached in for Kerrick and I noticed the window had been covered with iron bars at one time. The stumps of the bars appeared as if they had rusted right through.

Glancing around, I understood why these men had used this window. The back of the jail faced a pasture and stable for the watchmen's horses. Since the jail marked the edge of town, there were no other buildings behind it. Just the well-used north-south trade route.

Kerrick joined us. A crash echoed, a man cursed and then the pounding drum of many boots grew louder, heading toward us.

"Belen." Kerrick sighed the name.

"Flee or fight?" the young man asked.

Kerrick glanced at me. "Flee."

After hopping the pasture's fence, we raced to the woods. The herd of watchmen behind us sounded as if they would tread on my heels at any moment. The last remnants of the drowning sickness impeded my breathing and I gasped for air. For a second, I marveled that Fawn had lived as long as she had.

When we reached the edge of the forest, Kerrick shouted, "Become one with nature, gentlemen. We'll meet at the rendezvous point." He snatched my hand.

Kerrick led me through the dark woods, but my passage sounded loud compared to his. However, my stumbling noises became undetectable when the watchmen chasing us burst into the woods. The cracks of breaking branches and crunching leaves dominated.

They soon settled and moved with care, pausing every couple of minutes to listen for us. Holding their lanterns high, they spread into a line. I counted twenty points of light. Kerrick stopped when they did, but our progress remained agonizingly slow. I feared my recapture was imminent unless we encountered a Death Lily first and it consumed us. I shuddered at the thought. I'd rather go to the guillotine than be snatched by a man-eating plant.

"There they are," a voice called.

I froze, but Kerrick seized my shoulders, ordered me to stay quiet and flung us to the ground. We rolled through the underbrush. A strange vibration pulsed through my body. The sounds of pursuit approached. Convinced they would trample us, I clung to him as my world spun. We halted with me flat on my back.

Kerrick covered me from view. He kept most of his weight on his elbows. He peered to our right. Shadows bounced as boots stepped near us. A few watchmen came within inches.

My throat itched with the need to cough. I suppressed the overwhelming desire to squirm, to yell, to scratch. Then the rustling of leaves and tread of boots faded. I relaxed, but Kerrick kept his protective position.

"Once they realize they lost us, they will come back," he said.

So I remained still despite the cold dampness from the recent rains soaking into my clothes. Despite Kerrick's warm body pressed against mine. Despite his intoxicating scent tickling my nose. He smelled of living green, moist earth and spring sunshine. Two of the three made sense, since leaves and dirt covered his clothes as well as mine. I couldn't explain the sunshine. The fall season was in full swing. I suspected my lack of sleep played a role in altering my senses.

To distract myself from my uncomfortable position and his closeness, I watched the moon descend through the trees. It would set soon, leaving us in total darkness for a few hours.

As Kerrick had predicted, the watchmen returned. Light swept dangerously close. Footsteps crunched nearby. My heart thumped so loud, I swore it would give us away. And just when I wanted to scream, they were gone.

We waited for a while, listening for many nerve-racking minutes...hours...days. Or so it seemed. Finally, Kerrick stood and pulled me to my feet. I swayed. Icy air clawed at my skin through my wet clothes.

He scanned the sky. "We need to put as much distance between us and Jaxton before sunrise," he said. "Can you keep up?"

I drew in a deep breath, testing my lungs. The drowning sickness had finally gone. "Yes."

"Good." He took my hand.

A tingle spread up my arm. I debated breaking his hold, but Kerrick moved through the forest with confidence. Once the moon set, the trail disappeared. Kerrick slowed our pace, but otherwise he continued on as if he could see in the dark, leaving me stumbling in his wake.

By the time the sun rose, I had lost all sense of direction, I was frozen and exhausted. Trusting this stranger seemed like a good idea in the middle of the night, but in the light of day, I questioned my judgment. What would stop Kerrick from turning me in for the bounty after I healed his friend? Nothing. His promise not to hurt me hadn't included his accomplices. Still, for now, my head remained attached to my shoulders. A positive thing. I decided to stay alert and stick to my own survival instincts—taking it one problem at a time.

As daylight lit the red, yellow and orange colors of the forest, Kerrick increased his pace. I dug in my heels and tried to extricate my hand from his, but he wouldn't let go.

Stopping to glance at me in annoyance, he asked, "What's the matter?"

"I need to rest. Healers are not indestructible. If I'm too weak, I won't be able to cure your friend."

While he considered, I studied him. The color of his eyes matched the forest—russet with flecks of gold, orange and maroon. Blond streaks shot through his light brown hair. Most of his shoulder-length locks had escaped a leather tie. He was five inches taller than my own five-foot-eight-inch height. And I guessed he was five to ten years older than me.

"It's too dangerous to be out in the open. We're not far from the rendezvous point," he said.

"How long?"

"Another hour. Maybe two. If you'd like, I can carry you."

"No. I'll be fine."

He quirked a smile at my quick reply, causing his sharp features to soften just a bit. Some women might think him pleasing to the eye in a rugged way. Four thick scars—two on each side of his neck appeared to be bite marks from some beast.

As he pulled me along, I wondered what animal had had its teeth around Kerrick's throat. The ufa were reported to be thriving and breeding like rabbits. Feeding off the plague victims' dead bodies, the large carnivore possessed the strength and pointed canines to rip open a man's throat. Packs of them lived in the southern foothills of the Nine Mountains.

After another hour of hiking, I lost all feeling in my feet. I stumbled. Kerrick grabbed my arm, preventing me from falling.

"Another two miles," he said.

"Just…give me…a minute," I puffed while he didn't have the decency to even appear winded. "Aren't you tired?"

"No." He gazed at the surrounding forest. "In the past two years, I've walked thousands of miles, searching for a healer."

"No horses?"

"No. They're too big to hide." Seeing my confusion, he added, "We didn't want anyone to know about our mission. Healers are skittish."

"Most prey are."

"True."

"How many healers did you find in those two years?" I asked.

He met my gaze. "One."

My heart twisted. "But you heard of others. Right?"

"Yes. Pattric of Tobory, Drina of Zainsk, Fredek of Vyg and Tara of Pomyt."

Tara had been my mentor. I had lost track of her where-abouts during the awful plague years. "And?" I dreaded the answer.

"Executed before we could reach them."

Even though I'd braced for it, the news slammed into me. I sank to the ground and covered my face with my hands. My little delusion that the healers had been holed up together burst. They hadn't deserved their fate. Grief rolled through me, jamming at the base of my throat.

When the waves settled, I asked, "Anyone else?"

"Just you."

"How did you find me?"

"Later. We need to keep moving. It's not far." He pulled me to my feet.

In a daze, I followed him. My hands and feet were numb. It was a shame I couldn't say the same for my heart. There hadn't been many healers before the plague—about a hun-dred. When my family had learned that Tara agreed to take me in as her student, we'd all been excited. My tattooing ceremony had been the best moment of my life.

Kerrick's voice jerked me from my memories.

"In here," he said, gesturing to a narrow opening between two oversize boulders.

I glanced around. The stones were part of a larger rock fall, resting at the base of a steep cliff.

Kerrick grabbed my wrist, tugging me along as he

squeezed through the gap. Probably afraid he'd lose me. I guess I couldn't blame him. If I had been searching so long, I'd be extra-protective, as well.

We entered a dark cave. The wet smell of limestone mixed with the acrid odor of bat droppings. Lovely. Kerrick paused to let our eyes adjust. After a few minutes, I noticed a yellow glow coming from our left. He turned in that direction and soon we arrived at a small chamber.

A campfire burned in the center of a ring of stones. The two leg-holders from last night's rescue sat beside it. They scrambled to their feet with wide smiles when they noticed us.

"Loren, why didn't you post a guard?" Kerrick asked the man on our right.

The men exchanged a glance.

"I did," Loren said.

Kerrick flung me at him. "Watch her. Quain, you're with me." He pulled his sword and left with Quain right behind him.

In the tense silence, Loren studied me. "I'm watching. Are you going to do any tricks?"

I searched his expression, gauging if he was serious or not. "I can juggle."

Interest flared in his blue eyes. "How many balls?"

"Five."

"Impressive. Anything else?"

"Six scarves, but it can't be windy. And three daggers."

"Ohh. That would be something to see. Too bad Kerrick would never allow it."

"Why not?"

"You might cut yourself."

"So? I'm a healer."

"Exactly. You're the last one. From now on, our sole pur-pose is to protect you."

The last one. Loren's words sliced through me. Hard enough to be a healer, but to be the sole survivor increased the pressure and the fear. At least these men appeared to be safeguarding me. After all, they had rescued me from certain death. Loren's pleasant expression seemed genuine. He was older than Kerrick. Maybe thirty-five. His black hair had been cut so short, the strands stood straight up.

"What happens *after* I heal your friend?" I asked.

"You'll be a hero," he said.

CHAPTER 3

"Everyone hates healers, so why would healing your friend make me a hero?" I asked Loren.

"We don't hate you. And when he's better, he's going to—"

Loud voices interrupted him. Kerrick and Quain returned with the young man who had pulled me from the jail between them. The boy's long brown hair hung in his eyes, but it didn't cover his chagrined expression.

"What happened?" Loren asked.

"He fell asleep," Kerrick said. "Why would you assign him first shift?"

"He offered."

"He's sixteen, Loren. He's been awake all night."

"And so have we."

"Yet you were still awake when I arrived. Why's that?" Kerrick's flat tone was scarier than if he'd been shouting.

"We couldn't sleep. We were concerned about you and the healer," Loren said.

"So was I," the young man said.

"Yet you were fast asleep," Kerrick said. "You're growing,

Flea. Don't volunteer for the first shift until you're twenty. Understand?"

"Yes, sir."

Kerrick glanced around the chamber. "Has Belen arrived?"

"No," Quain answered. He swept a hand over his bald head as if he could smooth away the lines of worry etched into his brow. He had no visible weapons, yet Kerrick had taken him as backup. Perhaps the thick muscles barreled around his chest, shoulders and upper arms were all the weapons he needed. I guessed he was close to my age.

"Everyone get a few hours' sleep. Flea, make sure our… guest is comfortable. I'll stand guard," Kerrick said. He strode from the room without waiting to see if his orders were obeyed.

Flea shot me a lopsided grin. Between the locks of unkempt hair, humor sparked in his light green eyes. "Would you like to sleep on the right or left side of the fire, ma'am?" he asked.

"There's no need for formalities. My name's Avry." I stood near the fire, letting my hands and feet soak in the warmth.

"Oh, I know," Flea said. "Avry of Kazan Realm. We've been looking for you for ages."

The three men stared at me. "Should I juggle now?" I asked Loren.

He laughed, breaking the awkwardness. "Sorry, but it's hard to believe that we caught up to you. That you're standing here. With us. We've been following your, ah, adventures for almost a year."

I hadn't suspected. That alarmed me. "How?"

"Rumors, mostly," Quain said. "We'd hear about a child being healed in various towns across the Fifteen Realms. By the time we'd arrived, you were gone. A couple of times you were spotted leaving so we at least had a direction to follow. Sometimes we just had to guess which way you'd go."

"Pure luck we were in Jaxton when you were arrested," Flea said.

"Not really," Loren said. "Kerrick started catching on to her pattern a few months ago."

"My pattern?"

"Heading generally northwest, and stopping only in the bigger settlements. You'd last about…six, maybe eight weeks before healing a child and taking off." Loren settled on his bedroll next to the fire.

When I thought about it, he was right. A zing of fear traveled up my spine. If I survived this mission, I would have to be extra-vigilant.

"We're really surprised you weren't caught by the locals sooner," Quain said. He unrolled his blankets.

"Why?" I turned my back to the flames, hoping to dry my damp clothes.

"We had a list of healers," Loren said. "But by the time we learned of their location, they'd been executed. We always heard the same gossip. That they had been caught by doing something stupid."

"Like healing a child," I said. My obvious weakness. Although I'd tried hard to avoid it by keeping to myself and limiting how much time I spent with other people.

"Not that at all." Flea fussed with his bedroll. "You're the only one who was smart enough to take off after you healed a kid. The other healers figured the grateful person or parent wouldn't turn them in. They didn't bother to disguise themselves like you, either."

I tucked a short strand of blond hair behind my ear. Some disguise. I cut my hair and dyed it. I still used my own name. It was amazing I hadn't been arrested sooner. But then I remembered what Loren had said. "How did you get a list of healers?"

He shrugged. "Kerrick had it. He probably raided one of the old town halls for the records. Didn't the healers have a guild before?"

Before always meant pre-plague. "Yes." But my name shouldn't have been on it.

My apprenticeship with Tara had started when I turned sixteen—mere months before the first outbreak. Once the sickness raced across the Realms, she stopped teaching me. Instead of earning my membership in the Guild, I returned to Lekas, my home town in Kazan, to find my family gone. They were either dead or had left. None of the living could tell me. And when the rumors about the healers grew into accusations and turned into executions, no one wished to talk. I had spent my seventeenth birthday hiding in a mud puddle as my neighbors and former friends hunted for me. After three years with no word about my family, I'd lost all hope of ever finding them or even knowing what happened to them.

I glanced around the small cavern. A couple of leather rucksacks slumped in a corner, but other than stone walls and a fist-size opening in the ceiling high above our heads, there was nothing else.

At least the cave was warm and dry. However, I eyed the hard ground with dread, longing for my knapsack. It had held my thin bedroll, money, some travel rations and my cloak.

Flea finished setting up his blankets. But instead of settling in, he swept an arm out. "Ma'am, uh, Avry, your bed awaits."

I jerked in surprise. "No need to give up your—"

"Kerrick said to make you comfortable. If I don't, he'll kill me. Besides—" he flashed me that lopsided grin again "—these are Kerrick's."

"Won't he be mad?" From the way his men acted, he appeared to be someone you don't want to be angry with you.

"No," Quain said. "There is always one of us on watch. When he wakes me to take my turn, he'll just sleep in mine."

Loren hooked a thumb at the packs in the corner. "He can also use Belen's."

The men all sobered at the name.

"He's the one who provided the distraction last night," I said, guessing.

"Yeah," Flea said. His shoulders drooped and he hung his head so his hair covered his eyes. "He probably got lost or something."

"Belen doesn't get lost," Quain said. "He's probably leading the town watchman on a merry chase."

"How long will we wait for him?" I asked Quain.

"Not long."

"Why not?"

"Because you're more important than him. Hell, to Kerrick you're more important than all of us, and the longer we stay here, the greater the danger."

As I lay on Kerrick's bedroll, I breathed in his scent. That same mix of spring sunshine and living green. It felt as if the earth embraced me in her warmth. I cuddled deep into the blankets, letting the shock of being the last healer fade into an ache under my heart. And allowing all the questions I had for Kerrick and his men to be pushed aside for now.

A shout woke me from a deep sleep. I felt safe, which was odd considering my circumstances. The fire had died to embers and the other bedrolls were empty. Alarmed, I jumped to my feet. Voices yelled and echoed from the only direction of escape. I was trapped.

As the noise level increased, I backed away until I stood at the far wall. Something large and dark blocked the narrow entrance. If I could, I would have climbed the rough wall. My first impression was that an angry bear had returned to his cave and he wasn't happy to find it occupied. The second and more accurate but no less terrifying was a giant man who looked like he could wrestle a bear one-handed and win.

When he spotted me…not quite cowering against the far wall, he grinned.

"There you are," he said in a reasonable tone. He crossed the cavern in two strides and held out his hand. "Belen of Alga." Kerrick and his men followed behind him. All sported smiles.

As I shook Belen's oversize paw, er, hand, I noted he was from Kerrick's Realm. "Avry."

"Nice to meet you finally. Here." He thrust my knapsack into my hands. "I hope this is yours. Otherwise, I went to a lot of trouble for nothing."

"You shouldn't have risked going back for her pack," Kerrick said.

Belen frowned at him. "Nonsense. She needs her things." He gestured. "Winter's coming and she doesn't even have a cloak. You probably didn't even think to give her yours."

"I was a little busy saving her life."

Loren and Quain hid their amusement at Kerrick's annoyed and slightly peevish tone.

"Well, she's going to need what little she has if we're going to travel through the Nine Mountains before the first blizzard."

I clutched my pack to my chest. "The Nine Mountains? Why?" The plague had destroyed all form of organized government in the Fifteen Realms. It had taken a couple years before the survivors had grouped together to form the small clusters we had now. Law in Realms like Kazan and most others had ceased to be.

Too busy dodging bounty hunters, I hadn't paid attention to our current political situation, but even I'd heard that marauders had settled into the foothills of the Nine Mountains. Gangs who warred with one another and set their own rules to suit themselves. And if you managed to avoid them, the ufa packs would hunt you down.

"Didn't he tell you?" Belen jerked a thumb at Kerrick.

"No time last night for idle chat," Kerrick snapped. "Our sick friend is on the other side of the Nine Mountains."

It would take us more than two months to reach him. "How sick? He might not last."

"He's been encased in a magical stasis."

Interesting. There weren't that many magicians left. I wondered how long it took Kerrick to find one. "By a life magician?"

"No. A death magician."

Even rarer. I considered. "How bad is your friend? If he's on the edge of dying, I won't be able to help him."

"He's pretty healthy. Sepp was able to pause his life force just after he began the second stage."

The second stage? Dread wrapped around me. Had the plague returned? As far as I heard, there hadn't been any more victims in two years. Then I remembered Kerrick had been searching for me at least that long.

"He has the plague. Doesn't he?" I asked.

"Yes," Belen said. "We know you can heal him. With the whole world dying, how could a hundred of you save six million of them? You couldn't. The Healer's Guild sent that missive so they could organize their healers, set up a response based on need, but that's all in the past, Avry. It's only one sick man."

"But—"

Kerrick interrupted, "Belen, do you need to rest?"

"No, sir."

"Gentlemen, prepare to go," Kerrick said.

His men scrambled to pack. I checked my knapsack. All my belongings remained inside. I removed my cloak, draping it around my shoulders.

Should I tell them the real truth about the plague? They had saved me from the guillotine and I owed them my life. They seemed receptive to reason, unlike all the other survivors I'd encountered, who, at the mere mention of a healer, spat in the ground and refused to acknowledge the truth. I'd almost been caught a number of times defending healers so I'd stopped trying.

However, Belen was right. I could heal their friend of the plague, but then I couldn't heal myself.

What they asked of me would be essentially trading one death—swift and certain—for another—slow, painful and just as certain.

I decided to wait and learn who their friend was. Perhaps he would be like Fawn, worth my life to save. Hard to imagine. Children deserved to be saved. They hadn't lived, hadn't made bad choices and hadn't had time to harm others. That couldn't be said of a grown man, but I was willing to give him the benefit of the doubt.

Kerrick set a quick pace through the forest, heading north. Rays of the late-afternoon sun pierced the tree canopy, leaving pools of shadows on the ground. The crisp air smelled clean and fresh.

We walked in a single line. I stayed behind Belen, and Flea trotted at my heels like an overeager puppy. No one said a word. Leaves crunched under my boots, drowning out the slight noise the others made. The men held their weapons ready as if expecting an ambush at any moment. Kerrick and Belen held swords, Loren kept an arrow notched in his bow, Quain palmed a nasty curved dagger and even Flea brandished a switchblade.

Traveling through the Fifteen Realms was difficult, if not impossible, for small groups. When I moved to a new town, I'd try to hook up with a pilgrimage—a caravan of people searching for lost friends and relatives, collecting needed items from abandoned houses and burying any dead bodies left behind. Even well armed, a pilgrimage still kept to the major roads between Realms.

So it wasn't a surprise that in the middle of the forest, we encountered no one. No Death or Peace Lilys grew near our path, either. Odd that the gigantic flowers were nowhere to be seen. With the lack of manpower to cull them, they had spread like weeds everywhere, and had invaded farm fields, adding to the survivors' struggle to feed ourselves.

Unused to the pace, I tired after a few hours. We stopped a couple times to eat, but it was always in silence and didn't last long. My legs ached and eventually all I could focus on was Belen's broad back.

The sun set and the moon rose. It had climbed to the top of the sky when I reached my limit. Stumbling, I tripped over my own feet and sprawled among the colorful leaves.

Before I could push up to my elbows, Belen scooped me into his arms. He carried me like a baby despite my protests, claiming I weighed nothing. Exhausted, I dozed in his arms.

By dawn, I had reenergized. That was when I felt his injury. I squirmed from his arms and pulled his right sleeve up to his elbow.

"It's nothing," he said, trying to pull the fabric down and

cover the six-inch-long gash in his forearm before Kerrick and the others could see.

I stopped him with a stern look, then traced the wound with a finger as magic stirred to life in my core. The cut was deep and dirty—borderline infected. Belen kept his face neutral, although I knew my rough examination had to hurt like crazy. Impressive.

"Belen?" Kerrick asked.

"It's just a cut I got stirring up the town watch the other night. Nothing to worry about."

"It's going to get infected if it's not taken care of," I said.

"Can it wait until we find shelter?" Kerrick asked me.

"I can heal him now. It doesn't matter."

"That's not what I asked you. Can it wait or not?"

"How long?"

"A few hours."

No sense arguing with him. "It can wait."

There was really no reason to wait. I wouldn't let Belen carry me, but I rested my hand on the crook of his right arm. As we walked, I let the magic curl around his forearm, healing his wound as it transferred to me. The cut throbbed and stung as blood soaked my sleeve.

By the time we arrived at another cave to rest for the afternoon, Belen's injury had disappeared. Loren, Quain and Flea gathered around him, exclaiming over his smooth skin.

"There's not even a scar!" Flea hopped around despite having walked for the past twenty hours. I suspected this behavior was linked to his name.

Kerrick, though, strode over to me and yanked my sleeve up, exposing the half-healed gash. I hissed as he jabbed it with a finger.

"Why didn't you listen to me?" he demanded.

"There was no reason—"

"You don't make those decisions," he said. A fire burned in his gaze. "I do."

"But—"

He squeezed my arm. I yelped.

"No arguments. You follow my orders. Understand?"

Silence blanketed the cavern as everyone stared at us.

"I understand." And I did, but that didn't mean I would obey him like one of his gentlemen.

"Good." He gazed at his men. "Standard watch schedule."

Once Kerrick left the cave, Flea bounded over to me. "Look at that! It's the same size and shape as Belen's was."

Interesting how the men were more relaxed when Kerrick wasn't around.

"How long until it heals?" Belen inspected the cut as if my arm would break at the slightest touch. Concern in his brown eyes.

"About two days for it to fade into a pale scar."

Flea whooped and Quain looked impressed.

"You didn't need to heal me," Belen said. "It was just a minor cut."

I pulled my arm from Belen. "And you didn't need to risk capture by retrieving my knapsack. Consider it my way of saying thanks."

Loren met my gaze with an amused smile.

"Better than juggling knives?" I asked him.

"I'd have to see you juggle the knives first," he said.

"Gentlemen, your knives." I held out my hands.

After a brief hesitation, Loren, Quain and Flea all provided me with a leather-handled dagger. Perfect.

"When Kerrick catches you, I'll make sure to shed a few tears at your funerals," Belen said. He shook his head as if distancing himself from the whole thing.

I tested the weight of each knife. My older brother, Criss,

had taught me how to juggle. First with scarves, then balls, and then wooden sticks before he'd let me throw anything sharp. A pang of sadness touched my chest as I juggled the daggers. The firelight reflected off the silver blades as they twirled in the air. Flea enjoyed the show, laughing and begging to be taught when I finished.

"Not bad," Loren said. "But most anyone can learn how to juggle. No one else can heal."

Later that night we settled next to the fire. The men moved about in an easy routine, hardly speaking as they cooked the rabbits Loren had shot with his bow.

"Have you been doing this every night for two years?" I asked them.

Loren and Quain exchanged a glance with Belen.

"Not quite," Belen said. "Kerrick and I started searching for a healer right after the magician encased our friend. Six months in, we encountered those two monkeys in Tobory." He jabbed a thick finger at Loren and Quain. "Getting the snot beat out of them." Belen chuckled. It was a deep rumbling sound.

Quain jumped to their defense. "We were outnumbered!"

"Didn't stop you from rushing that whor—" Belen shot me a look. "That brothel."

"It's not a brothel when the girls are *forced* to be there," Loren said with a quiet intensity.

Another reminder of our world gone mad. Not all survivors desired a return to normal. Some took full advantage of the depleted security and turned small towns into their own playgrounds.

"What happened?" I asked.

"We lent a hand," Belen said. "Helped clean out that nest

of nasties, got the town back on track and picked up those two for our trouble."

"We're returning the favor," Loren said.

"Uh-huh." Belen stretched out on his blankets, sighed and was soon snoring.

Considering how long he'd been awake, it was amazing he'd lasted that long.

My bedroll was close to Flea's. He had been practicing the first step in learning how to juggle, tossing a stone from one hand to another. Flea mastered the motion of throwing the rock up to his eye level and letting it drop down to his other hand, making a path through the air like an inverted V while keeping both hands near his waist. I showed him the next step. Same motion, but using two rocks—trickier.

After a few tries, he started to get it. "That's it, Flea. When the first stone is at the tip of the V, you throw the second." I made encouraging noises.

He worked a while longer, then flopped back onto his blankets. "It's too hard."

Flea reminded me of my younger sister, Noelle. She would give up right away if a task proved too difficult. I wondered if she had gotten the plague and died just as quick.

No one who contracted the disease survived. Except those very first people the healers cured before they in turn died. Back when we hadn't known it would become a plague. There had been enough sanity for the Healer's Guild to send out notice to their members *not* to heal anyone who had those symptoms. Not even if there were a couple healers to share energy. It had been a logical decision. There were more sicknesses than healers. And it made sense to heal the ones we could. But that notice had been what condemned us all to death. Or rather, the wording of that missive. It hadn't clearly stated that a healer would die if he helped a plague victim. It had said, "Success was unlikely at this time."

I suppressed those dark thoughts, concentrating instead on the positive. Being with these men had renewed my interest in life. They'd been traveling throughout the Fifteen Realms, perhaps they'd heard of my family. Except Loren and Quain had also fallen asleep. Only Flea stared morosely at the cave's ceiling.

"Don't fret," I said. "With more practice, you'll be juggling in no time."

He groaned. "That's what those guys say all the time. Practice, practice, practice. It's boring!"

I hid my smile. "You're right."

He sat up. "I am?"

"It's very boring. Unfortunately, it's necessary."

Groaning, he plopped back onto his pillow. He waved a listless hand. "You can stop the lecture. I've got four fathers. I don't need a mother."

I gasped in mock horror. "You're right. I'm sounding like my mother! I promise never to do it again."

"Really?" Flea squinted at me.

"No. Sorry. An overdeveloped nurturing instinct comes with being a healer."

He shrugged. "Oh, well. I guess everyone has their faults."

"True."

He pushed up to an elbow and looked at me for a moment. "Do you like being a healer? That cut you took from Belen had to hurt."

"It does, but for less time than it would have hurt him." Plus there was the satisfaction of helping another.

Flea huffed. "I don't think Belen feels pain. I kicked him hard in the shins one time and he didn't even blink."

"Why did you kick him?"

"He wouldn't let me go." Flea's eyelids drooped and he yawned.

I sensed a longer story, but I stifled my curiosity. Instead, I gently pushed him down and pulled the blanket up to his chin.

Flea gave me a sleepy half smile and said, "Belen won't let you go, either."

It was an odd statement and he noticed my concern.

"Not like that… Once you heal Prince Ryne, you won't *want* to go."

I jerked wide awake. "Prince Ryne of Ivdel Realm? *He's* your friend? The one who's sick?"

"Yeah, he—"

"Flea, go to sleep," Kerrick said from behind me.

Flea grimaced an oops and turned onto his side.

Oops was putting it mildly. I gathered my belongings.

"What are you doing?" Kerrick asked. His voice low and deadly.

"Leaving."

"No."

"I'm not asking. I'm going." I rolled up my thin mat and stuffed it into my knapsack.

"No, you're not."

Slinging my pack over my shoulder, I faced him. "There is no reason for me to stay. Go find another healer."

"No."

It was like talking to the rock wall. I raised my voice. "Let me make this perfectly clear. I will *not* heal Prince Ryne. Nothing you do or say will change my mind."

The men stirred awake. Fury sparked in Kerrick's eyes.

"Easy, Kerrick," Belen said, sitting up.

"You *will* heal him." Kerrick's dangerous tone warned me not to argue, but I wouldn't back down.

"Never."

"That's enough, Avry." Belen stood. "We can discuss this in the morning."

"There's nothing to discuss," I said. "I'm not healing him. In fact, I'm glad he's locked in stasis where he can't hurt anyone ever again. The only thing that would make me happier is his *death*."

I'd gone too far. With a strangled cry, Kerrick lost his temper. Belen lunged toward Kerrick and I raised an arm to block Kerrick's strike, but we were both too slow. Kerrick backhanded me across my cheek. The force of the blow sent me to the ground.

CHAPTER 4

My cheek stung and throbbed. I remained on the floor of the cave. Belen stood between me and Kerrick.

"...temper in check. She's a sweet girl," Belen said.

"She's a healer, Belen. And no longer a girl. Healing Ryne is *all* I care about. *All* you should care about, as well. You know—"

"Yes, I know what's at stake." Belen spat the words. "But if you raise your hand to her again, I'll rip your arm from its socket."

Wow. I tilted my head to catch Kerrick's expression.

A flicker of surprise flashed across his flat gaze. "Make sure she keeps her opinions of Prince Ryne to herself and I won't have to." Kerrick glanced at me.

I met his cold gaze and realized I meant nothing to him. Unlike Belen, Kerrick must know I wouldn't survive healing Ryne and he didn't care.

"You *will* heal Ryne," he said before turning away. "Loren, your watch."

Loren shot to his feet. "Yes, sir." He dashed from the cavern. And I wished I could follow him.

Belen knelt next to me. He pressed a wet cloth to my cheek. "I'm sor—"

"Don't apologize for him," I said, leaning into the cool comfort of the cloth. I glanced around. By the rigid way they lay under their covers, I knew Flea and Quain pretended to be asleep. Kerrick shucked off his boots and settled into Loren's spot, ignoring us.

Belen played nursemaid, fetching me a drink of water and setting up my bedroll. I liked him. Too bad, I wouldn't be staying with them for long.

I waited for an opportunity to escape. It took two days. Two days of walking through the forests in silence and one night in yet another cave. A night I kept quiet and just listened to the men, nursing my bruised ego.

The second night's stop was far from ideal since Kerrick stopped at a big echoey cavern. I suspected he knew the location of every single cavern in the forest. But I couldn't stand being with him any longer.

"Remember when those three drunks challenged Belen to a fight?" Quain asked no one in particular during dinner and when Kerrick was out on watch.

"And Kerrick gave strict orders. No fighting or we wouldn't be able to go near a tavern again," Loren said.

Flea rolled his eyes. "I've heard this story a dozen times."

"Only a dozen?" Belen asked. He had stretched out on his back by the fire and rested his head on his crossed arms. "For some reason those two monkeys—" he gestured to Loren and Quain "—think that story bears repeating over and over again. Perhaps it's just an unfortunate manifestation of their low intelligence."

Quain snorted. "Manifestation? Oh, boy, look who's trying to impress the healer."

"He doesn't want us to finish the story. He's afraid we'll scare Avry," Loren said, trying to draw me into the conversation.

All four of them had been overly solicitous as the bruise on my cheek swelled, turned red, and faded to a mere smudge of greenish black. I reminded myself that *they* hadn't struck me. No need to hate *them*.

"I'm not that easy to scare," I said. "What happened with the drunks?"

"He clapped all three of their heads together, knocking them out. Thus, no fight," Quain said.

"Thus? Now look who's flinging the fancy words around," Loren said.

"*Thus* is not fancy," Quain shot back.

Flea sighed elaborately. "Here we go…again." He picked up his two rocks and practiced juggling them despite his claims of giving up the other night.

I had made sure my bedroll was close to Flea's. While Quain and Loren launched into a debate about the fanciness of certain words, I asked Flea about his name.

Keeping his gaze on the stones, he pointed his chin over to the others. "They, ah, gave me the name. Seems it was nicer than being called a parasite."

"What's your given name?" I asked.

"I don't have one. At least, not one I remember." Flea missed a stone and muttered a curse. "I grew up on the streets, thieving to survive. I've been called *boy, thief* and other uncomplimentary words." A flash of his lopsided smile. "How's that for a fancy word? *Uncomplimentary*."

"I'm suitably impressed," I said.

He managed to keep the rhythm of the throws consistent for a number of exchanges before the rocks collided in mid-air. Another curse and he started again.

"How did you get involved with this group?" I asked.

"About a year ago, they came to my town, asking questions about healers. They were discreet, but still word gets around and the local muscle didn't like them or me for selling information to Kerrick. Stealing secrets was one of my most lucrative abilities."

"It almost got you killed," Belen said.

"*That* time. I had a whole network of informers and these guys showed up and just blew it apart."

"Funny, I remember it differently." Belen tossed another log on the fire.

"You would. *Your* life and livelihood weren't at stake." Flea scratched his temple with the edge of one of his stones. "When things grew too hot, I helped them slip out of town and…" He glanced at Belen with affection, but masked it before the big man could see. "I just stayed."

"Ha. We *rescued* him from the stockade before they could hang him as a traitor. And then we stopped the idiot from going back."

Which would explain Flea's comment about kicking Belen's shins because he wouldn't let go.

"So who gave him his name?" I asked.

"Kerrick," Belen answered.

Not who I'd expect. "Why 'Flea'?"

A full-out grin spread across Flea's face. "'Cause I'm fast and hard to catch."

"Because he's a pest and hard to squash," Belen said.

"Because he jumps about three feet in the air when you scare him," Loren added.

"Because he's annoying and makes us itch with impatience," Quain said.

"Thanks, guys. I love you, too." Flea made exaggerated kissing noises and patted his ass.

They threw pieces of bread and pillows at him, laughing. I realized they had formed into a tight family. Guilt at what I'd planned welled, but it shattered the moment Kerrick entered.

I bided my time, keeping awake while Loren woke Quain for his shift and Quain roused Flea for his. After Quain's breathing settled into a deep rhythm, I crept from my covers. With one mournful look at my knapsack, I tugged my cloak around my shoulders and tiptoed away from the fire. If anyone woke, I hoped the presence of my knapsack would make them assume I had just gone to the privy—which was a stinky side cavern I hated to use.

Flea sat on the top of a large boulder a few feet away from the cave's entrance. As soon as he spotted me, he immediately slid down the side.

"What's wrong?" he asked in a whisper.

"Nothing. I just needed some fresh air."

"You shouldn't be out here."

"Is there anyone around?" It would be a surprise if there were. Since I'd been with Kerrick and his men, I'd seen no one at all, yet they still carried their weapons at the ready.

"Not close, but there's a group of merchants—we hope— about two miles due east of here. See the fire?" He pointed.

I squinted into the darkness. We stood on a slight rise. A tiny pinprick of orange-yellow dotted the mound of trees.

"How do you know they're merchants?"

"Wagons loaded with goods, horses and armed guards. They could be mercenaries, but they have too much…stuff. Mercenaries usually travel lighter."

"How do you know all this?"

Flea grinned. "Kerrick's already checked them out and determined they're probably harmless. We have to be more careful now. I'm sure the rumors about your rescue and our involvement have spread faster than the plague. Twenty golds is a huge sum. There are a few mercenary groups who would love to take you from us."

Curious, I couldn't help asking, "Can they?"

"Not many," he said with pride. "But don't worry, Avry. We're too smart to walk into an ambush."

My heart squeezed with guilt and I hesitated.

"You better get inside. If Kerrick finds you out here, I'm a goner."

"All right." I turned to go, but stopped. "Flea, don't move."

He froze. "What?"

"Kissing Spider. Hold still." I touched the back of his neck with my hand. I found the small area between the vertebrae and shot my healing power into his spine. He arched back in silent surprise before collapsing.

Catching him, I laid him down. I arranged his limbs so he would be comfortable. My stomach twisted as I pushed a lock of hair from his eyes. Healers had a few ways to defend themselves, but we hated to use them. And some, like the one I used on Flea, needed to hit the precise location or it wouldn't work.

I considered his size. He'd wake in two, maybe three hours. However, Belen's watch shift would start within an hour. I needed to go. Now.

Should I head toward the merchants and hope they'd protect me?

No. Basic survival—trust no one. I ran west.

I discovered within minutes that running full speed through the forest at night wasn't my best idea. After I wiped the dirt from my face and hands and regained my feet, I slowed my pace. It would be hard to follow my trail in the dark so I hoped Kerrick would wait until dawn.

If I was lucky, I'd have a three- or four-hour head start and wouldn't stumble into a Death Lily. If I wasn't, I'd have one hour at most or become plant food. I focused all my energy and concentration on putting as much distance between me and Kerrick as possible.

My luck held for once. When the sun's rays diluted the darkness, I was able to see better and I increased my pace until I smelled smoke. Skidding to a stop, I turned in a slow circle, seeking the direction of the fire. When I found it, I crouched and crept toward the source.

It wouldn't be good if I accidentally ran into a band of mercenaries. Better to know where they were and how many than try to guess. My progress through the underbrush was far from utter silence. However, aside from a few rustles, I managed to get close enough to see into a clearing.

I counted ten sleeping bodies around the dying fire. No horses. But one guard slumped against a tree trunk with his mouth hanging open—also asleep. Would they set two guards? I searched the surrounding woods, seeking movement. Nothing.

Satisfied, I backed away and bumped into someone. I froze as the edge of a sword touched my neck.

"Gotcha."

CHAPTER 5

"Turn around slow," the sword's owner ordered me.

I obeyed. Perhaps he didn't know who I was. Yeah, right. And perhaps this was all a dream and I would wake up in my house, surrounded by my family.

By the exultant smirk and greedy glint in his dark brown eyes, I had only the possibility that they wouldn't kill me outright.

"Put your hands where I can see them," he said. His sword still rested on my neck.

I held my hands out.

"Wake up!" he yelled. The shout roused the sleeping men in the clearing. "Today's our lucky day!"

Voices and loud calls cut through the forest. Not good. As the sounds drew nearer, I stepped back in panic.

"Relax, sweetheart. The bounty for you is double if we bring you in alive."

That stopped me. "Forty golds? Why?"

"Don't know, don't care. As long as Tohon pays us in full."

"And if he doesn't?"

"There are other interested parties. I'm sure—"

Hands wrapped around the mercenary's head and yanked. The sword's blade nicked me as a loud snap vibrated through the air. The man fell, revealing Kerrick. A scarier sight by far.

Kerrick lunged toward me. Knocking me to the ground, we rolled through the underbrush with ease. But this time, I was aware enough to realize we shouldn't be able to do that. When we stopped, Kerrick was once again on top, but this time he pressed his hand over my mouth.

After my head cleared from the spinning, I noticed Kerrick's skin and clothes matched the colors of the forest floor. Exactly. Even his hair. Magic tingled inside me as he drew it from the earth, using it to camouflage us. Kerrick must be an earth magician. Which explained so much—like how we avoided all the Lilys.

We lay there for what seemed like ages. Men's boots pounded past us. Voices called and anger over the dead mercenary rippled through the forest. My senses expanded and I felt a connection with the living essence of the forest.

To the forest, the men were invaders, a blight on a healthy organism. It knew where each irritant was located. When the men moved farther away, Kerrick yanked me to my feet. He used the forest's aversion to keep track of the mercs and escape the area without being seen, dragging me with him.

When we were far enough away, he broke the magical connection with me. I staggered with the shock of being cut off from the soothing green. He let me fall.

I regained my feet with the intention of running away, but Kerrick grabbed my wrist. By this time, his skin and hair had returned to normal.

I said, "Thanks for the help, but you're not going to change my mind about Prince Ryne."

"You'd rather be handed over to Tohon of Sogra?" he asked as if I lost my senses.

"No. I'd rather be left alone."

"Not going to happen." He tugged me along behind him like a disobedient child.

Digging in my heels would be useless so I gathered magic and sent a blast of pain into his hand on my wrist.

Instead of dropping my arm like a normal person would, he squeezed harder and pulled me toward him. More skin contact meant more pain for him. What the hell was he doing? I increased the intensity. He dropped to his knees, but kept his hold on me.

Damn it. I focused all my strength and directed it at him. He pitched over to his side, bringing me with him. Kerrick's muscles convulsed with the pain, but he still wouldn't let go.

I stopped when I had exhausted my energy. We lay locked together, panting as if we both had run for miles.

"Is that all you have?" His voice rasped. "Because you're not going to get another chance."

I ignored his comment. "Your earth magic must have protected you or else you'd be unconscious and drooling right now." Except I suspected that wasn't quite true.

"I'm not letting you go. Do you understand?"

Unfortunately, I did. "You can't force me to heal him."

"True. However, I can make you so miserable that you'll be happy to heal him in order to get away from *me*."

Fear swirled in my heart. "You promised you wouldn't hurt me. Yet—"

"I did." He stared at me a moment. "I'm sorry I hit you. I lost my temper. It won't happen again."

"I don't believe you."

"Do you really think I'd risk getting my arm torn off? Belen never makes an idle threat. And neither do I."

★ ★ ★

Kerrick kept an iron grip on my wrist, towing me at a fast pace. I jogged to keep up and was soon winded. My failed escape attempt had drained me.

Loren joined us when we neared the cave. He shot me a hard glare. "Any trouble?" he asked Kerrick.

"Mercs—at least a dozen. She walked right into them."

If I had the energy, I would have protested.

Loren glanced behind us. "Did they follow you?"

"Not yet, but they'll find our trail soon." Kerrick pulled me through the entrance and flung me down by the fire. "Get your stuff packed."

As I gathered my things, I noticed Quain's glowers and Flea's hurt-puppy pouts. Belen, though, smiled, and would have come over except Kerrick intercepted him.

"No helping her," Kerrick said.

"But—"

"That's an order, Belen."

Belen stared at him. "It won't work."

Kerrick didn't back down. "Not your decision."

The air thickened as the tension emanated from them. I stood and slung my knapsack over my shoulder. "Don't worry about me, Belen. I'll be fine."

My bravado sounded good. Even boosted my energy a bit. But after Kerrick clamped his hand around my sore wrist, and I endured another endless quick march through the forest, I began to wonder if I had been overly optimistic.

We stopped…sometime. It took me a few moments to realize we had indeed halted for the night in a tiny clearing. Kerrick only allowed me to eat half rations before manacling my hands behind a tree. The cold metal cuffs cut deep into my wrists. I leaned against the rough bark just happy to be sitting.

The men's voices surrounded me as I drifted into and out of sleep.

"...get sick." Belen's soft concern.

"...can't, she's a healer." Kerrick's dismissive bark.

I opened my mouth to educate him—healers sickened like everyone else. We just recovered faster. And if the injury was severe enough or the disease too quick, we'd die. But I pressed my lips together. Let him figure it out for himself.

The next morning, Kerrick shook my shoulders.

"I'm awake," I said when he didn't stop.

He rested his hands on my shoulders and gazed at me. "Will you heal Prince Ryne?"

"No."

Kerrick didn't say a word. He unlocked the manacles. After I gulped a few mouthfuls of bread, he reclaimed my wrist. And once again my world blurred to a smear of orange, red and yellow as I struggled to keep up with him.

That night he confiscated my cloak before securing me to a tree. Curled up on my side with my arms bent uncomfortably around the trunk, I shivered.

Voices worried over the mercenaries drawing nearer. I would have felt bad about alerting the mercs if I had the energy.

The next morning, Kerrick shook me awake. "Will you heal Prince Ryne?"

"No."

And that was my life for...I'd no idea. Wake, answer Kerrick's question, eat, hike all day, eat, doze, shiver and repeat.

Funny how a person's body could adapt to the harshest of circumstances. Eventually, I wasn't as exhausted at the end of the day. I kept up without being half dragged. But each night grew a bit cooler, and my teeth chattered a bit harder.

On the sixth—seventh?—night, I huddled close to the small fire, sucking in as much warmth as I could before Kerrick pulled me away. Flea sat next to me. He wouldn't meet my gaze and hadn't since I'd attempted to escape.

"Flea," I said.

He poked the fire, refusing to acknowledge me. I touched his arm. He yelped and jerked it away.

"Relax. I'm not going to hurt you."

He huffed, stabbing a stick deep into the embers. Bright orange sparks flew up.

"I didn't hurt you before," I tried. The neck zap didn't cause pain, just unconsciousness. "I'm sorry."

"Doesn't mean anything," Flea said. The firelight illuminated his profile. A few hairs sprang from his chin and small red pimples dotted his cheek. "You used me to escape. You pretended to like me and teach me to juggle. I was stupid to fall for it. But I won't make that mistake again."

"I wasn't pretending."

"Not listening."

"If your friend had been anyone else…"

Flea turned his back to me, asking Belen a question. Belen lounged on the other side of him.

When Kerrick hauled me over to a tree for the night, I decided I'd heal anyone else, except Kerrick. He could die a slow and painful death—preferably while cold and shackled to a tree.

The next night, I tried again. But Flea refused to talk to me. I wondered why I bothered. Guilt, I supposed. I hadn't deceived him, but I did use him to escape.

Belen had kept his distance all this time, but tonight he sat near me. "Why won't you heal Prince Ryne?" he asked.

I sensed interest from everyone even though they acted casual. Kerrick stood watch, but when we camped out in the open, he stayed closer. In other words, he could hear me so I chose my words with care. "Before the plague, he…invaded Casis Realm and burned the city of Trenson to the ground, killing thousands and leaving the rest homeless."

"That's an ugly rumor," Belen said. "Trenson's priests planned to start sacrificing nonbelievers. Ryne sent his troops in to stop them and the priests started the fire."

Hard to believe. Every major town in Casis had been ruled by a sect of priests. They wouldn't destroy their own town or they'd have nowhere else to rule. Each sect had been very territorial.

"Give me another reason," Belen said.

"He annexed the Nine Mountains. Stole all those natural resources from the Vyg Realm, which is his neighbor."

"He bought the rights to the mines. Vyg's operations were losing money so Ryne purchased the companies from the government and made them profitable. Vyg owned the land and they received twenty-five percent of the profits."

"If that's true, then he made them profitable by not spending any money on safety," I said. "He lured workers from the other Realms with promises of high wages, except he sent them into dangerous mines without the proper equipment and he wouldn't give them any time off. Hard to spend your wages when you're not allowed to leave the mines. Not even to visit your family."

Belen's gaze turned inward as if he considered my words. "There was a horrible cave-in before the plague." He took my hand. "Who did you lose?"

I jerked my hand back. "I didn't *lose* anyone. I know right where they are. They can both be found under millions of pounds of rock." I stood and planned to storm off into the woods for some privacy. But Kerrick blocked my way. I resisted the urge to punch him. Instead, I sat next to the nearest tree. He manacled my wrists.

Later that night as I curled up, I let the tears leak from my eyes. I didn't make a sound. I wouldn't give Kerrick the satisfaction. Or the hope.

On the tenth—twelfth?—night, something changed. Instead of one ladle, Kerrick filled my bowl with stew. He returned my cloak. The morning question remained, but he slowed his pace as we traveled through the forest. He stopped more often, listening, and he seemed distracted.

He had multiple whispered conversations with Belen, who kept glancing at me in concern.

Kerrick wouldn't let Belen light a fire that evening. He paced. Not a good sign. Furrows creased Quain's bald head and Flea was extra jumpy.

"What's going on?" I asked Belen.

"Mercs closing in."

"Sorry."

He waved my apology away. "They would have caught up to us eventually. They started following us soon after we left Jaxton."

I considered. "You're trying to make me feel better."

"What are you talking about?"

"We were overnighting in caves before I escaped, but since then, we've been out in the open so we don't get trapped."

Belen beamed with pride. "Smart girl."

"Not smart enough to get away from Kerrick," I mumbled.

His smile didn't falter. "No one gets away from Kerrick in the woods."

"Found that out already." I glared at Kerrick, but he didn't notice, which caused me quite a bit of alarm. Grudgingly, I admitted being Kerrick's prisoner was my best option at this moment. Which said a lot about my life.

When Kerrick stopped pacing and crouched to place his palms on the ground, my concern increased.

"We won't make it to the ravine in time," Kerrick said to the others. "We can't outrun them and they outnumber us, so we'll have to outsmart them." He issued orders.

We packed our belongings and headed north toward the ravine. After an hour or so, Kerrick stopped. When he let go of my wrist, I about fainted. He spoke with Belen in a low whisper and then thumped him on the back.

With a strange sense of doom, I watched Kerrick, Loren, Quain and Flea continue north, leaving Belen and me behind. Belen held out his arm. I hooked my hand around his elbow. We walked east.

Stopping hours later, Belen found a dent in a rocky hillside. I couldn't call it a cave as it wasn't deep enough, but it cut in just enough to protect both of us from rain or wind. However, it failed to protect us from mercenaries.

According to Belen, the plan had been for Kerrick and the others to lead the mercs north to the ravine. They could travel faster without dragging me along. Belen and I would go west and wait for them to loop back after losing the mercs.

Not a stellar plan, but one that had worked for them before. Belen filled me in on the details as we rested in the shallow shelter. It didn't take long for the mercs to find us. A noise alerted Belen. He stood, pulled his sword and stepped in front of me, blocking me from view.

I peeked around him. Six men fanned out in front of him. All armed. The seventh hung back, and the way he crinkled his nose when he met my gaze told me why this time Kerrick's plan hadn't worked.

The mercs had a magic sniffer—a person who had no

magic of his own, but could smell it in others. The stronger ones could track the scent, sometimes hours after, and these could also distinguish the types of magic by the aroma. Before the plague, magic sniffers had been employed to find children with magical powers.

There were eleven different types of magicians in the Fifteen Realms, and all but one of them were born with power. Young children and magic were a dangerous combination. The sooner a child started training, the better. Healing powers were the exception. It could lay dormant for years, undetectable by the sniffers. Mine hid until right after I had turned fifteen. My sister, Noelle, had cut her hand and this urge bloomed in my chest, tugging me to her as if I had been hooked by a fishing line. My mother had started searching for a teacher for me that day.

Belen waited for the mercs to make the first move. Even though they outnumbered him, they hesitated. Not surprising, considering he was a foot taller and two feet wider than their biggest man.

"Look," the man with the red beard said to Belen. "Just give us the girl and we'll be on our way."

"No."

I touched Belen's elbow. "Take the offer. I don't want you getting hurt."

When he didn't move, I stepped around him to give myself up. But Belen stopped me with his arm.

"Stay behind me," he growled.

No arguing with him. As my heart did flips in my chest, I thought fast.

"She's smarter than you," Red Beard said. "Last chance."

Belen tightened his grip on his broad sword—a two-handed weapon that he held easily with one hand.

"I don't suppose you have a trio of knives hidden somewhere?" I asked him.

"It's a little late for a distraction," he said.

"Juggling isn't the only thing I've learned to do with knives."

He yanked his dagger from his belt, handed it to me, then pulled another from his boot. "That's all I have."

Better than none.

"I guess that's your answer," Red Beard said. "Don't kill the girl," he ordered his men.

Red Beard stepped forward to engage Belen. Two others also joined the fight. Because Belen kept me and the rocky hillside behind him, there wasn't room for the other three, and they couldn't grab me, either.

The fierce intensity and the speed of the fight surprised me. Belen's calm demeanor remained, and for the first minute, it appeared he had the upper hand. Then the men switched places in one smooth move and now Belen faced three fresh opponents.

That was how they wore him down, by taking turns. I waited for an opportunity to throw my knives, thinking I'd hit their arm or shoulder, but no one would stand still long enough. I had always practiced with a stationary target. No reason not to; I'd never imagined I'd be in this situation in my lifetime.

When Belen's swings slowed, I knew I had to help him. Even if it was accidental, killing a person went against my nature, so I aimed low and hoped for the best. My first knife pierced one man's thigh. He yelled and staggered away from the fight. Beginner's luck didn't last as the second dagger sailed right by another man.

Then all I could do was watch as they harried Belen, tiring him out. I offered to surrender again, but he just growled.

Red Beard entered the fray again. He feinted left and dipped his thinner blade under Belen's and straight into his stomach. Belen grunted as I yelled. But he kept swinging. Red Beard continued to snake past his defenses and stab his blade's tip into Belen's gut. Eventually, Belen collapsed.

With a cry, I knelt next to him.

Blood soaked his tunic. He thrust his sword into my hands. "Don't give up."

I staggered to my feet, holding the heavy blade. The men smirked until I charged, letting my fury over Belen's injuries fuel my attack.

CHAPTER 6

The men sidestepped, avoiding the tip of Belen's sword. I turned to charge again, but this time Red Beard knocked the heavy blade aside with his, redirecting my momentum. Belen's weapon dragged me to the side. Red Beard moved in close and yanked the hilt from my hands.

Then he grabbed my upper arm. "Come on, let's go."

I resisted. "I have to heal—"

"No time. He…" Red Beard squeezed my biceps as he scanned the area.

I copied him. Glancing around, I counted five. The magic sniffer had disappeared.

"Where's Conner?" Red Beard asked his men.

At first they exchanged confused glances, but then they realized the danger. Red Beard pulled me to where Belen lay, keeping his back to the rocks and me in front of him like a shield. His men fanned out in front of us, facing toward the woods. Red Beard sheathed his sword and drew a knife. He pressed it against my throat. Without thought, I grabbed his wrist, trying to pull the weapon away from my neck, but he rumbled a warning. Stopping my efforts, I left my hand on his arm.

"I have your girl. Come out now or I'll slit her throat," Red Beard called.

Nothing.

"I can collect the bounty whether she's dead or alive."

A rustle and then Kerrick emerged from the brush. The fabric of his tunic and pants blended in with the surrounding landscape, but his face, hands and hair remained normal. I was impressed with his level of control despite myself.

The knife cut into my skin and I hissed at the sharp sting.

"Keep your hands where I can see them," Red Beard ordered.

Kerrick appeared to be unarmed. His gaze dropped to Belen's prone form, then returned to Red Beard's. "I have enough gold to pay you the bounty. Take it and go."

Red Beard laughed. "She's worth forty golds if brought in alive. I doubt—"

Moving slowly, Kerrick dipped his hand into his pocket and pulled out a black bag. Coins rattled within.

Red Beard sucked in a breath. "Axe, check it out."

One of the men snatched the bag from Kerrick. He opened it and poured gold coins into his hand. The young man's voice squeaked when he reported the count. Forty.

Red Beard tensed. "Where's my sniffer?"

"Does it matter?" Kerrick asked.

A moment passed. "No."

Just when I thought he would let me go, Red Beard tightened his hold on me. He laughed. "You're a fool," he said to Kerrick. "Now we'll get eighty golds. Forty from you and forty from Tohon."

Kerrick's gaze flickered to my hand still resting on Red

Beard's—a warning. Magic grew inside me, pushing to be released, but I waited for Kerrick's signal.

"That's rather greedy," he said in a conversational tone. Kerrick gestured to the young man drooling over the gold coins in his hand. "You're not setting the proper example for your young friend here. I would never do that. Isn't that right, Flea?"

"That's right," Flea called from above. We all glanced up. Flea, Quain and Loren stood on the rocks above.

"Now," Kerrick ordered.

I sent a blast of pain into Red Beard as Flea and the monkeys jumped down. Red Beard swore. I twisted away from his knife and held on to his arm with both hands, sending in another intense wave of pain. Red Beard collapsed onto his knees. Sounds of fighting increased for a moment before dying down. By the time Red Beard slumped to the ground unconscious, the others had been...I wish I could say disarmed, but they had been killed.

I rounded on Kerrick in outrage. But he knelt next to Belen so I swallowed my accusations. All color had fled Belen's face. His lips had turned a bluish-gray. I sank next to him and put my hand on his sweaty forehead.

"Is she safe?" he asked Kerrick.

"Yes." As usual, Kerrick showed no emotion.

Belen sighed wetly.

"No," I said. "I'm not safe, Belen. Who is going to tear Kerrick's arm off if he hits me again? Come on," I urged. "Stay with us."

Kerrick met my gaze. "Can you heal him?"

"I don't know. I need to examine the wounds."

He shot to his feet. "Gentlemen, we need a litter. Now."

The others had been hanging back, but they surged into action. I held Belen's hand. My magic swelled and pressed to be released, but I kept it in check. If he was savable, I would need complete concentration.

Faster than I thought possible, they constructed a litter. Rolling Belen onto the lattice of branches, Loren and Quain pulled the big man. We didn't go far. Kerrick knew of a cave system—of course.

The men made torches, but maneuvering the litter through the tight passages of the cave slowed our progress. I kept talking to Belen, encouraging him to keep awake and stay focused. When we reached a cavern that met Kerrick's approval, I ordered the others to build a fire and heat water. I didn't really need the water, but it gave them all something to do. Except Kerrick; he hovered over my shoulder, providing light.

I yanked Belen's shirt up. His stomach resembled a ball after a dog chewed on it. It was amazing Belen had lasted this long. The rank odor of blood, stomach acid and feces wafted off of him. Kerrick stifled a cough.

Lightly rubbing my hand over the wounds, I let my power seek how deep his injuries were. Deep. His intestines had been damaged, his stomach torn. If I healed him, there was more than a good chance I wouldn't live through it.

I settled back on my heels, considering.

"Well?" Kerrick asked.

I turned and looked at him. He might argue and disagree with Belen, but I knew Kerrick cared for his friend.

"Whose life is more important? Belen's or Prince Ryne's?"

His expression hardened. "Why are you asking?"

"Because if I heal Belen I may not survive and you'll have to find another healer for Prince Ryne."

Understanding brought pain. I stared at Kerrick, knowing I was being cruel to ask him to choose between them, but not caring.

"You might not survive? What are the odds?" he asked.

"I'd give myself a fifty percent chance of living." More like ten percent, but I wanted Kerrick to choose.

I waited as a range of emotions flashed. He had such good control, no wonder he exploded when he lost his temper. While he weighed the risks, I sent my magic into Belen's wounds, flooding them. Yet I kept my gaze on Kerrick.

His decision hurt him deeply. "Don't heal Belen," he said in a low voice. "It's too risky."

Wow. I hadn't expected that. I thought for sure he'd choose Belen over Ryne. I drew my magic back inside me.

"Go," Kerrick ordered. "I'll stay with him until..." His voice broke.

I left quickly. Pain stabbed deep into my stomach, blood ran down, soaking my waistband. I made it to the small fire before I collapsed. My muscles felt as if they'd been shredded and I couldn't breathe. Now I know why Tara *never* talked about the Realm wars, and when she healed the warriors near the border. It was an experience like no other.

The pain increased as acid leaked from my pierced stomach and burned my flesh. My magic fought to heal the damage, but it wasn't fast enough. There would be no recovery from this one. I had no regrets. Belen deserved to live.

Shouts. Curses. A buzz of noise. Flea beside me. His mouth moved, but I couldn't hear a word he said. The edges of my vision blurred. Black and white spots swirled, turning the world into a chaotic snowstorm. I reached out blindly, clasped a warm hand, faded from life and into peace.

Well, that was what was supposed to happen. Waking in the blissful afterlife, joining all my loved ones who had died before me. Except an annoying, distracting tug kept pulling and yanking. Pain lingered in that direction. Hurt and anger and harsh words waited on that side. I resisted, but damn it all to hell, I wasn't strong enough.

When I woke, I thought I had overcome the pull and stayed in the afterlife. Whiteness billowed over me in soft waves. My body was cushioned and cocooned in warmth. I stretched my legs and then tried to raise my arms, but my left arm wouldn't budge. Rolling over, I encountered a number of very unpleasant realities.

I was alive. I was in a room. I was naked except for a bloodstained bandage wrapped tight around my stomach. Kerrick lay beside me. And his hand trapped mine.

Kill. Me. Now.

The only saving grace—he was asleep. I glanced around, searching for my clothes. No luck. Figures. Hiding them was an excellent way to prevent me from running away.

I studied him, wondering if I would wake him if I tried to free my hand. Asleep, he looked four or five years younger— around twenty-five or twenty-six. The harsh lines were gone. His nose was a little too hawklike for my taste, but it worked well with his sharp chin. His eyebrows were on the thicker side, but at least they were smooth and not creased together, which they did every time he looked at me. Plus they matched his long eyelashes.

I remembered my little brother, Allyn, had appeared so innocent and angelic when he slept—similar to Kerrick. It must be a survival tactic. If Allyn hadn't looked so sweet, we would have killed him while he slept. He had been pure evil when he was awake—similar to Kerrick.

Not pure evil, but close. At least as far as my brother was concerned. Kerrick, on the other hand—pure evil.

Thinking of my brother, I smiled. Allyn had a rare gift of talking his way out of trouble. I dearly hoped he had survived the plague along with Noelle and my mother. I wish I knew where they were. A wave of loneliness rolled through me. As I told Belen, I knew right where my older brother, Criss, and Father were—buried under a million pounds of rock. At least they died quick. Unlike the plague victims. Some of them took two weeks to succumb. Fourteen days of pain and the knowledge that their life would end.

Jerking my thoughts back to my present problems, I decided to extract my hand from Kerrick's. He woke the instant I moved my fingers.

I froze, waiting for his anger. I had disobeyed his order. I almost died healing Belen.

He studied me and I wanted to pull the covers over my head. After all, someone had to remove my clothing. When he moved, I flinched, causing him to pause for a moment.

Why wasn't he yelling at me? The anticipation was worse than his fury.

But he sat on the edge of the bed with his back to me. He didn't have a shirt on or an ounce of fat—just lean, hard muscles. At least he wore pants.

Without saying a word, he left my room. I stared at the closed door in shock. I expected a lecture. I expected punishment for my actions.

Not one to let an opportunity pass me by, I slid out of bed and searched for my clothes or any piece of clothing. At this point I'd wear whatever I could find. Nothing. I wrapped the sheet around me and tested the window. The shutters had been latched, but they opened without trouble. My room was on the second floor, facing a forest. Perfect, I could climb down the drainpipe. In a sheet? I laughed. It could be worse.

Someone knocked on my door. I closed the shutters and dove into bed just as a woman with pure white hair bustled into my room.

"Glory be. Mr. Kerrick was right. So happy to see you

awake. Oh, you had us all so worried, you did." She carried a bundle in her arms. Dropping it on the bed she hustled over to the windows and flung open the shutters. "Get dressed and I'll fetch you some vittles. You must be starved. A skinny little thing like you, going days without food." She tsked, heading for the door.

"Days?" I squeaked. "How many?"

"Four or five. The boys brought you in."

"Where am I?"

"In Mengels, dearie." With a wave she disappeared as fast as she had arrived.

From the amount of time we'd spent traveling, I'd thought we'd gone farther than Mengels. Oh, well. Not my problem. I fingered the clothing the woman had left. A long dark green skirt with a thin pattern of tiny light yellow flowers, growing as if on a vine. A light yellow tunic, some under-garments and black wool leggings. With no other options, I dressed, hoping my own clothes would show up soon.

Catching my reflection in the mirror, I stared at the strange woman on the other side of the glass. My hair had grown to my shoulders. The dark auburn roots a stark comparison to my dyed-blond strands. It stuck up on one side and was matted flat on the other. I combed my fingers through and realized my hair was clean. Who had washed it?

Curious, I lifted my tunic and pulled the bandage down, inspecting my stomach. Ugly reddish-purple circular scars peppered the skin along with burn marks from the acid. I remembered when Tara had shown me her scars, noting each one was a source of pride and not censure. Since I had been an apprentice, I only had one scar from when I healed Noelle. Now, I had the ones from Belen.

The woman returned with a tray. I hurried to cover my-self. She exclaimed over my clothes. "Yours were ruined. That nasty boar tore it to shreds. The boys did a nice job picking out the right size for you. Your boots are below." She set the tray down and pulled a chair over. "I'll bring them up, but a nice girl like you should wear something more... feminine. I can send Melina out?"

"No. Thank you, Ms...."

"Call me Mom. Everyone does. When you stay at the Lamp Post Inn, I take care of you, just like your own mother."

"Thank you, Mom."

"You're very welcome. I'm so glad you lived. Frankly, when Mr. Kerrick brought you in, I was about to call the undertaker. It's a miracle you survived." Mom shooed me into the chair.

At least she didn't suspect I was a healer. My stomach grumbled as I smelled the food. The tray held a bowl of steaming soup and a hunk of bread and cheese.

"Don't wolf it down or it'll come up just as quick." Mom hovered until I started eating. "I'll be back in a bit. We'll do something about your hair."

I tucked a lock behind my ear. "What's wrong...?" But she had left. Other questions came to mind, but I enjoyed the meal and the solitude. I'd been on my own for three years, and grown used to quiet. Now I'd been with Kerrick's men for the past twenty-five days at least. Probably more.

Mom returned with my boots, two bottles, towels, scissors and a helper carrying a washbasin and large pitcher. Mom called the young girl Melina and she looked to be around Flea's age. She filled the basin with water, and waited for orders.

I stood. "You don't need—"

"Mr. Kerrick wants your hair one color so you don't stand out so much."

Mr. Kerrick could kiss my ass. I tried to be stubborn, but Mom didn't bat an eye. She handled me as easily as a pouting two-year-old. Before I could even protest, she had me just where she wanted with my head in the basin.

"Auburn or blond?" she asked me.

"No orders from Mr. Kerrick?"

She ignored my sarcasm. "He said he preferred your natural color, but you could decide."

Gee, what a swell guy.

"The reddish brown sets off your beautiful sea-green eyes better," Mom said. "But if you choose blond, I'll give you the dye so you can do your roots."

I imagined trying to touch up my hair while camping in the Nine Mountains and almost laughed aloud. "My natural color is fine."

It was sort of nice to be fussed over. After Mom dyed my hair to match my roots, Melina trimmed the ends with the scissors. My hack job had grown in uneven.

When they were finished, Mom stepped back. "Much, much better, my dear. You look lovely. The boys won't recognize you."

Good. Maybe I could escape for real this time.

"I'll fetch them," Mom said, dashing any hope. "They've been pestering to visit, but I wouldn't let them until you were decent."

Her comment reminded me of one of my questions. "Was it you, er...did you...?"

"Not to worry. Me and Melina took off those bloody clothes and did what we could for you. There were a few scary nights where I swore we would lose you, but Mr. Kerrick stayed by your side all night."

That explained the annoying tug. Kerrick couldn't even let me rest in peace. But as much as I would like to blame him for keeping me from the afterlife, earth magicians didn't have any healing magic.

"Thank you, Mom, and thank you, too, Melina."

Melina blushed prettily. After they left, I shoved my feet into my boots and strode to the window. My cloak and knapsack were still missing, but I could—

The door banged open and Loren, Flea and Quain charged me. I backed away until I realized they wore smiles and appeared to be happy to see me.

"Told you she'd live," Loren said. "You owe me fifteen silvers."

"You said 'in no time.' I believe it took her five days to recover. That's not 'in no time,'" Quain protested.

Flea beamed at me. "Wow, you look like...a girl!"

Belen plowed through them all, knocking them aside. He wrapped me in a tight hug, lifting me off the ground.

"Easy, Belen. My ribs..."

He set me gently down. "Avry, why did you risk your life for me? Kerrick ordered you not to heal me. You suffered for days! You shouldn't have done it."

The room grew quiet. I spotted Kerrick near the doorway.

"Belen, *I* decide who I heal. *Me.* Not Kerrick. Not you. Not anyone. It's *my* decision. The only one I have left." I put my hand on his cheek. "You *deserved* to be saved. I had no doubts."

He covered my hand with his own, pressing it against his face. "Thank you."

"Anytime." And I meant it.

Mom entered. "You've visited. Now shoo! We don't want her to have a relapse."

Everyone filed out except Kerrick. Mom crossed her arms, waiting. Kerrick didn't move. She sighed with such exasperation, I couldn't keep from smiling. But after warning Kerrick not to tire me, Mom left, taking my good humor with her. Kerrick closed the door behind her and faced me.

Here we go. Time for the lecture. I braced for his recriminations.

"Did I see you actually smile?" he asked.

Thrown, I stared at him.

"I know you can smile," he said, as if we were having a pleasant conversation. "You gave that little girl one even after her family turned you in to the town watch. Why?"

I stammered a moment before I collected my wits. "It wasn't her fault her father turned me in. She's a delightful child and I was glad to see her well."

"Even though it almost led to your execution?"

"The two aren't connected. *I* decided to heal her. *I* took the risk of being captured. It was my fault."

"I see."

I didn't. What game was Kerrick playing now?

"We're leaving Mengels a few hours before dawn." He gestured to the bed. "I suggest you enjoy the comforts while you can. We won't be overnighting at an inn again."

"You're still planning on taking me to Prince Ryne?"

"Yes."

"Can you?" I asked.

He bristled. "You haven't escaped."

Not yet. "That isn't what I meant. Mercs and bounty hunters are searching for me. They almost succeeded and Belen almost died. Can you really escort me to your prince without losing more of your men or me? Forty golds is a fortune to these people."

"Almost succeeded isn't succeeding. If you remember, we rescued you. Again."

"And killed all those men. Even the magic sniffer, he's—"

"Working for the enemy. If I didn't kill them, they would attack us another time."

"But there are more to take their place. You haven't neutralized the source. As long as Tohon of Sogra dangles those forty golds, they'll just keep chasing us like ufas after fresh meat. Eventually, someone's going to succeed."

Kerrick's gaze turned contemplative. "What are you suggesting?"

I hadn't realized I was. But as I chased the logic, I knew what should be done. "That we find out why Tohon wants me. Maybe if you turn me in—"

"That's insane. I don't need—"

"Not for the money. If you turn me in, then there's no reason for the mercs or hunters to chase us anymore. We can learn why Tohon wants me alive. Maybe he's like you, and wishes me to heal a sick friend or loved one. I could heal that person and then we won't be bothered."

"And if there's another reason he wants you alive?"

"Then we escape. You have your earth magic."

"Won't work. I'm a forest mage not an earth magician. It's a common mistake. My magic is a gift from the living essence of the forest. Tohon·lives in the Sogra castle. I can't do a thing surrounded by stone and dirt. Besides, I doubt Tohon cares enough for another to offer forty golds to save his or her life."

"You know him?" I asked.

"Unfortunately. Why do you think he's put a bounty on the healers?"

"I figured he lost someone to the plague and held a grudge against us."

"No. He knows Ryne is sick and only a healer can save him. He wants the prince to die."

So did I, but I wouldn't go to such extremes. "Why?"

"Ryne is the only one who can stop Tohon."

CHAPTER 7

"Stop Tohon from what?" I asked Kerrick.

"From turning the Fifteen Realms into his own personal kingdom."

Not what I expected. "First, one man can't change or stop anything. And second, why would Tohon's attempt be bad? In case you missed it, our world has fallen apart. Peace throughout the Realms would be a step in the right direction."

Kerrick shook his head. "You've been in hiding so long, you've no idea what's really going on. Tohon is not trying to *help* the plague survivors. He's gathering them into an army so he can invade all those towns that have managed to reform. Towns like Jaxton. All so his army can grow. And if his forces encounter anyone who refuses to join, they kill him or her. Tohon is...mentally unstable, and for him to be king of all...would be a living nightmare."

"Why do you think only Ryne can stop him? Why not raise your own army?" I asked.

"Because Ryne is a brilliant strategist, and has outsmarted Tohon before."

I huffed in disbelief. "Probably because Ryne and Tohon are both megalomaniacs." I realized my mistake when Kerrick's entire body stiffened. Expecting him to lose his temper, I stepped back.

Instead, he said in a flat monotone, "We're going to cross the Nine Mountains. I suggest you get some rest while you can."

I tried again. "We've been traveling for over twenty-five days and we've only reached Mengels. Do you really think we can get to the Nine Mountains?"

Annoyance creased his brow. "Dodging mercs, keeping off the main roads and dragging along an unwilling healer has slowed us down. However, I've no doubt we *will* reach Prince Ryne." He opened the door, then paused. "And don't worry about anyone disturbing you. My men will take turns staying with you."

I bit back a sarcastic reply. After he left, I went to the window. I drew in the cool air and gauged the distance to the ground. Would the drainpipe hold my weight?

Even if I escaped, how long would I be free before Kerrick tracked me down? Or before the mercs found me? If I turned myself in to Tohon, would he give *me* the forty golds? A ridiculous prospect, but interesting to contemplate nonetheless.

"Avry?" Loren stood in the doorway. "What are you doing?"

"Taking in the view."

"Uh-huh."

"What's the matter, Loren? Afraid I'm going to jump out the window?"

"Something like that."

I sighed. As much as I would love to part company with Kerrick, I was smart enough to know he was better than being dragged to Tohon by a group of mercenaries. I shuffled over to my bed, kicked off my boots and squirmed under the covers.

Loren closed and locked the shutters before settling into a nearby chair. I enjoyed the warmth and comfort of the bed, but couldn't fall asleep.

"Why did we come to Mengels?" I asked Loren.

"Do you want the ugly truth or for me to sum it up nice and neat?" His words were punctuated with anger.

I propped up on my elbow and studied Loren's expression. "Did you want Belen to die?"

"No…yes…no." He rubbed his face. "It wasn't *my* decision."

"That's right. It was mine and it was easy. I'm sorry it caused you such…trouble. And don't expect me to promise not to do it again."

Loren laughed. "I wouldn't dream of asking you *that*. Wouldn't want you to make our lives easier or anything."

"You'd be bored." I flopped back onto the pillows. "Although I'm not too sorry. I ended up in this lovely bed."

"You can thank Kerrick for that."

"Ugh. I'd rather not."

"He probably saved your life."

"Oh?"

"He packed leaves and mud into the holes in your stomach and wrapped a bandage tight around your waist. We used Belen's litter and ran here. Mom's famous for her healing herbal remedies and she forced spoonful after spoonful down your throat."

"Should I thank Mom, then?"

"Not funny."

Kerrick only worked so hard to save my life so I could save Ryne's. He didn't care about me. "You're right, it isn't."

"Get some sleep, Avry."

Despite Kerrick's promise of a peaceful rest, a commotion outside my door woke me in the middle of the night. The lantern had been turned down low, and Quain had replaced Loren. He stood near the door with his dagger in hand.

"What's going on?" I asked.

He shushed me, and cracked the door open. Mom's frantic voice pierced the darkness. Pounding steps drummed past my room. Other voices joined Mom's. Unable to wait any longer, I slid from the bed and crept beside Quain. He shot me a dark look before returning his attention to the hallway.

"Well?" I whispered.

Quain pointed his dagger at me. "Go back to bed."

After being on Kerrick's bad side, Quain's attempt to intimidate me didn't work. It fact, it had the opposite effect. "No."

He jerked in surprise. Opening his mouth, he paused, then shut it.

The noises from the hall died down. Then Kerrick pushed into my room with the others behind him. Their expressions told an interesting story. Belen concerned, Loren uneasy, Flea angry and Kerrick impassive as usual.

"Since we're all awake, we'll leave now," Kerrick said.

Flea swallowed his squawk of protest when Kerrick glared at him.

"Why's Mom so upset?" I asked.

"It's not our concern," Kerrick said. "Belen, do you have her cloak?"

Belen nodded.

"Belen, tell me," I said.

"Melina's missing," Flea answered. "Over the past six weeks, someone's been kidnapping girls and disappearing into the woods. None of the town watch has been able to find them." He stared at Kerrick.

"It's not our concern," Kerrick repeated. "We don't have time for this."

I rounded on him. "You're a cold, heartless bastard."

He remained calm, but I sensed his fury simmering. It would soon boil. Too bad.

"Of course it's our concern! Mom took us in, she helped me. *You* can find them."

"In case you haven't been paying attention, if Ryne is more important to me than Belen's life, then he's certainly a higher priority than some girl."

"*Girls,* Kerrick. Not girl. The beast has done it before and will do it again. You hold your prince in such high esteem, what would he think about you abandoning Melina and Mom for him?"

Anger twitched on his face, but Kerrick held his temper.

Belen answered for him. "Ryne would be appalled."

That was the first good thing I'd heard about Ryne. Unfortunately, the argument had no effect on Kerrick.

Time to make a concession. "Find Melina, and I won't make any more escape attempts. We'll be able to travel faster if I cooperate," I said.

"And you'll heal Ryne?" Kerrick asked.

"No, but I'll give you until we reach him to change my mind. How's that?"

"Will you swear to it?" he asked.

"I, Avry of Kazan Realm, give you my word."

"Agreed." He held out his hand.

When I clasped it, a strange tingle of magic zipped up my arm. I let go quickly.

"Okay, gentlemen, looks like we're going hunting," Kerrick said.

Everyone rushed to get ready. Before Flea hustled from my room, he touched my shoulder. "Thanks, Avry."

"Are we friends again?" I asked.

"Yep." He flashed his lopsided grin and ran after Quain.

I stopped Belen. "Do you have my knapsack? I need to change into my travel clothes before we leave."

"You're staying here," Kerrick said.

"No. Melina might need me."

"We'll bring her back here."

"*If* she goes with you. She might be traumatized and not trusting a bunch of men. Forcing her will only make it worse."

He considered.

I added more incentive. "The town watch is combing the woods—there'll be no one here to protect me if the mercenaries catch up to us."

Belen hid his smile as Kerrick's shoulders drooped just a smidge. "Fine."

When Kerrick left, Belen shook his head. "Flea argued and begged Kerrick to help Melina. I tried and so did Loren. No luck. But *you* changed his mind."

"Only because I gave up my freedom."

"I don't think so. You can really get under his skin. This has been a most interesting trip. I can't wait to see what else happens."

"I can."

When Belen returned with my knapsack, I asked him why Kerrick was the one in charge. Belen was a few years older, stronger and more personable.

"Prince Ryne asked him to find a healer." Belen turned his back so I could change into my extra set of black travel clothes. Which were now my only set. I folded the tunic and skirt, tucking them into my pack just in case.

Belen handed me his two daggers. "Keep them with you just in case."

"Won't Kerrick be upset?"

"He never ordered us not to give you a weapon."

I smiled, thinking how he and Kerrick acted like brothers. "Kerrick and you are both from Alga Realm. So how did you meet Ryne?" I asked.

"Long story. Let's find Melina first."

Easier said than done. Despite Kerrick's magical connection, we couldn't find the man who had taken Melina. When dawn woke the colors of the forest, I hoped we'd find a trail to follow. No luck.

I worried that Kerrick would give up the search, seeing it all as a colossal waste of time. When we encountered yet another large group of people, I remembered how the forest reacted to intruders. Finding two people among all these searchers would be almost impossible.

"We need to talk to Mom," I said to Kerrick during one of our breaks.

He sharpened his sword with a stone. "Why?" he asked without looking up.

"Only she can empty the woods for you."

"What do you mean?"

"You know." I gestured at the surrounding trees. "How the intruders feel to the forest, like an infection or pox on a sick patient."

Kerrick stopped in midstroke, glancing at me with suspicion. "How do you know that?"

"From you."

"I didn't tell—"

I huffed. "When you grabbed me from the mercs. Remember? Your skin and hair turned the colors of the forest, and—"

"I know what I did. I just didn't know you could…feel it, as well. I never could explain the experience to anyone." He considered. "You're right. We should ask Mom to empty the forest of searchers."

Shocked that he admitted I was right, I almost missed the next thing he said.

"But Mom doesn't know," Kerrick said.

"Doesn't know what?" Belen asked. He had returned from scouting and sat down next to me.

Kerrick stared at me with a hint of amusement as I realized Belen didn't know about his forest magic, either. And Kerrick wasn't inclined to tell him. Though he didn't seem worried I'd tell Belen. Hell.

Magicians tended to be skittish, as well. When a family discovered their child was gifted with powers, they kept it quiet until the child learned control of his magic and could protect himself. Kidnapping of young mages had been an unfortunate problem before the plague. Children with magic could be sold for a thousand gold pieces to the northern tribes living in the wildlands.

"Mom doesn't know I'm a healer, so if we find Melina and she's injured it would be better not to have anyone around." I don't know why I covered for Kerrick. Perhaps I could use it to my advantage someday.

"Oh."

We sat in silence for a while. I thought about the problem.

"The kidnapper has gone to ground," I said. "We'll tell Mom we know where, but he won't emerge until everyone has given up. Mom will understand and order everyone but us out."

"And what if we still don't find them?" Kerrick asked.

"Do you have another idea?"

"No."

Kerrick followed my plan, asking Mom to bring in the searchers. Since there had been no signs of Melina, she was happy for any bit of good news. Guilt churned in my stomach over our little deception. Little—how was that for trying to make myself feel better?

After all the watchmen and volunteers returned to the Lamp Post Inn, Kerrick ordered his men to stay behind, as well. "We will go alone," he said, gesturing to me.

They protested and I wondered what Kerrick was up to. He didn't change his mind. As we headed out, I tucked one of the daggers Belen gave me into my belt and the other into my boot. Kerrick noticed the action, but didn't say a word.

When we reached the door, Belen stepped in the way. "If any harm—"

"Comes to her, you'll rip out my arms. Got it," Kerrick said.

"I'm serious," Belen said.

"I know. Do you really think I'd put her in danger?"

"Not on purpose, but things happen that are beyond even *your* control."

Kerrick gave him a tight smile. "You mean I'm not omnipotent?"

"You're not even semipotent."

"Is that even a word?" Kerrick asked.

"He probably meant you're impotent," I offered.

It was worth Kerrick's glare to hear Belen's deep chuckle. He pushed Belen aside. The big man's laughter followed us as we left the inn.

Kerrick paused just after entering the forest. "We don't have much light left. We'll need to move quickly. How committed are you to finding Melina?"

An odd question. "Very."

He held out his hand. "Two is better than one."

Understanding rolled through me. I really didn't want to touch him, but this wasn't about me. When his fingers wrapped around mine, magic zipped along my skin, connecting me with the forest.

My awareness expanded into the trees and along the ground. The living green rustled with unease. Unwelcome irritants had trampled its young shoots. It pulsed with pain from broken branches and cut foliage. Deep in its heart, a splinter throbbed. A sore spot the forest wished to remove.

United through the forest's essence, we searched for that thorn without saying a word. No need. I was no longer Avry, but an extension of green.

Together we found the path of a dangerous intruder. Light at first, it darkened as if rotting with excessive moisture. The smell of decay hung in the air.

And then it loomed before us. An infection oozing with an unnatural bile. Kerrick released my hand. I sank to my knees as the living essence retreated and Avry returned.

I sucked in deep breaths to clear my head, letting my eyes adjust to once again being an observer and not a part of the forest. I mourned the loss of the forest's state of being, and I wondered how Kerrick could be so grumpy and mean when he had that ability to sink into the living green at will.

He crouched next to me, pointing to a hillside. "See that?"

"The hill?" I squinted in the semidarkness. The shape had an odd...bump.

"That's how he's managed to avoid capture. He built a cabin into the hillside and camouflaged it with moss, grass and dirt. Stay here." Kerrick crept through the woods, keeping well away from the hidden cabin. No sound marked his passage. Soon he disappeared from my sight.

I waited as the air cooled and darkened. My concern about Melina grew with each minute I spent doing nothing. We should storm the cabin before that bastard could harm her. What if she was dead?

Kerrick returned after full dark. A satisfied smirk twisted his lips.

"Where have you been?" I whispered.

"Did you miss me?"

"Not possible. However, there's a girl—"

"I looped around the cabin. There isn't another entrance or any windows. But I found a chimney of sorts. He's using a small metal pipe to vent the smoke from a fire."

"And this helps us how?"

"Think about it. There is only one way to get inside. If we try to go through that door, he'll be waiting for us. He has the advantage."

But if he came outside, we would have the upper hand. What would force him to leave? "You blocked the pipe?"

"Yep. We'll smoke him out."

Clever. But I wouldn't admit I was impressed.

"When he emerges, *I'll* take care of him. You find Melina and help her. Understand?"

"Yes."

Kerrick positioned himself near the entrance while I crouched a few feet behind him. It didn't take long for the moss-covered door to swing open. A shaft of firelight pierced the darkness as white smoke billowed out. A tall man waved his arms to clear the haze. He coughed once before Kerrick pounced, wrapping his hands around the man's neck.

I straightened. Intent on telling Kerrick not to kill the guy, I stepped closer but froze as three more men ran from the cabin.

Chapter 8

The three men rushed Kerrick, knocking him and the tall guy to the ground. Even surprised by them, Kerrick managed to land a few blows before he was overpowered. Two men sat on him, while the third took his sword. They questioned him, but Kerrick remained silent.

I stood in the open, unnoticed for now and afraid to call attention to myself. I stepped back into the shadows, but I caught the tall guy's attention. Recovered from his near strangulation, he dashed forward and clamped a hand on my arm, hauling me into the firelight streaming from the cabin.

"What do we have here?" he asked.

I was getting tired of being manhandled all the time. My fear transformed into anger. "Are you blind?" I asked. "Oh, that's right. You've been playing with girls so long, you've no idea what a *woman* looks like."

Instantly angry, he backhanded me. Expecting the attack, I leaned away and caught a glancing blow. The force knocked me to the ground. While there, I pulled the dagger from my belt and held it close to my body. Tall Guy pulled me to my feet by my hair.

I pressed his fist against my head, trapping his hand. Not only did the move stop the pain, but I now touched him. Skin to skin. Magic exploded from my core. I channeled it into him. He screamed, but I held on.

The man with Kerrick's sword charged. I spun, putting Tall Guy between us. He dropped to his knees still yelling, which made it easier for me to press the tip of my knife against his throat. Sword Man stopped in midcharge. I reduced the amount of pain, quieting Tall Guy.

Nice to have everyone's undivided attention. "Release the girl, or I'll slit your buddy's throat."

The two squatters on Kerrick jumped off and yanked him to his feet. Sword Man aimed the blade's tip at Kerrick's neck. "I can play that game, too," he said.

"You're assuming I care about *him*." I laughed. "Go ahead. You'll be doing me a favor."

By their stunned silence, I guessed they hadn't been expecting that response. Kerrick kept his expression neutral, but I felt his glower. His gaze flicked to the ground for a second before he resumed looking bored. Turning the dark gray color of the forest, Kerrick's boots and legs seemed to disappear. Vines twisted around the squatter's ankles as Kerrick used his forest magic.

I zapped my captive. He jerked and cried out. "Go get Melina or he dies," I said.

As far as distractions go, it wasn't the best, but it worked. Kerrick faded into the surrounding woods. When the squatters realized he had gone, they moved to chase after him, tripping over the vines. As they rolled on the ground in panic, the ivy twined around their legs, tightened their hold. Sword Man tried to cut them free with the blade.

The scene would have been comical except Kerrick ap-

peared behind Sword Man and grabbed his head the way he
had trapped the merc's.

"Don't kill him!" I yelled.

Instead of snapping Sword Man's neck, Kerrick squeezed
until the man stopped struggling and slumped to the ground.
I released the pressure on Tall Guy's fist. His hand dropped.
I pushed his head forward, exposing the back of his neck.
Quickly finding the sweet spot, I knocked him out.

I checked on Kerrick's victim. He still had a pulse.

"Take care of the others," Kerrick said. Strain tightened
his voice. He leaned against a tree with his eyes closed.

I hurried to the two squatters. The vines had trapped their
arms. I touched that sensitive spot on each of their necks,
rendering them both unconscious.

"How long?" Kerrick asked.

"They'll be out three hours at least."

"Good." He collapsed.

I knelt beside him. "What's wrong?"

He batted my hand away. "Go check on Melina." But
when I wouldn't move, he added, "Vines are stubborn in
autumn."

"Oh." I glanced at the two prone forms. The leaves had
already turned brown and the vines looked brittle. Kerrick
had sapped his energy.

"Go," Kerrick ordered.

I rushed to the cabin's entrance and paused for a second,
dreading what I might find inside. She had been alone with
four men for almost a day. I entered into an open sitting area.
A fire burned inside a stone hearth built into the left wall. A
row of cots lined up near the right wall. Smoke rolled along
the ceiling and spilled out the door. Along the back wall was
another door. Running across the sitting area, I fumbled to
unlock it. I yanked it open, revealing blackness. I hesitated

in the threshold, afraid of what I might find. "Melina?" I called.

"In here," she said with a sob.

I sagged with relief. "Hold on, I'll get a lantern."

I rushed to light one. Holding it in front of me, I entered the dark room. Melina flinched as the yellow glow illuminated her bleeding and battered face. Her left wrist was chained to a cot and she wasn't alone. Two other girls sat on other beds. They were similarly shackled. One of them also sported bruises, but otherwise they appeared to be unharmed. They stared at me in surprise.

"Are you hurt?" I asked.

Melina touched her cheek. "Not bad."

"Did they…" I couldn't finish.

"No," the girl with the bruised face said. "We're to be sold. But if you give them trouble, then…" She slammed a fist into her palm.

"Sold for what?" I asked horrified.

She looked at me as if she couldn't believe how naive I was. "Wives if we're lucky. Slaves or prostitutes if we aren't."

The other girl gestured toward the door. "Are they gone?"

"They've been, uh, neutralized. Do you know where the key to the cuffs is?" I asked.

"One of *them* carried it with him," Melina said.

I placed the lantern on a nearby table. "I'll be back."

Outside, the men remained where I'd left them. Kerrick appeared to be asleep, but when I neared, he asked, "Is she…?"

"She's alive, but injured, and there are two others." I explained what I learned while I searched the men's pockets for the key.

"Unfortunately, selling women is not limited to this area.

The plague has left many places with an uneven population. There're gangs who will find wives for survivors for a price."

I glanced at the men. Bastards. Maybe I'd let Kerrick kill them, after all.

"Did you heal Melina?"

"Not yet." This earned me an appraising glance. I dug my hand into Tall Guy's back pocket and finally found the key.

"Good. Release them and take them to Mom's right now." Kerrick pushed up on one elbow with obvious effort.

"Why?"

He huffed. "Can't you just follow orders for once?"

"Do you really want an answer?"

"Only if it's, 'Yes, sir.'"

"Not going to happen."

He paused as if summoning the willpower not to bark at me. "There's a group of people—seven men and two women—heading this way. I can't tell if they're friendly or not, so you and the girls need to leave well before they arrive."

"What about you?"

"I can handle myself."

I pushed on his shoulder. He fell back onto the ground.

"Uh-huh. Want to try that again?" I asked.

"No one's after *me*," he said. "*You're* the one in danger. Plus you'll be risking the others."

"What happens when these four wake up?"

"I thought you didn't care. They'll be doing you a favor."

"I'd love to leave you. Believe me. But I gave my word. Come on." I helped him to his feet.

Even though Kerrick was taller than me, my shoulder ended up being the perfect height for supporting him.

"Now what?" he asked.

"We'll hide inside the cabin until the others pass us by."

"What about the prior occupants?"

"I'll drag them inside."

"Your plan—"

I pulled him along. He was too weak to resist. Fun. I dumped him onto one of the cots in the sitting room before releasing Melina and the other girls. They rubbed their wrists and followed me out to the main room. They froze when they spotted Kerrick.

"You remember Kerrick from the inn, don't you?" I asked Melina.

"Yes."

"He's part of the rescue team."

She glanced around. "Are there others?"

"Ah... No. We had been expecting one man. Not four." Melina shuddered.

"And we have a bit of a problem." I explained our situation to the three of them.

They offered to help.

"Where's the chimney?" I asked Kerrick.

Although dubious of my plan, he explained how I could find the metal pipe in the dark. It took me longer to locate the chimney than I had hoped. Kerrick had shoved a clump of muddy leaves to block it. I cleared it and hurried back.

While I was gone, Bianca—the girl with the fading bruises—Peni and Melina had dragged the unconscious men into the hideout. They'd shackled the men to the cots in the back room and locked the door. Nice.

Empowered, they discussed what they'd like to do to the men in great detail. Kerrick muffled a horrified croak. He had one foot resting on the dirt floor. "If you ladies are done plotting revenge, you might want to cover our tracks outside before the others reach us."

"How long do we have?" I asked him.

"Ten, maybe fifteen minutes max."

Damn. I rushed outside and let my eyes adjust to the darkness. Between the scuff marks from the fight and the drag marks, even I could figure out which way we went. They would discover the hidden cabin in no time.

Melina relayed instructions from Kerrick as I smoothed the ground with my hands and... "Are you sure he said to *sprinkle* the leaves?" I asked her.

"Yes."

I worked as fast as I could to hide the marks, backing up until I reached the cabin. Standing in the threshold, I studied my efforts. We were in big trouble.

Nothing more to do, I closed and latched the door. I gave Bianca my knife before picking up Kerrick's sword. Both Melina and Peni armed themselves with kitchen knives.

"Give me your other knife," Kerrick said.

I had forgotten about the one in my boot. But he hadn't.

When I handed it to him, he said, "Help me stand."

"But you're too—"

"They don't know that."

Good point. I grabbed his wrists, pulling him to his feet. A weak pulse of magic traveled up my arm. I had a brief sense of the travelers close by before I let him go. He wobbled, but steadied himself with a hand against the dirt wall.

Bianca and I positioned ourselves on each side of the door. Ready for... I wasn't entirely sure. I strained, listening for any sounds, but I watched Kerrick's expression.

A few minutes passed without incident. Then Kerrick straightened.

"They're suspicious," he whispered.

"What are you doing?" I asked, pitching my voice low.

"Increasing the camouflage around the door."

All color drained from his face. "I..." He swayed and reached for the cot. "They're..."

I debated for a second before abandoning my post. Kerrick sat on the edge. Taking his hand in mine, I released my healing power, sending it into him. Energy flowed through him as it drained from me. Through Kerrick, I learned the moss on the door had thickened and grown over the bare spots that would have given us away.

Magic surrounded two of the nine people searching outside. Kerrick's awareness stretched farther into the forest. Finding what he searched for, Kerrick shook a tree about a mile away. A dead limb crashed to the ground. I felt the impact through Kerrick. The noise drew the others away.

He released my hand.

"But I can—"

"No. Save your strength." His voice rasped.

Melina came over. "Are they...?"

"Gone." Keeping one foot on the ground, Kerrick lay back on the cot and fell asleep in an instant.

I stood on unsteady legs.

Melina twisted the bottom of her tunic. "Can we leave now?"

"No. We have to wait for Kerrick to regain his strength. Sorry."

"He's a magician, isn't he?" she asked in a low voice.

"Yes. Although I don't think it's common knowledge."

She nodded as if she understood. "I don't blame him. With ten golds being offered for information on the whereabouts of magicians, I'd keep quiet, too."

"Ten golds? Why?"

"Mom told me that since many of the Realms' legitimate leaders have died, the remaining powerful people are all scrambling to amass armies, grab Realms and stockpile resources, including magicians."

"I thought that was just one of those paranoid rumors."

"Where have you been?" she asked, but didn't wait for an answer. "We had a customer from Grzebien who told us his town was in the middle of reorganizing when a large army arrived to help. Except they set up their own town watch and declared the city an official member of the Ozero Realm, and under the protection of the High Priestess's holy army."

"Was there any resistance?"

"I doubt it. If Grzebien is anything like Mengels, there's not enough people or energy to put up much of a fight." She glanced at the back door. "If the High Priestess's army can stop bastards like them and bring peace back, I'm more than happy to wear one of those red robes and give thanks to their creator."

Which, from what I'd learned from Tara, Melina would be forced to do. The High Priestess, also known as Estrid of Ozero was intolerant of other faiths, and required her subjects to be members of her cultlike religion. Was she better or worse than Tohon? I mulled it over as I rummaged for food. Bianca and Peni helped me cook a simple vegetable soup. Melina's pale face worried me. She sat nearby, holding a wet cloth to her bleeding cheek. I asked her who the other powerful survivors were to distract her from the pain.

"Tohon of Sogra and Prince Ryne of Ivdel until he disappeared. I've also heard a couple Algan princes, President Lyady's daughter and a few other minor nobles lived, but they're not looking to rule, just survive like the rest of us. Oh, and some guy claiming he's the Skeleton King has a small army in Ryazan Realm."

"That's it?" Now Kerrick's comment about Tohon wanting Ryne dead made more sense. As I thought about the problem, I wondered how greedy Tohon could be? Fifteen Realms split three ways would give each leader five Realms. But who would decide which five? Each Realm had its own assets and drawbacks. The richest ones would be the most desirable.

I found a loaf of bread and a wedge of goat's cheese to go with the soup. Melina picked listlessly at her portion while I tore into mine. I saved a hunk of both for Kerrick.

When I suggested we get a few hours of sleep, Melina shot to her feet. "No. I'm not... I can't... I want to go home." Her body shook.

I embraced her as she broke down. She had been so strong earlier and hadn't complained at all that I had forgotten how young she was—at least three years younger than Bianca and Peni. Guiding her over to a cot, I lay down next to her. Magic pulsed under my ribs and I released it. Melina had been punched repeatedly in the face. While I could heal her wounds, I couldn't erase her memories. At least she'd have Mom to comfort her.

A hand shook my shoulder. I jerked awake. Kerrick leaned over me. Annoyance creased his brow. Melina stood behind him. She covered her mouth with her hand, staring at me with wide eyes as she put the clues together. She felt great and I had bruises covering my face. I wondered if Melina or the other girls would turn me in, but I couldn't produce the energy to care.

"My men will be here soon," Kerrick said, straightening.

"The ones you ordered to stay at the inn?" I asked, suppressing a grin.

"Yes. They're leading Mom and half the town watch straight here. Quain is tracking our trail—which should be impossible to follow." Disgruntled, he glanced at the door. "I taught him too well. Either that or Quain is half eagle."

"A bald eagle?" I quipped.

Kerrick smiled a genuine smile. One that reached his eyes. Good thing I was already lying down or I would have fainted in surprise. It faded as he studied me.

"Will you be able to travel?" he asked.

"Yes."

"Good." He strode to the door and unlocked it. With his hand on the knob, he paused and looked at me. "My men had *never* disobeyed an order before we found you."

Even though his comment was meant to be a complaint, I said, "Thank you," just to annoy him.

It worked. He decided to wait for his men outside. Sunlight streamed in from the open door. I blinked in the brightness. Morning already?

"Avry, what happened?" Melina asked. "Your face... Are you...?"

I sat up and made room for her to sit next to me. "Yes, I'm a healer." I spoke in a low voice so the others didn't overhear, not that it would matter once they saw me.

"Is that why those people from last night are after you?" she asked.

"Unfortunately."

"Is Kerrick protecting you so he can turn you in for the bounty?"

She had a quick intelligence, and, out of curiosity, I asked, "What do you think?"

Tugging on the hem of her tunic, Melina considered my question for a few minutes. "He's protecting you, but not for the gold." She put her hand on my cheek. "Does it hurt?"

"No." The truth.

"*Did* it hurt?"

"It doesn't matter."

"Of course it does."

"No, Melina, it doesn't." How to explain it? I searched for the right words. "Your pain was a reminder of what happened to you. But the pain I felt was connected to you—a bright young lady. By healing your injuries, I was helping you and that transforms how I perceive the pain, making it bearable."

She still looked unconvinced.

I tried again. "It's like when I held my newborn sister. Noelle was heavy and my muscles ached, but the discomfort paled in comparison to my awe over her presence in my arms. I would have been content to hold her...." Sudden grief choked off my words. I had been six, but I'd never forget the intense desire to hold and protect her forever. As she grew, she had been full of impish curiosity. And she'd follow me so much that I'd called her my little shadow.

"They're here," Kerrick said behind me.

I startled and turned, but he had already left. He needed to wear a bell or something, I grumbled as voices called. In no time, Mom barreled past everyone and gathered Melina in her arms.

The town watch took the four men into custody. Mom squinted hard at me, and I immediately felt guilty. But she didn't comment on my bruises. As Melina and the others told their tales, no one mentioned my healing powers.

Belen and the others waited outside. They had brought all our travel gear. We could leave from the cabin and not have to backtrack to the Lamp Post Inn first, which made Kerrick a bit happier.

When I joined them, the guys appeared to be glad to see me. Belen inspected my face.

"Good thing I wasn't here," Belen said in a low growl. "I

would have ripped the four of them apart and scattered the pieces for the scavengers to eat."

Quain scanned the ground at our feet. "It looked like quite a fight. What happened here?" He pointed to a long scuff mark.

"That's where she made good use of Belen's—or should I say her—knife," Kerrick said. He turned to me. "You can keep them if you promise not to use them against us."

I copied his flat expression. "First, it's not *your* decision if I can keep them or not, it's Belen's. Second, I am *not* going to promise—"

"The knives are yours," Belen said. "And we should teach you how to swing a sword."

Kerrick coughed. "No, we shouldn't. She's dangerous enough." He ended the discussion by ordering us to gather our packs.

We said goodbye to Bianca, Peni, Melina and Mom.

"You're welcome to come back anytime," Mom said to me. "We'll always have a room for you. No charge. I know what you must have done for my daughter, but don't you worry, we won't say a word."

I hugged her in thanks. It felt good to be embraced even if it was for only a moment.

We headed north. No clouds marred the bright blue sky. The air held a cool crisp scent of leaves and earth—gorgeous weather that was perfect for hiking. Kerrick led, and for the first time since I'd been rescued from Jaxton's jail, I felt… not quite content since anxiety, worry and fear still shadowed me. But more alive.

When I used my magic to heal others, I had a purpose and felt satisfaction over helping another. I was needed. Even if this "adventure" didn't last long, it had roused me from the nothingness that my life had been before. Three wasted years.

Even though I'd healed a few children, I could have done so much more, but had been too afraid.

Despite the men's routine, I decided to help when we stopped for the night. As the designated cook, Loren prepared the meal. His concoctions were edible, but plain, so I went in search of something...tastier.

Of course Kerrick followed me. "Where are you going?"

I bit my lip to trap my sarcastic reply. Instead, I said, "If I had intended to break my word, I would have done it last night after you passed out."

He didn't respond right away. Finally, he said, "Don't wander too far." He returned to camp.

Interesting. I looped around, inspecting the plants. Tara had taught me which ones could be used for fevers and other maladies. She explained that in a few cases like minor injuries, plants worked just as well and would save our healing energy for the more dire cases. In the six months I'd been her student, I had learned so much. But to her, it had only been a small portion of her vast experience and expertise. I not only mourned her death, but the loss of all her knowledge, as well.

I found a few sprigs of rosemary and returned. Ignoring the collective sigh when I appeared, I stripped off the leaves and handed them to Loren.

He sniffed them in suspicion. "What's this?"

I guess it would take more than my word for them to trust me. "Rosemary." No glimmer of recognition. "It's to make your stew taste better. Don't you know the basic herbs and spices?"

"No. I took this job in self-defense. Quain burns everything. Belen thinks jerky is all we need to survive. Flea's idea of a good meal is something that hasn't been in a garbage can first. And Kerrick poisoned us—"

"Not on purpose," Kerrick said. "The meat looked done."

I realized then that Kerrick had assigned Quain first watch. Another oddity. "Well, my cooking skills are rudimentary, but I know herbs and can help you if you'd like."

Loren glanced at Kerrick, before he said, "Sure." He returned the leaves to me.

I broke them into little pieces and sprinkled them into the stew.

"Speaking of food," Kerrick said. "Belen, do you remember when we were in school and Ryne had gotten upset over the amount of wasted food?"

Here we go. Kerrick was as subtle as a thunderstorm.

Belen chuckled. "Yeah. He'd been assigned garbage duty for fighting."

The real story.

"I wouldn't call it fighting," Kerrick said. "He was protecting the new kid from Stanslov."

"Good thing Master Fang came when he did. Otherwise, Ryne would have been turned into pulp."

"Instead, his punishment was two weeks of dealing with garbage." Kerrick placed another log on the fire. "By the end of those two weeks, Ryne had worked out a way to donate all the extra food to the poor in town."

I debated ignoring them, but this could be a good opportunity to get more information. "Did you meet Ryne in school, then?" I asked Belen.

"Yeah. The three of us attended boarding school for brats."

"Brats? I can't believe *you'd* fit in that group," I said.

Belen's deep laugh vibrated in my chest. "I didn't." He jabbed a finger at Kerrick. "Even though I'm four years older than him, his father insisted I go along so I could keep him out of trouble." Belen huffed. "Didn't work. And every time he caused problems, I'd be sucked in and we'd both be punished."

"You'd have been bored otherwise," Kerrick said.

"Are you two related?" I asked Belen.

"No. My parents worked for his family for years. We grew up together." Then Belen sobered. "The plague took my mother and my older sister. But my younger sister survived, and Izak, one of Kerrick's brothers, lived."

Quiet descended over the campsite.

"As far as I know, my great-aunt Yasmin is still alive," Kerrick added. "Which doesn't make sense since she's ancient and has been ill for as long as I can remember."

Nothing about the plague made sense. The healers had tried every herb and tonic they knew to heal the victims to no avail.

"Where is your sister now?" I asked Belen.

"Sayen is guarding Prince Ryne. He has many loyal supporters. We were expanding our reach and bringing order to the chaos, but once he sickened, everything stopped. There's no one else like him."

"You're right. No other Realm leader has executed as many prisoners as Prince Ryne." The words popped from my mouth before I could stop them. I glanced at Kerrick, but he kept his relaxed position by the fire.

"His father ordered all those executions," Belen said.

"Come on. Everyone knows King Micah was just a figurehead during the six years after his accident. And he died before the plague struck."

"A figurehead who still had loyal generals despite his erratic behavior. When Micah decided to clean out the dungeons, they followed his orders. By the time word reached Ryne, it was too late."

Flea started throwing stones to practice juggling. I joined him, glad for an excuse to end the conversation about Ryne.

Except it picked up where we had left off the next night and the following three nights. I had made a mistake in directing my questions to Belen on that first night. He had a sincere honesty that was hard to ignore, and, after getting the topic steered to Ryne, Kerrick let Belen take over the reminiscing.

However, on the fifth night Kerrick took first watch. Belen paced around the campfire and even Flea remained quiet. During the day, I had noticed the strain in Quain's face and witnessed a couple intense, but private discussions between the men.

"What's going on?" I finally asked Loren.

He heated water over the tiny fire—all that Kerrick would allow. Loren exchanged a glance with Belen.

"If you're trying to protect me from bad news, stop it right now. I don't like secrets," I said to both of them. "I can't help if you keep me in the dark."

"We've a couple bands of mercs on our tail," Belen said.

Having already warned Kerrick of this possibility, I wasn't surprised. We then played hide-and-seek with the three different groups of mercenaries for the next two days. Our rest breaks shortened until we skipped them altogether. Cold food and a scant few hours of sleep during the day became our new routine.

Kerrick didn't have to say that the mercs were closing in. I knew from the others. No one smiled. No one spoke more than a few words. No one put their weapons down.

When the sun rose on the third day, Kerrick stopped. We were at the edge of the forest. Spread before us was an abandoned village. A carpet of thick thorny vines had grown over all the wooden structures, obscuring the streets. White, man-size Lilys dotted the greenery. Peace or Death Lilys—it was impossible for anyone to tell them apart.

"Damn. They've been herding us like cattle to the slaughterhouse," Kerrick said.

Belen noticed my confusion. "The mercs knew this was here." He swept a hand out, indicating the buried village. "They've must have coordinated their efforts because the mercs have us boxed in on three sides. The only way we can escape is through the Lilys."

Fear energized my tired muscles. Too bad it wouldn't do me any good.

"We're trapped," Loren said.

"We're dead," Quain said.

CHAPTER 9

"Those thorns look sharp, but what's wrong with going through the Lilys?" Flea asked.

"Nothing if they're all Peace Lilys," Belen said.

"Unfortunately, there is no way to know if there's even one Death Lily hiding among them," Quain said.

I met Kerrick's gaze. "Did you know this was here?"

"No. The town is outside the forest. Besides, I can't tell if a Lily is benign or lethal."

"No one can," Quain said. "That's the problem. You don't know until the flower opens, and by that time it's, See you later, sister!"

Staring at the barrier, I tried to find a route that would avoid the white flowers. No luck. When we had plenty of workers, they would pull out the new shoots of all the Lily plants before they could grow a flower. With its deep root system that covered miles, eradicating the plant had been a full-time job. The Lilys also grew in unexpected places and the Death Lilys killed the unwary.

"Now what?" Flea asked.

"We stage an ambush of our own. If we move fast enough,

we might be able to fight our way through one side and escape," Kerrick said.

"Not going to work," Belen said. "Too many of them."

"I'll surrender and they shouldn't hurt the rest of you," I said.

"No," Kerrick and Belen said together.

"We'll take our chances and go through the Lilys," Kerrick said.

"You're crazy." Quain gestured with his knife. "I'd rather take my chances against the mercs."

"What are the odds?" Loren asked.

"It's more like a ratio," Kerrick said. "Approximately one Death Lily for every hundred Peace Lilys."

Everyone turned to the field. I estimated there were about three hundred Lilys.

"Approximately three Death Lilys," Kerrick said. "I'll pick a route with the least number of Lilys and go first. Belen, keep her close to you. You'll be last. Who wants to go second?"

This was the first time Kerrick asked for volunteers.

"I'll take second," Loren said without hesitation.

"Third," Quain said.

"Then Flea," Kerrick said. "If one of those flowers so much as twitches, run."

Lining up in order, we followed Kerrick. The flowers' scent misted the air. A combination of sweet honey and tangy lemon that evoked a strong feeling of déjà vu in me. We climbed through the vines, avoiding the thorns with little success.

When we reached the halfway point, the crash and rustle of many boots sounded behind us. A line of mercs spread out along the forest. No going back now.

The mercs cursed and called us idiots with good reason.

If a Death Lily grabbed you, it would do one of two things. Either consume your flesh and then spit out your bones, or spit you out whole. But don't get too excited about being released. You'd most likely die later. Only ten percent survived the toxin the flower injected into them.

And if you were caught, your friends wouldn't be able to cut through the petals. They were thick and fibrous. Plus they would need to get close to the plant. Then the vines would ensnare them, saving them for the Lily's next meal. Nice, huh?

With the arrival of the mercs, Kerrick picked up the pace. We skirted many of the white flowers, but couldn't avoid them all.

Memories of my younger brother kept surfacing in my mind. Something about the Lily's scent reminded me of Allyn. He had gone from crawling to running in a matter of days and all before he turned a year old. Once mobile, he'd never stopped moving unless asleep. My family had constantly chased after him. I remembered bolting after Allyn with my heart slamming in my chest. He had wandered into a copse of trees and had been too young to know what traps to avoid. I couldn't recall if I had caught him or not. The rest of the memory remained elusive.

Funny how one sound could bring everything back. A low hiss. I froze. How could I have forgotten? The shushing noise grew. Flea paused under a big bloom. Kerrick and the others had gone ahead.

The petals above Flea parted. I shoved Flea out of the way as the Lily attacked. A whoosh echoed. White petals surrounded me. Then all was black silence.

Cocooned within the Lily, I waited for the pricks. The toxin was supposed to kill me so the plant could digest me at its leisure. I should be terrified, except this wasn't my first time inside a Death Lily.

My brother had finally stopped running long enough for me to catch up to him. He'd pointed to a huge hissing white flower, and in a heartbeat the Lily had grabbed me. Obviously, I survived. However, I had no memory of being released.

Two thorns pierced my arms. A familiar feeling flowed over me. I drifted as if transformed into a wisp of smoke. Forgotten memories sprang to life. After being spat out, I'd endured two weeks of sickness. However, the toxin must have blocked the memory of my time inside the Lily, and since no one, except Allyn, had seen me snatched, they didn't know what had caused me to be sick. The symptoms matched a bad bout of stomach flu.

My consciousness now spread along the plant's roots and into the plant's soul. Through this strange mental link, I peered beyond the petals. Kerrick and the others had tried to cut the Death Lily down only to be caught tight in its vines. The mercs had watched them with amusement even though they had been upset over losing me. Or more accurately, over losing their share of forty golds.

The Death Lily dipped to expel me.

Wait, I thought. *Keep me until the mercs leave.*

It stopped. I sensed its contentment at knowing me again. Its pride over my life since we'd been together. I felt its regret over unsuccessful encounters. Yet it was ever hopeful. It had sensed potential in Flea, aiming for him.

I asked it to allow me to remember. The Death Lily wasn't truly a predator; it was trying to help, but its efforts either killed a person right away, or they died later. Only a few survived. Time passed. The mercs left with the setting sun.

Don't take Flea, please, I asked. *Let us pass.*

Agreement flowed along with sorrow over parting. It pulled the thorns from my arms. I snapped back into my body, feeling heavy, blind, stiff and awkward. Its petals opened and I tumbled out. Belen caught me in midair.

"Avry, what happened?" he asked.

The vines retreated, releasing the men.

"Run before it picks a new target," Kerrick ordered.

Belen wouldn't put me down as they bolted to the far side of the village. No other Lilys attacked and soon we reentered the forest. Kerrick kept a fast pace until we reached a small clearing.

"Oh, man!" Quain said. "I thought we were Lily food for sure." He rubbed at the creases on his neck where a vine had pressed against his skin.

I squirmed from Belen's arms. Kerrick strode over to me. I stood my ground even though I wanted to duck behind Belen.

"Do you have a death wish?" he asked me. Anger spiked each word.

"Of course not. It was an automatic reaction."

"Can you survive the toxin? How long do you have until it kicks in?" he asked.

The Lily had granted my wish. I remembered the entire encounter, but I needed some time to sort it all out. "I'm immune to the toxin." I expected my news would be well received. It had the opposite effect.

Kerrick stepped closer as pure fury rolled off him. "And why didn't you tell me this earlier?"

"I didn't know earlier."

My answer threw him. He sputtered before reining in his emotions. "Why do you know now?"

"Common sense. I was in that flower for hours. If I didn't have a reaction by now, I'm not going to."

Kerrick let the topic drop, but he barked orders for his men to set up camp. His ill humor lasted through dinner.

I finally barked back at him. "You should be happy. The mercs think I'm dead. They won't be chasing us anymore."

My comment earned me a glare from Kerrick.

Belen slapped his leg. "She's right! What a day. I thought we'd all die. Killed by a giant plant. Not the way I'd want to go."

"How would you want to die?" Loren asked.

"Doing something heroic and not something stupid," Belen said.

"Not like you get a choice," Flea said. "Starving to death isn't heroic or stupid, it's just plain sad."

It wouldn't surprise me if Flea had personal experience with starvation. During the two years of the plague, no one tended the fields or cared for livestock. Many people who had survived the disease died of starvation.

Flea sat across the fire, juggling two stones. He'd mastered the technique. I offered to teach him how to include the third stone.

"Sure, that'd be great."

We searched for a rock that matched the size and weight of the others. When we found a good stone, I demonstrated the motions.

"Hold two rocks in one hand, and one in the other. Remember how you threw the second rock when the first reached the top of the inverted V? When the second rock is at the apex, you throw the third with one hand and catch the first with the other. And just keep throwing so one rock is always in the air."

He rushed his first attempt. A rock whizzed by Loren's head. On the second and third try, he pelted Belen's shoulder. The big man tossed the stones back good-naturedly.

When Flea almost clipped Kerrick, we were *ordered* to move farther away.

At least Flea considered this new step a challenge and wasn't getting frustrated yet. After twenty tries, Flea performed one successful juggle before dropping all the stones.

"That's it!" I said. "Now all you need to do is—"

"Practice, I know." He paused for a moment, sobering. "Thanks, Avry."

I waved my hand dismissively. "This is fun for me, too. It reminds me of happier days."

"Not just for teaching me to juggle, but for, you know… saving me from the nasty giant flower."

"Anytime," I said.

"No." His body stiffened as all joviality fled, replaced by a dead-serious intensity. "Don't risk yourself for me again. I'm willing to die for Prince Ryne. It's my choice. Not yours."

Surprised by his demeanor, I considered his words. "You haven't even met Ryne. Why are you so willing to give up your life for him?"

Flea gestured toward the fire. Quain, Belen and Loren exchanged insults. Kerrick had taken the next shift of guard duty.

"*They* are willing. I trust them. It's that simple." He crossed his arms. "Promise me you won't risk your life for me."

"No. Because it's not that simple for me."

Flea huffed just like Kerrick. I almost laughed.

"Well, it should be simple for you, as well," Flea said.

"Why?"

"Don't you trust Kerrick?"

This time I couldn't muffle a laugh. "No."

"What about Belen? You trust him, don't you?"

"That's different. Belen sees good in everyone. I know that

he's not lying to me about Prince Ryne, but I don't trust his judgment."

Flea gave up and stormed back to the fire. I stayed behind, mulling over our conversation. When Kerrick's men had found Flea, he'd been on his own for as long as he could remember. They'd protected him and all but adopted him. Of course he would be grateful and loyal. They were in essence his family so his judgment was suspect, as well.

"It's getting late," Kerrick said.

I jumped a foot. "Will you stop doing that!" I spun in the direction of his voice.

"Doing what?" He stepped from the shadows, but halted a few feet away.

"Sneaking up on me."

"I wasn't. You're just deaf to the sounds of the forest." His reasonable tone at least meant he'd gotten over his earlier snit.

"I don't have your forest magic."

"You don't need it. The forest has its own unique…song. I taught my men how to listen for notes that are off-key, and for those silent pauses which means danger."

Curious, I couldn't help asking, "Did you teach them how to move without making noise?"

"Yes. Except they do make noise. It just blends in with the forest's song so it doesn't stand out. I could teach it to you if you'd like."

I searched his expression, but I couldn't tell if he joked or was serious. Instead of responding, I asked him, "Why didn't you tell your men about your magic?"

"I don't want them to rely on it."

"But you use it all the time."

"Only since *you've* been with us. I don't want them getting lazy or sloppy, believing I can protect everyone. There's a reason I taught them how to navigate the forest. If something happened to me, they need to be able to protect themselves."

"What about Belen? He's been with you the longest. Doesn't he suspect?"

"We've never talked about it. He may."

"He probably felt you using magic at some point."

A strange queasy expression, almost a flinch, creased his face for a second. "Those without power can't feel it. In fact, I was under the impression that only a fellow forest mage could sense it, and only when we were both in the forest. I can't feel others' magic unless they use it when we're both in the woods."

That would explain his queasiness. "When you grabbed my hand, I not only felt the magic, but I sensed what you did. Is it your power or mine that makes that…connection possible?"

"I don't know. I've encountered a few other magicians, but nothing like that has happened to me before."

"And I've only been around other healers. We can share power—like when I sent you a portion of my energy, but that connection has been…unique." Except when I had been inside the Death Lily. Interesting.

Thinking about magicians reminded me of the night we had rescued Melina. "Why didn't those two magicians who searched for us sense your power?"

"They aren't of the forest. One is a water mage and, I think, the woman drew hers from the moon."

The plague had decimated the ranks of magicians, as well. No wonder they traveled with seven others for protection.

"Were they powerful?" I asked.

"Hard to tell for sure."

With every merc and bounty hunter searching for me, it seemed odd Tohon would send two valuable supporters. And where were they earlier when the Death Lily had me? I don't remember sensing them among the mercs. Remembering what Melina had said about Grzebien, I made an unpleasant connection.

"Those two magicians aren't from Tohon. Who else is chasing us?" I asked.

"How did you make that leap?"

I paused. Was he testing my logic or was he indeed surprised by the possibility of another faction? Probably testing me. I repeated Melina's story. "Estrid of Ozero's people could be hunting us, as well. She's giving gold for information, and I'm sure she doesn't want Tohon or Ryne to have a healer, either." I suppressed a sigh. "It's all a big game, isn't it? A power struggle to see who can grab the most between the three of them." Sadness filled me. If I wasn't a pawn in this game, I'd be free to heal those who needed me.

"Ryne wanted to organize the survivors and help them rebuild their towns even before the plague died out. He knew if no one stepped up to enforce the laws that criminals would take full advantage, forming gangs, and marauders would wreak havoc," Kerrick said. "If he hadn't gotten sick, I think we'd still have Fifteen Realms."

"But he did get sick and now he'll need a large army and magicians to disband the mercenaries and all the other factions, and to stop both Tohon and Estrid. An impossible task."

"Ryne *will* find a way."

"You can't know that for certain."

"I can." His gaze burned into mine. "I wouldn't have spent two years searching for you if I didn't have utter faith in him."

The next logical question would be why Kerrick had this

faith. But I squelched it. I didn't want to know. Or was it because I was afraid to know?

I glanced away.

He said, "You're right about Estrid. She sent her dogs to stop us from reaching Ryne. They're moving to block the pass through the Nine Mountains as we speak."

"I thought there are other routes across them." All infested with dangerous marauders and ufa packs. Swell.

"Not in the winter."

"Can we beat them there?" I asked.

"No. We've had too many delays." He gave me a pointed stare.

"What's next, then?"

"As you pointed out, the mercs believe we're dead. If we lay low for a few weeks, then word of our demise should reach Estrid and she'll recall her troops."

My heart skipped a few beats. "Lay low as in hide?"

"Yes. It shouldn't be a problem for you. You're adept at running and hiding." He turned and disappeared into the shadows.

Oh, joy. The nasty jab from Kerrick paled in comparison to the thought of spending even more time with him and his loyal companions.

I returned to the campfire. The others had fallen asleep. Squirming under my blanket, I stared at the clear night sky. Kerrick's hideout would probably be inside a cave, which would obscure this fantastic view. Sleeping under so many stars felt magical. Although sleeping through an ice storm would be horrible. In that case, a cave would be welcome.

Tonight was the perfect night to see the various star patterns. I found the cluster my father had called the bull's horns. Grinning, I remembered his story about the absentminded bull who had lost his horns. The stories had been his way of teaching us various life lessons, but at the time, I had believed poor Yegor still searched the earth for his horns. If only the bull had looked up, all would be well.

I hadn't fully appreciated those late nights, sitting on the porch with my two brothers and my sister, Noelle, tucked in my lap, listening to my father's stories. He'd been a romantic stargazer. Looking back, I realized it must have been terrible for him to work so deep underground in the mines. He'd taken the high-paying job so we could afford the apprentice-ship fee for me.

What a brat I'd been then, complaining about having to wait a few months before I could start my lessons. Not even thanking my father for his hard work and sacrifice. And I didn't even consider Noelle's feelings. She'd been my almost constant companion since she was born, and I had left for the month-long trip to Galee without any thought to how she would react to me being gone. The distance between my home and Tara's had been too great for visits, although I had planned one about halfway through my four-year ap-prenticeship with Tara.

It was difficult to sleep with guilt lodged under my heart. I tossed and turned until daybreak erased the black sky.

We traveled east for five days. I was right. Kerrick stopped at a cave system close to the town of Grzebien, and pro-claimed it home.

"Isn't this Pomyt Realm and occupied by Estrid?" Loren asked. He built a fire ring as Quain and Flea fetched rocks for him. Belen had been sent out to collect firewood.

"Yes." Kerrick sorted through his pack.

"Then why—?"

"Estrid's searching for us."

Loren glanced up, but Kerrick didn't offer to explain further.

"Logically, we should head west away from the people intent on harming us." I tossed a few sprigs of parsley into the soup—my first attempt at cooking. "Which makes hiding in her occupied lands a strategic move. I'm guessing this area isn't well-known to the locals or used. Right?" I aimed my question at Kerrick.

"Right," he said.

"Still seems too risky to me," Quain said.

"Consider it from Estrid's point of view." I tapped the spoon on the pot. "She believes we're intent on reaching Ryne, and she has blocked the route. When we fail to arrive, she'll think we're either dead, captured by Tohon or holed up somewhere nearby so we could dash across the Nine Mountains at the first opportunity."

"You don't dash across those mountains," Kerrick said.

"That's beside the point."

"And what *is* the point?" Flea asked.

"You tell me," I said.

He chewed on his lower lip. "This is probably the last place she'd search for us?"

"That's right."

"I still think it's dangerous," Quain said.

"Dangerous would be getting too close to Tohon," Kerrick said.

"Or trying to go around the mountains," I said.

Kerrick shot me a surprised glance as if he hadn't considered that idea before.

"No," I said. "It would add *months* to the journey and the Ronel Sea is treacherous even in the summer. It would be suicide in the winter."

When he kept his contemplative purse, I added, "And we'd

have to cross Pomyt. It's one thing to hide out just within the border, but to travel in the open..."

"Is asking for trouble." Quain supplied.

"Who's asking for trouble?" Belen asked. He entered the cave carrying a huge pile of firewood. Dumping it in a corner of the cavern, he collected a handful of thin branches.

"Guess," Quain said. He smirked, pointing to me behind Belen's back.

Belen bent over the fire ring, building a lattice of kindling around a few thicker branches. Without looking at Quain, Belen said, "I'd say *you're* looking for trouble, Quain. Because that's what you'll get if you keep teasing Avry."

Unaffected, Quain challenged. "From who? You or Kerrick?"

"From Avry." Belen straightened. "She can hold her own, don't you forget that."

My turn to smirk. Quain opened his mouth to retort, but Kerrick silenced him with a single raised eyebrow.

Belen had the fire roaring in no time. The smoke vented through a natural chimney in the ceiling. I wondered how Kerrick had found all these caves. Water had eroded parts of the bedrock, forming them. I'd think sensing holes in the ground would be part of a rock magician's skills and not a forest mage's. However, I wasn't an expert. I'd learned the eleven different types of magic—forest, earth, water, fire, air, life, rock, death, moon, sun and healing—but my education hadn't gone beyond the basics.

I could ask Kerrick, but that question would have to wait until we were alone. Not likely now that we were "home." Considering he hadn't said more than a few words to me since that night we talked about Ryne, I doubt he'd talk to me.

"We're getting low on supplies," Kerrick said. "There's a market in Grzebien, but a few of us would be too recognizable."

"The monkeys can go," Belen said.

"Except they made quite an impression on the town watch the last time we were here."

The monkeys exchanged confused glances.

"Whiskey Wendi," Kerrick said.

"Oh, yes," Loren said. A slow smile spread on his lips. "That was Grzebien? Wow that was…a wild time."

"That was also over a year ago before Estrid and when the Booze Baron ruled the town. Do you really think the people would remember us?" Quain asked.

"Whiskey Wendi," Loren repeated, looking at Quain with a gleam in his eyes.

"Oh, yeah." Quain grinned. "Yeah, they'd remember."

"We have enough provisions for a week," Kerrick said. "Then Flea can take her if…" He focused on me. "If she can learn how to move through the woods without sounding like a buck protecting its territory."

"I think she sounds more like a brown bear defending her cubs," Loren said.

"You guys are nuts," Quain said. "She sounds exactly like a troop of watchmen after some poacher."

With a wide grin, Flea joined in the teasing. "When I hear her, I'm always reminded of when we were chased through Horse Shoe Forest by that pack of wild dogs."

Everyone turned to Belen. "I think she does pretty good considering she hasn't had any training."

"Thank you, Belen," I said, giving him a sweet smile.

The rest groaned. Quain threw a rock at him. Belen caught it in one hand. While the men joked, I added the remaining ingredients to my soup. I fished a few hot embers from the fire and placed the pot over them. As I stirred the liquid, my thoughts returned to Kerrick's comment. My excitement over the chance to go into town warred with the unappealing prospect of Kerrick teaching me how to match the forest's song. Perhaps Belen could instruct me instead.

When the soup was done, I made a show of letting Belen try it first since he had defended me.

"Fine with me," Quain quipped. "He'll also be the first one to keel over, killed by Avry's cooking."

"But what if I used a heavy poison?" I asked. "One that sinks to the bottom and only kills the men who eat the last couple of bowls?"

Quain stared at me as if he wasn't sure if I joked or not. "You have an evil mind," he hedged.

"Thank you." I grinned.

"Aren't healers required to take an oath not to harm anyone or something like that?" Loren asked.

"After we complete our apprenticeship, we travel to the Guild House and work there for a year, demonstrating our knowledge to the Elders. At the end of that year, we graduate. During the ceremony, we swear an oath not to intentionally cause harm or death to another." Unless in self-defense.

"But *you* zapped Flea, and hurt the merc leader," Loren said.

"I didn't graduate. Therefore, I haven't taken the oath."

My revelation caused a ripple of…not quite concern, but unease. Belen's hands suddenly went to his throat. He wheezed and gasped, then slumped over.

Everyone but Kerrick jumped to their feet. I knelt beside him. Was he allergic to parsley? His body shook and I touched his shoulder. He was laughing.

I played along, fussing over him, apologizing for not waiting long enough for the poison to sink.

When the three men inched closer, he sat up. "Gotcha!"
They yelled, then scolded him for his prank.

Still laughing, he said, "I can't believe you fell for it. Why
would Avry poison us when she could have let me die, and
Flea get eaten?"

"Besides," I added, "I wouldn't want to waste good poison
on you guys."

"Ha. Ha. Not funny," Flea said.

"Is there such a thing as a good poison?" Loren asked.

"Actually, there is," I said. "The fulip plant is poisonous,
but if you dry it, crush it and mix it with ginger water, it
becomes a remedy for an upset stomach."

"You seem to know what you're doing. Why didn't you
graduate?"

"The plague came before I finished my apprenticeship."

The humorous mood faded in an instant. The plague had
ruined all our futures. I served the rest of the soup, but noticed everyone but Belen waited until I swallowed a few
mouthfuls before they ate. Joking aside, they still didn't trust
me.

"Stop overthinking it. Your head is getting in the way of
your feet," Kerrick said.

"That makes no sense," I said, stifling my frustration.

I had been walking through the woods all morning and
getting nowhere. Back and forth outside the cave, I tried to
copy Kerrick's silent movements.

"It's all in how you step and how you distribute your
weight."

He watched while I made another pass.

"Use your hips more."

"Like this?" My hips swayed with each step. I felt ridiculous.

"No. Not like that." He came up behind me. "Let me show you."

When Kerrick grasped my hips, his magic flowed over me, igniting a tingling warmth in places it shouldn't.

"Why are you pulling power?" I asked.

"Am I?" He sounded surprised.

"Yes."

"Habit, I guess. Keeping my connection with the forest just in case. Ignore it."

Easy for him to say. He didn't have someone leaning against his back sending him distracting vibrations.

"Walk like you did the last time," he said.

As I stepped, he corrected my gait. We did a couple passes. I understood what he had been trying to explain, but when he released me, I wasn't so sure.

"That's better. Try again."

I did. Again and again and again. All afternoon, which normally would have been unpleasant, but there was a big difference in personalities between Kerrick the teacher and Kerrick the leader.

"That's it," he said. "You got the technique. Now you need to—"

"Practice." My words to Flea had come back to haunt me.

"Right. I'll give you two days."

"And if I don't improve?"

"I'll go with Flea to the market. But if you do improve, you'll graduate." Humor lit his gray eyes—they had changed color to match the winter forest.

"As long as graduating doesn't involve swearing an oath."

"Oh, no, wouldn't want to do that. Besides, you've been true to your word. That's all I need."

I spent the next two days practicing in the woods on my own. It was refreshing to be by myself for a few hours. And without the pressure of someone watching me, I could focus all my energy into listening to the forest's song. Once I knew what sounds to listen for, I wondered how I had missed them before.

After my two days of practice, Kerrick announced we'd all play a game of hide-and-seek. "If she can find everyone, she wins."

"Sweet," Flea said.

"The rules are…" Kerrick waited for everyone's attention. "You can't stay in one hiding place too long. You have to switch spots to give her a chance to hear you." He paused dramatically for a moment. "Ready. Set. Go!"

CHAPTER 10

The game of hide-and-seek was on. The men scattered into the woods. I turned my back to the forest, facing the outer rock wall of the cave.

"And no cheating," Quain called. "Make sure you count to a hundred before seeking."

"Don't forget to shout out the 'Ready or not' at the end," Loren said.

Half of me felt foolish, the other half reverted to my childhood days—when no other worries sullied the pure thrill of the hunt. I embraced my childish side, pushing away the dull adult sensibilities. I counted faster. Long-forgotten strategies surfaced in my mind. Too bad all the…boys—couldn't call them men when playing this game—wore gray, black or dark brown clothing. It made sense for blending in with the winter landscape, but it gave them an advantage for now.

"Ready or not, here I come." I spun around, hoping to catch a flash of movement as one of the boys dashed to a hiding spot. Nothing. Not even a branch swayed. I listened to the forest for a moment. Off to my right, an unnatural off-note sounded.

Despite the cold air, I removed my cloak. I wore my black clothes, but I had taken the time to smear gray clay I had found at the bottom of a shallow pool in the caves over sections of my shirt and pants, equalizing the playing field.

Instead of going right, I walked with the special—what to call it?—gait straight for a while before veering right, hoping to come in behind the unnatural spot. I stopped often to make sure my quarry hadn't moved. As I drew closer, I noted a dense little thicket that would be perfect to hide behind. I stood nearby and waited. Sure enough, Flea slipped out, searching for another spot. I followed.

Once Flea found a place to hide, I crept up on him and pounced. His yell of surprise echoed throughout the forest.

Sputtering with indignation, he said, "You didn't have to scare me!"

I feigned innocence. "I thought you heard me."

"Yeah, right. You have that evil gleam in your eyes. Have you've been pretending to be noisy all this time?"

"No. But you don't know everything about me. Like the fact that when I was younger, no one could hide from me. I was Queen Seeker." I had grown up in a small city, but a few of the strategies for seeking someone in an urban environment worked out here, as well.

Flea grumbled, but I shooed him back to the cave. "Hurry up so I can find the rest."

"You won't find Kerrick," he said.

I waited until the forest settled, then honed in on another off-key area. This time I caught Quain.

"At least I'm not the first one," he said. He wore a gray wool cap over his bald head. "You're a fast learner, but you won't find Kerrick."

If Quain and Flea had been trying to discourage me, they failed. I continued to stop and listen. But when I encountered the perfect hiding spot—a dried creek bed hidden under the branches of a fallen tree, I knew one of the boys wouldn't be able to resist this place. I squirmed below the thickest part of the branches and pressed against the bank. My years on the run hadn't been a total waste. A couple of the skills I had learned aided me today. The biggest one was patience.

After twenty or thirty minutes, Loren slid under the tree.

"Ah, hell," he said. "I should have known this spot was too good to be true."

Three down, two to go. I made half-circle sweeps farther and farther from the cave and, on my tenth pass, I sensed a strangeness. Boulders jutted from the ground. A few were in mounds while others stood alone. As my gaze traveled over the area, something seemed wrong. Not the color, not the size, but one shape kept snagging my attention. One large boulder had soft lines and a symmetry to it.

When I touched the boulder, it chuckled. Belen peeked out from under his cloak.

"With my size, I didn't have a lot of choices," he said.

"You blended in," I said. "But one thing I did learn as a healer's apprentice was to be observant. A rash could be just an ordinary rash, but if it had blurry edges, it was a sign of a more serious illness."

"I knew you were smart, so I'm not surprised you found the four of us. But—"

"I won't find Kerrick. Everyone seems to delight in telling me that."

"Don't take it the wrong way," Belen, ever the peacemaker, said. "His ability to disappear in the forest is impressive. We're just proud of him."

As Belen returned to the cave, I wondered if they'd still be proud of him if they knew about his magic.

I considered the problem. Kerrick wouldn't make any

noise, and the forest wouldn't give him away with out-of-tune notes. He would be camouflaged, but not by magic. That wouldn't be fair unless he used it unconsciously, keeping contact with the forest just in case. I might be able to feel it and follow it to him.

Except I only felt it when we touched. Skin to skin. I searched my memories. Something Kerrick had done…when he knew about the mercs… An image formed in my mind of him crouched down, touching the ground with his hand.

I pressed my palm to the earth. A slight tingle rolled along my fingers. Was it going in any certain direction? Concentrating, I thought it might be coming from my left. Which didn't help since I couldn't crawl because he'd hear me. I needed to stay on my feet. Of course!

Sitting down, I pulled my boots and socks off. I stood, cringing as my soles touched the cold ground. After my skin adapted to the temperature, I felt that tingle pointing to the left. I'd have to find him before my feet froze and lost all sensation.

The vibrations intensified as I walked. I covered a good bit of ground before the tingle stopped. Which probably meant Kerrick had seen me with bare feet, figured out what I was doing and ceased using magic, or my feet were numb.

Kerrick must be close. I turned in a circle, scanning the forest before remembering he wouldn't stand out. Frustration swelled, but I shoved it down. What were my options? I couldn't use sight, touch or sound. What's left? Taste and smell.

Not about to taste the dirt, I sniffed the air. The cold damp scent of earth with a slight rotten taint filled my nose. With no other options, I returned to the cave and did sweeps again, but instead of listening, I drew in deep lungfuls of air. Ten, twelve, fifteen, twenty, twenty-three sweeps later, I caught a hint of spring sunshine. Like a hunting dog, I followed it, sucking in so much air I was dizzy.

The scent increased and I focused all my energy into staying with it. It led me to a huge briar full of thorns. I remembered when Kerrick had rolled me right through the underbrush. But then he had used his magic. Of course, he could have pulled power to get inside, then stopped. Except his scent wasn't coming from the patch, but seemed to surround me. Odd.

I circled the briar a few times, puzzling over the inconsistency. No brilliant solution came to mind. I'd lost him. That one word—*lost*—jolted me. Yegor the bull had lost his horns. I scanned the trees above my head.

Kerrick lounged on a limb. His amused half smile grew into a full-blown grin. "What took you so long?"

"Well, I napped a couple hours this afternoon so the boys would believe they were hard to find."

"Ah, yes, the fragile male ego. Always good to keep it intact." Kerrick swung down from the limb and landed beside me without making a sound. "So what gave me away? My magic?"

"At first, but you stopped using it."

"Once I realized I'd connected to the forest, I had to stop. Otherwise, it wouldn't have been fair."

"Uh-huh. Keep repeating that, and maybe one of us will eventually believe you." Now that the game had ended, I relaxed and woke to other sensations. The cold air assaulted my exposed skin. My hands and feet were numb. I retraced my steps to where I'd left my boots.

Kerrick followed but kept quiet as I pulled on my wool socks. I shivered. My cloak was back at the cave. Of course Kerrick had gone the farthest.

We headed back "home."

After a few minutes, he said, "You didn't answer my question. How did you find me?"

I feigned confusion. "I didn't answer? Odd. Doesn't sound like me."

"You're not going to tell me, are you?"

"Why would I do that?"

"Because if you tell me, I might change something and you won't be able to find me next time."

And I was too embarrassed to tell him I sniffed him out. I shouldn't know he smelled of spring sunshine, shouldn't care and shouldn't tell him a damn thing. But, knowing him, he would pester me for an answer.

I asked, "Remember when Belen was injured by the mercs?"

"Hard to forget."

"You distracted them while Flea and the monkeys positioned themselves up on the rocks. It was a good strategy. People don't usually look up. When I lost your trail, I remembered it."

"Interesting." He didn't say anything else for the rest of the trip.

The others waited for us outside the cave. Their expressions remained uncertain as they looked from me to Kerrick and back, searching for some hint of what had happened. They hoped I'd failed. After all, they had boasted about Kerrick's superior forest skills.

Finally, Quain asked, "Well?"

"You were right," I said before Kerrick could open his mouth. "I couldn't find him."

I endured a few "told you so's" from the monkeys and Flea. They whooped and were obnoxious. Belen, though, gave me a shrewd look. I met his gaze without flinching or glancing down. I'd learned to lie while on the run. My life had depended on it. Funny, my mother didn't even have to see my face to know when I'd been lying.

Once the boys were done crowing, they returned to the cave for a special surprise. I grabbed my cloak and moved to follow, but Kerrick clasped my shoulder, stopping me.

"Explain," he ordered.

"I couldn't disappoint them."

"That makes no sense. *I* let them down. Not you. Besides, it's just a silly game. And they won't let you forget it. You did boast you were Queen Seeker."

"It may have been a silly game to you, but not to them. *You're* their leader. They have complete confidence in you, which they should. Any doubt, no matter how small or silly, can be detrimental to their trust. *You'll* be ordering them to risk their lives, not the Queen Seeker."

Kerrick stared at me so long I grew uncomfortable and wondered what he was thinking about. I almost swayed in relief when he glanced away.

He swept a hand out, gesturing to the entrance to the cave. "After you, your majesty." He bowed.

I punched his arm. "Don't start. I'll take the ribbing from the boys, but not from you."

"Who said I was teasing?"

Now it was my turn to stare at him.

"Hey, what's taking you so long?" Quain called. "Can't Avry *find* the entrance?"

Laughter erupted from inside the cave.

"I warned you," Kerrick said.

"I grew up with two brothers. I can handle harmless teasing. Besides, laughter heals the soul. You should try it sometime." I walked into the cave without looking back.

Cheers and a few good-natured taunts greeted me. The men stood in a line with their hands hidden behind their backs, fidgeting like kids who had been caught stealing sweets. Their attention focused on Kerrick, who had followed me inside. He nodded.

"Okay, boys. What's going on?" I asked.

Belen stepped forward. "We decided that even though you didn't find Kerrick, you did catch the rest of us and should graduate. Congratulations!" They hooted and hollered.

"Thanks. Now stop blocking the heat, I'm frozen solid."

"Not so fast," Belen said. "We still need to give you our graduation gifts."

"But—"

Belen approached and brought his hands forward. With a dramatic flourish, he opened them, revealing a pair of black gloves. "I noticed you didn't have a pair."

"Where—?"

"They were mine, but they had holes in the fingertips. I just cut them down for you and sewed them." He gave them to me. "Try them on."

They fit, but all I could say was, "You sew?"

"After two years on the road, someone has to. Do you like them?"

"Yes. They're lovely...thanks."

Quain and Loren presented me with a piece of leather rolled up and tied with twine.

"Untie it," Loren said.

I had to take off my gloves to loosen the knot. Unrolling the leather, I exposed the inner side. Pockets lined the material. I puzzled over it.

"It's for your plants and herbs," Quain said. "You can store them in separate pockets and, when you roll it up, you can carry it in your knapsack."

"That's..." Unbelievable. Unexpected. "Perfect. Thanks."

Flea came up next. With a shy smile he flourished three

rocks and proceeded to juggle them. He performed a whole routine, with high throws and low throws, ending the show with one rock going up to the ceiling while he spun around in a circle before catching it behind his back.

The others cheered and clapped. I couldn't speak for a long moment. When the cave grew quiet, I said, "You've been practicing."

"A little," he said.

"Wow, that was…amazing. Thank you."

Kerrick handed me a piece of paper. I squinted at the words with suspicion. Was this an oath? But it was a list of supplies.

"Things to buy at the market," he said. Then he dropped a pouch full of coins in my hands. "You and Flea can go tomorrow. I suggest you wear your green skirt and tunic to match the market crowd."

"And clay-caked clothes are *so* last year," Quain said.

Lying in my bedroll that night, I couldn't sleep. The unexpected gifts from the guys had shocked me. They didn't think of me as just a healer for Ryne like Kerrick. They cared about me. All those years I had avoided forming close relationships because I knew they would make it difficult for me to keep moving on. Eventually, I would have to leave the guys and that would cut deep. Damn. I hated being right.

Even knowing Kerrick and company crouched in the nearby woods just in case we ran into trouble, I planned to fully enjoy the day. Another bright cold morning had arrived with the dawn. I wore the skirt and tunic to keep the peace, but my cloak covered the clothes, anyway, so there was no real reason to wear them.

Located in the center hub of the city, the market bustled with shoppers, merchants and various undesirables seeking to prey on the unwary. Most of the merchants had set up their tables in three-sided huts with wooden roofs. Others hawked their wares from wagons, carts and blankets spread on the ground. Children dashed between legs. The general noise of voices arguing and haggling blended together into a happy, prosperous hum. I basked in the market's energy, filling my lungs with the heady smell of fresh bread.

Flea and I walked a circuit first to orient ourselves to the sellers and goods available for purchase. Although we had agreed to stay together—well, Kerrick had insisted—I held the list. I also brought along my remaining coins, hoping to secure a few needed items.

At one point, Flea touched my shoulder. "See that kid?"

"The girl with the red hat?"

"No, the boy with the long black hair."

"Yes, I see him by the applecart."

"Watch."

When the customers around the cart captured the owner's full attention, the boy pocketed as many apples as he could before slipping away unnoticed.

"Nice technique," Flea said.

"How did you know he was going to steal?"

"Coat too small. Pants threadbare with holes. No hat or gloves. Plus he had that look."

"A hungry look or an I'm-about-to-do-something-illegal look?"

Flea laughed. "He doesn't consider what he just did illegal, Avry. It's survival. He had the worried look. Worry over where he'll find his next meal. It's constant. It doesn't stop even when you have a full belly and a few slices of bread tucked away."

My enjoyment of the day faded. "You'd think with the town back on the mend, no one would starve."

"You might think that, Avry, but I know better. Even before the plague, people starved." Flea glanced around. "At least there's no immediate danger. According to Belen, it was pretty much every man for himself when the Booze Baron ruled the town last year." Flea gestured to a pair of well-armed soldiers, watching the market with keen interest. "Estrid's men."

"Then her presence here is good for the town."

"If everyone is so happy, then why are there so many soldiers around?" Flea asked.

I peered at him with suspicion. It sounded like Kerrick had schooled him on what to say to me today. "You have a point," I said. "But we can't linger too long or Kerrick will have a fit. I suggest we purchase the lighter items first and save the heavy stuff for last."

"Now *you* have a look," Flea said.

"What kind?"

"The shopper's glow. If I were still a street rat, I'd try to pick your pocket *before* you spent your money."

"Good thing you're no longer one."

"Thanks to Kerrick."

Ignoring Flea's comment, I strode to the merchant selling jerky. We moved from stand to stand, buying the items on the list—basic supplies and travel rations. Flea caught one of the street rats before she could steal the bag of coins from my pocket. He admonished the girl for her poor technique and pointed her toward an easier mark.

But I stopped her before she could dash off. "Here." I gave her a few of my coins—I didn't really need a comb or new undergarments; the ones I had would last a few more months. I still had enough to buy another set of travel clothes.

She stared at me as if I had lost my mind, then nodded a

quick thanks before disappearing into the market's crowd. Flea peered at me, as well.

"What?" I asked.

He didn't say anything.

"That's one meal she doesn't have to worry about."

"No. That's five or six meals."

"All the better. Come on."

We shopped for the rest of the morning. I was surprised that only a few people wore the red acolyte robes that marked them as devout believers in Estrid's creator. Perhaps she had relaxed her laws.

At one point I asked Flea, "Do you think Kerrick would mind if I bought a few spices? Herbs are going to be harder to find as it gets colder." The winter season was in its infancy. The real nasty weather lurked a few weeks in the distance.

"If it improves the food, no one will mind."

Almost finished with the list, we waited for the beef merchant to settle with the elderly lady in front of us. My arms ached from carrying our purchases. Flea was also loaded down. Now I was glad Belen and the others waited nearby.

After the lady paid for her rib eye, she turned toward us and stopped in astonishment. "Noelle! I thought they took you. When did you get back?" she asked.

"I'm sorry. You must be mistaking me for someone else." Named Noelle, like my sister.

"Oh, sorry, dear. With my old eyes, you looked just like her. But now I can see you're older."

My insides turned to ice. "Do you know where she's from?" I asked. The woman appeared uncertain, so I added, "I have a cousin named Noelle. She's about fourteen, and my family lost track of hers during the plague."

"Oh, yes. So many lost." The woman tsked. "I know she was on her own. She'd do odd jobs for me, such a sweet girl.

But when Estrid of Ozero's army arrived, they recruited the young men and women without families." She lowered her voice. "More like conscripted." The wrinkles on her face doubled when she frowned. "That's why I was so startled—I thought she escaped. Bah! More bad times."

"Did she say anything about her family?" I asked.

"No. She never said a word about anyone. Just did the work, thanked me for the coins and left. When the money ran out, she'd show up, asking if I had any work for her. I sure miss her. My legs are getting too old to be gallivanting around the market."

"Thanks for your time," I said.

The woman waved goodbye and headed home.

"Do you really have a cousin named Noelle?" Flea asked me.

"No, but I have...had a younger sister by that name."

"You don't know?"

I told him a condensed version of my arrival home from Tara's. "For all I know they could be buried in the mass grave in Lekas."

"That's tough."

I tried to shrug it off. "Lots of girls have that name. The odds that it's her are low. Besides, you heard the lady—the girl's gone."

"Still..." Flea scanned the market. He put his packages down. "Wait here. I'll go make a few inquiries for you."

"We don't want to attract notice by asking a bunch of questions."

"I won't. The street rats don't care about politics. I'll be back."

Before I could protest, he slipped into the flow of people and was gone from sight. Various emotions churned in my stomach as I waited for him.

What if she wasn't my sister? Then I'd return to wondering where she might be.

What if she *was* my sister? Nothing I could do. Estrid's army had her. Unless she wasn't taken. Then we might be able to find her in town. Hope wanted to grow, but I squashed it flat. Hope led to despair.

What if Flea was caught? Kerrick would kill me. No. He would make me wish I were dead.

Unable to just stand there, I organized our purchases, redistributing the heavier items to make it easier for us to carry. Flea still hadn't returned by the time I finished. Worry swirled. My muscles itched for action, but I forced myself to remain in place.

What if Flea didn't come back? Do I search for him? Get Kerrick? I sorted through my meager options when Flea appeared.

"Where have you been?" I demanded.

"I've been gone for ten minutes," he said.

"Ten torturous minutes." I drew in a deep breath. "These are yours." I gestured to a pile of packages. "Let's get moving before Kerrick comes looking for us."

He gathered his half. "Don't you want to know what I found out?"

"I do. But move first."

We headed toward the road leading east. When we had put the market behind us, I asked Flea what he'd learned.

"Lots about Estrid's army. The people they gathered were mostly street rats. And they're all being held at a training camp about five miles north of town."

I sensed he had more. "Don't keep me on edge, please."

"Noelle was one of the street rats taken. No one knew much about her. But they knew where she came from."

I stopped to face him. "And?"

"She's your sister. No doubt about it."

CHAPTER 11

"How can you be so sure?" I asked Flea.

"The street rats kept mistaking you for her—except the one who tried to pick your pocket. They said she was from Lekas. That's in Kazan, isn't it?"

"Why did they tell you all this?" I'd been searching for any sign or clue to my family's whereabouts for three years. For this to just pop up now...seemed suspicious. Perhaps a trap?

"I was a street rat."

"Uh-huh."

"And I spread a few coins around. Happy?"

"That makes more sense." I kept a firm grip on my emotions. Flea might not doubt who she was, but I did. "Did you learn anything about the training camp?"

"It's guarded, but not locked tight. Let's face it, most of the recruits went from worrying about their next meal and where they would sleep when the snows came to having food, shelter and warm clothing."

"But they have to fight for Estrid."

"Like I said before, street rats don't care about politics.

Treat them good, and they'll be loyal. Besides, it's not like anyone's at war or rebelling or doing much of anything."

"Now. What happens when Tohon and Estrid decide they want to occupy the same town?"

Flea didn't respond. He put a finger to his lips just when I heard the sour rustle to our left. I grabbed the hilt of my knife, but relaxed when Belen emerged from the forest. We were soon surrounded by the others.

"You were gone longer than expected," Loren said. "Did Avry have a hard time finding the market?"

Quain chuckled.

I glanced at Kerrick to gauge his mood. Nothing. I'd get more information staring at a stone. Belen tried to take all my packages, but I kept a few. Loren and Quain helped Flea.

Finally, Flea said, "We had an opportunity to discover a few more details about Estrid and her forces." He explained about the training camp as we headed to the cave. "And we need to rescue Avry's sister."

This last bit was met with stunned silence, including me. Then the questions started. Flea told them about Noelle.

"There's no proof it's her," I said.

"We'll do a reconnaissance first," Flea said. "We'll verify she's there, then we'll sneak in—"

"No. It's too dangerous," Kerrick said, as if that ended the discussion.

I had been thinking the same thing, but when Kerrick said no, my first instinct was to argue with him. "It wouldn't be that dangerous to go have a look. If it's her, then I don't have to keep wondering if she's alive or dead."

"We're not going near the camp. You can come back after…" An evil gleam shone in Kerrick's eyes. "Promise you'll heal Ryne, and we'll take a look and see if it's her."

I felt as if he shoved his sword deep into my chest. Perhaps this was payback for making him choose between Belen and his prince.

"No deal," I said. Proud my voice didn't squeak, I increased my pace so I led the group back to the cave. So they couldn't see the tears blurring my vision.

We returned and the others unpacked the supplies. It was my turn to cook, and I focused on the task at hand. With fresh ingredients, spices and herbs it would have been difficult to ruin the meal. Loren, Quain and Flea made appreciative noises. Belen proclaimed the roast the best he'd ever had. But I had no appetite, and I slid into my bedroll as soon as I could.

My thoughts returned to Noelle. If she was the missing street rat, being able to see her or even talk to her would be beyond wonderful. She probably knew the fate of Allyn and our mother, although just the fact she was alone meant bad news. They would never leave her if they were alive. Unless they had gotten separated by unexpected circumstances. Too many questions without answers. Were they worth my life? If she trained with Estrid's soldiers, then she was relatively safe. And what if I'd promised to heal Ryne, and the girl wasn't my little shadow?

I'd made the right decision. Although the desire to sneak away to see the camp for myself throbbed in my heart. Even if I hadn't given my word not to escape, I wouldn't be able to go very far before Kerrick dragged me back.

The knowledge that my choice was based in logic failed to remove the sharp knife of pain in my chest. Over the next couple days, I picked at my food, and stayed under my blankets as much as I could.

On the third day, Belen hauled me to my feet and cajoled me into leaving the cave. I squinted into the bright sunshine as fingers of cold air stroked my face and ruffled my hair. Loren and Quain practiced sparring with sticks instead of swords. Flea napped in a patch of sunshine. Kerrick, of course, was gone to I–couldn't–care–less.

"See that target?" Belen asked.

A red circle had been painted on a tree trunk about forty feet away. "Yes."

"Here." Belen handed me my knives. "Even though my memories are fuzzy, I seem to recall someone needs to work on her aim."

I stared at the daggers. Both gleamed. I wondered which one had embedded into that man's thigh.

"That someone is you, Avry," Belen said. "Try to hit the target with the knife."

"I'm not in the mood for this. Maybe later…"

He refused to take the weapons or to move out of my way.

"You're not going back to the cave until you hit the target," he said.

I glared, but he remained unaffected. "Fine." I grasped the end of the blade and threw the knife. It missed. So did the next one and the next and the five after that. Frustration welled. Focusing, I pushed all distracting thoughts and problems to the side and concentrated on the red circle. The knife hit the target and bounced off.

"There. I hit it." I moved to leave.

Belen's huge hand clamped onto my shoulder, stopping me in midstep. "Not so fast. It has to stick."

"That wasn't part of the deal."

"Too bad. So sad. Try again."

My aim had improved, but none of the blades would pierce the bark. "It's too far for me. I'm not strong enough." My voice whined. Normally, I would have been appalled. Not today.

"No. You're not putting enough heat behind it."

"Heat?"

"Yeah, heat." Belen scratched his arm as he searched for the right words. "Heat like energy, desire, emotion. Think of that target as a giant spider and then throw the knife."

"I like spiders."

"Then think of it as something you don't like. A snake or a Death Lily. Anything."

I aimed at the red circle and imagined an image on the tree's trunk. Anger and annoyance in equal measure flowed through me. Whipping the knife, I put heat into the throw. A satisfying thunk sounded.

"That's what I'm talking about," Belen said. "What did you think of? The Death Lily or the snake?"

"Neither." Could I do it a second time? Conjuring up the feelings the image evoked, I sent the second blade deep into the trunk next to the other.

"Nice. See, you *are* strong enough."

I pulled the knives from the bark, returned to Belen's side and buried them both again.

"You got it. What gave you the motivation?"

"Kerrick's face inside that target." I sucked in a deep breath. Pain no longer stabbed quite so deep. Perhaps I needed to throw a few dozen more knives right between his eyes.

"That's not nice," Belen scolded.

"Too bad." Thunk. "So sad." Thunk.

"At least you're smiling again. Think you can hit a moving target?"

"Maybe."

"For any task, you need two things above all else. Confidence and practice. When you have those two, you can do anything."

"A cheesy motivational quote. Kill. Me. Now."

"Being nasty will only prolong your knife-throwing lesson."

I shrugged. "Not like I'm doing anything else."

"You could be running laps to get into shape. Climbing the Nine Mountains is strenuous in any weather, but particularly difficult in the winter."

Ugh. "Sorry. How do you plan to mimic a moving target?"

"Quain rigged up a board with some ropes. Quain, are you ready to take a break?"

He and Loren finished their bout.

"Yeah, I'm tired of winning," Quain said, wiping the sweat that dripped off his smooth head.

"You call that winning? I'd call it barely keeping up." Loren's red face and damp tunic told another story.

Flea woke, stretched and yawned. "Yep, that was a super exciting match. I'm glad you guys invited me to observe—I needed to catch up on my sleep." He ducked as they flung their sticks at him.

We all walked to an area that had a long thin line of sight. At the end, a square piece of wood with a red circle on it hung down from the trees. Quain wrapped his arms and legs around a tree's trunk and climbed into the lower limbs.

"Ready," Quain said.

"Start slow," Belen ordered. "Side-to-side motion."

Quain yanked on the ropes, causing the board to sway.

"It's all in the timing," Belen said to me. "The aim and throw are the same, but now you need to release the knife at just the right moment."

Flea and Loren watched. Guess I would have an audience. Yippee. Gripping the blade, I counted beats as the board swung one full circuit. No real reason why, just seemed like the thing to do. It didn't work. After a few misses, I clipped the wood. I adjusted my timing and had another near hit.

When the knife's tip stuck inside the circle, the guys cheered. Quain increased the pace of the swing. Again, I struggled to find the right release point. Eventually, I hit the mark. Then Quain became creative with the motion. Pulling on the ropes, he resembled a puppeteer. The board moved up and down and side to side. Once I hit the target, he changed the speed or the motion or both.

I hated to admit this, but I enjoyed the challenge. Belen no longer offered advice. Either that, or I didn't hear him. My world shrank to me, the knives and the moving red circle.

When the light faded, Belen stopped the session. "That's a good start." He clapped me on the back and almost knocked me to the ground. "Kerrick was right. You are a fast learner. Soon, you'll be dangerous with those knives."

"As long as my opponent stands forty feet away," I said.

"One thing at a time. After you mastered the art of throwing, I can teach you how to fight with and defend against a knife."

We returned to the cave. My arms ached from the exertion. My stomach grumbled for the first time in days, although my appetite soured when Kerrick entered. Mr. Ghost of the Forest. He could run circles around that training camp with no one the wiser, yet he wouldn't. Bitter? Who me?

I forced half a bowl of Loren's stew down my throat before crawling under my blanket.

Voices whispering intently woke me sometime later. I guessed by the low light that the fire had burned down to embers. After a few minutes, I identified the voices as Kerrick's and Belen's. No surprise.

"...never agree to heal Ryne if you don't show her some kindness," Belen said.

"What do you call teaching her how to move through the forest, or how to throw knives?"

"Survival skills because *we* put her in danger."

"And locked in a jail awaiting execution wasn't dangerous?" Despite the whispering, his sarcasm rang clear.

"You know what Tohon's capable of. I'd rather she go to the guillotine than be captured by him."

A flurry of fear swirled at his words. That didn't sound good. Not at all. No answer from Kerrick, which made it worse. I wished I could see his face.

"I helped her find that girl," Kerrick said in a more subdued tone.

"Doesn't count since Avry made a deal with you."

"But she's being so stubborn. And we're running out of time. Every day he's trapped in stasis is another day Tohon and Estrid have to strengthen their armies."

"Even if we reached him tomorrow, it won't matter. She'll refuse to heal him and then what do we do?" Belen asked.

Silence.

"It'd be better to take the time and show her what happens to the people under Tohon's rule."

"No. Too dangerous." Kerrick sighed. "There has to be another way. She's too smart to believe those rumors about Ryne, but I don't know why she won't agree."

"There's another reason why. We need to find out, but she won't open up with you being all stony silence and brooding anger. Jael's been gone for four years…she's not—"

"Don't start." Boots scraped on the ground. Footsteps faded.

Belen settled into his blankets with a muttered curse. It didn't take him long to fall asleep. I wish I could say the same thing. Their conversation replayed in my mind.

I wondered who Jael was. Although it was better for me if

Kerrick kept being a cold heartless bastard. He made refusing to help Ryne easy. Belen had been right; I had many other reasons to hate Ryne besides the rumors.

When I'd apprenticed with Tara, she told us about the time when Queen Alvena had requested her to heal King Micah. After traveling across the Nine Mountains, Prince Ryne blocked Tara from seeing his father, claiming healers were unnatural and upset the world's balance. Disease and sicknesses were nature's way to regulate our population.

Ryne's reasons had sounded like bullshit to me. Ryne wanted his father's throne, not natural order. Tara had said he'd been nasty, rude and had his guards escort her from the castle even though it was late at night. He hadn't allowed her to talk to his mother, either.

It was pointless to share this story with Belen. He'd been countering all my objections about Ryne, explaining away all his bad behavior. I wondered if he knew about Ryne's dislike of healers even before the plague. But, if I thought about it, it wasn't up to Belen or the others to change my mind about Ryne. That was Ryne's job. Too bad he couldn't speak for himself.

My thoughts blurred until sleep took over. Images of Noelle at various ages haunted my dreams. I tried to reach her, but giant flowers kept blocking my path. She yelled for me to save her. Shoving petals out of the way, I muscled closer to her. When I was about to grab her, vines circled my wrists, stopping me. I struggled but they tightened, pulling me back. The vines grew from Kerrick's arms and twisted around me until I couldn't move.

My dreamworld melded with reality when I woke.

Kerrick knelt next to me, holding my flailing wrists. "Easy. It's just a dream."

I stopped fighting.

He let go and sat back on his heels. "Nightmare?"

"Something like that," I mumbled, still half-asleep.

"Is your sister's name Noelle?"

"Yes, why?"

"You were yelling her name."

"Oh." What else could I say to that?

"Who is Allyn?"

"My younger brother. Did I shout his name, too?"

"Not tonight, but sometimes you mutter his name when you're sleeping."

Wonderful, I thought sourly.

"Did he survive the plague?" Kerrick asked.

"I don't know. He disappeared with my sister and mother."

"Do you have any other siblings?"

I caught on. "If you think you can use my family as a way to get me to agree to heal Ryne, it won't work. I've been on the run for three years, and during that entire time I hadn't discovered a single clue to where my family might be. Learning that my sister might be alive and in some training camp is astounding. But even that didn't work for you, so I'd suggest you find another way."

"You really have a low opinion of me, don't you?"

"No one else has backhanded me, starved me, manacled me to a tree and let me freeze each night. Therefore, I don't have anyone else to compare you to."

"And what about the rescues from jail, the mercs and the lessons?"

"All for Prince Ryne. Not me. You made that perfectly clear. Ryne is your priority."

"Fair enough. Consider this. It's obvious you care for Noelle. What if she was sick, and I was the only one who could save her life? And you knew if she lived, she would do great things for thousands of people. What would you do after I refused to cure her because I heard she punched her brother?"

Hitting a sibling wasn't quite the same. "I wouldn't resort to violence or intimidation. But I understand your point and, yes, I would put every effort into changing your mind about Noelle. I don't object to the stories, the lessons or being a prisoner—not like my life before was any better. What I don't like is being treated as a means to an end. That what I think or feel doesn't matter at all as long as I agree with you. That might work for your gentlemen who choose to be here, but it won't for me."

Kerrick gaze grew distant, and I wondered if he would finally understand. Which would complicate my life since his bully tactics only strengthened my resolve not to heal Ryne. But, as usual, he didn't give me any indication that I had gotten through to him.

"Belen was whittling knives from branches tonight. He has a busy day planned for you tomorrow. Go back to sleep, Avry," Kerrick said.

Shock rolled through me. Kerrick had said my name, and I suspected things between us would change. But would it be in a good way or bad?

Even warned, I didn't think Belen would work me quite so hard. He had me repeat the knife throwing with both stationary and moving targets until he was satisfied. Then he drew smaller circles and asked me to aim for them. Once I managed to hit the smaller targets, we started with basic knife defense, using the wooden knives he had carved.

Bruised, sore and tired, I had no trouble falling into a deep sleep that night. No nightmares disturbed my rest, but Kerrick shook me awake, anyway. I blinked at him in confusion.

"Come on," he said.

"Why? Did they discover our hiding spot?"

"No. But we need to leave now if we're going to make it back by daylight."

"Leave for where?" My thoughts felt as if they'd been dipped in honey.

"To visit your sister."

CHAPTER 12

I snapped awake. Did Kerrick just say…? "Visit my sister?" I repeated.

"Yes."

"And what do I have to promise you in exchange?"

"Nothing."

I stared at him, seeking the real truth. But he returned my gaze with a rare open expression. Belen stood behind him with a wide smile on his face. Interesting. Not one to waste a golden opportunity, I threw back my covers, yanked on my boots and wrapped my cloak around my shoulders.

"You're in charge until we get back," Kerrick said to Belen.

"And if you don't arrive by morning?"

"Come find Avry at the training camp. Don't worry about me."

"Yeah, right."

Kerrick muttered under his breath.

I gave Belen a quick hug. "Thanks," I whispered in his ear.

He tried to act innocent. "For what?"

"Belen, promise me you won't *ever* play poker."

"Too late. The monkeys cleaned me out months ago."

"Oh, Belen."

"It's only money, Avry. Get moving or Kerrick'll leave without you." He waved me off.

Now it was my turn to mutter as I followed Kerrick from the cave and into the dark forest. No moon hung in the cloudless night sky.

Kerrick turned to me. "Do you want to…?" He held his hand out. "We can move faster if…"

I blinked a few times. Kerrick being shy? Normally, he would just grab my wrist and drag me along. Nice Kerrick was scarier than Mean Kerrick.

In answer to his unfinished question, I laced my cold fingers in his warm ones. Magic buzzed up my arm and the objects in the forest became clear as if the sun had just risen.

He set a quick pace. For the first time, keeping up was easy. Through his magic, I sensed we were alone in this part of the woods, and I had a number of questions. "How do you know she's my sister?"

"I've been watching the camp." He glanced at me. "She resembles you, and she fights with a familiar tenacity. I've seen her take on bigger opponents and win. If she isn't your sister, then I'll relinquish command to Flea."

Hope mixed with pride. A dangerous combination, but I couldn't suppress those feelings anymore. "How am I going to talk to her?"

"The security around the barracks is lax. I've gotten inside without trouble, encountering no one. It's an old facility that used to house thousands of soldiers so all the recruits have their own rooms."

He'd been busy. I considered. Being able to talk to her would be unbelievable, but what if she was unhappy? How could I leave her there? "What if she wants to come with us?" I braced for his answer.

"Then we'll come back for her."

I skidded to a halt. "What's going on?" I demanded. "I told you before, I won't promise—"

"I know. Despite what you think, I wouldn't be that cruel." He drew in a deep breath. "My behavior has been... inexcusable. This is a way I can show you that you're more than a means to an end."

Even though I remained suspicious, I couldn't refuse his help. "You'll let her travel with us?"

"No." He held up a hand to stop my protest. "It's too dangerous for her. Hell, it's too dangerous for us. I thought we'd leave her with Mom."

He'd thought this through! Going back to Mom's would add weeks onto our journey. I should be terrified about how he might use this act of kindness in my future, but Noelle's safety was all that mattered.

"What should I tell her, then?" I asked.

"To pack a bag and hide it. When we leave this area, we'll come for her. Warn her, it'll be in the middle of the night again, and it may be a couple weeks before we can leave."

We continued to the training camp, slowing as we drew closer. As Kerrick had said, only a few security guards patrolled the dilapidated wooden fence. When two of them disappeared around a corner, we climbed through a gap between boards. Just inside the fence, a ring of torches burned, creating pools of light. We sprinted into the shadows hugging the barracks. Sliding along the wall, we reached one of the side doors.

Kerrick used his lock picks and popped the lock. He slipped inside and I followed, closing the door behind us. He headed straight to a door halfway down the corridor. I didn't bother to ask how he knew where Noelle's room was located.

"I'll wait here," he whispered. "Don't be long."

Suddenly nervous, I turned the knob, entering the room. Kerrick shut the door. A single bed, night table and desk decorated the small space. A weak yellow glow shone through the window, illuminating black hair spilled over the pillow. Stepping closer, I worried. What if she wasn't Noelle? What if the girl screamed? Not wanting to scare her, I stopped about two feet away.

"Noelle," I whispered.

"Hmm?"

Some things never changed. We had shared a room, and I used to wake her up in the middle of the night to discuss a matter that, at the time, seemed so important it couldn't wait for morning. I sank to my knees at the familiar response.

"Noelle," I said a little louder.

She jerked up with a yelp.

"It's okay. It's me."

"Me who?"

"Avry."

Shock replaced fear as she met my gaze. "You're alive?"

A silly question, but considering the circumstances... "Yes. I've been searching for my little shadow for years."

She lunged. For a split second, I thought she meant to attack me, but she wrapped me in her arms and squeezed so hard, I feared for my ribs. Noelle buried her face in my neck. I held her, drinking in her scent as a flood of emotions overwhelmed me.

Aware of Kerrick waiting outside, I reluctantly pulled her away. Her eyes glittered, but, unlike me, she hadn't cried.

"How did you—?" she started.

I cut her off. "What happened to Mom and Allyn?"

She stiffened as her gaze turned icy. "Dead."

I jerked as if she had punched me. Suspecting they were dead felt far better than the truth. The confirmation cut through me, rendering me unable to draw a breath.

"Why didn't you come home?" Noelle demanded.

In that moment she no longer resembled my little shadow, but acted like a stranger.

I gazed at her in confusion. "I did come home, but you were gone."

"Why did you wait so long? I sent you a dozen letters as soon as they got sick, begging you to come home."

"Letters?"

"Don't pretend you didn't get them. I described their symptoms in detail. You knew they had the plague before we did. I can't believe you'd listen to the Guild. Nothing's more important than your family."

It took a long moment, but I realized Tara must have hidden or destroyed Noelle's letters. She knew I would run home to help my family despite the Guild's directive about the plague.

"Noelle, I don't have time to explain right now. But give me the chance." Talking fast, I outlined our plan to rescue her, giving her a brief summary of Kerrick and his men.

"Prince Kerrick of Alga?" she asked.

"He's no prince. Believe me." I took her hands in mine. "Please come with us. We'll have lots of time together and I can tell you everything."

"Of course I'll come. I hate it here."

I hugged her as relief melted my heart. "I missed you so much."

The door opened. Noelle pulled away as Kerrick poked his head in.

"We need to go," he said, then ducked back out.

I relayed his instructions to her. "It could be a couple weeks, but I promise we'll be back for you."

She nodded. "I'll be ready."

We returned to the cave an hour before dawn. The guys had waited up for us. To me, everything had changed even though nothing had changed. Lying in their bedrolls around the fire, Loren and Quain still argued, Flea greeted me with his lopsided grin and Belen was still Poppa Bear, smiling as he followed us in. He had been on watch.

Flea sat up. "Was it her?"

"Yes," I said.

"Knew it! And *you* didn't believe me."

"It just seemed too big a coincidence. It could have been a trap."

"Why can't a coincidence be a good thing?"

"I think there's a law against it in Ryazan," Quain quipped.

"I'm all for avoiding Ryazan," Kerrick said.

"Don't want to run into Xane's skeleton crew again?" Belen asked.

"Do you?"

"Not without another hundred armed men by my side. Those people…"

"Are sick bastards," Quain said.

"How so?" I asked.

"For one, they use the bones of the dead as weapons, armor, tents and two—"

"That's enough, Quain," Loren said, then asked me, "Did you find out about the rest of your family?"

Quain swatted him. "Nice segue, Loren. You basically implied Avry's family is crazy."

"Only you would make that connection, bonehead. I was

trying to change the subject. Unless you want to reminisce about the time Xane's men almost skinned you alive?"

"No," Quain, Flea and Belen all said together.

"Any more good news?" Flea asked me.

Grief welled as I shook my head. "More victims of the plague." This they all understood. "Noelle is all I have left."

"Sorry to hear that, Avry," Belen said. "I've lost a sister and my mother. My younger sister and father survived."

"Parents and sister gone. One brother and a great-aunt left," Kerrick said.

"My wife and..." Loren closed his eyes. "And the baby she was carrying died with her."

I bit my lip, losing his child seemed extra cruel. This listing of the dead and the living was inevitable whenever survivors become comfortable with one another. I was touched they shared their lists with me.

"It was just me and my dad," Quain said into the silence. "He lasted a couple years, then the plague got him in the end."

Flea stared at us. "I can't decide what's worse. Losing family members or not having a family to lose."

"Not having a family to lose," I said. "It's heartbreaking, but better to have some time together than none at all."

"And they live on in your memories," Belen said.

Flea hunched down. "I don't have any memories."

"Sure you do," Belen said.

Confused, Flea glanced at us.

"Like when you kicked Belen in the shins," I said.

"And when we rescued Avry," Belen said.

"Oh." Flea brightened.

Kerrick suggested everyone get a few hours of sleep.

"I'll stand guard," Belen offered.

"Have you been on duty all night?" Kerrick asked.

His sheepish expression answered for him.

Kerrick sighed. "Belen, being in charge doesn't mean you stand guard all night."

"I couldn't sleep."

Loren flung back his blankets. "I'll take the next shift. I had a few hours earlier."

I slid into my bedroll as exhaustion caught up to me. Fresh grief for my mother's and brother's deaths played tug-of-war with joy over finding my little shadow alive. My heart felt torn in two. Eventually, I didn't have the energy to stay awake any longer.

A couple days after we'd visited Noelle, Kerrick announced his plans to travel north to find out if Estrid's ambush had returned from the pass. "The bulk of her army is camped outside Zabin. The group from the pass would most likely travel down the border road between Pomyt and Vyg to meet up with them. Since we've already lost so much time, I don't want to waste more guessing if they've left." He looked at me.

I wouldn't feel guilty about the delays. No reason for me to hurry to Ryne's bedside only to refuse to heal him. I dreaded Kerrick's reaction when that happened.

"If I don't return in ten days, leave this location immediately," Kerrick said to Belen. "Find a hiding spot and hunker down until spring, then take Avry across the Nine Mountains."

"You shouldn't go alone," Belen said.

"I can move faster on my own. Don't worry, Belen, I won't get too close." He glanced at me again before he left, and I wondered how far his forest magic stretched.

Belen kept me busy during the next nine days, teaching me how to fight with a knife, defend against a knife and practicing all that I learned. I worked with Flea at night, showing him how to juggle four objects.

"Two in one hand, throw and catch them with the same hand." I demonstrated the motion. "When you master that for each hand, you put it together so it looks like the stones are going back and forth between hands, but you're really just throwing the same two rocks with the same hand."

Flea hefted the stones. "This is just going to get more and more complicated, isn't it?"

"Yep."

"Just like you," he said.

"What do you mean?"

"It was supposed to be simple. Find you, take you to Prince Ryne and it's done. But it's all complicated now. And what if Kerrick doesn't come back?"

A strange little feeling tugged deep within me. Flea had voiced what I'd been unconsciously worried about—Kerrick. Which was utter nonsense. I concentrated on Flea's question. "Then we'll go find him and rescue him if we can."

"But Kerrick said—"

"Think about it, Flea."

He didn't take long. "Belen won't listen."

"Not that complicated when you stop to consider all the variables."

"No, but...sometimes I don't have an answer for all the variables."

"No one does. We do the best we can with what we have. And good leaders stay about two steps ahead of the rest of us. I'm beginning to understand why your prince assigned this mission to Kerrick and not Belen. A certain amount of ruthlessness is needed."

Kerrick failed to arrive on the tenth day. Belen paced and fretted and growled at anyone who dared suggest we pack up or we search for Kerrick. He kept his angry bear routine all during the eleventh day, as well.

Near sunset, Quain, Loren, Flea and I gathered outside the cave and out of Belen's sight and hearing.

"Do we follow Kerrick's orders despite Belen's…ill humor?" Loren asked.

"Or do we find out what happened to Kerrick?" Quain asked.

"We should leave," I said. "If Estrid has him, she'll eventually learn where we're hiding. We can launch a rescue attempt from our new location. If he's delayed, he can easily track us to our new hiding spot."

"Leave tonight or in the morning?" Loren asked.

"Tonight, under cover of darkness," I said.

"What about your sister?" Flea asked.

"She's safe enough where she is. If there's a chance to get her before the spring, I will, but I won't risk all of you. I can always come back for her later." Without thinking, I had assumed the leadership role, and, like I had said to Flea, a certain amount of ruthlessness was needed. In this case, my sister would have to wait.

The men returned to the cave to start packing despite Belen's protests. Before I entered, the wind shifted and I caught a whiff of spring sunshine and living green. I turned into the wind, expecting to see Kerrick standing there. Disappointment panged until I remembered I hated him. Until I realized he had probably been hanging around to see what we'd do without him. Typical.

Breathing deep, I walked north, following Kerrick's scent until I lost it as quick as I had found it. I pulled off my gloves and pressed my palms to the cold ground. Strong magic tingled along my skin, pulsing to the south. He had moved downwind of me.

I straightened and spun around. No one, but I wasn't going to trust my eyes this time.

"I know you're there. No sense wasting any more energy," I said.

Kerrick appeared next to the tree a few feet in front of me. He had used his magic to blend in with the darkening forest. His expression was unreadable.

"How long have you been back?" I asked, trying to sound annoyed in order to cover my relief.

Instead of answering, he said, "You sniffed me out, didn't you?"

"I asked first."

"You had to," he mused more to himself than me. "You didn't resort to feeling for the magic until I—"

"Yes, I followed your stench. It's not that big a deal. Not when *you've* been playing around, making *your* men worried and considering mutiny."

"*My* men? As of an hour ago, they were *your* men, willing to take on Belen so they could carry out *your* orders." He cocked his head to the side. "Funny, I didn't put you in charge when I left."

I crossed my arms. "Did you or did you not order Belen to leave this place if you didn't return in ten days?"

"I did."

"In case you missed it, we're still here. A dangerous place to be if you were in Estrid's or even the mercs' custody. Belen is too kindhearted to leave without you. Someone had to be the voice of reason."

"You? The voice of reason? That's hard to believe."

His nasty comment was uncalled for. I struck back. "Since I didn't care if you returned or not, I had no trouble making decisions based on logic."

Not wanting to continue this useless conversation, I

headed toward the cave. Belen's angry voice reached me well before I arrived. He held Quain in a headlock. Bedrolls and blankets had been strewn about the cavern. Flea and Loren kept their distance from the raging Poppa Bear.

"Belen," Kerrick said.

Everyone turned. The tension dispersed as grins of relief replaced the strained expressions. Belen released Quain, who puffed for air and rubbed his neck.

"What happened?" Loren asked Kerrick.

Kerrick shot me a look before saying, "I was delayed. But I've good news. Estrid's people are returning home, and there's no sign of mercs, either." He scanned the mess. "We'll leave tomorrow night after Avry and I fetch her sister."

Flea and the monkeys gathered their belongings, but before Belen could join them, Kerrick said, "Belen, a word." He led Belen outside.

We all exchanged glances.

"Belen shouldn't get into trouble," Flea said. "He was right. There wasn't any danger."

"This time," Loren said.

I packed my knapsack early the next morning. It didn't take long. Too many hours remained before I would be with my sister. I'd endured three long years without her, but the thought of waiting until midnight seemed unbearable.

An unusually subdued Belen worked knife-defense drills with me, which helped to pass the time. But after dinner, I couldn't keep still.

"You should rest," Kerrick said. "It's going to be at least a full day before we can sleep again."

"Why don't you tell her another Prince Ryne story," Quain said. "That always puts her right to sleep."

I muffled a laugh over Kerrick's sour expression.

"Tell her about Jael," Belen said in a quiet voice. He stared at the flames and not at Kerrick. "Tell Avry how if it wasn't for Jael, you would have killed Ryne."

I glanced at Kerrick, expecting an angry retort. But he had shut down. Kerrick stood without a word, and left. A minute later, Loren arrived. He rubbed his hands over the fire to warm them.

Sensing the mood, Loren asked, "What did I miss?"

"Nothing." Belen threw a log onto the fire. "Absolutely nothing."

I lay in my bedroll, but I couldn't sleep. When Kerrick approached to wake me, I sat up. No one else had fallen asleep, either. As I stuffed my remaining things in my knapsack, the others also packed the rest of their belongings.

"We'll meet you just south of Zabin around midday," Kerrick said to Belen. "If we don't arrive by after—"

"I know," Belen said.

We left the cave together. Taking our packs, Belen led the others northwest, while Kerrick and I headed north. He offered his hand and I took it without hesitation. Through his connection with the forest, I sensed the location of the others. Handy.

It didn't take long to reach the training camp. Nothing had changed. Once again we slipped inside the barrack without trouble.

I woke Noelle.

She stared at me a moment. "You came back."

"I said I would."

"Is Kerrick with you?"

"Yes, he's in the hall. Are you ready to go?"

Pushing her covers off, she sat up. Instead of wearing nightclothes, she wore her training uniform. Smart girl.

"It's nice of him to help us," she said.

I agreed. "Where did you hide your pack?"

"No one in our neighborhood would help me when Mom and Allyn were sick."

"Noelle, we need to go. You can tell me this later."

"I was ten years old. No one would help me. They died and left me all alone. I've been alone for the last three and a half years."

I sat next to her and put my arm around her shoulder. "You're not alone now, little shadow."

She shrugged me off and stood. "Don't call me that. And you're right. I'm not alone anymore." Noelle crossed to her desk, grabbed what looked like an oversize hairbrush and banged it repeatedly on the wood.

The sharp slaps splintered the quiet night, rattling the window. I jumped to my feet, and rushed to stop her. "What are—?" I froze in horror.

Voices yelled, boots drummed, doors slammed and the unmistakable sound of steel striking steel rang from the hallway.

Noelle stopped pounding on the desk. She gestured toward the door with the mallet. "You're too late. *Again.* I don't need or want your help."

CHAPTER 13

Noelle swung the mallet at my head. "You…"

I ducked.

She reversed direction. "Abandoned…"

I ducked again.

Lunging forward with her weapon, she aimed for my stomach. "Me!"

I hopped back, but stepped in close when she raised the mallet above her head. As she brought her arms down, I grabbed her wrists. Skin on skin. Noelle struggled, but I held tight.

She cursed. "I hate you. I want to kill you, but you're too valuable." Noelle nearly growled the words.

They burned through my heart like acid. I kept my grip on her wrists, but in the end I couldn't hurt her. She had endured so much, I wasn't going to cause her any more pain.

The door banged. Voices ordered me to release her. I ripped the mallet from her hands and spun her toward the soldiers. Then I yanked my knife from my belt. Before anyone could react, I threw the weapon at the closest soldier, burying the blade into his shoulder. He yelped.

I hurled the mallet at the window. The glass shattered with an explosive crash. In two quick strides, I reached the broken window and dove through it. Hitting the hard ground with my shoulder, I rolled. Despite the pain, I gained my feet and ran. Shouts and curses followed, but I didn't stop until I climbed over the fence.

Instead of racing into the woods, I turned left and hugged the fence. When I encountered a dark section, I pressed up against the wooden boards, hoping to blend in.

I muffled my gasps for breath as the fastest soldiers reached the barrier. My heart ceased its frantic beat when the soldiers landed on my side. They glanced both ways. And just when I felt on the edge of passing out, they headed into the forest.

Sagging in relief after the last of them disappeared, I fought to regain my composure. Everything had happened so fast, but once again, those years spent on the run had trained me not to hesitate even when my own sister tried to beat me over the head with a mallet.

When my heart slowed from panicked to scared, I ghosted along the fence until I found a crack big enough to peer through. Soldiers searched the compound. After a few minutes, the door at the end of the barracks flew open. Men spilled out. And in the middle of a tight group was Kerrick.

Blood flowed from a gash on his forehead. He scowled as they hustled him along. His hands had been manacled behind his back. They took him to a square building in the northwest corner of the camp. Probably a jail or a place where they could interrogate him.

What now? Catching up to Belen and the others would be the smart thing to do. It would be what Kerrick would want me to do. But guilt wouldn't let me be smart. Oh, no. Guilt knew we had come here for me. And that I had to fix this. The problem of how to rescue him remained.

I considered what I had in my favor. The element of surprise—since they would hopefully assume I had escaped into the forest—my defensive powers and a knife. In order to keep my optimism, I skipped the longer list of things against me.

Waiting for the camp to return to normal, I wiggled into a comfortable position and spied through the crack. As I shivered in my cloak, my thoughts kept returning to Noelle. The venom in her voice and the rage in her gaze still burned in my mind. More guilt swelled. I remembered thinking it was odd that I hadn't gotten a letter from home in a while, but I had been so wrapped up in my studies that I hadn't spared the time to discover why. Noelle was right to hate me. I had abandoned her. Desire to make amends, to explain, to hold her until she forgave me, pulsed in my chest. However, Kerrick was first, and later, if I had a later, I would find her again.

The soldiers who had run into the woods returned. Slowly, the compound emptied of searchers and settled. A few men left the square building, but too many for me to handle remained inside. Torchlight glowed from the ground-floor windows.

When I felt as confident as possible considering the circumstances, I climbed the fence and dashed into the shadow of the building. No cries of alarm pierced the air. I drew in a deep breath. Hugging the wall, I crept to one of the windows and peered inside.

The bright light blinded me for a moment. Despite the glass, I heard a man ask, "Where is she going?" No answer. Then a loud slap.

My vision adjusted, and I had an unobstructed view of Kerrick's bloody back. I closed my eyes, but I couldn't block the image of him with his wrists chained to two posts. He stood between them without a shirt. The man asking him questions held a whip. And each time Kerrick refused to answer, another ugly bleeding slash joined the others.

Five more soldiers witnessed the whipping. Too many for me to fight. Unable to watch, I sank to the ground. I bit down on my knuckle as the torture continued. Tell him something, I silently urged Kerrick. But the stubborn man wouldn't say a word. He didn't make a sound the entire time. It went on for an hour or more, but felt like days. The only thing keeping me from surrendering was the fact he would have suffered for nothing if I just waltzed in there.

The soldier finally stopped. He promised to return with a magician, and he left along with three others. Two remained. Could I handle two? I would have to.

I removed my cloak and hid it. My black shirt and pants resembled the training uniform. I twisted my hair up into a knot. Now the hard part. Walking as if I belonged there, I headed to the drinking well. My luck held. No one called out and I found an extra bucket and ladle. Filling the bucket, I returned to the square building.

The door was locked so I knocked on it. A soldier peeked out. "What?"

I held up the bucket. "Captain ordered me to bring the prisoner water, sir."

He stepped aside, letting me in. The other leaned against the far wall. He peered at me with a contemplative purse on his pudgy lips. Kerrick no longer stood, but hung limply between the posts.

"Would you like a drink first, sir?" I asked the guard.

"Sure."

I held up a ladle full of water. He took it from me and bent his head to drink. One chance only. I touched the back of his neck with three fingers, and sent a blast of power. The soldier tipped forward as the other one yelled his name. I let him fall, pulled my knife and turned in time to meet Pudgy Lips.

He hadn't drawn his weapon. Skidding to a stop, he reached for his sword. I didn't wait; I threw my knife, aiming for his right shoulder. Hard to swing a heavy blade with a knife embedded in flesh and muscle. Then I rushed him. Grabbing his arm, I poured magic into him, overloading his senses. He screamed, then collapsed to the ground.

Not wasting any time, I went to Kerrick. He had passed out. I laid my hands on his chest and shared my energy with him. Kerrick groaned and opened his eyes.

He squinted at me. "Avry, what—?"

"Can you stand?" I put my shoulder under his arm to help him get to his feet. On tiptoe, I inspected the cuffs around his wrists. "Do you know where the key is?"

"No."

I searched the two guards and found a ring of little silver keys. Dragging a chair over to the post, I stood on it. Of course the right key had to be the third to last one I tried. At least unlocking the second cuff took mere seconds.

Kerrick's short cape and ripped shirt had been tossed in the corner. By the time he dressed and we slipped from the building, the predawn light had crept over three-quarters of the night sky.

Halfway to freedom, we were spotted. "Hurry," Kerrick urged as the soldiers chased us.

We scrambled over the fence and dove into the woods. As soon as we entered, Kerrick grabbed my arms. Magic zipped along my skin as we rolled together through the underbrush. Our pursuers crashed through the brush. I marveled over how close they came to stepping on us.

This was the third time Kerrick had used this trick. It

was effective, but he wouldn't last long. My magic stirred in response to his weakened physical condition and burning pain. Instead of sending my healing power, I shared more of my energy.

Hours passed before we felt safe enough to move. By this time, Kerrick could barely stand.

I searched my memory for a mundane way to ease his pain. "Is there a stream or creek nearby?"

He nodded. I supported him as we shuffled east. When we reached a small tributary, I sat him down and helped him remove his cape. The back of his shirt was soaked with blood. It clung to the gashes and in a few places it had dried.

"This is going to hurt," I warned him.

He barked a laugh. "Hard to imagine anything worse."

I scooped icy water from the stream and poured it down his back.

Kerrick hissed. "I stand corrected."

Once his shirt was dripping wet, I pulled the fabric from the lacerations and over his head. Then I grabbed fistfuls of muddy sediment from the stream's bottom. I smoothed the mud over the raw cuts. Kerrick paled.

When I finished, we were both shivering in the cold late-morning air. The temperature was the only thing keeping him from passing out. He had his short cape, but the mud needed to dry first. My cloak was back at the training camp and his shirt was sopping wet. I hung it over a tree branch.

"Should I build a fire?" I asked.

"No. The wind is wrong. Lean-to," he said.

I collected branches, vines and leaves with numb hands. He called instructions and I built a small shelter. Using mud to plug the gaps between the branches, I completed the structure.

Kerrick collapsed inside it. I crawled in to cover him with his cape, but he drew me down next to him.

"You're frozen." He draped the cloth over us both, pulling me close.

Our combined body heat eased the shivers. He fell asleep, but I could still sense the forest around us even though he slept. Nice to know no one came close to our hiding spot.

Should I heal him? I debated. He wouldn't want me to. Low on energy and with no food the past twelve hours, I wouldn't have the strength to defend myself if I assumed his injuries. However, his forest magic was more useful right now than my healing power. Plus he shouldn't suffer any- more. It was my fault he'd been captured in the first place. If we were discovered, he could camouflage us. I really hoped it wouldn't come to that.

His arm was wrapped around my waist. I laid my hand on his forearm, releasing the magic. It flowed into him. The cuts on his back throbbed, but didn't sting as sharp as before. I collected the power, pulling it into me. My back blazed. My tunic irritated the lacerations. And my temple throbbed.

Then it seemed as if the roots in the earth swelled, envel- oping me in a cocoon of living green and spring sunshine. The pain eased, and I drifted to sleep.

"Avry." Kerrick managed to pack my name with both an- noyance and exasperation.

I opened my eyes, but the darkness remained.

Kerrick's hand pressed on my back. "Can you move?"

Stretching, I tested my range of motion. My muscles were tight. The fabric of my shirt stuck to my skin.

"Do I need to cover your back with mud?" he asked.

I sat up and reached under my shirt. Touching the welts along my lower back, I felt a line of scabs. "No."

Kerrick slid from the lean-to. "Come out in the moonlight and let me see."

An achy stiffness slowed me. I felt like an old grandmother as I joined him outside. A brisk wind sent goose bumps along my skin. He pulled up the back of my shirt. The icy air bit deeper. I shivered.

"The wounds are already half-healed." His tone carried a note of awe. "Why? I thought you hated—"

"I do." I yanked my shirt down and stepped away from him. Even for me, the cuts shouldn't be so far along. Unless... "How long did we sleep?"

"About ten hours."

Not enough time. But I wasn't about to credit the faster recovery to Kerrick's forest magic. That wouldn't change anything. However, a little voice in my head wouldn't be quiet. It reasoned he must have saved my life back when I had taken Belen's injury. I threw the annoying voice down a deep well in my mind and locked the lid.

"What's wrong?" Kerrick asked.

"Nothing. Shouldn't we go? We need to intercept Belen and the guys before they storm the training camp."

He offered me his cape, but his shirt hadn't dried. It was frozen.

"I'll be fine as long as we keep moving." I ignored his hand, too.

But after stumbling through the woods for an hour, I didn't protest when he laced his fingers through mine. Nor did I complain later when he wrapped his arm around my shoulder and pulled me in close, sharing his warmth.

We stopped at dawn. Without a word, we built a shelter and ate the nuts Kerrick had found. Lying next to him, I stared out at the gray landscape. Once again his arm hugged my waist, but I felt the tension in his muscles and knew he wasn't asleep.

"I'm sorry about my sister," I said.

"You couldn't have known she'd ambush us."

"She'd survived years on her own and had changed so much, but still, she'd given me plenty of clues when I talked to her the first time. I missed them. And look what happened…"

"It worked out."

"Not without considerable…consequences. And it makes me wonder, what else am I missing?"

"Not much gets by you, Avry."

"But my sister—"

"That's different. She's your sister. We all have blind spots when it comes to family."

I felt a little better.

"And there was one positive thing from all this," he said.

"Hard to believe."

"I know, I'm a bit shocked myself. But I figured if you came back for me, who you hate for all the right reasons, then there's hope you'll heal Ryne, who you hate for all the wrong reasons. In fact, I'm quite certain your own quick intelligence will change your mind."

I huffed. "Quite certain? You sound like Belen."

"I'll take that as a compliment."

We caught up to Belen, Loren, Quain and Flea the next night. They had been en route to the training camp. Belen demanded an explanation for our delay.

"We ran into a bit of trouble," Kerrick said.

Flea looked around. "Where's Noelle?"

"She changed her mind," Kerrick answered for me. "Let's get moving."

Glad to have my knapsack, I used my blanket as a cloak. Kerrick took the lead, heading northwest through the dark woods.

As we traveled, Loren walked next to me. "I'm assuming there's more to the story than a bit of trouble," he said.

"Not much," I said. Even following Quain, I felt as if I would trip over an unseen root and fall at any moment. I missed the connection to the forest.

"Uh-huh. So where's your cloak, what's with that cut on your forehead and why aren't you glaring at Kerrick anymore?"

"My sister has it, I fell and I'm saving my glares for the next time he pisses me off."

Loren grinned. "That won't be long."

I agreed. Although I did wonder why he didn't tell them about the ambush or the whipping. And why was I reluctant to mention it? I kept many of Kerrick's secrets. Why? No immediate reason sprang to mind. Perhaps I could use them as leverage. Something along the lines of if Kerrick didn't do X, I would tell the others about his magic. Except, it wouldn't work. As I'd just seen, he wasn't the type to cave in to threats or demands.

We stopped near dawn. Lying low during the day and traveling at night would be our new routine. Loren built a small fire. I sat as close to the flames as possible, trying to drive out the cold that had settled deep in my bones. My muscles ached, and the healing cuts on my back itched like crazy.

"What's the plan?" Belen asked Kerrick.

Everyone had gathered close to eat Loren's squirrel soup.

"We'll stop at Zabin and purchase a few provisions." Kerrick tapped his spoon against his lower lip.

"But you said the bulk of Estrid's army was camped outside Zabin," I said.

"They're camped east of the city. As long as we avoid them and not linger in town, we should be fine."

"Then what?" Belen prompted.

"Then it gets a bit...tricky."

Belen glanced at me as if I knew what Kerrick meant, but I was also in the dark.

"Tricky how?" Loren finally asked.

"Estrid will soon know Avry's not dead. And what Estrid knows, the mercs and Tohon will also learn," Kerrick said.

"So that bit of trouble was Estrid's people discovering Avry's miraculous survival?" Belen asked.

"Yes."

"Then we need to get to the mountain pass before they do," Belen said.

"That would be the logical next step."

"I sense a *but* coming," Quain said.

"But," I said, "everyone knows that's the next logical step."

"Right. Estrid's and Tohon's mercs will head to the pass," Kerrick said. "And there are two possible outcomes. We reach it first and we're chased over the Nine Mountains. The pass is treacherous in good weather. If we rush, we could fall, and these past two years are for nothing."

"What's the second outcome?" Belen asked.

"Estrid or the mercs reach the pass first and we're blocked."

"We might as well wait for spring," I said. "Then we have a few different routes to choose from." Ugh, more time spent with Kerrick and his men all trying to change my mind about Ryne.

"Wouldn't that be obvious, as well?" Loren asked. "Estrid has plenty of soldiers. It'll be three months until the snow thaws, she could block all the passes."

"Not if we're already hiding in the foothills," Kerrick said.

"I think I'd rather take my chances crossing the mountains in winter." Quain voiced what I'd been thinking.

"I remember a certain gentleman who hugged the cliff climbing down into a hundred-foot-deep ravine. I wonder how he would fare climbing a steep icy path that's only a foot wide with a two-thousand-foot drop on the right and a sheer rock wall on the left?"

Quain looked queasy. He swallowed his next comment.

"I don't like hiding in the foothills, either," Kerrick said.

Quain and I said, "But…"

Kerrick gave us a wry smile. "But it's our best option at the moment."

We arrived in Zabin early the next morning. Located northwest of Grzebien next to the border between Pomyt and Vyg, the town was bigger than Grzebien. I tucked my blanket back into my knapsack before we entered the town's limits. As we headed toward the center, the sight of so many people in the streets was overwhelming after spending so much time with just the guys. Unfortunately, uniformed soldiers and robed acolytes also walked among the citizens.

"Should we leave?" Belen asked when we spotted a trio of soldiers watching the market stands.

"We need supplies. There's not another market until Peti, and that's too far," Kerrick said. "We'll split up so we don't attract undue attention. Flea, you're with Belen. Loren and Quain. Avry's with me." He distributed coins and a list of items for each team to purchase. "We'll meet up along the northern road."

Kerrick and I headed to a woman selling cloaks, capes and gloves. He didn't waste time looking through the goods. "Do you have any gray traveling cloaks in her size?" He pointed to me.

The woman peered at me over her glasses. "Goodness, dearie. Aren't you frozen?" She shot Kerrick a nasty look.

I liked her right away. She reminded me of Mom.

She sorted through a rack. "I've a dark gray that might fit." Pulling out a cloak, she wrapped it around my shoulders. "Fur-lined and lots of pockets inside, dearie. Two big pockets on the outside. Do you have gloves?"

"Yes." I had shoved Belen's gift in my pants pocket when I'd rescued Kerrick.

She fussed around me, checking the length. "Those boots are too thin for this weather, dearie. The hair on the Lilys is thicker than last year. We're in for a bad one."

"They're fine," I said.

But she was determined. "I've a pair so soft..." She uncovered calf-high boots the same color as the cloak. "Try them on."

I glanced at Kerrick.

"Go ahead," he said.

The woman had been right. Not only soft, but the fur inside cushioned my feet in warmth. The soles gripped the ground nicely.

"You can walk all day in those and nary a blister." She brandished her own boots. "I won't wear anything else. I thank the maker every day that the cobbler survived the plague."

Which meant the boots probably cost a fortune. I shouldn't have tried them on. "They're wonderful." I agreed. "But I don't have any...enough money."

"Don't you worry, I'll give you a good price for both."

"But—"

"We'll take them," Kerrick said. He didn't bother to haggle over the price because the woman was true to her word.

He paid her and we continued along the row of merchants. I needed the cloak, but not the boots. What was Kerrick up to now? Trying to bribe me? Not his style, but I wondered about the gold. When the mercs attacked Belen, Kerrick had forty gold. Considering they've been on the road for over two years, he probably started with a fortune.

"Did Ryne give you the money?" I asked.

"Yes. He also gave me a list of healers he had gotten from the Guild." Kerrick's gaze grew distant. "You wouldn't have been on that list. How did Ryne know your name?"

Because I've had the misfortune of meeting the bastard. But I wouldn't tell Kerrick that. Why? Cowardice? If he convinces me Ryne's worth saving, then I'd die. Scary, right?

Or was it anger? Kerrick was well aware of what would happen to me after I healed Ryne and yet he showed not the slightest regret. I'd even listen to a speech about the greater good, or about being a martyr, or a hero like Loren had claimed. Yet, I'd gotten nothing. Perhaps he was worried about Belen's reaction. Perhaps he shouldn't keep so many secrets from Belen.

"Avry?"

I met his gaze. "They must have listed the apprentices, as well."

No answer. My thoughts lingered on the Guild. They had been collecting information about the plague until they'd been overwhelmed. I wondered if the Guild House survived. Hoping to change the subject, I said, "The Guild House is a few miles east of the border between Vyg and Pomyt. Won't we pass it on our way to the foothills?"

"We'll come close. Why?"

"If any of their records survived, it could help us."

"How?"

I explained about the medicinal plants. "And since we'll be hiding for a couple months, it will give me something to do besides practice knife fighting."

"As long as there isn't any danger, we can stop. It's a good idea."

He had agreed too quick. That worried me.

We bought a few more supplies. Then Kerrick stopped at a stand selling weapons. "Last place." He sorted through the daggers, hefting a few.

Sensing a sale, the owner approached. "They're all crafted from the finest Zainsk steel."

"They're too heavy. Do you have any throwing knives?" Kerrick asked.

"Yes, sir." The man rummaged under the table and returned with a black pouch. Unrolling the case, he revealed a half dozen narrow blades with small leather-wrapped hilts. "These were hand forged and blessed by the priests of Casis."

Kerrick slipped one out and handed it to me. "What do you think?"

I covered my surprise by gauging the weight and fit of the weapon in my hand. "Easier to handle than Belen's."

"I have a target in the back. You're welcome to try them out," the owner said.

He showed us a red circle painted on a wooden fence. I flipped the right side of my cloak over my shoulder to free my arm. Aiming for the middle of the circle, I snapped my wrist. The knife flew straight and fast. Fun. I sent the other five. They clumped together in the center.

"Your aim has improved," Kerrick said as he yanked the blades from the fence.

"They're so light. It makes it easy," I said.

The owner beamed.

"Do you have any that are a bit sturdier, but still lightweight—more for self-defense?" Kerrick asked.

"I have a sweet little stiletto that's like a feather in your hand, but it's strong. Come." He bustled back to his stand. Pulling a short leather sheath from a box, he handed it to Kerrick. "Made from liquid metal extracted from the bottom of the Nine Mountains, the edge never dulls."

Kerrick drew the weapon. It looked small in his hand. He inspected the shaft before giving it to me. "It weighs nothing."

I wouldn't go that far, but it was well-balanced.

"As you can see," the owner said, "the blade is a few inches longer than a standard dagger, which will give your wife an advantage if she's attacked."

Keeping my gaze on the stiletto, I wasn't about to correct the man—better for us if he thought we were a couple. And I had no interest in Kerrick's reaction. None. Instead, I swung the weapon like Belen had taught me.

"How's the grip?" Kerrick asked me.

The round leather hilt fit nicely in my hand. On the end was a ball-shaped counterweight, and the protective guard wasn't too long. "About perfect."

"I'll take the stiletto and two sets of throwing knives," Kerrick said.

The owner's eyes about popped from his head. "Yes, sir!" He bustled about, gathering the weapons together. Kerrick haggled this time, seeming more comfortable with the price of weapons than clothing.

He handed me the stiletto and its sheath. "Thread it through your belt."

I did, settling the sheath on my right hip.

Giving me the leather pouches of knives, he said, "Put a few in those inside your cloak and the rest in your knapsack."

We cut through the market as we left. Warm and well-armed, I felt better until I glanced back at the arms merchant. He talked to a couple of soldiers, then pointed our way. The soldiers headed in our direction, calling to their colleagues for assistance.

"Kerrick—"

"I see them. Thought we might have trouble. I'm sure the soldiers keep a close eye on the weapon seller's customers."

He didn't seem concerned. I hurried after him as we entered the side streets leading away from the town's center.

"We'll lose them, then meet up with Belen and the others," he said.

A good idea, except the soldiers kept multiplying as they chased us through the town. Surrounded by buildings, Kerrick didn't have access to his forest magic.

Halfway down a rank alley, he stopped. Three people waited at the far end. They just stood there as if they knew we'd be coming. The drum of many boots sounded behind us, echoing off the bricks.

I didn't know why he'd hesitated. There were only three in front of us. "Should I use my knives and clear the way?"

"Won't work," he said.

"Why not?"

Kerrick didn't answer. Instead, he walked up to the three. I followed a step behind. When we drew close, I saw two of the three were women. The lady in the middle was stunning. Tall and slender with long glossy blond hair, large blue eyes and full lips that stretched wide into a smile, she radiated beauty and powerful magic.

"Hello, Kerrick," the lady magician said in a soft purr. "I see the rumors of your demise have been greatly exaggerated."

"Sorry to disappoint you, Jael."

Jael? The same woman Belen had mentioned? The soldiers had stopped a few feet behind us, as if waiting for orders.

"Oh, I'm not disappointed. Not a bit. After all, you've brought me a present." She stepped toward me and extended her hand. "You must be Avry of Kazan. I'm so pleased to make your acquaintance. I'm Jael of Alga. Kerrick's wife."

CHAPTER 14

Kerrick's wife? Quite the surprise, but that would explain why he refused to talk about her. Jael's gaze remained on my face as I shook her hand.

She clasped my fingers in both of hers and held on. "Interesting. No heartbreak. What have you been telling her about me, Kerrick?"

He didn't answer.

"He said nothing to me," I said. "Why would I be upset?" Aside from the dozen soldiers behind us.

She pursed those full lips, considering. "Because I might steal him back."

I laughed. "Please do. He's been a pain in my ass for the past two months."

Jael dropped my hand. "I see you haven't changed in four years, Kerrick."

"Neither have you. You can still lie with a straight face." He glanced at me. "She's not my wife. Jael enjoys playing head games."

"Still bitter after all these years?" She tsked. "No wonder the pretty healer is happy to be rid of you. Kerrick and I were betrothed and almost to the altar when a stronger suitor stole my heart."

"It's been unpleasant reminiscing with you, but we need to go." Kerrick grabbed my arm and stepped around her.

The air surrounding us thickened until we could no longer move. Magic rolled along my scalp like static.

"Cute," Jael said. "You know better, Kerrick." She faced us. "My magic is a gift from the air. It obeys me. I can even take your breath."

My confusion lasted until I felt the air being pulled from my lungs. I struggled to keep it and to draw in more, but couldn't. My lungs strained as black and white spots swirled in my vision. My healing magic flared to life, fighting Jael's power. The wall of air holding me up disappeared. Weak kneed, I sank to the ground, sipping air. But not enough.

"She's strong." Jael sounded impressed.

"Jael, stop," Kerrick said.

"Ohh... You care. How sweet. But she needs to learn who is in charge."

On the edge of consciousness, I reached to gather my magic, but healing Kerrick had depleted my strength. The world faded as I suffocated.

I woke with a blinding headache. Unfortunately, my encounter with Jael hadn't been a dream. She sat on an overstuffed armchair reading a book. Groaning, I rolled over. Someone had dumped me onto a couch.

"There's tea on the table next to you," she said. "Drink it. It will help with your headache."

I fumbled for the cup. Sitting up, I fought off nausea and gulped the warm liquid. The pounding behind my eyes eased a bit. I downed the rest in two swallows. Feeling better, I scanned the room. Bookshelves, desk, chair, another armchair and glass tables filled the room. Afternoon sunlight streamed in, illuminating a beautiful black-and-silver rug underneath the desk. A fire crackled in the stone hearth. No guards stood by the door. If it wasn't for the powerful magician sitting across from me, the room would be quite cozy.

Jael closed her book with a thud. "Now we can have a private chat."

I wondered where they had taken Kerrick. If she liked to play head games, I wasn't about to ask her about him and give her something to use against me.

"Don't look so frightened, Avry. I'm not some Death Lily ready to swallow you up. If you cooperate, no one will harm you. In fact, I'm hoping you will join us."

"Us?"

"My mother-in-law, High Priestess Estrid of Ozero, has been helping the poor plague survivors to put their lives back in order. We've amassed quite an army. And we have a few magicians working with us. However, we've had some skirmishes—it's an unfortunate side effect of progress, and we've had our fair share of injuries. Plus disease and infections have taken a toll." She leaned forward. "We're in need of a healer. And it seems you are the last alive."

Sweeping an arm out, she said, "You will be treated well, given every comfort and well protected. The High Priestess gives you her word that no harm will come to you."

A dream job. So what was the catch? Stalling for time, I asked, "You can speak for her?"

"Of course. I married her oldest son, Stanslov of Ozero. He was first in line for the throne, but he left me a widow."

Interesting how she appeared more upset about being a widow than in losing her husband. "Doesn't the High Priestess have another son?"

"She did, but he died of the plague along with his wife.

They left a little girl, the High Priestess's only grandchild, but she's very ill. In fact, we'd been searching for you for some time. She would like you to heal Nyrie first, if possible."

"How far away is Nyrie?"

"She's upstairs."

Surprised, I asked, "Isn't she in danger?"

"Oh, no. Our efforts to restore peace have expanded throughout Pomyt, so she's quite safe. And when we heard you were in the area, we took a chance that we might catch up to you."

I stood. "Take me to Nyrie."

She gained her feet. Shock blanketed her face and I knew that was the first true expression she'd shown me.

"Does this mean you'll join us?" Jael asked.

"I need some time to think about it, but I'm not going to use a sick child as a bargaining chip."

"Oh."

I had caught her off guard.

It didn't last. "This way."

I followed her down a plush hallway. Flames flickered from gold sconces, and elaborate paintings hung on the walls.

"You mentioned hearing about me," I said. "From who?"

"We had a report from our training camp near Grzebien."

My apprehension about being here turned into fear. They knew about my sister. Which meant they could use her to force me to work for them. Thankfully, Jael had the decency not to mention it at this time.

We climbed a grand staircase. The child's room lacked for nothing. Her nanny sprang from a chair beside the canopied bed. She had been reading to the girl. Long copper hair fanned around the girl's pale face. I guessed she was around five years old.

Jael introduced me to her niece. Nyrie gave me a wan smile despite the pain shadowing her eyes.

I perched on the edge of her bed and took her small hand in mine. She shot Jael a frightened look.

"What story was your nanny reading you?" I asked her. Healing magic swelled from my core, and I sought the source of the girl's sickness.

"The story of Neil, the First Queen's champion who crossed the Ronel Sea. He was the only one brave enough to request help from the sea dragons." Her thin voice matched her skeletal body.

She had the wasting disease.

"Is that the story where he brings back fifteen dragon scales that turned into warriors when the First Queen's grateful tears touched them?" I asked as I gathered the black fibers of the disease and drew it from her.

"Yes. The warriors chased the tribes into the wildlands and the First Queen gifted land to each of them. That's why we had Fifteen Realms."

I noted her use of the past tense. If Estrid kept expanding, then it was more than a possibility that the Fifteen Realms would cease to exist outside of stories. Pain bit down on my intestines as the wasting disease settled deep in my guts.

Nyrie sat up. Her warm brown eyes glowed. "My stomach doesn't hurt," she marveled.

Releasing her hand, I said to the nanny, "Don't let her eat too much or else she'll throw it up. Start with soups for a day, then gradually increase to thicker food." I turned to Jael. "Is there some place I can lie down?"

"Of course. There's a guest room." She led me to another opulent room.

I slipped into the bed. Despite the needle-sharp pains in my lower stomach, I enjoyed how the mattress cushioned my back and the comforting weight of the supple blanket over me. Now this was luxury.

"Can I get you anything?" Jael asked.

"Nothing for now, but in about five or six hours I would like more of that tea."

Only when she left did I wonder what happened to my knapsack, new cloak and weapons. Those thoughts led to Kerrick and the others. What were they doing? Was Belen organizing a rescue? I worried about them, but it wasn't long before the fight to cure the disease consumed all my energy.

When I woke hours later a servant appeared with a pot of tea. She fetched more when I had drained it, and then brought me a tray overflowing with food. As soon as the scent of hot stew reached me, I felt ravenous. I devoured the stew, bread and cheese in no time.

After the girl cleared the tray, she waited for more instructions. The girl looked to be about thirteen. She wore an acolyte's ruby-colored robe. I wondered if she had applied for this job or been conscripted.

Not wanting to start with personal questions, I asked, "Do you know where my knapsack has gotten to?"

"What do you need it for?"

"I'd like to change my clothes."

"Would you like me to draw you a bath?"

I froze. "A bath as in a bathtub?"

"Yes, miss."

"That would be *wonderful*."

She smiled at my enthusiastic response. When she finished filling it, I eyed the tub as if it was the peaceful afterlife.

"I'll still need clean clothes," I said.

"Yes, miss. While you're soaking, I will inquire about your effects."

"Thank you."

This time her grin included surprise before she darted from the room. Poor girl acted like she had never been thanked before.

I shed my smelly clothes and dipped a foot into the steaming water. All thoughts about the servant, my situation, Noelle, Kerrick, Belen and Jael disappeared as I sank into paradise. Lulled by the warm water, I dozed.

When the girl returned, I jerked awake. She carried my knapsack. "The High Priestess wishes to see you, miss. Do you have appropriate attire for a meeting with the Blessed One?"

The Blessed One? "What is considered appropriate?"

"Not travel clothes, miss. An acolyte's robe would be best."

"I have a skirt in my pack."

"I can fetch you a robe."

"No, thanks. I prefer my own clothes."

She clutched my knapsack a little tighter to her chest.

"Would the High Priestess be upset with you if I showed up wearing inappropriate attire?"

"Don't worry about me, miss. I'm just—"

"In a bad situation and trying to survive? Forced to be a servant for the High Priestess's family to avoid being sent to a training camp?"

"I..."

"What's your name?" I asked.

"Inari, miss."

"Inari, how about a compromise?"

She gazed at me in astonishment.

"I'll wear my skirt and tunic, but I'll wear the robe like a cloak."

Inari considered.

"And I'll let you do my hair."

The clincher. She brightened. "That would be acceptable,

uh, yes, miss." Setting my pack down, she grabbed a towel and held it out for me.

I stepped from the tub, turning so she could wrap it around my shoulders.

Inari gasped. "Your back…"

Probably looked horrid. "Doesn't hurt." Curious, I asked, "What color are the marks?"

"A deep red, almost purple."

Farther along than they should be. At least, that's what I thought, having no real experience with such deep lacerations. I examined the scars on my stomach. It had been about forty days since I healed Belen. Visible but not red, the puckered skin shone a bit lighter than my beige skin.

Inari drew the towel around me. "Who would do such a thing to you?"

"I did it to myself."

The girl covered her mouth with both hands. I suppressed a grin. She was too young to remember when healers had been respected. When all the big cities had at least one healer who lived and worked there.

"I healed a…" What to call Kerrick? Not a friend. "Someone who had been whipped." By the High Priestess's soldiers, but I didn't want to increase Inari's apprehension. Instead, I explained how my magic worked as I dried and dressed in my green skirt and yellow tunic.

Inari swept up my hair into an elegant knot. She pulled a few tendrils down and curled them with a hot iron rod. Then she fetched a robe and soft leather shoes. I eyed the shoe heel. Not too bad, but I wouldn't be able to run far with those things on.

Finally ready, I followed Inari to the High Priestess's receiving room. Two oversize soldiers guarded the ornate double door. Inari tapped on the wood. The doors swung

inward. Inari knelt and bent forward so her forehead pressed
on the floor.

I couldn't see too far inside, but Inari waited until a voice
gave her permission to speak. My opinion of the High Priestess slipped several notches.

Inari introduced me, and if the Blessed One thought I'd
kneel for her, she was in for a surprise. I entered and Inari
left, closing the doors behind her. Estrid sat on a divan, reading a story to her granddaughter. Nestled in her lap, Nyrie
stared at the pictures in the book. Estrid's powerful gaze,
though, was focused on me.

Should I curtsy? Or bow? I decided to remain standing.
The High Priestess gestured to the nanny who had been
sitting in an armchair by the window to take Nyrie for her
afternoon nap. The woman rushed to obey.

When we were alone, I braced for… I didn't know, but
predicted it wouldn't be pleasant. Except I was wrong.

Estrid smiled. "Please sit, Avry." She gestured to a seat near
her.

The room matched the others I'd seen. Dark furniture,
gold trimmings, lush carpets and bookcases lined the walls.
I perched on the edge of the cushion.

"Thank you for healing my granddaughter," Estrid said.

"You're welcome."

"If I had lost her, too…" She glanced away as grief creased
her face. After a moment she continued. "Have you considered our offer?"

"I have."

"And?"

"I'm sorry, but I cannot accept at this time." I waited for
the threats.

Instead, she asked, "Why not?"

"I gave my word to Kerrick to travel with him until we reach his sick…friend."

"I'm well aware of Prince Ryne's condition. Will you be able to heal him?"

"I can heal him, but I haven't decided *if* I will."

She laughed. "His reputation is worse than mine." She tapped long elegant fingers on her lips. "Are you aware Tohon of Sogra is after you?"

"Yes."

"He's trouble. And I don't think my army will be able to hold him back once he decides to move into Pomyt."

Not about to get into a discussion of the trouble she had caused, I kept quiet.

"If Tohon succeeds in gaining all the Realms south of the Nine Mountains, then my rules to keep a pure heart in the name of the creator will seem a mere nuisance to the populace in comparison." Again her gaze grew distant. "Do you think Kerrick is capable of getting you to Ryne?"

"Yes."

"What would you do if I threatened your sister's life if you didn't stay here and heal my warriors?"

And just when I thought she wouldn't resort to threats… Grief filled my heart. I had caused Noelle so much pain already. "I would stay." Until I figured out a way to escape with Noelle and Kerrick.

A side door opened and Jael strode into the room. She wore a uniform and a sword. "We just caught Belen and three others trying to rescue Kerrick from the jail," she said to Estrid. "Perhaps one of them will—" She noticed me.

At her announcement, I slumped against the back of the chair.

"We have all your companions now. And your sister is on her way here so we can keep a close eye on her," Jael said.

"Jael, that's enough." Estrid seemed to mull over the news. "Was Belen that commoner they allowed in school with you and Stanslov?"

"Yes. He was supposed to be Kerrick's bodyguard, but Kerrick treated him like an equal. Kerrick spent more time protecting Belen than the other way around."

"Is that how you met Kerrick?" I asked Jael.

"Yes. And how I met Stanslov. We were in boarding school together. All the children born to the leaders of each Realm attended. As future leaders, it was supposed to teach us tolerance and cooperation of the other Realms. But all we did was make alliances and fight."

"Which was a more accurate representation of how the Fifteen Realms interacted," Estrid said. "Now, all bets are off."

Silence descended as we mourned the past. Jael's comment about the students being future leaders sunk in. Kerrick, a prince? Hard to believe, but Noelle had called him by that name. It didn't matter. It wouldn't change how I felt about him. And just how did I feel about him?

Jael said, "If you're finished with Avry, I'll take her down to the infirmary."

"Not yet. Leave us," the High Priestess ordered her daughter-in-law.

Jael gave her a curt bow and left by the same door she had entered. From the fire in her eyes, I knew she was angry. I wondered why she obeyed Estrid's orders. She commanded the very air, while her mother-in-law had no magic. But then I realized that power came in many different forms, and Estrid commanded the army.

As if she could read my thoughts, Estrid said, "Avry, how about a compromise?"

Estrid used the same word I had with Inari, which made

me wonder if she had sent an acolyte to spy on us. Wary, I asked for details. She explained her terms. I agreed. We shook hands. When I left, Inari appeared beside me.

"Can you direct me to the infirmary?" I asked her.

"Yes, miss. Do you wish to go now?"

"I need to change first."

Inari looked strickened. "I...took your clothes to be washed. They—"

"Stank?"

"Oh, no."

"We're going to be together for a while. I'm not like the High Priestess and Jael. I want you to be honest and to call me Avry," I said.

"They reeked and were stiff with dried blood, Avry," she said as if reporting battle statistics.

"That's a start. Where can I find some clothes that I can get dirty? I'm sure it's a major sin to get blood on the robes."

Inari led me to a laundry. They had a few extra sets of plain tunics and pants that the infirmary workers wore.

I worked in the infirmary for two weeks, teaching the caregivers how to bandage wounds, clean cuts, set bones and how to recognize and use medicinal plants. I healed those who wouldn't survive without my magic. And even though I returned to my room exhausted and sick every night, I felt happy that I was able to help others without the fear of being executed. If I wasn't in a bad situation, I would be quite content to stay here. This was my future before the plague ruined it, healing people. Too bad I would never have an apprentice to show my scars to with pride.

Also during that time, I half expected Kerrick to escape, arrive in my room and drag me away, claiming we wasted more precious time. While I didn't care if we'd reach Ryne or not, my desire to leave increased each day.

Not because of the effort to heal her people, but because I learned Estrid's strict rules for a pure heart, which included no music, dancing or any form of entertainment. No lying, swearing or violence against fellow acolytes. Laughing was bad. Also, all unmarried women must be virgins or they were sent to the monastery in Chinska Mare to spend the rest of their lives praying for forgiveness. If it hadn't been for the timely arrival of Inari, providing a distraction, Estrid's Purity Priestess and her four goons would have had spread my legs and inspected me. Although I would have passed, I still shudder at how close I'd come to being examined.

Noelle arrived in town at the end of the first week, but she refused to see me. Instead, she was assigned as Jael's page. The magician delighted in taking Noelle under her wing. And Noelle went to great lengths to avoid me.

When Estrid was satisfied that I was true to my word, she had two of her personal guard escort me to the jail early the next morning.

Kerrick and his men each had their own cell. When I entered the block with my two guards, various expressions rippled through the guys. Loren and Quain didn't bother to get up from their beds. An air of hopelessness surrounded them. Belen's worried frown deepened. Flea jumped to his feet and hung on to the bars, grimacing. Kerrick's gaze stayed wary.

"About time you joined the party," Quain said.

"I see you've been lazing around here doing nothing for the past two weeks," I said. "Unless there's a tunnel you've dug hidden somewhere?"

"I wish," Flea said. "I'm so bored, hard physical labor sounds like fun."

"Well, then, gentlemen. Are you ready to go?" I asked.

Their reaction was worth the collection of extra scars

I'd earned in Estrid's infirmary. The monkeys leaped from their beds. Flea whooped. Belen transformed back into happy Poppa Bear. However, Kerrick remained the same.

My escorts unlocked the cells, returned all our possessions and led us outside. The guys reveled in the fresh air and sunshine.

"We can stay in town until the passes melt," I said to them. "We'll be safe behind Estrid's front line."

When we were a few blocks from the jail, Kerrick rounded on me. "This—" he gestured at the surroundings "—doesn't come without a price. What did you promise Estrid?"

He still didn't trust me. I decided to let him sweat for a bit. "Let's see. I promised her that Loren and Quain will babysit her granddaughter anytime. That Flea would give her soldiers lessons on how to pick pockets and that Jael can use you for target practice. I offered to keep Jael company for that one."

The others suppressed their grins, but Kerrick failed to find it amusing. "Avry," he growled.

"Lighten up, Kerrick," I said. "I just spent two weeks teaching her medical staff how to care for their injured and in exchange she let us go. Actually, *you* benefit the most from all this."

"I find that hard to believe."

Anger boiled. "You shouldn't. I swore an oath, and I've stuck to it all this time. But you're right. There *is* a catch. If I heal Ryne, I'm to tell him Estrid wants to join forces with him to fight Tohon. Does that sound bad to you?" I didn't wait for an answer. "No, it doesn't. It sounds like an ideal situation. Happy, happy for everyone."

"Even you, Avry?" Belen asked.

His concern doused my fury. "No. Not me." I walked away, heading in no particular direction. Estrid was scared of Tohon. Kerrick, too. If Estrid, who enjoyed being in charge, was willing to make an alliance with Ryne, that weighed heavier in Ryne's favor than all of Belen's school stories.

"Where are you going?" Kerrick asked.

I stopped. The guys had followed me. "To find a tavern. I need a drink."

"Estrid has banned alcohol. She calls it the devil's drink," Loren said.

Quain gasped. "We can't stay here! The next thing you know, we'll be wearing those red skirts and promising our souls to the creator."

"You'd look good in red, Quain. And you can show off those shapely legs," Loren teased.

"Estrid provided us with fresh provisions," Kerrick said. "There's plenty of daylight left. We'll head north toward the Nine Mountains as planned."

The others looked at me, which didn't make Kerrick happy. Although, as far as I knew, nothing made him happy. Having no interest in leading, I said to Kerrick, "Lead on."

We walked through the streets of Zabin. I noticed how the citizens who didn't wear the robes kept their gazes on the ground. They hurried along as if afraid someone would stop them.

Exiting the city, we followed the border road so named because it paralleled the border between Vyg and Pomyt. Without having to worry about Estrid's soldiers, we could use the road and camp on the Pomyt side. Most of Vyg was still disputed territory.

An hour outside Zabin, we encountered trouble. Kerrick cursed and pulled his sword, warning us before six horses broke from the forest. I yanked one of my throwing knives as everyone grabbed their weapons, but it didn't matter. Jael led the ambush. No weapon could match her magic.

Armed soldiers rode on the other five horses. And, as an

added bonus, Noelle shared Jael's mount. Sitting behind Jael, my sister wouldn't meet my gaze, but she stared with a cold disgust at my companions.

"Estrid was a fool to let you go," Jael said. "Our army is more than capable of handling Tohon's."

"Did you come all this way just to say goodbye?" Kerrick asked.

"Oh, yes. This is goodbye," Jael said. "Unlike Estrid, I'm not a fool. You're too dangerous to leave alive."

"Estrid won't be happy," Kerrick said.

"That's why I'm not dragging the healer back with me. She'll just squeal to the High Priestess, and I don't want to tip my hand just yet."

"But you trust Avry's sister?"

"My little protégée has been surprisingly helpful. She's also proving to be quite valuable and loyal. We agree on so many things."

Not good. Noelle finally met my gaze and I was the one to glance away. Pure joy over my imminent demise shone from her face. Not only had she changed, but she'd found another person to shadow.

"You don't need to kill my men," Kerrick said.

"And leave them to avenge your deaths? Didn't you hear me when I said I wasn't a fool? Goodbye, Kerrick, I'm afraid there's no chance of us ever getting back together."

In desperation, I threw my knife at her, aiming for her neck. But the air thickened, stopping the weapon in midair. It dropped to the ground.

Jael tsked, shaking her head at my lame attempt before a wall of air slammed into us, knocking us to the ground. When the wall retreated, it sucked all the breath from our lungs. This time Jael wasn't playing around.

CHAPTER 15

Lying on the ground, I strained to draw a breath. Familiarity with this particular situation didn't prevent my panic from rising, but knowing Belen and the others also suffered kept my fear from dominating.

My healing magic surged and fought to keep air in my lungs. Jael's power pressed harder, but another magic tingled along the back of my hand. I looked to my left. Kerrick lay next to me with his arm outstretched. Jael either didn't know about his forest magic or didn't believe it would make a difference. On its own, it probably wouldn't, but combined with mine...

I grasped his hand and it felt as if I had just been struck by lightning. Instead of sharing my energy with him, he sent his to me. And, damn, the man was strong. The forest's vast energy waited for me to tap into it. Air flowed back into my lungs as the healing power won the battle. I "healed" Kerrick and reversed the flow of energy, letting Kerrick tap into mine.

Not quite understanding what had happened, Jael frowned at us. Suffocating six people required all of her strength, but now she only had four. And if we didn't stop her soon, she would kill them.

Keeping a grip on Kerrick's hand, I grabbed one of my knives and flung it at her. It struck her upper arm. She yelped and I sent another into her thigh. The horse reared at the scent of blood. Noelle clutched Jael's waist, but they remained in the saddle. My attack did break her concentration. Noisy gasps erupted behind me.

Her soldiers drew their weapons. Kerrick dropped my hand in order to engage the soldiers while the others recovered. Heavy branches dropped from the trees above us, scaring the horses. Against five on horseback, Kerrick was holding his own. It was impressive, but I knew with the energy he spent he wouldn't last. I wounded two of the soldiers. By then Belen, Loren and Quain joined in the battle.

Although boastful, Jael's claim of not being a fool proved accurate. She called for a retreat and the six horses galloped away.

We cheered and congratulated ourselves until we realized Flea remained prone on the ground. He stared at the sky, but he wasn't moving. I raced over to him. Blue lips, eyes vacant and the pasty pallor of the dead greeted me.

I touched Flea's slack face. No magic swelled from my core. "Kerrick," I yelled.

He knelt next to me and covered my hands with his. Magic flowed into me, but I couldn't funnel it into Flea. I tried until exhausted. And I would have kept going, but Kerrick pulled me away. Healers couldn't bring the dead back to life, but I had hoped just this once I could.

Numb with grief, I sat next to Flea as Kerrick and Belen discussed the macabre yet necessary task of burying him. Loren and Quain stood nearby, looking miserable.

"…ground's too hard, scavengers will dig him up," Belen said.

"…a pyre will alert every merc in Vyg of our whereabouts," Kerrick said.

"…cave…seal off the entrance?"

I tuned them out as I remembered Flea's energy and enthusiasm. His lopsided grin, puppy-dog pouts and utter joy as he mastered juggling three rocks. He had such potential… The word caused a flood of memories, but not of Flea. The Death Lily had wanted him. It said he had potential.

Scrambling to my feet, I interrupted Belen and Kerrick. "Offer Flea to a Death Lily."

Their reactions matched. Shocked, repulsed, upset and angry. I explained as much as I could without sounding like a lunatic. They argued. Not surprising, it went against logic and compassion and plain old moral decency. But, damn it, I knew it was the right thing to do.

"Avry, you're grieving and not thinking clearly," Belen said.

"Belen, I spent hours inside a Lily. This is what we need to do for Flea."

Belen, Loren and Quain shook their heads sadly. They thought I had lost my mind. And maybe I had.

"How can you *not* trust me?" I asked, attempting one last time. "Did you even see my sister's joy at the prospect of my death? I could have stayed with Estrid and tried to repair the damage between us. But no, I…" My throat closed as tears threatened. "Forget it." I turned my back to them so they wouldn't see me cry.

"There's a cluster of Lilys about two miles west of here," Kerrick said.

I wiped my face and glanced back. Kerrick pressed his

hand to the ground. "It's in Vyg, but there's no one else around."

"Are you nuts?" Quain asked. "You're not going to—"

"We are. Belen, get Flea's blanket."

Belen wrapped Flea in the blanket and carried him over his shoulder. No one said a word. By the time we reached a grove, darkness had descended.

Gently laying him down, Belen told a story of how he had taught Flea the facts of life and how the boy thought it was disgusting, but a few months later, he had changed his mind and asked for more details. Loren and Quain took a turn relating how they taught him to fight.

"My son in all ways but one," Kerrick said.

The others agreed.

I couldn't speak.

Kerrick removed the blanket and carried Flea over to a pair of trees. I went with him just in case the Lily attacked. The base of the tree trunks almost touched, but the upper trunks bowed away, making the trees look like a giant V. The Lily grew right behind them. Death or Peace? We'd find out soon enough.

It didn't hiss or move fast, but the petals parted, dipping toward Flea. The tips of the petals bent under his body. The Death Lily gathered Flea as if it were his mother. Then Flea was gone.

We traveled north along the border road for the next six days. Encountering no resistance from Estrid's platoons, or mercs, we covered roughly two hundred miles. Conversation was kept to the minimum. No one smiled or laughed or teased.

At night, we followed a routine, gathering firewood, cooking a meal and sitting by the fire. Except we stared at the flames instead of talking. My thoughts dwelled on Flea or on one of the empty villages or farmsteads we passed that day. There had been so many. By the end of the night, I would be leaning against Belen. He'd wrap his heavy arm around my shoulder and we'd comfort each other. Poppa Bear had lost one of his cubs, and I think he suffered the most. Although, half the time I would fall asleep on him and he'd tuck me into my bedroll.

Why Belen? His steady solid presence eased my pain. I considered him an ally and a protector. But more important, he was my friend. The first one I'd had since…before I left for my apprenticeship with Tara. Loren and Quain relied on each other. Not physically, but they were brothers in all but name. And Kerrick didn't need or want anyone as far as I could tell. Jael had crushed his heart. It had shriveled and died in his chest four years ago. Yet, he strived to find a healer for Ryne. Perhaps he wasn't beyond hope, after all.

As I grieved for Flea, I began to believe Kerrick had it right. Keep a distance. Especially during this mission. It was dangerous. Too late for me. After having no friends or family for three years, I had grown quite attached to these three guys. Or was that four?

On the seventh day, Kerrick veered to the east, taking a small road that branched from the main one. An icy wind blew, biting into exposed skin, reminding us that it was midwinter's day. Before the plague, cities and towns across the Realms would celebrate the halfway mark to spring. Now, it passed with a sense of relief that we had gotten halfway through another winter without starving.

Two hours later, Kerrick stopped at a large ruin. Three magnificent buildings had stood here at one time. Their fancy stone columns had toppled, their roofs had collapsed and their interiors had burned. Other smaller structures filled the area. All had met the same fate.

"The compound of the Healer's Guild," Kerrick said.

I had forgotten about visiting it. No surprise that it hadn't survived. The people had been angry, miserable and grieving. We poked around the wreckage, searching for anything useful.

Memories from my single visit to Guild headquarters bubbled to the surface of my mind. Healing, research and teaching had been their three goals. Each of the three grand buildings was dedicated to one goal. If I had graduated, my ceremony would have been in the building of teaching. Those seeking medical aid entered the building of healing. The last one housed those who worked to learn more about our healing powers and about the plants that could provide relief.

The researchers shared the information with others, but they had also been careful in protecting all they had learned. One of Tara's comments tugged. Something about a room known only to the healers. A place sheltered from the elements and secured. A room not located in the building of learning.

I walked over to the smallest structure in the compound, but stopped. That would be too obvious. It would be an unremarkable building sized to match others around it.

Kerrick followed me. "What are you looking for?"

I explained about the hidden room. "It probably didn't survive."

He considered. "If it is underground and protected by stone, it might still be here." Instead of focusing on the buildings, he scanned the forest around us.

I wondered why until I realized the forest had broken through the edges of the compound. Kerrick pressed a palm to the ground. If the roots had grown in far enough, he might be able to sense an oddness.

Kerrick stood and headed east of the main buildings. I trailed behind him. He stopped at a building that met my criteria—basically unremarkable.

"An underground room?" I asked.

"Maybe. There's something underneath this building."

We called the guys over. Everyone helped to clear the rubble. Belen's strength continued to amaze me as he hefted large pieces of the broken stone wall with ease. As we worked, a sense of purpose formed. And for the first time in days, I wasn't brooding over Flea's death. After a while, I noticed the others making a few comments. Quain teased Loren for his girlie arms. Belen growled good-naturedly at Kerrick to stop supervising and to get back to work. It wasn't the same as before, but it was a start.

It took us a day to unearth the top half of a potential doorway. As we cleared the debris, dark gray clouds crept over the ice-blue sky. Quain frowned at the approaching front and studied the clouds. He sniffed the air, claiming a snowstorm was on its way.

"How soon?" Kerrick asked him.

Quain gauged the wind by scattering dead leaves. "Half a day at most."

"How bad?"

He pulled a strange glass vial that resembled a skinny teapot filled with a silver liquid. Tapping on the glass, he whistled. "A midwinter howler."

Kerrick cursed.

"You shouldn't complain," Quain said. "It's been unusually dry. Otherwise, we'd have been hiking though two-foot drifts the past few weeks."

Sensing Kerrick would stop our efforts, I said, "Perhaps that door leads underground and we can shelter in there."

"What happens if we can't?" He didn't wait for me to answer. "Then we wasted all that time and will be caught out in a blizzard." He scanned the darkening sky, then the forest. "You can keep working for now. I'll scout out the area, see if there's a cave nearby."

Not another cave! But I stifled a groan. In this situation, it would be ideal. After Kerrick left, we exposed the door. It had been made of iron and was locked. Belen pulled out a set of lock picks with a sly grin. He worked on the lock.

After about twenty minutes, he sat back on his heels and gave up. "It's one of those complicated ones with double pins to make it all but impossible to pick."

"Could Kerrick open it?" I asked.

Belen huffed. "What makes you think he would be better than me?"

"Uh, more practice?"

"He's certainly gotten into more trouble than me. That's for certain."

"Really? Jael said Kerrick was constantly getting *you* out of trouble."

"Don't you believe her, Avry. Everything she says is a lie. In fact, almost all the skirmishes and problems we had in school were because of her. With her beauty and intelligence, she played us all like she was conducting Queen Jenna's ninety-six-piece orchestra. And it took us many years to figure it out."

"But she kept Kerrick from killing Ryne. How?"

"That's not my story to tell." Belen lumbered to his feet. "And even Kerrick couldn't open this door. The blasted lock is also rusted tight."

Disappointment stabbed. Rust had destroyed… The word

triggered a memory. When the guys had rescued me, the bars to the window appeared to have rusted away, but all the other ones had been fine.

"What did you use on those bars?" I asked Loren.

"What bars?"

I explained.

"Oh! Quain, do you still have some of that lightning juice?"

His eyes lit up. "Yes. It's in my pack." He strode over to where we had dumped our stuff. "Too bad I didn't have it with me when we were rotting in Estrid's jail for two weeks." Rummaging in the pockets, he brought out a glass jar filled with a clear liquid. "We need some way to pour it into the lock."

We all searched. Belen found a broken piece of pipe that worked. The lightning juice filled the keyhole. Metal sizzled and the smoke smelled like brackish water.

When the sound stopped, Quain told Belen to give it a try. He pressed his shoulder to the door and pushed. Nothing happened. Quain poured in more juice. Belen tried again. Nothing.

"Perhaps we should douse the hinges?" Loren asked.

Before Quain could move, I said, "Wait." The door's hinges were visible. "Belen, try pulling on the handle."

He grasped the heavy latch. With a screech of metal, the door opened, revealing a staircase that descended into blackness. A musty odor with a hint of decay wafted from below followed by a faint rustling sound. Rats? Or the wind?

We all peered into the darkness.

"We're going to need torches," Belen said.

"Maybe there are some hanging just inside," I said.

Quain walked down the first few steps. "Hooks are here, but no torches."

Loren and Belen went in search of materials, while Quain and I waited. The winds died. Soon after, fat flakes of snow drifted down.

"I thought you said it would be a howler," I said.

"It will. First the storm dumps piles of snow, and then the winds come, blowing all that white stuff into drifts and creating more problems. Otherwise, it wouldn't be fun for the storm if the winds came first. Nothing for it to swirl around."

"I don't think the storm cares."

"Probably not a normal storm."

I searched Quain's face to see if he teased. "Aren't they all normal?"

"No. Some are influenced by air magicians to do more damage than they would on their own."

"Do you think Jael sent this storm?"

"She killed Flea and tried to kill us. This could be another attempt."

I shivered at the memory.

Quain focused on me. "We need to talk about what happened with Flea."

"What do you mean?"

"I've been replaying Jael's attack and the aftermath in my mind, thinking of nothing else. Why did you yell for Kerrick to help you with healing him? And how did Kerrick know the exact location of a Death Lily?" Quain started making more connections. "In fact, all those months we hiked through the woods, we've never encountered a single Lily. Except for that village. What's going on, Avry?"

His questions were inevitable. "You'll have to ask Kerrick."

"Why?"

"It's not my story to tell." I used Belen's line.

Loren and Belen returned in time to see Quain scowling at me.

"What's the problem?" Loren asked.

I answered before Quain could. "We can discuss it when we're stuck in some cave for days because of the storm."

Belen brushed the snow from his hair. "We'd better hurry." He handed out torches and Loren lit them with his flint.

We descended the dust-covered steps. It spiraled down for two, maybe three stories before the walls opened up, revealing a storage room. Rows of shelves lined the floor. The shelves had been filled with wooden crates. A list of each box's contents had been burned into the outside wood.

I read the titles as we walked between them.

Dissection notes on twenty-two-year-old female—cause of death: childbirth.

Dune grass seeds from Bavly Realm.

Results of Apgull Poison test.

Maps of known Red Tiger trees.

As we continued, it became apparent that the room was huge. We hadn't reached another wall, and the shelves disappeared into the darkness.

"We found the secret record room. Now what?" Belen asked.

"I was hoping to find some information that could be useful," I said.

"You don't think the 'contents of an ufa's stomach' is useful?" Loren asked.

"Only if the report lists what killed the ufa." As we neared the foothills, ufa packs would become another danger.

"We could split up," Belen suggested. "Cover more ground. What would be useful, Avry?"

"Anything that mentions medicinal plants or herbs." I

hesitated, but decided to throw it out there. "Or mentions the plague."

Silence, then Belen said, "Okay, everyone take a row."

After a few minutes, I realized we would need days to go through the entire room. And it might take that long just to find valuable information. Perhaps after the storm we could come back. If the door wasn't buried beneath a snowdrift.

I scanned crates until my vision blurred. My torch sputtered a warning. It wouldn't last long. Besides, it seemed we had been down here a long time and Kerrick still hadn't returned. Worry swirled as I followed my trail of dusty footsteps back to the entrance.

No one else had returned. With a hiss and pop, the flames, and therefore my light, died. Then the distinct tap of boots on the stairs sounded. Kerrick? Or one of the others? Or someone new? Pressing up against a shelf with my knife in hand, I waited as the taps grew louder and a black silhouette appeared. Kerrick.

Relief rushed through me. I slid my knife back into its sheath, stepped away from the shelf and surprised him without meaning to. He knocked me to the ground and sat on me, pinning my arms until he recognized me. I hadn't realized my eyes had adjusted to the dark, but his hadn't.

"Don't surprise me like that," he said.

"Already figured that out," I said. "Can you get off me now?"

He stood and pulled me to my feet. "Where are the others?"

I rubbed the back of my head. "Searching for something useful. My torch died." I peered into the darkness, hoping to find a sign of one of the others.

Kerrick cupped his hands around his mouth and called, "Gentlemen, time to go."

Rustlings and footsteps approached. Quain and Loren appeared. Only Loren's torch still burned.

Quain carried a crate. "It's really creepy in here when the lights go out."

"What did you find?" I asked.

"Notes on all the failed remedies for the plague. I wasn't sure if it would be useful, but it was the only one I saw."

"It's a start."

Kerrick gave me his care-to-explain look, but I ignored him as we waited for Belen.

"Why can't we shelter in here?" I asked Kerrick.

"No back door."

"There could be one," I said.

"Without more torches, we won't be able to find it. Belen's probably stumbling around in the dark by now." Kerrick called to him.

No reply. Loren offered to search, but Kerrick said no. Another fretful ten minutes passed, then Kerrick emitted a high-pitched and painfully sharp whistle.

"Over here," Belen called back. "I've found something!"

We followed his voice. He stood at the far end of a row of shelves. The torchlight made a yellow puddle around his feet. When we drew closer, he moved the light, revealing a desiccated body on the ground.

Dried-out flesh clung to the bones. The man, I think, lay on his side. I bent closer to examine the corpse. Quain made a disgusted sound. As part of my healer training, I had assisted in autopsies and dissections in order to learn about the internal parts and organs of a body.

However, it didn't take a healer to figure out what killed this man. A sword had been shoved between his ribs, piercing his heart. He had been murdered. I sat back on my heels, mulling it over. If the grieving public had gotten in here, they would have burned all the records. The door had been locked. Someone who had a key perhaps, or knew of this room's existence. Too many unknowns at this point to determine why he had been murdered.

"There's a broken crate underneath him," Belen said. "Maybe he was protecting the contents." He rolled the man onto his back.

I swept out the pieces and connected the ones marked with letters. There weren't many. The crate had held Death Lily seeds.

CHAPTER 16

"Why would anyone want Death Lily seeds?" Quain asked.

"Or more important, why would the Healer's Guild have these seeds in the first place?" Loren asked.

"To study them," I said.

"Or to find a way to kill them," Kerrick added.

Belen moved the dead body and the last bits of the broken crate to the side as if searching for something. "I don't see the seeds anywhere. They're gone."

"How do you know what they look like?" Quain asked him.

"When that Death Lily had us in its grip, I had an up close and personal view of its seedpods."

Loren cocked his head, staring at the body. "So, public sentiment turns on the healers, and it's the last days of the Guild. Again, why are those seeds worth protecting? Do you think they might have something to do with the plague?"

Belen shrugged. "Possible."

"Are there any records?" I asked, scanning the crates stacked on the shelves nearby. Nothing.

"This puzzle will have to wait," Kerrick said. "The snow is piling up outside."

"What about the body?" Quain asked, hefting the crate he had found. "Should we feed another Death Lily? Or don't they like the crunchy ones?" No one was amused by his sarcasm.

We retraced our steps and climbed the stairs. Belen closed the door, and leaned a large piece of stone against it. "That should keep the snow and wind out."

About four inches of snow had fallen since we entered the record room. Following Kerrick, I noticed the quiet stillness of the forest. I was glad for my fur-lined boots, but worried about our tracks. They would be visible until the winds swept them away.

Quain saw me glance back and said, "If Kerrick's not fussing about our tracks, that means no one is close enough to us." He gazed at his leader. "He always knows where the mercs are hiding in the woods. Do you know anything about that, Avry? Or is it his story to tell?" He shook the crate in his hands. "What other secrets are you hiding from us?"

I didn't want to increase his agitation so I didn't answer. Instead, I wondered if he would have the courage to question Kerrick directly or just make sarcastic comments until I or Kerrick told him.

No one was surprised when Kerrick led us to a cave. I watched Quain add another uncanny skill to Kerrick's list. The snow made it difficult to find firewood. All our piles, except Kerrick's, were meager.

Dinner was a quiet affair, more so because we were tired from uncovering the records room than because of an all-consuming grief for Flea. The grief would never go away completely, but it would fade into a background ache. Being survivors of the plague, these men had so many people to grieve for; it had to be numbing. Me, too, but I couldn't claim to be a survivor of the plague since, in another odd quirk of the disease, healers were immune to it.

Why hadn't the healers caught the plague, too? We sickened with other ailments like everyone else; we just recovered faster. But there had been no reports of a healer contracting the plague unless they'd assumed it from a victim. At least once we sickened, we were never contagious to others.

Quain started his questions soon after we had finished cleaning the stew pot. Loren gave him a warning look until he realized that Quain was determined. Then his focus shifted to Kerrick. Belen, too, kept his gaze on Kerrick. I couldn't read Belen's expression, which was unusual, or Kerrick's, which wasn't.

"You *are* going to explain what's going on," Quain said. It was a statement not a question.

Kerrick looked at me.

"Don't blame Avry. She didn't say a word," Quain said. "I just started putting things together."

"What do you think is going on, then, Quain?" Kerrick asked.

"Don't you pull that stunt on me. I'm not Flea."

"How can you be so smart and so dumb at the same time?" Loren asked him.

Quain hopped to his feet and loomed over Loren as if he wanted to punch him. Unfazed, Loren peered up at him in amusement.

Belen chuckled. "He found all the pieces, but can't put them together."

Quain whirled on him, clearly upset.

"Avry isn't the only one here gifted with magic," Belen said.

Understanding dawned. The furrows in Quain's brow and bald head smoothed. "I'm such an idiot."

"Can I quote you?" Loren asked.

Quain tackled him and they wrestled, rolling on the ground.

Kerrick peered at his friend. "How long?"

"Since you were sixteen. Loren and Flea didn't figure it out until Avry came along and made things...interesting."

"Hey," I said, pretending to be affronted. "If you don't want interesting, I can leave," I teased.

However, his response was dead serious. "But would you? If I sat on Kerrick and let you go, would you?"

"I gave my word."

"Under duress. I'm offering you the chance to walk away. Would you take it?"

The monkeys stopped wrestling. Everyone's attention focused on me, burning into my skin.

Belen wouldn't shut up. "I watched them arrest you back in Jaxton. You didn't resist or try to get away. Not the Avry I've come to know."

"What do want me to say?" I whispered.

"Do you want to leave?" Belen asked.

Don't do this to me.

"Do you want to leave?" he asked again.

Conflicted emotions knotted in my throat. I wished to go back and make amends with my sister, but I didn't want to leave the guys, either. They had become my family.

"The truth, Avry."

"No. Pathetic, isn't it?" Unable to meet anyone's gaze, I stumbled out into the snow.

Breathing in deep lungfuls of damp air, I kept close to the cave's entrance. Storm clouds blocked the moon, and a silent blackness surrounded the area. Snowflakes struck my face with tiny pricks of cold. While I wished to put distance between me and the others, I knew I'd just get lost in the darkness.

Although, I already felt lost. Perhaps *confused* was a better word. Belen forced me to admit I had a reason for living. Since I'd been with them, I'd healed people, found my sister and made a friend. As I gained more incentives to live, I also learned more about the uncertain future of our world. It would be so much easier to agree to heal Ryne if I had nothing to lose.

Belen's heart was in the right place. He didn't know the consequences if I healed Ryne. If he had, it would tear him apart. I was sure that's why Kerrick hadn't told him, and I wouldn't, either. However, I'd made the mistake of getting too attached to them. I needed to keep my distance. To stay uninvolved.

No one said a word when I returned to the cave. I brushed the snow from my hair and cloak, then set up my bedroll. Pulling my blanket up to my chin, I vowed to keep my emotions in check. To keep my distance from everyone. To gather as much information about Ryne as I could to make an informed and logical decision regarding him. I would also learn more about the plague, if possible. My confusion was replaced by determination.

After another full day of snow, the winds came. The fire pulsed, and the cave echoed with the shrill keen of the wind. I passed the time by sorting through the crate Quain had found in the records room.

The Guild healers had listed all the remedies, medicines and techniques that had failed to heal the plague. Scanning the list, I was impressed by the sheer number of different things they had tried. Each trial had exhaustive notes about the patient's response. Nothing cured the disease. Although crushed ginger root mixed with white birch sap helped ease the horrible stomach pains—a small concession.

I created my own list of what I had learned about the plague. It hadn't discriminated as far as age or gender. No one survived. Those living now never had any symptoms at all. The last known case had been over two years ago. I wondered about the magicians who had survived. Did the plague strike only certain types of magicians?

"I don't know," Kerrick said when I asked him. "A few are in hiding, although I've no idea who they are. The others have either joined up with Estrid or Tohon." He sat next to the fire, repairing the leather tie on his boot.

"Do you know what their specialties are?"

He paused, frowning. "Tohon has one earth mage, one rock hound and one fire. Estrid has Jael, a water mage and a moon mage."

"What's a rock hound?" Quain asked between gulps of water. He was taking a break from his practice bout with Belen.

"They're magicians whose power is a gift from rocks, gem-stones, ore, coal or any hard substance found in the ground or mountains. They can also cause earthquakes if they're strong enough."

"Wouldn't they be called earth mages?" I asked.

"No. Earth mages are linked to the soil and the creatures that live in the soil."

"I'd rather be a hound," Quain said.

"You certainly smell like one," Loren teased. He stirred the stew.

After more than a week on the road without being able to do more than splash a few handfuls of water on us, I sus-pected we all did.

"Why the nickname?" I asked Kerrick.

"They're called hounds because they're good at finding precious metals and stones. Ryne lost... Three rock hounds died in the Vyg copper mine cave-in. They had helped direct operations." He glanced at me as if to gauge my mood. "Ryne suspected the cave-in had been caused by sabotage, but then the plague arrived and turned all our other problems into trivialities."

Sabotage? That was a little too convenient. "How many magicians are loyal to Ryne?"

"One."

"What about the death mage?"

"Sepp was on my father's staff before. He's loyal to me now," Kerrick said.

Ah. Time to ask the big questions. The ones I had been avoiding all along. "You met Ryne in boarding school and would have killed him except for Jael. Now you're his champion. Why? And what about your own Realm, *Prince* Kerrick? Why can't *you* stop Tohon?"

Loren and Quain exchanged a surprised glance. They hadn't known Kerrick's royal background.

Kerrick didn't react. He studied me for a moment, then looked at Belen.

"Perfect time for you to convince her Ryne's worth saving," Belen said.

With a slight sigh, Kerrick shifted his gaze to the fire. Just when I thought he wouldn't answer my questions, he said, "We called it boarding school for brats, but calling the students brats was being kind. Everyone starts when they're fifteen years old. The school was supposed to be a neutral ground for the future leaders of the Realms, but all the students brought along their prejudices and grudges. Pranks were aimed to hurt. Alliances, double crosses and fights marked a typical school day." He quirked a smile at Belen.

"Belen and I tried to stay out of it, but it was impossible to avoid it altogether. Jael, Tohon and I became close friends, since we had special classes—"

Belen coughed.

"Since we had magic classes together for all six years. We were the only ones in our year gifted with power, but we hadn't been allowed to tell anyone or use it when we were with the other students. I avoided Ryne. Our fathers didn't get along, and had been fighting about the location of the border between our Realms for years. Plus it seemed Ryne was always in the middle of all the intrigue."

"He was," Belen said. "But not for the reasons you had thought."

"At the time I didn't know that Ryne was always one step ahead of the various plots and schemes, and he ruined most of them. He has a unique talent for strategy and tactics. He tried to keep the peace, but everyone hated him, anyway. Even me."

"What changed your mind?" I asked.

Kerrick stared at the fire. "During the final year of school, the instructors give the senior students a challenge to crown a king of the school. Basically, a few people try to convince, bribe or intimidate their peers to pledge allegiance to them until they have the majority. Ryne, Tohon, Stanslov and Cellina of Lyady all campaigned to be king. I didn't care who won. By that time, Jael and I were engaged. We pledged our support to Tohon early in the year and I planned to stay uninvolved with the whole king nonsense." He added another log to the fire, sending sparks flying. His movements were stiff with tension.

I sensed he wouldn't finish the story. "Then what happened?"

"Stanslov happened." Kerrick growled the words.

"Stanslov's king campaign," Belen said. "About midyear, Tohon told Kerrick that Ryne had bet Stanslov three supporters that Stanslov couldn't get Jael to break off the engagement. Stanslov was supposed to leave her after the contest, but he fell for her. Hard."

"And when Kerrick found out about Ryne's bet, he lost his temper and tried to kill him," I said, guessing how the rest of the story played out.

"Almost succeeded, too," Kerrick said with a tight voice. "Jael stopped me. She told me Ryne hadn't made the bet with Stanslov. Tohon had, after *he* failed to lure her away from me."

Double betrayal. No wonder he kept his distance.

"Tohon wanted me to go after Ryne since he was Tohon's strongest competition for king. Too bad I couldn't kill Tohon."

"Not for lack of trying," Belen said.

Kerrick rubbed the scars on his neck.

"What happened?" Quain asked. He and Loren had been intently listening to the story.

"Life magicians have an affinity with all living creatures," Belen said. "Tohon called an ufa to protect him against Kerrick's attack. They were fighting outside, behind the stables so the teachers couldn't see them. The ufa almost ripped Kerrick's throat out. I spent two weeks nursing Kerrick—who should have known better to challenge a life magician—back to health."

Seemed odd the school wouldn't have a healer on staff. Especially with such important students. "Wasn't there a healer there?"

"Called away for an emergency," Belen said.

I mulled over the information and found an inconsistency.

"Why was Ryne winning when you said everyone hated him?"

"He convinced his supporters with logic and honesty," Kerrick said. "By that time everyone was sick of being deceived and not knowing who to trust."

"And how did he convince you?" I asked.

"He visited me every day when I was recovering. He exposed the people who had orchestrated and caused the most trouble over the years. Jael and Tohon. As the youngest of three siblings, Jael would never gain power of Bavly Realm. She planned to marry me so she'd eventually be Queen of Alga. When she realized Stanslov would be easier to manipulate, she changed her strategy." Kerrick fisted his hands and tapped them against his thighs. He met my gaze for the first time since telling his tale. "I ignored and refused to see what was going on around me all those years."

Was he implying I had been doing the same thing?

"Who became king?" Loren asked.

"Ryne won," Belen said. "He had gained all but three students' support."

Easy to guess the three. Interesting how Jael and Tohon were still causing problems.

"Okay, so you and Ryne graduated and returned to your respective Realms. Why aren't you there? Helping your people?" I asked Kerrick.

"I was there for two years, dealing with the plague and the waves of marauders." He rubbed his face as if he could wipe away the memories. "We didn't have the manpower to keep them out, and they terrorized and stole provisions from the survivors. They killed, as well. But they were hard to find and counter. They fought like the tribal people in the north."

"Smart bastards," Belen agreed. "They were in position to

storm Alga castle and there was nothing we could do other than dig in and die fighting."

"I sense a happy ending," Quain said.

"We were saved by—"

"Ryne," I said, guessing.

"Not him in particular," Belen said. "But he sent a... What did he call it?"

"An elite squad," Kerrick said.

"That's it. They were just a handful of very well-trained soldiers, but man, they outsmarted the marauders, striking at night, targeting the leaders. By morning, the marauders were gone. Amazing."

"He sent a few more elite squads, and in a couple months Alga was free of the threat and we started rebuilding," Kerrick said. "After everything settled down, I handed leadership of the Realm over to my younger brother, Izak, so I could join Ryne in helping the other thirteen."

"So *we* could help," Belen said. "We spent a year with Ryne, and the three Realms north of the Nine Mountains were safe and prospering when we crossed over two years ago. You won't find the horrors we have found on this side over there."

"This side has Tohon and we already discovered Ryne's elite squads can't counter his...army," Kerrick said. "Ryne was in the process of collecting more information when he sickened. And I've no gift for strategy. Ryne outsmarted Tohon five years ago—he can do it again."

Which made Kerrick twenty-six years old. Which I didn't care about. I should care more that they seemed so certain that Tohon needed to be stopped, or at least contained to his Realm. Except I didn't quite understand why.

I remembered Tohon had worked at the Healer's Guild for some time. As a life magician he was an invaluable resource to the Guild and he helped out before the plague. How bad could he be? Well, besides the whole bounty on healers. Hating healers wasn't unique to him. Ryne hated them as well, and that was before the plague. And why didn't I want to know more about Tohon? Cowardice again?

Everyone watched my expression.

I tried to keep it neutral as I asked Kerrick, "After the snowstorm, can we return to the Guild's record room?"

"If it's safe and not buried under tons of snow, we can stay there a couple days before heading north."

Despite his claim, Kerrick knew enough strategy. He had linked my newfound interest in Ryne with the crate of documents we had uncovered. The best strategy would be to go back and look for more. Perhaps we would discover another box that would convince me to heal Ryne.

The storm blew for the next two days. We emerged from the cave on the third morning, squinting in the bright white sunlight. The forest had been transformed. It looked as if the clouds in the sky had descended to the earth. Piles of fluffy snow mounded on the lee side of trees and bushes, while open areas were bare.

Kerrick frowned at the drifts. "This is going to slow us down."

"We have at least thirty days until the passes open," Belen said.

"And over two hundred miles to travel. Let's go."

We skirted the deeper drifts and kept to the bare spots when possible. At times, the snow was knee-deep, and others it reached as high as our waists. The snow might appear to be fluffy, but it felt quite dense as I trudged through it, reminding me of the air and how Jael had been able to thicken it so much it had stopped my knife in midair. Worried she might send another storm, I glanced at the sky. Nothing but blue.

"What about our tracks?" I asked, puffing from the exertion.

"Not much we can do," Kerrick said.

We reached the Healer Guild's ruined buildings in the afternoon. About a foot of snow had collected in front of the slab holding the door closed. It didn't take long for all of us to clear it. Belen moved the slab with ease. While Kerrick scouted the area, the rest of us descended into the record room with torches to search for more information.

That night, we camped at the foot of the stairs, so our small campfire could vent and we remained close to the exit.

"What happened to 'no back door'?" I asked Kerrick.

"It's not snowing."

"What does—"

"It's too hard to sense intruders in the forest during storms," he said.

"Why?"

"The forest doesn't like the wind snapping its limbs and branches. During a storm, it reacts as if being invaded by an army of intruders. But now, I'm pretty confident no one is nearby."

I offered to take a turn on watch. Kerrick laughed at first, but when he realized I was serious, he allowed me to man the first shift.

Nothing happened during my inaugural shift. It was simple to guard a single door. However, the few hours alone, breathing in the crisp night air and watching the snow sparkle in the moonlight, was a much-needed respite from the pressure. Even when no one talked about Ryne, I felt their gazes on me and their hopes weighed on my conscience. Worry for Noelle clung to me as well, but out here in the quiet stillness,

I could pretend for a little while that all was right with the world.

Eventually, Kerrick arrived to take the next shift, and all my problems rushed back. Reluctant to join the others, I lingered at the top of the stairs.

"What's wrong?" Kerrick asked.

Nothing. Everything. "Will...Jael hurt my sister?"

"I wish I could say no, but you've seen what she's capable of." Kerrick stared out at the snow. "As long as your sister is useful to her, she should be fine. Jael's probably hoping that you'll return to rescue her. Once Ryne is healed, at least Tohon shouldn't bother you anymore."

In that particular case, I would have taken myself off the chessboard. "Unless there is another reason he wants me. He did change the bounty so I'm captured alive." I paused, considering. "Which is better than being dead."

"You told me before that some things are worse than death. Do you remember?" Kerrick's gaze now focused on me.

Surprised he had, I nodded.

"Do you still feel that way?"

I searched my feelings. "No."

"Good."

We camped in the record room two more nights. During those days, we searched the entire room. No one spotted another crate that might hold information about the plague. Dejected, we gathered around the campfire until Belen returned from his final sweep. He carried a crate labeled *Olaine Poisoning*.

"Thinking of learning the assassin arts, Belen?" Loren asked.

"Isn't that a rare flower? Maybe he wants to get into gardening. I hear that's what older people do when they reach their dotage," Quain teased.

Belen shook his head. "Two brains and not a bit of intelligence between them. Good thing the monkeys are entertaining or I'd have left them back in Ryazan."

Before they could defend themselves, Belen held the crate up. "Olaine poisoning is what the healers thought was wrong with the people before they realized it was the plague."

I remembered Tara's consternation over how the symptoms matched, but no olaine plants could be found near the patients. It had been one of many diagnoses suggested during that chaotic time.

"Another deadly plant?" Quain asked, looking a little green.

"In this case, it's the pollen," I said. "Anyone living downwind of the plant when it flowers sickens. But they recover about ten days after being exposed to the pollen."

"Why haven't we heard of it?" Loren asked.

"It's a very rare plant that only grows in the foothills on both sides of the Nine Mountains," Belen said.

Which was why Belen knew about it. However, olaine poisoning had been quickly ruled out. I took the crate from Belen. We'd found nothing else. It might be useful.

That evening, I sat close to the fire and sorted through the crate. Most of the contents detailed the cases of olaine poisoning over the years. There had been twenty-two confirmed sufferers the last year that had been recorded. A map of the foothills of the Nine Mountains had been marked with the location of each case. The majority had been on the northern side in Ivdel, with six in Alga and one on the southern side in Vyg.

Shoved in the back of the crate was another map. This one showed all the Realms. Red dots also marked the map, but the concentration of them were located in Vyg, Pomyt and Sectven. The page had been titled, *Recent Outbreak of Olaine Poisoning.* However, it had been crossed out and *First Plague Victims* had been written on top in a different hand.

I dug a little deeper into the records and found a list of dates and locations that matched the red dots.

I borrowed Belen's stylus and ink. Using dates to link cases, I connected the dots for each date. When I finished I had a series of concentric circles that grew bigger with each date.

They resembled the target Belen had painted on the tree during our knife-throwing lessons.

A finger of ice slid down my back as I stared at the target.

The bull's-eye hovered right over the Healer's Guild.

Proof that the plague started at the heart of the Healer's Guild.

CHAPTER 17

Breathing became difficult. The first victims of the plague had lived within ten miles of the Healer's Guild. And like ripples in a still pond, the disease radiated out in circles. Whoever had marked the map stopped after a couple months so the last circle crossed through the border between Pomyt and Casis down through Tobory, sweeping past Lekas—my hometown—going up through Sectven, Sogra, Zainsk and Vyg and past the Nine Mountains, touching on Alga and Ivdel.

I calmed my emotions and viewed the information with a clinical eye. What did these circles tell me? The plague hadn't been an airborne virus or else the marks would have been concentrated downwind of the prevailing wind direction. Since it had been the spring, the winds would have been from the west.

The plague must have been transmitted person to person. The marks were centered on the more populated areas, which supported that theory. I checked the date of the circle near Lekas. It matched when Noelle said she had sent those letters.

"You've been staring at those papers for hours," Belen said. "Did you find anything useful?"

"A few things," I hedged.

Then I considered the timeline of the plague. This spring would be five years since it began. It took two years to sweep through all fifteen Realms, and another year to reach the remote areas. Ryne's castle was near the coast of the Ronel Sea, overlooking a busy port town. So why did it take so long to affect him?

"Belen, where was Ryne living when the plague broke out?" I asked.

"I don't know." He glanced at Kerrick, who had appeared to be sleeping, but now pushed up on his elbow. "Do you?"

"No, why?" Kerrick asked me.

"He contracted the plague late. I was just curious if he had been living in northern Ivdel or far from populated areas."

"There weren't many people living up near the wildlands," Belen said. "Mostly just the border sentries on duty. People were afraid of being too close to the tribes."

Who we had assumed also caught the plague and died in large numbers. But no sentries walked the border, guarding against attacks. No rumors of invaders, either. At least, not yet. If it had been transmitted from person to person, then perhaps the people of the tribes were all healthy. A scary thought.

I considered. "Before he became sick, was he with anyone who had the plague?"

Once again Belen met Kerrick's gaze. "No."

"Did anything happen to him? Where was he at the time?"

"One of the elite had uncovered a spy working for Tohon," Belen said.

"We *suspected* he was loyal to Tohon," Kerrick added. "He was being questioned when he broke free and wrapped his hands around Ryne's throat. He was yelling in Ryne's face, promising to kill Ryne when one of the elite sent a knife through his heart. We never confirmed who he had been spying for."

"It was just a small group of us. Ryne always insisted on traveling light despite the danger. We were camped in the southern foothills of the Nine Mountains in Vyg," Belen said.

It was possible Tohon had sent a sick spy to infect Ryne, but that still didn't explain how he managed to survive so long. Did it matter? Probably not. But… "When he got sick, how long after that incident was it?"

"A few days," Kerrick said.

"I need a number."

"Didn't we change locations after that?" Belen asked Kerrick.

"Yes. We didn't know how long the spy had been watching us. Ryne ordered us to move east and we hiked through the foothills for two—"

"Three days?" Belen cut in.

"Two," Kerrick said. "Remember, we stopped because of the spring?"

"How could I forget unlimited hot water?"

"Sounds nice," I said.

"It was, but that night Ryne started vomiting and had stomach cramps," Kerrick said. "We thought it was just a reaction to spoiled meat, but when it went on longer than a day, we knew he was in the first stage of the plague. At that time, there were still a couple victims."

The first stage resembled a stomach bug, and once the person's stomach and bowels were empty, the symptoms transformed into all-over aches, pains and a high fever, which was stage two. The final stage involved convulsions, delusions and large white blisters on the skin that itched at first, then burned. Many of the victims screamed nonstop in pain during the third stage. They reacted as if they were burning alive.

We didn't know much about incubation periods, but the general timing of the illness had been four days for stage one, five for stage two and two for stage three. Eleven days to die. Healers took longer. According to Tara, the healers had lasted for twenty days before passing away.

It hadn't been a surprise to learn many people who had known they had the plague killed themselves before entering the third stage.

"What happened when you knew?" I asked.

"I sent a message to Sepp," Kerrick said. "We met up with him in the mountains and encased Ryne in stasis about five days after the first symptoms. Then we transported him to a safe location."

It didn't matter how far along Ryne was, I would start at the beginning if I healed him. Was he worth twenty days of suffering? I couldn't say.

We headed north the next morning. Even though we had Estrid's promise of safe passage to the Nine Mountains, Jael remained a threat. Avoiding the main road, Kerrick chose a route that paralleled it in Pomyt Realm. He kept to the wooded areas, which made sense, but occasionally we would pass through an abandoned town or skirt around a populated one.

As we drew closer to the foothills, all the towns we saw were empty. After five days on the road, we encountered towns that had been recently burned. Evidence of an attack marked the buildings and stained the ground.

Belen noticed my concern. "Marauders."

"Like the ones who attacked Alga?" I asked.

"Yes. Except these live in the foothills. They invade a town, steal everything that's worth anything, burn the place down and retreat back to the foothills. When they run out of provisions, they target another."

"What about Ryne's elite squads? What have they been doing all this time?"

"One is protecting Ryne. The rest are protecting the three northern Realms, keeping them safe while Belen and I searched for a healer," Kerrick said. He quirked a wry smile. "We had no idea it would take this long."

"In the meantime, Estrid's been gaining momentum in the eastern Realms," Belen said. "And Tohon has been creeping in from the west."

I gazed at the destroyed homes. If Ryne hadn't gotten sick, his men might have stopped those marauders. That thought led to another, which had been bugging me for the past couple days. "Why couldn't the elite counter Tohon's army?"

"We don't know. None of the squads returned from a reconnaissance mission in Sogra," Kerrick said. "That's why we were in Vyg, to find out what happened to them."

"Not even one solider?"

"No."

Later that afternoon, I stopped and glanced around. The area looked familiar, but I'd no idea where we were exactly. Each day we had covered as much ground as possible, traveling about twenty to thirty miles before halting for the night. I calculated the approximate distance to be one hundred and twenty-five miles in five days.

"What's wrong?" Loren asked me.

"How close is Galee?"

Everyone looked at Kerrick. He always knew our location. Quain had once teased that Kerrick was a living map, and I had wondered if the information had come from his forest magic.

"Galee is about eighteen miles east of here. Why?" Kerrick asked.

"My mentor, Tara of Pomyt, lived there. She had known so much about plants and herbs that she had written everything down so she wouldn't forget. That book would be invaluable. It's not far—"

"We spent three days in the Guild's record room. Wouldn't that information have been there?"

"No. The records are of past experiments and studies. Something that was used daily would have been near where the healers worked, not put away. It would have burned."

"And Galee probably has been burned to the ground by marauders," Kerrick said.

"Even if the town wasn't," Loren said gently, "her house would have been torn apart if her neighbors knew she was a healer."

True. "And Tara probably carried it with her when she went into hiding. Never mind."

But Kerrick didn't move. "Tara didn't go into hiding."

"How do you know?" A cold emptiness swirled inside me.

"She was on the top of Ryne's list, and close to our starting point. Belen and I arrived in Galee a few days after we left Ryne, but she had been executed the month before. Her house had been looted, but not burned."

Grief swelled along with an impotent fury. Killed by the very people she had loved and cared for. Whose scars she proudly wore. Whose sickness she had assumed so they didn't have to suffer.

I pushed my useless emotions down. Nothing would change because I was angry. "The book's long gone. Probably burned for warmth that first winter."

"Perhaps. Or she could have hidden it," Kerrick said.

"Maybe. But the odds are so slim there's no sense going eighteen miles out of our way." I was well aware that Kerrick and I had changed roles even before I caught the monkeys' smirky grins.

"Still worth stopping," Kerrick said.

I stared at him knowing full well he only agreed because he hoped it would sway me to decide in Ryne's favor.

As expected, the town of Galee had been destroyed. Burned-out buildings lined the streets. Nothing left except the stone foundations. However, Kerrick was determined to find Tara's house.

I led them to her place by memory. As her newest apprentice, it had been my job to go to the market every morning. I had gotten all the jobs no one else wanted, but I had treated each task as if it had been essential to do well—a trick I had learned from my father. Tara had called me her hardest-working apprentice, and had eventually started coming to me to help her with the more interesting cases.

Her house resembled the others—a pile of burned rubble. Kerrick and the others poked around, clearing sections. I stayed on the street, trying and failing not to recall how the six months I had lived and studied here had been the happiest of my "adult" life.

"Found something," Kerrick said, joining me. He held a small dented metal box coated with ash.

My heart jolted in recognition. It had survived!

"It's locked." He shook the box and it rattled. "Hold it so I can pick the lock."

"No need." I dug into my knapsack and withdrew a small silver key. "The box is mine. I'd left it here when I returned home, hoping I would be back. I'd forgotten about it."

"Yet you carry the key."

I shrugged. "Just couldn't bring myself to throw it away. Strange, I know."

The key fit, but opening the lock proved difficult. Kerrick helped and soon the contents that I had thought vital at the time were revealed. Coins, a necklace and a notebook.

Kerrick held up the necklace. The pendant hanging from it was a pair of hands. He gave me a questioning glance.

"My brother Criss sent that to me a month before I left home to start my apprenticeship. He's the one who taught me how to juggle." I smiled at the memory. "His letter said he knew I would be the best healer in all the Fifteen Realms because I had always been good with my hands and that he was so proud of me." Tears filled my eyes, blurring my vision. "That was the last time we heard from him or my father." I turned so Kerrick couldn't see me wipe my cheeks.

"What's in the notebook?" Kerrick asked.

I flipped the pages. My crooked handwriting filled each one. Reading through a few, I realized that what I had thought was a silly diary of events actually was an account of what I had learned each day. I had already forgotten many of these lessons.

"Anything useful in there?" he asked.

"Tara's would be better, but there's more here than I had thought."

"Worth going out of our way for?"

"Yes."

"Good. Now turn around."

"Why?"

"Can't you just—"

"Okay, okay." I spun, wondering what he wanted me to see.

Instead of pointing something out, Kerrick hooked the

necklace around my throat. He pulled my hair out, letting the clasp rest on the back of my neck. The touch of cold metal on skin sent a shiver along my spine.

"There. Now you won't lose it again."

We overnighted in Galee, camping on the lee side of a large stone wall that hadn't been knocked over. After so many days on the road together, we gathered wood, cleared snow, set a fire, cooked, ate and took turns on watch without having to say a word. However, once we settled under the blankets of our sleeping rolls, conversation would start, usually after Kerrick left for his shift. Tonight was no exception.

"Has anyone else noticed that we've encountered no one in the past two days?" Quain asked.

"The people living around here are not the type we'd want to encounter," Belen said.

"The trees are probably telling Kerrick where they are, and we've been avoiding them," Loren said. "No sense letting Tohon or the bands of marauders know our location."

"What about the mercs?" I asked.

"Them, too," Loren said.

I mulled it over. "Except for today, we've been traveling pretty much straight north for days. You'd think we'd have to skirt areas to avoid them. And we haven't seen any tracks in the snow. Quain may be onto something. It's too quiet."

"What's wrong with quiet?" Belen asked. "Not everything has to be a struggle."

"What are you thinking, Avry?" Loren asked, ignoring poor Belen. "Ambush near the main pass in case we try to cross it before spring?"

"It's a bit obvious, but logical."

"Wouldn't Kerrick be able to use his tree mojo to detect them?" Quain asked.

I grinned at his word choice. Kerrick had tried to explain to the monkeys how his magic worked, but unless they felt it like I had, they wouldn't be able to fully understand how the forest communicated with him. Magicians in general kept the details about their powers quiet. Either they were afraid a person would figure out how to counter them, or they liked being viewed as mysterious. Although once everyone knew, Kerrick had been open and frank with the guys.

"For his tree mojo to work, it would depend on where the ambush is. If they're hiding above the tree line, then we'd be out of luck."

"What about the ex-girlfriend?" Quain asked. "Do you think Jael's going to come after us again?"

"No. Jael lost the element of surprise and she knows her power can't counter ours."

Quain sat up and stared at me. "Ours?"

I cursed under my breath for my slip.

Belen chuckled at Quain's confusion. "Think about it."

So Belen knew. Did Loren? I glanced at him. He had a faraway expression.

"Is that why you yelled for Kerrick with Flea?" Quain asked. "You wanted to combine your magic?"

"We didn't combine it, we shared magical energy," I said, then explained how Kerrick and I had fought off Jael's attack. "Healers often linked together if a patient was on the edge of dying, giving one healer the strength to save the patient's life. Since Kerrick and I have different types of magic, I was surprised we could do it at all."

"Could Kerrick heal Ryne using your energy?" Belen asked.

"No. It just gives his own magic more power."

"But it has a price, right?" Loren asked.

"Yes," I said. "Using magic is draining and can be physically exhausting." Their thoughtful and intense expressions worried me. I didn't want to discuss Kerrick anymore. I tried to change the subject. "I'm usually starved afterward and craving my mother's cinnamon apple crisp. Does anyone know if the survivors are taking care of the apple orchards in Zainsk?"

No one fell for it.

Watching their faces, I knew Belen was the first to make the connection, although Loren wasn't far behind.

"Kerrick helped you heal me. Didn't he?" Belen asked.

I should just say yes and be done with it. However, I couldn't lie to Belen. "Not quite."

"Avry." Belen's voice held a warning tone.

"I healed you. But Kerrick gave me the energy to heal myself. Otherwise, I would have died. I admit it. Okay? Can we talk of other things?"

They did, but my thoughts lingered on my personal plague—Kerrick. In the list of attempted remedies for the plague, the Guild had tried sharing the energy of half a dozen healers to cure a sickened colleague. It hadn't worked. So there was no chance a lone magician could pull me back once I had the plague.

From Galee, we traveled northwest and reached the southern border of the foothills three days later. The craggy snow-topped mountains filled the sky, looming over us, yet at the same time the peaks looked impossibly far away.

In the foothills, we saw no one. Only small animal tracks marked the snow. As for the infamous reputation of the area, the rolling terrain and thick clusters of pine trees caused us the most trouble, slowing us down. Not bands of lawless marauders, ufa packs or mercs. All remained quiet.

I tried to believe the quiet meant good things. After two

uneventful days, I was almost convinced, but everything changed the next morning when Kerrick tripped.

We had been following him as he searched for a place for us to hide in until the spring melt, which hopefully would be in three to four weeks. Without warning, he sprawled forward, doing a face-plant in the snow.

At first, we laughed and teased. The normally sure-footed Kerrick brushed snow off his cape, grumbling good-naturedly. The culprit appeared to be a tree limb. A curved gray branch arched from the disturbed snow. We would have stepped over it and continued on our merry way except Belen paused and peered at the branch closer.

He cursed and dug around it, sweeping the snow away. The rest of us exchanged confused glances until our brains deciphered the object Belen had exposed. A dead body. Which, considering the plague's speed and the marauders, wasn't a surprise.

"That's why I tripped," Kerrick said. "The forest doesn't consider a dead body to be an intruder."

"Yeah, it's plant food now," Quain muttered.

Belen discovered more lumps in the snow. Again, no big shock. Every survivor had seen or found a plague victim. As the others brushed the snow away, revealing more bodies, I examined the man who had tripped Kerrick.

Thick beard, long hair and scars on his face, he appeared to be around twenty years old. He was curled up on his side with his arms crossed over his stomach. A futile gesture since most of his intestines lay next to him. I looked closer at the jagged flesh and bite marks on his body. Scavengers or killers?

"Something munched on this one," Belen called.

"Half this guy's face has been eaten off," Loren said.

"Uh, guys." Quain's voice shook. "I think I found one of the culprits."

We joined him. He had uncovered a huge ufa. Kerrick took a step back as soon as he saw it. An automatic reaction, but I couldn't fault him. The beast was six feet long with gray and black brindled fur covering about two hundred pounds of pure muscle. Two nasty-looking teeth curved down from its upper jaw. Black blood stained its front claws.

We uncovered fourteen bodies, but only one ufa. Although there were signs of many more animals. But it was hard to determine if the animals killed them or just stopped by for an easy meal.

"Marauders out on a raid, or returning from one," Kerrick said.

"How can you tell?" I asked.

"Unkempt appearance. Well armed. Battle scars. Mostly men. They leave the weaker members back at their base camp."

"What should we do with the bodies?" Belen asked.

"Nothing. As Quain said, they're plant food."

"Come spring, they'll reek. Aren't there any hungry Death Lilys around?" Quain asked, half joking.

"They don't deserve the honor," I said with surprising vehemence.

The guys peered at me as if I had lost my mind. Perhaps I had.

As we hiked west through the foothills, we encountered two more bands of snow-covered dead marauders that day. And another three the next. But no slain ufas. Kerrick's scowl deepened with each discovery. The snow meant they all died before the big storm seventeen days ago, far enough in the past to give us some comfort, but any consolation we scraped together slipped away by the sheer number of dead.

"Now we know why it's so quiet," Quain said.

When we set out on the third morning, we braced for more carnage, but nothing could prepare us for the next discovery.

This group of marauders had been killed like the others. However, their bodies were not covered by snow. Blood, guts, mud and bodily fluids stained the white snow. Ufa tracks marked the edges.

Kerrick ordered us to remain behind while he followed the tracks.

While he was gone, I examined the dead. Same story as the other groups we had found. The only difference was the timing. I estimated they had been killed about ten to twelve days ago.

"Avry, you do know how creepy that is. Don't you?" Quain asked.

"What's creepy?"

"Your fascination with the dead. It doesn't take a healer to know these guys were killed by packs of wild ufas."

"It's not a fascination. More like curiosity. Besides, I'm beginning to suspect they weren't killed by the animals. Don't you think it's unusual for all of the victims to be lying on their stomachs?"

"Or what's left of their stomachs." Loren pointed to mangled pile of intestines next to one body. "Actually, I think it's odd that the ufas keep attacking when they should be well fed by now."

"Unless there's more than one pack," Quain said.

"Oh, there's a happy thought." Loren scowled at him. "If it wasn't ufas, then who or what attacked them?" he asked me.

"I'm not sure." I crossed to the man Loren had indicated, and tried to roll him over. He was too heavy and stiff.

"That's gross," Quain said.

"Come help me," I said.

"No way."

"Sissy," Belen said. He grabbed the dead man's shoulder and hip, pulling him over. "What are you thinking?"

I studied the gaping hole that had been the man's stomach. Unlike some of the others, the cuts appeared to be from a blade and not teeth. "From the extent and location of the damage, he would have fallen onto his back if attacked by an ufa." I examined the snow around the victim. "The ufa wouldn't have turned him over."

"Why not?" Quain asked.

"All the tasty parts are in front."

"Disgusting. Remind me not to ask any more questions."

Loren huffed with amusement. "As if that would work."

"Shut up."

"Make me."

"Gentlemen," Belen warned. "If the ufa didn't flip the body, then who did?"

I walked around the other bodies. "There are drag marks in the snow." Backing up so I could see the whole scene, I noted how the bodies had also been lined up so their heads pointed one way. Northwest. "Why go to all the trouble of arranging them?"

"Because it's a message," Kerrick said as he returned.

"Something other than 'run as fast as you can in the opposite direction right now or you'll be ufa food'?" Quain asked.

"The main pass through the mountains is northwest, isn't it?" I asked Kerrick.

"Yes."

"A message warning us away from the pass?"

"No. I found another set of remains quite close to here. The bodies have also been arranged."

"How's that a message?" Quain asked.

Belen answered, sounding stunned. "Tohon's clearing the way for us so we will reach the pass without running into trouble."

"That doesn't make sense," Loren said. "Wouldn't he want to *prevent* us from reaching the pass?"

"Are you sure it isn't a warning *away* from the pass?" I asked. "After all, Ryne's safe on the other side."

"He's not on the other side," Kerrick said. "He's hidden within the Nine Mountains. The easiest way to reach him is via the main pass, but the others work, as well. They just take longer and can only be accessed in warmer weather."

I put a few clues together. "Does that mean—?"

"Can someone tell me what's going on?" Quain asked.

"Tohon knows where Ryne is," Kerrick said.

CHAPTER 18

"That's a big leap in logic. Just because the bodies had been arranged a certain way doesn't mean Tohon has found Ryne," Belen said. "Tohon could just be playing with your mind, capitalizing on your fears. Let's consider other possibilities."

"All right, Belen. What do you think it means?" Kerrick asked.

"Maybe he's guessing that we're headed to the pass and is being cocky about it, letting us know he knows. It's typical of him."

"It could be a trick," Loren said. "He wants us to think he has Ryne so we rush to him, leading Tohon right to him."

"Either way, it's a heck of a message," Quain said. "There's lots of bodies. He's not fooling around."

"And how did he know you'd see it?" I asked. "Yes, he could guess we'd enter from Pomyt, but the foothills span for miles."

"We've been following the animal paths, just like the marauders had," Kerrick said. "It's easier than trying to push through the dense pine trees. He knew we'd stumble upon them eventually." Kerrick paused. "I'm changing our plans. We're not going to hunker down, but take the main pass."

Just what Tohon wants, but I wasn't going to say it aloud.

"What about the steep icy path and thousand-foot drops?" Quain asked with a slight quaver of nervousness.

"Be careful where you step and don't look down," Kerrick said.

"That's not funny."

"It wasn't supposed to be."

The change in plans felt wrong. Belen and Loren had both made excellent points. And there was always the possibility that Tohon was goading Kerrick so he'd rush right into an ambush. They had been friends for years; Tohon must know how to provoke Kerrick. Heck, I knew how to upset him and I'd only been around a little over three months.

Regardless of our opinions, Kerrick led us straight to the pass. We encountered a couple more bands of dead marauders, but he wouldn't let us stop.

We reached the base of the main pass two days later. Wider than the animal paths, the road snaked through the pine forest. The snow had been packed down by previous travelers.

Kerrick pointed at the thin lines made by wagon wheels. "A caravan came through here a few days ago. Otherwise, there's no one else on the trail."

"What about above the tree line?" Quain asked.

"We'll have to send a scout ahead," Belen answered.

"How would that work?" I asked. "Not much up there to hide behind."

"He'd have to travel at night and wear camouflage," Belen said. "There's a rock fall before it gets steep. Once the road turns high and tight, there's no room for an ambush."

Quain glanced up at the mountains. "What about room for a camp?"

"None. We'll push through until the road widens."

"How long?"

"Worried about your beauty rest, Quain?" Belen teased.

"If you really wanted, you could take a nap," Loren added. "Just be careful not to roll over in your sleep."

"Not funny." Quain pulled his cloak tighter.

"I wonder if you'd wake up in midair?" Loren mused more to himself than his friend. "Once you hit bottom, then it's lights out forever."

Quain shot Loren a sour look while Belen chuckled.

As we hiked, the forest thinned as the path rose in elevation. My calves burned with the extra effort. At least with the rolling terrain there was a break between uphills.

Although worried about Ryne, Kerrick was confident that no one waited to ambush us among the trees. And no ufas, either. He sensed a pack of them far to the west.

We stopped five miles before reaching the tree line and planned our next move. Loren volunteered to be our scout. Belen was too big, Kerrick too recognizable, Quain too uncomfortable with heights and I was too valuable. We set up a small camp a hundred feet off the main road while Loren prepared for his night mission. He removed his cloak and sword. Wearing all black clothing, he smeared a dark gray goo on his face, neck and hands.

"Flea's concoction," he said with a sad smile. "He taught us some cat burglar tricks." Loren scanned the darkening sky. "Now if only the moon cooperates and stays behind the clouds."

Half a dozen streaked the expanse, but they didn't appear thick enough to block the moonlight.

When complete darkness filled the area, Loren waved

and said, "See you in a few." He strode away, then stopped. "Found them." Loren backed up as two men holding swords approached.

Kerrick and the others were on their feet in an instant, weapons in hand. I grabbed my stiletto.

The trees around us rustled with movement. A quick glance confirmed we were surrounded. And outnumbered. As the circle tightened, Loren grabbed his sword and joined us. Clustered in the middle, we kept our backs to one another.

"Damn, Kerrick," Quain said. "I thought you said no one was around."

"No one is," he growled. "I don't feel them."

An odd statement. But there was no time to contemplate it as the ambushers engaged us. One thing was in our favor; Kerrick and his men outmatched them as far as fighting skills. I sent knives into shoulders, thighs, stomachs and upper arms.

Despite the lopsided numbers we had the upper hand. Except these men and women wouldn't stop when slashed with a sword. They didn't react when a knife embedded into their skin. Injuries that should have knocked them down failed to affect them at all.

They fought in utter silence. Eventually, the attackers closed in, rendering swords useless. Belen switched to hand-to-hand combat, tossing them around like rag dolls. But they kept advancing. Kept shambling to their feet with a mindless determination.

Two made it past Kerrick and grabbed me, dragging me away. I suppressed my revulsion and panic. Pressing my hand on freezing cold flesh, I summoned my power. Nothing happened. No magic swelled in my chest. Kerrick's comment echoed in my mind. *I don't feel them.*

Horrified, I met the gaze of one of my captors. Death stared back. Shocked to my core, I ceased struggling.

Shouts filled the darkness. Poppa Bear roared. Then silence.

The dead men kept a fast pace as they pulled me along. My mind reeled over the impossible. No magic could bring the dead back to life. Not a life magician or a death magician had that ability. It had been proven.

Yet the impossible held me tight. Grasped me with icy fingers. Filled me with a terror so strong it hurt.

When I could no longer keep up the pace, one of them carried me over his shoulder. Their repulsive touch grew unbearable and my sanity threatened to take a holiday without me. I closed my eyes and concentrated on the living. Thought of Mom and Melina. Fawn and her mother. I couldn't worry over Kerrick and the others' fates right now or else I would go insane. Instead, I envisioned Nyrie's sweet smile and remembered Noelle as she was before the plague robbed her of her childhood.

The night blurred in one long test of endurance. Dawn broke, but my captors kept their fast pace. They hadn't said a word all night. Nor did they stop for food or water or rest. My throat burned with thirst and my head ached from hanging upside down. Eventually, I passed out.

Ice-cold water slapped my face, filled my nose. I woke, choking and disoriented.

A man peered down at me. "Easy there."

I struggled to sit up. He held out his hand. When I grasped his fingers, I almost sighed in relief at the touch of a living, warm person. He helped me to my feet, but I leaned against him, drinking in his pulse of life. It filled me like a glass of warm wine, dulling my senses.

He raised his eyebrows. Humor sparked in his deep blue eyes. "Are you going to zap me?"

"Should I?" Confused, I glanced behind him. Two men and one woman—all armed—watched me intently. I was in danger. My muddled thoughts cleared a little.

"No, you shouldn't. My companions wouldn't like it and would stop you."

"But I could threaten to harm you if they don't back off," I said.

He smiled sadly. I guessed he was around twenty-five years old. A few inches taller than me, he had short black hair, long dark eyelashes and a killer smile. His good looks had a royal quality, while Kerrick's was more rugged. This man wouldn't lack for admirers.

Hooking a thumb at the three hovering nearby, he said, "I wasn't referring to them, but to *them*." His gaze slid past my shoulder.

I turned and jerked as if he had thrown more ice water on me. The dead stood in precise rows, staring at nothing. Terror welled, clearing away my confusion in an instant. I counted six of them.

"Creepy, aren't they?" His tone remained friendly and conversational. "But efficient and obedient. I thought more would return from the mission, but it doesn't matter—they're easily replaced. And they were successful. You're here."

"What...? Who...?" I couldn't form a coherent question.

"They're King Tohon's special soldiers. Impressed?"

"Horrified."

He smiled again. "There's that, too."

"Are you working for Tohon?"

"You could say that."

"What does he want? Does he need me to heal someone for him?"

"Your healing power will certainly be an asset, but he has other plans for you. And, of course, keeping you from healing Prince Ryne is another benefit."

Compared to the six dead standing nearby, the thought of being Tohon's prisoner failed to produce anything other than mild concern. Or was it because I still held the handsome mercenary's hand? And why couldn't I draw away? Obviously, I wouldn't harm him. Not if it meant being grabbed by those repulsive things again.

Since he seemed content to talk, I asked him, "Were the dead marauders in the foothills a message?"

"No. They're part of the cleanup. King Tohon will not allow such undesirables to infest his kingdom."

Movement behind him drew my attention. His three living companions jerked and flailed as if fighting an invisible opponent. One by one they crumpled to the ground.

My captor didn't draw his sword in response to the noise. Instead, he sighed and turned as Kerrick appeared. Disheveled, bleeding and pissed off, he stood next to the three now-prone forms with his sword in hand. The sword looked as if it was coated with Flea's dark gray goo.

Belen and Quain broke through the trees and joined Kerrick. They all sported cuts, bruises, stained swords and very determined demeanors. Where was Loren?

"I should have sent twice as many dead," the merc said.

Kerrick's gaze dropped to my hand intertwined with the merc's. This would be a perfect time to zap my captor. Yet, I didn't. Kerrick's anger burned on my skin.

My merc glanced between me and Kerrick. He laughed. "Have I stolen another from you, Kerrick?"

"We figured out how to neutralize your abominations, Tohon. As I see it, you only have temporary custody."

Tohon?

He quirked a smile at me. "I prefer King Tohon. And have you noticed that Kerrick and his goons haven't come any closer?"

No, but now that he'd mentioned it… "Why not?"

Tohon lifted our linked hands. "He knows if he moves to attack me all I have to do is apply a touch of power and you're dead. He also knows I don't wish to kill you, so we're at a bit of a stalemate."

I wanted to be afraid, but couldn't produce the emotions. Instead, a detached curiosity flowed through my veins. "One touch? Death? But you're a life magician."

"Which makes me able to take a life at will. But not yours, my dear." He stroked my cheek with his other hand.

I had to make a conscious effort not to lean into Tohon's intoxicating touch. Kerrick's hatred, jealousy and fear zipped through my body. Strange that I should feel it.

Tohon said, "Besides influencing emotions, another facet of my power is sensing emotions. I could share Belen's and Quain's emotions with you as well, but I prefer to focus on Kerrick. He can be quite amusing for a stick in the mud."

I laughed. I couldn't help it.

"I really wanted to steal you away from him, but I think it will be so much more delightful when you leave Kerrick and come to me."

"Why would I do that?" I asked.

"He's grandstanding, Avry," Kerrick said. "He knows we have the upper hand and it's his way to soothe his damaged ego."

Tohon shrugged. "Think what you will." Then he met my gaze. "My dear Avry, I shall look forward to our next meeting." Tohon kissed the back of my hand.

A wave of heat slammed into me.

"Kill the men," he ordered his dead soldiers. They surged forward, aiming at my friends.

I tried to zap Tohon, but another wave hit me. This one burned, turning my muscles into goo. Tohon caught me and laid me on the ground.

"Come to me, Avry. Soon. Or I'll send a whole company of my special troops to fetch you and to take care of your annoying companions. For good." He kissed my forehead and a liquid blackness washed away the world.

Sounds and colors returned in little splashes of light.

"...ice-cold," Kerrick said.

"Locked in a stasis?" Belen asked.

"I don't think so."

"Then what's wrong with her?" Poppa Bear sounded worried.

I wondered who they talked about. Patches of blue pulsed in and out over me. Green bushy blobs flashed in my peripheral vision. Feeling languid, I enjoyed the kaleidoscope of colors.

"I don't know." Kerrick's frustration cut through my fuzziness.

"We need to get back to Loren," Quain said.

Loren's name gave me another jolt. The world around me snapped into focus. Kerrick bent over me. He clutched my hand. My skin burned where he touched it, but the rest of me felt like it had been dunked in ice-cold water.

"Are you all right?" Kerrick asked.

His concern pressed on me like a physical thing. I didn't know how to respond to his question. I didn't feel any pain. But an oddness tingled through my body as if Tohon's life magic remained inside me.

"Avry, answer me."

"I'm..." My voice rasped.

Belen offered me his canteen. Kerrick helped me sit up. I gulped water until my arms shook. Thrusting the canteen into Belen's hands, I curled into a ball as uncontrollable shivers racked my body. Too much had happened. Memories of being held by the dead coated my skin with ice. For a moment, I craved Tohon's warm touch, which did more than share Kerrick's emotions with me. It had dulled my reaction to the horror.

"Don't just sit there," Belen chided Kerrick.

With stiff arms, Kerrick gathered me close and held me tight. Even with his body heat, I still shook, convinced I would never be warm again. Or sane. Those...abominations. That they existed... That they obeyed Tohon's orders... That they attacked us... Loren had been injured. He needed me. I pulled my emotions in, reeling them into one neat little ball and tucked it away. My muscles relaxed, the shakes settled and I drew in a deep breath.

Wiggling from his grasp, I sat on the ground. My hair clung to my cheek; I swept it behind my ear and realized I had been crying. Mortified, I wanted to turn away, but everyone stared at me. "Sorry, I just—"

"Don't apologize." Belen handed me a handkerchief. "It's been an utterly gruesome day."

I scanned the area. Tohon's dead lay in pieces. Broken by decapitation. Black blood pooled on the snow. The putrid odor of decaying flesh soiled the air. At least there was a way to stop them. There was no sign of the other three who had been with Tohon.

Struggling to stand, I brushed snow and dirt from my cloak. I met Quain's gaze. "How bad is Loren?"

"Bad, but not critical," Quain said. "We should get back."

"How far?"

"About half a day."

I wouldn't last an hour. No one carried their packs. They probably left them with Loren and the other dead dead. What else could we call them? The truly dead? Dead for real? Dead again? I shivered. Now wasn't the time to think about it.

"Does anyone have any food?" I asked, although I doubted the guys thought of food when they had chased after me.

Belen produced a handful of beef jerky.

I pounced on the food and munched it as we headed east at a fast pace. Walking next to Belen, I asked, "Canteen, handkerchief, food…what else do you carry?"

He blushed. "Just a few essentials."

"Thanks. I can always count on Poppa Bear."

"Poppa Bear?" he asked in a neutral tone.

Uh-oh. Did I hurt his feelings? "Yes, like a bear protecting his cubs."

"Isn't that what the mother bear does?"

"Would you rather I called you Momma Bear?"

He laughed. "That would offend my fragile male ego." He remained quiet for a while. "I guess that's an accurate nickname." Belen jabbed a thick finger at Kerrick's back. "I've been protecting that cub since he was born."

"When you were like…four? Five?"

"Four. And before you pish at me, isn't Noelle six years younger than you?"

"Yes."

"Then you know what I'm talking about."

"I do. Point taken." I lowered my voice. "He's lucky to have you."

"And Noelle is—"

"Screwed up because I wasn't there. Let's not go there." I mulled over his comment. "But you are always there for

Kerrick. Wasn't there a time you wanted to do your own thing?"

"No. I swore an oath."

Wow. "But what about if you had met a girl? What if you wanted to get married?"

He shrugged. "Then I would have gotten married. But I didn't meet anyone. And once the plague hit, there were more important things to do."

"How about when things settle down?"

"Perhaps. If I meet the right person." He smiled. "Then I might have cubs for real."

"They'd be the luckiest cubs alive."

"I don't know about that. But if they get hungry, I'll have that covered."

"No doubt."

"What about you, Avry? Is marriage and children in your future?"

Fingers of ice gripped my heart as images of Tohon's dead soldiers filled my mind. I focused on Belen, pushing the horror back. "No."

We reached Loren as the sun sank in the west. He huddled next to a small fire. Bandages covered with blood had been wrapped around his right thigh. A sheen of sweat coated his forehead.

"Avry, I'm so glad to see your beautiful face," Loren said.

"How nice. Let's see if you still think I'm beautiful in the morning."

Loren tried to mask his pain, but couldn't suppress a yelp when I touched his leg. A sword had cut the muscles behind his right leg almost to the bone. My magic flared to life.

"Don't you want to rest first?" Belen asked me.

I glanced at Kerrick. He gave me a slight nod.

"I'll be fine." My power surged.

Loren yelled as the magic stitched his muscles back together and repaired the damaged tissue and skin. It rushed back into me and pure fire stabbed my right hamstring. I had thought nothing could hurt as bad as Belen's stomach injury—I was wrong. Loren's was a whole different animal.

I stumbled and hit the ground hard. But compared to the agony in my leg, it didn't even register. My opinion of Loren went up as I realized he had dealt with this for almost a day.

Then a warm wave of spring sunshine and living green dulled the pain as Kerrick pulled me into his arms.

Kerrick and I needed a couple days to recover. I fell into a deep healing sleep that lasted both days. When I woke, Loren cooked a big pot of stew. He rationalized that since we weren't hunkering down in the foothills, we didn't need to lug around so much meat.

When we were ready to continue up the pass, Loren scouted ahead even in the woods. We could no longer rely on Kerrick's forest magic to warn of ambushers.

Each time Loren reported back, we'd climb another mile or two. The path narrowed as the trees disappeared. Rocks poked through the snow and we slowed so no one would twist an ankle.

The wind keened between the mountain peaks and cut right though my cloak. Just as Belen had said, when the trail was high and tight, we pushed on without stopping. Quain hugged the rock wall on our left. I didn't blame him. The drop to the right made me dizzy.

We crested the pass. When the trail angled down, the ache in my calves transferred to my thighs. Loren's injury throbbed. After a couple hours going down, I slipped, fell on my backside and slid down the path, gaining momentum.

The trail ahead of me snaked to the left. If I didn't stop, I wouldn't make the turn. Instead, I'd fly off into the abyss.

Shouts echoed, warning me of the danger. I dug in my heels and stopped inches from the edge, but my heart continued its fast tumble.

"Were we going too slow for you?" Loren teased when they caught up to me.

"Hold on to me from now on," Belen said, hauling me to my unsteady feet.

"Yeah, it would take an avalanche to move him off this mountain," Quain said. "Can I hold on to you, as well?"

Belen ignored him, but tucked me in close.

When we reached the tree line, Kerrick led us off the pass.

"I thought you said Ryne was hidden within the Nine Mountains?" I asked Kerrick.

"We're still in the mountains." He pointed north. "There's the next ridge."

I groaned. "How many more of them are there?"

He smiled. "After that one, there's seven more. Nine ridges in all."

Quain paled. "Holy shit."

"Why did you think they're called the Nine Mountains?" Kerrick asked.

"I never thought about it."

"Oh, man, Quain. You make it easy," Loren said.

"I thought it had to do with the war with the tribes in the north," I said, jumping in before Quain could dig himself in deeper. "My father told me the mountain chain kept the tribes from invading our land. But once they learned how to cross them, it took us nine years to push them back into the wildlands."

"I thought it had to do with the nine gemstones that can be found in the mines underneath," Belen said.

"That's a better reason than war," I said.

"Anything's better than war," Belen agreed.

As we traveled deeper into the woods, I noticed there wasn't any snow on the ground. That night, we camped in a small clearing. Kerrick assigned two people to be on watch at all times.

I had no trouble falling asleep, but my dreams haunted me. The dead chased me as Tohon laughed. I woke with a start. My heart slamming in my chest. When I returned to sleep, the dream continued as if I hadn't woken.

Come to me, Avry. Tohon's voice held me immobile as the dead closed in. I thrashed and screamed, caught in their icy grip.

Kerrick woke me. "Nightmare?" He settled next to me.

Belen snored on the other side of the campfire. Loren and Quain must be on watch.

I clutched my blanket to keep my hands from shaking. "I wish."

"Tohon's dead?"

Come to me, Avry. I ignored the voice inside my head. "Yes. They're a nightmare you can't wake from."

"I knew he was...depraved, but I'd never thought he'd resort to bringing the dead back to life."

"They're not alive. Or else you would have sensed them, and I would have been able to zap them."

"Then what are they?"

I considered. "I didn't feel any magic. Perhaps he found a medicine that animates them, gives them enough intelligence so they can be trained."

"You might not be able to sense his magic. What else could have prevented you from zapping him when he held your hand?"

Reviewing my encounter with him, I hadn't felt his magic, but my reaction to him had to be due to his influence. "I couldn't feel it, but you're right, he had me in a…thrall. Can you sense his power?" I asked.

"No, but I can't feel Jael's, either." He stared at the fire.

Come to me, Avry.

No. Tohon, I won't. You have to be stopped.

"Kerrick."

He looked at me.

"Can Ryne stop Tohon?"

"He'll find a way. Yes."

"Okay."

"Okay, what?"

"I'll do it. I'll heal Ryne."

CHAPTER 19

I had thought Kerrick would be happy I'd decided to heal his prince, but he frowned instead.

"And it only took an encounter with Tohon's dead. Gee, what a swell girl," Kerrick said. His tone was sharp with sarcasm.

My initial reaction was to turn away, let him think what he wanted about me. I shouldn't care, especially since he knew my fate and wasn't upset by my impending death at all. Except I couldn't keep quiet. "Did you ever wonder how Ryne obtained that list of healer names?" I asked.

If he was surprised by the change in topic, he didn't show it. "The Guild—"

"Doesn't give out that information."

"So he stole it. No big deal."

"You're right. Except he also stole a *confidential* correspondence between the Guild and its members."

Understanding softened his scowl just a touch. "The document detailing the plague symptoms?"

"Yep. That also informed the healers not to heal those

sickened with those symptoms. The one that was misinterpreted."

"They sent them out to every Realm. Anyone could have intercepted it," Kerrick reasoned.

"True. However, during those early days, Prince Ryne brought his very sick sister to Tara in Galee, hoping she could heal her. This is the same man who wouldn't let her help his father. Did you know that?"

"Yeah. But he thought all magicians went against nature, not just healers. He used to lecture us about it at school all the time."

"Yet, you are friends."

"He's matured since then and understands."

"Swell," I said, copying Kerrick's sarcastic tone. "When she refused, he demanded to know what was going on. At that time, Tara didn't know and had been following the Guild's orders. She showed him the letter, hoping it would explain her situation." I stared at the embers, remembering.

"He flew into a rage. His men dragged all of us out of bed, tossed us together in the living room and held us at sword point." The image of Ryne furiously waving a document in Tara's face came unbidden. "Ryne harassed her and…" I swallowed. "Threatened to harm us if she didn't heal his sister." I'd never seen a man that angry, including Kerrick. My father had been the sweetest soul and never lifted a hand to us. His disappointment had been the worst punishment. We'd behave just so we wouldn't disappoint him.

"Let me guess," Kerrick said. "That's about when you interfered."

I pulled my shirt, exposing my left shoulder. An old scar marked my skin. "This one's mine. Not one taken from another. And before Tara could give in to his demands, his sister died. The poor thing. After he finally left, he started the rumors. By that time, the public was in a panic. Ryne handed them someone to blame. You know the rest."

"Is that why Ryne knew your name?"

"Yes. Tara had three apprentices at the time, and he learned all our names."

Silence. Then Kerrick said, "I'm sorry I was angry."

"You didn't know."

"I didn't. What else are you hiding from us?"

"I promised Estrid I would return after I healed Ryne." I didn't wait for the lecture. "You were right. Our freedom from Estrid came with a price. But you already know it won't be an issue once Ryne is healed." Fear of dying churned in my stomach, but it wouldn't change my mind.

"I agree. You *won't* be returning to Estrid." Kerrick stood and roused Belen for their watch shift.

Shocked at his comment, I stared at him as he earned a good-natured growl from Belen. He left with his friend in an almost jovial mood. Kerrick really was a cold heartless bastard.

As I thought about what I'd promised to do, fear once again twisted deep inside me. I knew healing Ryne was the right thing to do. I'd known since Estrid offered an alliance with him. However, my heart remained unconvinced. Stupid heart.

We entered a cave system the next day. The damp air smelled of minerals and dirt. Daylight filtered through holes in the ceiling, but unlit torches lined the walls of the first cavern. Loren lit them, and we continued deeper, leaving the relative brightness of that initial room behind. We traveled through tunnels and the occasional cavern. The solid darkness pressing against the torchlight reminded me of Tohon's inky magic.

Come to me, Avry. His voice seemed to conjure invisible hands, stroking my cheek with icy fingers. Shivers threatened.

"So you've had elite soldiers and a magician living here for the past two years?" I asked.

"And my sister," Belen added cheerily. He'd been in a great mood since learning of my decision and, of course, seeing his sister again.

"Kind of dreary. Do you think they're still here?"

"Why are you asking?" Kerrick asked.

"It's been so long. Wouldn't they be worried?"

"No. We've stopped by a few times. They're aware of the healer situation."

Quain snorted a laugh. "Healer situation. That's putting it mildly. Wait until they hear—"

"Nothing," Kerrick snapped. "All they need to know is we found Avry and have returned."

I picked up on Kerrick's warning tone, but Quain didn't— unless he chose to ignore it. "Are you embarrassed by all the problems Avry's caused us, or—oof!"

Kerrick had slammed Quain into a wall. "Not another word. That's an order," he said.

Quain stared at Kerrick for a moment. "Yes, sir."

Kerrick let him go. Quain shot me a nasty look. Wonderful. I wouldn't miss Kerrick's bad moods or Quain's pouts.

We continued for another hour. Just as the torches sputtered, we reached another large cavern equipped with fresh torches. Smart.

"Are they allowed to leave?" I asked.

"There should be enough food for another year, and fresh water flows in a cavern nearby," Belen explained. "But they take turns going outside for fresh air and sunshine. Or they'd go insane."

I understood that. I wouldn't miss camping out in caves, either. After a couple hours, I wondered why we hadn't seen any guards.

"Don't need them," Belen said, answering my question. "This place is a labyrinth. Beyond those living here, only Kerrick and I know the way."

"But what if something happened to you two?" I asked.

"Loren and Quain knew to bring you to the woods outside the entrance. Then it'd be a matter of waiting until someone came out."

They certainly had everything covered. Or so I thought. As the hours blurred past, I worried we were lost. At one point Kerrick and Belen exchanged a concerned look. When we entered yet another cavern, Kerrick ordered us to wait as he disappeared down a dark tunnel.

I leaned against a stalagmite. "How much farther?" I asked Belen.

"Not far now," he said.

"Then why are we waiting?" Loren asked.

"A precaution."

If I had hackles they would be up. Belen was a lousy liar.

Kerrick returned. His face ashen. He pulled Belen aside and whispered in his ear. Belen roared, pushed Kerrick away and dashed down the tunnel. Kerrick gave chase and we followed with weapons drawn.

The smell hit us first. A putrid rotting stench like no other. The reek of death. Loren and Quain stopped, covering their noses and mouths, coughing and choking on the odor. They retreated. I opened my knapsack. Pulling Belen's handkerchief out—he had let me keep it—I rubbed the cloth on my bar of soap before tying it around my nose and mouth like a bandit.

Belen roared again. Anguish and heartache clear in the

sound. I hurried to catch up and paused at the entrance to the largest cavern we'd seen. Dead bodies littered the floor. Belen cradled one in his arms as he rocked and cried. No doubt his sister. Kerrick checked the others. A few had been decapitated and I guessed they were Tohon's dead. No wonder he hadn't been too upset to lose me. A numb horror settled on me.

A lone figure lay on a cot in the back. Ryne? I wove through the carnage, trying not to step on anyone. The man on the cot wasn't the prince, but he was alive. Barely. He had multiple cuts on his torso and arms. One deep gash along his rib cage had become infected. His skin burned with fever. My magic swelled and pushed to be released.

"Kerrick," I called.

He joined me.

"Is anyone else alive?" I asked.

"No." A whisper full of pain.

"Is Ryne…"

"Not here. The bastard must have him."

No need to ask who the bastard was.

"Did he say anything to you about Ryne?" Kerrick asked.

"No."

"Will Sepp live?" he asked, pointing to the man.

"With help. I need to heal him now."

"I'm cut off from the forest."

"I'll be fine." I gestured to Belen. "Although, as soon as Sepp can walk, take us back outside. It'll be…healthier. And make sure I drink plenty of water."

Kerrick nodded. I released the energy inside me and assumed Sepp's injuries. My torso blazed with pain. Suddenly overheated, sweat poured down my back and soaked my shirt. I sank to the ground as my magic fought to heal the wounds.

Delusions swirled. Tohon's voice—*Come to me, Avry*, repeated over and over as his dead soldiers chased me.

Someone—Loren or Quain…or both—helped me as we navigated the darkness.

The fresh air roused me for a few minutes. We had left the caves, but the sky remained black. I sensed movement near me; voices talked and argued, flames danced along dead limbs. My body shook with fever. Sweat coated, then froze on, my skin. Someone covered me with a blanket. Another tipped cups of water into my mouth.

Eventually, the grip of infection loosened and I slipped into sleep. Tohon's dead waited for me, but I lacked the energy to run. They surrounded me, trapping me as the cold soaked into my bones. The circle of dead parted to let Tohon enter. Images from the cavern flashed in my mind. Tohon smiled and gestured to his special soldiers.

Come to me, Avry, or they will hunt you down.

I jerked awake. My heart jumped in my chest. Filling my lungs with fresh air, I lay still as my pulse settled. Fever dreams. Nothing more than that. Yeah, right.

When I calmed, I glanced around the campfire. Kerrick sat next to Sepp, their heads close as they talked in whispers. Loren and Quain slept next to the fire. Belen must be on guard duty. No sense in posting double watch now. Tohon had Ryne.

Kerrick's conversation grew heated. No surprise. I closed my eyes and eavesdropped.

"…saved your life," Kerrick said. "We just can't—"

"He wants her and it's our best chance to save Ryne. You of all people know sacrifices have to be made."

"No. There has to be another way."

Didn't take a genius to guess what they were arguing about. I sat up, surprising them into silence. "Sepp wants to use me as bait, doesn't he?" I asked.

"Uh…" Sepp said.

He looked like an older version of Kerrick. Broad, but not bulky, graying hair and the same nose. Interesting. Was he his uncle? I couldn't sense his power. "Kerrick?"

"Yes. He thinks we can trick Tohon into leaving Ryne behind while he comes for you. While you lead Tohon on a merry chase, we'll go in and retrieve Ryne."

"Won't work," I said.

"I know. Tohon's too smart to fall for it. Plus, his dead found you before. If he sends enough of them, they can again. So why this elaborate game?"

"I think you answered your own question," I said.

"Tohon likes to play games. It makes him feel powerful to manipulate people." Kerrick rubbed his hands over his face. Deep circles of exhaustion hung from his eyes. "We're at another stalemate."

Until he sends a company of dead after me. Bad enough in the hands of two, but with more than a hundred chasing me... Revulsion snaked along my skin as I realized that I would have to go to Tohon. But I couldn't give myself up without knowing more.

"Can Tohon wake Ryne?" I asked.

"No. Only a death magician can," Sepp said. "Tohon can take a life, but I can stop life and only I can restart it."

"You or another death magician?"

"Anyone with that power, but I'm the only one."

"Are you sure?"

He bristled at my question.

"Think about it. Tohon's special soldiers are not alive. I had thought a medicine might be the reason they can move and obey orders, but maybe there is another explanation. Could *you* animate the dead?"

Sepp sputtered. "It's...an affront to life. It's...perverted. I've never tried it, nor would I ever!"

"She didn't ask you if you would, but if you *could*," Kerrick said.

Opening and closing his mouth a number of times, Sepp huffed. "I think I can."

Kerrick leaned forward. "Are you thinking a death magician is working with Tohon?"

"Not possible," Sepp said. "I'm positive I'm the only one, and have been for years."

I considered. "Was Tohon in the cave during the attack?"

The magician squinted as if he peered into the past. "I don't think so. Unless he came after I'd been knocked out."

"So he might think that you're dead," I said.

"It doesn't matter," Kerrick said. "We can't reach Ryne, and even if we do find him, we won't be able to leave Tohon's castle alive. We should join forces with Estrid and hope for the best." Kerrick's shoulders sagged. "Sepp, can you unanimate the dead?"

"I believe so. My powers are basically the opposite of Tohon's. But I don't know for sure. When they stormed the cave, we were taken by surprise. By the time I figured out what they were and how to stop them, it was too late."

"How to stop them as in decapitation?" I asked.

Sepp nodded.

"How would you unanimate them? If only you can wake Ryne, doesn't it make sense that only Tohon can stop the dead?"

"I don't know. I haven't had any experience." Sepp's tone bordered on snippy.

"Did you sense them before they attacked?"

"Are you deaf or just stupid? I just said we were surprised." He'd skipped over snippy and went straight into nasty.

I decided to follow Kerrick's example and keep my expression neutral even though I wanted to slap him. "Allow me to elaborate. Before they attacked, did you feel uneasy or feel something wasn't quite right and just dismiss it?"

"Of course not. I can't *feel* through stone walls."

"What about when they were in the room with you?" I asked.

Sepp appealed to Kerrick. "This is a waste of time, we should—"

"Answer her question," Kerrick said.

Sepp gaped at him. "Don't tell me that you've—"

"Answer her question," Kerrick ordered.

I wondered what Sepp was going to say to Kerrick.

With an elaborate sigh, he said, "Yes, I could. When they were in with us, I knew no life breathed inside them. Although I don't see why *she* needs to know."

Perhaps Sepp thought I'd overstepped my place in this little group. As Belen would say, Too bad, so sad.

Kerrick studied me and I caught a glint of humor in his gaze. "What are you thinking?"

"You're not going to like it."

"No surprise."

"Just think it through before you dismiss it. Okay?"

"All right."

"You, Belen, Loren and Quain will join Estrid's army. You spread the word that Sepp died and Ryne is lost. I'm sure Tohon has spies in her organization. Then you convince her to rally her troops and prepare them for an attack against Tohon's army."

Kerrick opened his mouth. I shot him a warning look. He kept quiet.

"Meanwhile, Sepp and I will travel to Tohon's castle. And, hopefully while he's distracted with Estrid's preparations, we'll slip in, heal Ryne and take off."

"Just like that?" Kerrick arched an eyebrow.

"That's an utterly ridiculous plan," Sepp said.

"You've never been to his castle before. How are you go-ing to find Ryne in Tohon's vast complex?" Kerrick asked.

He had me there. I mulled it over as Sepp smirked. What was his problem?

I ignored the magician, focusing on Kerrick. "Tohon's expecting me. He threatened to send his dead to fetch me if I didn't go to him." Holding up a hand, I stopped Kerrick's retort. "Too many for you and the guys to counter. What he won't be expecting is a man he believes is dead."

"No," Kerrick said.

"Insane," Sepp said.

"Think about it. Tohon's been wanting a healer for a rea-son. If it's just me there, then he has no one to use against me. Sepp can hide nearby, and when I've gained Tohon's trust and learned where Ryne is, then I'll figure out a way to make it work."

"You can't expect us to do anything based on you finding 'a way to make it work,'" Sepp said.

Kerrick shook his head. "Tohon will just manipulate you."

"He'll try, but—"

"He'll succeed. He got to Jael and me in school. You won't be able to resist or hide anything from him."

"Yet Ryne outsmarted him. Ryne with no magic at all."

"You're not Ryne," Sepp said.

Ouch.

"No." Kerrick crossed his arms as if that ended the discus-sion.

I bit back a sarcastic comment. "Okay, then. What's your plan?"

"We *all* go to Estrid's, mount an attack and—"

"As soon as you get close, he'll move Ryne to another location. Sepp? Got anything?"

He blinked. "We could all go to Tohon's and rescue the prince."

"And we all get caught because there is nothing to distract him. Then Tohon threatens to harm Belen or Loren, and I've no choice but to cooperate." I shuddered at the thought.

"We could distract him," Sepp said.

"How? There are only five of you. And the problem of finding Ryne remains."

"Your plan has just as many holes," Sepp said. "It's ridiculous to think you can trick Tohon."

More preferable than waiting for his dead to find me and drag me to him. However, Kerrick's stiff posture meant I had a better chance of convincing Estrid to denounce her religion. At least I tried. If we reached Estrid's army, maybe I would be safe from the dead. Then I'd be physically closer to Noelle.

"You're right," I said to Sepp. "I couldn't possibility trick Tohon. I hope you can last a few weeks without sleep."

"What is she talking about?" he asked Kerrick.

"Only you can sense the dead. You'll have to alert us of ambushes," Kerrick said.

"You can't believe this silly girl. She's planning her schemes based on a rumor that I've died! I thought you learned your lesson with Jael, Kerrick."

The look he gave Sepp made the mountain air feel downright toasty. Glad I wasn't on the receiving end of Kerrick's ire this time, I laid back on my bedroll. Sepp's injury throbbed with pain, still sapping my strength. Kerrick hadn't shared his energy for this one. Perhaps he was too preoccupied with Ryne's kidnapping. Yeah, right. The chance of rescuing Ryne was slim to impossible, so I was no longer valuable to him.

I dreaded falling asleep, but I needed the rest to finish

recovering. Giving in, I slipped into a deep, senseless void. Too bad it didn't last all night. Nightmares of Tohon's dead plagued me. Eventually, they trapped me and converged, grabbing me with their cold hands.

"Avry." Icy fingers circled my wrists.

I yelled as the grip tightened and tried to pull away.

"Avry, wake up." The hands shook me. The voice sounded upset. "Now."

I opened my eyes. Kerrick straddled me, pinning me down. The horror of the nightmare faded, but his expression alarmed me.

"Are we under attack?" I asked.

"No." He released me, moving off, but he sat on his heels.

Dawn balanced on the edge of the mountains. So close, I expected the sun to crest the rippled peaks in seconds.

"We will be," I said. "Tohon will send his army for me."

"I know. That's why we're going to follow your plan."

CHAPTER 20

I sat up. "We are?"

"Don't act so surprised. I thought it through and you're right, it's the best chance we have to rescue Ryne," Kerrick said as if it pained him to admit it.

"And how does Sepp feel about it?"

"He's going to be pissed off as hell, but he swore loyalty to me."

And I had thought traveling with Kerrick was difficult. A resentful death magician made Kerrick's moods nothing but a trifle annoyance.

The sun crested the mountains. Kerrick glanced past the fire. "Belen wishes to bury his sister this morning. The ground's frozen, but he dug a shallow grave and plans to cover her with rocks. He was waiting for you to be strong enough."

I sagged back. "I'll never be strong enough for that."

"Me, either. But we'll pull it together for Belen, won't we?"

"Yep. Not much I wouldn't do for him."

Kerrick gave me an odd look. "Really?"

"Of course, Belen's my friend. The same would go for Loren and Quain, as well."

"But not me." A half smile tugged.

"No. I hate you. Remember?" I teased.

"Couldn't possibly forget." He grinned. "Just so you know, the feeling is mutual."

"Gosh," I said with mock horror. "We actually have something in common."

Kerrick laughed. "Let's not let it happen again."

"Agreed."

Way too soon, Kerrick sobered. Belen had returned to the fire. We roused the others and the six of us walked to the rocky grave. A small pile of stones sat next to the grave.

Hunched over as if the Nine Mountains pressed down on his shoulders, Belen said a few words about his sister, Sayen. She sounded as sweet and tough as Belen. Then Kerrick stepped forward. He picked a rock from the pile and spoke to Belen before placing the rock on the grave. He turned and left.

Loren, Quain and then Sepp copied Kerrick's actions. When it was my turn, I grabbed the last stone.

I touched Belen's sleeve. "I'm so sorry about Sayen. I'm sorry I caused such trouble and delayed the trip back here. If I hadn't, maybe we would have gotten here in time to—"

"Avry, ifs and maybes can't change the past," Belen said, covering my hand with his own. "Sayen knew the risk. I wanted her to go with Kerrick while I stayed behind, but she told me to get my lazy fat ass out of her sight." He smiled at the memory. "Don't feel guilty, Avry. It's not your fault."

Belen might believe it, but I didn't. My stubborn refusal to heal Ryne could be linked to so many of our current problems. When I placed the stone on Sayen's grave, I made a promise to her. I would do all I could to rescue and heal Ryne.

After the burial, we packed and prepared for travel. Sepp's sullen anger burned on my skin whenever he thought I wasn't looking at him. However, Belen's fury over the plan was unexpected.

"Did you not see how those…things affected her?" Belen asked Kerrick. He shook with rage. "You can't just let her—"

"It's her plan. Besides, she has a slight chance of succeeding," Kerrick said, keeping calm.

"A slight chance? Let's break out the champagne."

Belen's sarcasm was impressive. I didn't know he had it in him.

"At what cost, Kerrick? Are you willing to risk her freedom and sanity? You know Tohon will just claim her."

Claim? That sounded bad. Unease swirled around my heart. Why did I think I could resist Tohon when I had had no willpower before? Perhaps Belen was right.

Kerrick's expression flattened. He pulled Belen away from us for a private chat. I watched Belen's face. Whatever Kerrick said mollified him. He still seemed upset, but not as furious as before.

When Kerrick returned, he detailed the route Sepp and I needed to take to Tohon's, what we should look for and avoid.

"If you can, don't let Tohon touch you," Kerrick said to me. "His power is like yours—he needs skin contact for his magic to work."

My stomach twisted with fear, remembering Tohon's touch. How I had no control over my emotions. "I don't think… I… Sepp's right, I can't… I'm not—"

Kerrick took my hands in his. His warmth steadied my nerves.

"You're the most strong-willed person I know. More stub-born than my great-aunt Yasmin, and I didn't think that was possible. Just pretend Tohon is me. You never listen to me, so you'll have no trouble ignoring him."

That surprised a laugh from me. "I'd like to meet your great-aunt Yasmin someday."

"Well, she's eighty-nine, so don't linger too long in To-hon's castle. Get in and get out. Okay?"

"Yes, sir."

Kerrick just shook his head and muttered under his breath as he walked away. I said goodbye to the monkeys. They each gave me a hug.

Belen still wasn't happy about our plans, but he pulled me aside to say goodbye. "Be careful. Be smart. And be strong. Here." He handed me an almost perfectly round stone that fit in my palm. Flea's name had been carved in the stone. "It was one of his juggling rocks. He was searching for three perfect ones as we traveled. When he found this, he marked it as a keeper." Belen swallowed. "He didn't have a chance to find any more, so I kept looking for him." Belen handed me two more stones that closely matched the first. One stone had Lo-ren's and Quain's names carved on it. The other had Belen's and Kerrick's. "They're keepers, too. Remember that."

Grief, guilt and awe churned, tightening my throat. "I will." The words squeaked out.

"Good. I'll see you in a few months." He enveloped me in a hug and joined Kerrick and the others.

I put the gifts in my cloak's pockets. The extra weight pulling on my shoulders gave me a boost in confidence as Sepp and I headed west.

Normally, the smaller passes would be impossible to navi-gate at this time of year. However, the dry winter helped, and the official start of spring was only sixteen days away. If we arrived at the Orel Pass too soon and it remained impassable, we'd just have to wait.

Sepp was a horrible traveling companion. He complained about the cold, the steep terrain, the wind and my crazy scheme. When he was supposed to be on watch, I'd wake and find him fast asleep.

Nightmares still disturbed my rest, and I couldn't shake the image of Tohon's confidence. My scheme seemed crazier as we drew closer to Tohon's castle. And I realized that if I was going to prevail, I needed more information about Tohon and life magicians. Perhaps Sepp could help.

The next night, as we shared a meal, I asked Sepp a number of questions.

"Tohon doesn't have too many weaknesses," Sepp said, dipping a piece of hard bread into his stew. "He's cocky and tends to be compulsive. Although he does have a soft spot for a pretty woman, just like Kerrick."

I almost choked on my food. Not how I would describe Kerrick at all.

Sepp ignored my sputterings and continued. "Magic-wise, Tohon's probably the most powerful mage living."

Regaining my composure, I asked, "What about the three magicians that are working for him?"

"His fire mage barely qualifies. All Aidan can do is start small fires and has probably been assigned to keep the hearths warm in the castle. Pov is the strongest. As a rock hound, he could cause a serious earthquake, or—" Sepp gestured to the mountain peaks around us "—start an avalanche, blocking the pass, or bury us alive if he wanted. Ulany's earth magic could find you the best worms for bait, and the richest soil for crops, but otherwise she's not useful in a fight."

"Who is the next strongest mage?" I asked.

Sepp slurped the juice from his bowl. "It's a toss-up between Jael and Kerrick. Their powers are so different, it's hard to compare them." He considered. "Jael, probably, since she can access her power anywhere. Then Pov, me, Marisol— she's a water mage working for Estrid—Aidan, Ulany and Selene, the moon mage. She's only good for one thing—influencing the tides."

Interesting commentary. I wondered how he knew everyone's names and strengths. "What about me? Where do I rank?"

"You?" He seemed taken aback. "Uh, you're a healer... not really a mage. I guess you'd be after Selene."

Which meant good for one thing only. Sepp underestimated healers, but I wasn't about to educate him. "Are there any other mages in the Realms?"

"No."

"But Kerrick had said a few were lying low."

"No. They're dead. Tohon killed any mage who wouldn't swear loyalty to him. The exceptions are Estrid's mages, who are protected by Jael."

"Why would Kerrick lie to me?" I asked.

"Probably so you wouldn't be afraid."

No. Kerrick made sure I had been well aware of Tohon's despicable actions. More incentive to heal Ryne. He hadn't told Sepp about my reluctance and I wondered why. Perhaps Kerrick didn't fully trust Sepp. Not good, considering I needed to trust him.

"Sounds like Tohon will be hard to beat," I said.

"One on one, yes. But when you combine me, Kerrick, Jael and Marisol, then the odds are very much in our favor."

I didn't believe Jael would join forces with the others, but perhaps she'd change her mind when she learned about the dead soldiers. "What about his special soldiers?" I shuddered.

"They're easy to stop. Don't worry about them, they're my problem." He waved a hand like a king granting a boon.

"But how did Tohon create them? Any ideas since that's more your…area of expertise?"

His scowl reminded me of Kerrick. A pang of loneliness touched my heart. It had been only a few days and I missed the guys. Even Kerrick, but I wouldn't admit that to anyone.

"A skill I've *never* exercised," Sepp said, sounding insulted. "My magic allows me to see death. If a person is sick, I can sense if the illness will kill them or not. When a dead body is found, I know at a touch what killed him or her. I can't take a life like Tohon, but I can pause it, freeze it, so the person is in a fake death."

Good information, but I noticed he hadn't answered my question. Either he didn't have a clue how Tohon "woke" the dead, or he knew, but didn't want to share. Which led me to wonder, why not?

We crossed the Orel Pass four days later. As we descended into the foothills and into the Realm of Sogra, the possibility of encountering Tohon's dead soldiers and his living army increased a hundred percent since we hadn't seen any of them in the Nine Mountains.

After a mile, I realized Kerrick never taught Sepp how to travel through the woods. Dried leaves crunched under his boots. Twigs snapped. Convinced the whole Realm heard us, I held my stiletto ready for a fight.

Sepp also didn't seem worried about being ambushed. The first day, he paused around midday and sniffed the air like a bloodhound. I copied his actions. The weather had been cold yet fair, but today it warmed up to comfortable. Listening for any strange noises, I noted the increase in bird activity. Spring was only ten days away.

The second day, Sepp stopped early in the morning. He pulled me behind a clump of pine trees. We crouched as a squad of dead shuffled past. They were led by a few living soldiers. I bit on my sleeve to keep from crying out. I really needed to clamp down on my panic. I knew I'd have to be "caught" soon, but I would not surrender to a squad of abominations. When they were gone, Sepp resumed our trek. At least the near run-in with the dead answered one question about Sepp's abilities. One of the dozen knots in my stomach loosened.

Sepp appeared thoughtful the remainder of the day. That night as we huddled in the dark—a campfire was too risky— he speculated on whether he could unanimate the dead.

"I don't think my powers will have any effect on them. There's nothing there. Death is a threshold," Sepp said. He made a grabbing motion with his right hand. "I can snatch a person just before they enter that threshold. Once they've crossed it, I know what pushed them through. But these... dead. There's nothing to grab."

"Can you freeze them?" I asked.

"Maybe."

Not very comforting. "Then best to avoid them alto-gether."

For the next four days, we dodged the dead and a few squads of living soldiers. The groups broadcasted their pres-ence miles away. Their noise was loud to me, but Sepp didn't hear them until they were almost on top of us.

On the fifth morning we slowed our pace as the forest thinned. Farm fields dominated the rolling landscape. A cou-ple had been plowed, but winter wheat covered the rest. We kept away from the edges of the fields. Death Lilys tended to grow there, hoping to catch a farmer unaware.

"Not that I have to worry about Death Lilys," Sepp said in his superior tone.

The tone I loathed. I considered ignoring him, but his knowledge, no matter the way it was imparted, could be vital to our mission. "Why not?"

"They don't attack me. They recognize a kindred soul."

"But you don't take life. Wouldn't Tohon be more compatible?"

Annoyance creased his large forehead. "I know death well, that is what they respond to. I've no idea if they'd go after Tohon or not."

I debated if I should ask the next question, but I was too curious not to. "Have you…been in…communication with them?"

Sepp stared at me as if I had asked him to make friends with Tohon's dead. "They don't communicate. They grab and kill all but a few lucky souls."

Which meant he'd never been inside one, or else he would have bragged about living through the experience. "What I meant was, can you pick out the Death Lilys among the Peace Lilys?"

"Yes. The Death Lilys smell…different."

"How different?" Lilys emitted a strong scent of honey and lemon.

"Why do you want to know?" Sepp asked.

"Didn't you ever think others could smell it, too?"

"No. I'd assumed it was due to my magic. Plus I have to be almost on top of it. Too close for another to risk."

"Does it smell like death?"

"Morbid curiosity?" Sepp asked.

Not sure how much I should reveal, I hedged. "Before the plague, the Healer's Guild had been trying to figure out why a healer couldn't heal a person poisoned by the Death Lily's toxin. As you can imagine, experimenting with the live plant is impossible." Although they had managed to get the seeds.

"I remember. They asked me to assist. When I found out what they needed me for, I refused on the grounds that the Death Lilys are a natural part of our world. They cull the idiots who don't have the sense to avoid them."

As if it were that easy. I clamped down on a sarcastic retort. Sepp was one cold bastard. I had called Kerrick that, but even he wouldn't agree with Sepp's sentiment.

"In my opinion, the Healer's Guild were delving into areas they shouldn't," Sepp said. "Performing experiments and calling it research, they kept pestering me to help."

Made sense. His powers would have been a great benefit to the healers. Yet, he'd refused. While Tohon had worked with the healers when he had time.

Sepp continued despite my silence. "They were mucking about with things they should have left alone. I wouldn't be surprised if the Guild had really started the plague by doing one of their experiments. And by the time they realized what they'd done, it was too late."

His speculation touched on one of my worries. The map of the early plague victims appeared to prove his suspicions. Yet, I needed more evidence. Either that, or I was in denial.

When we reached another set of fields, instead of bypassing them, Sepp led us along their edge. No doubt he wanted to prove his claims about the Death Lilys. We passed a number of the huge flowers. None reacted, but their perfume filled the air. I wondered if a Death Lily would recognize me or attack me. The flowers were all linked through their roots. Perhaps I'd be safe.

Sepp stopped at the corner of the field. "Smell that?"

I inhaled. Honey and lemon dominated. Ignoring those scents, I focused on a slight spice in the mix. "Anise?"

"That's what it is! I knew it was familiar, but couldn't put a name to it."

I scanned the area, counting four Lilys nearby. "But which one smells like anise?"

He turned this way and that, sniffing the air. Sepp pointed to a Lily to our left. "That is a Death Lily." Striding up to the plant, he stood underneath the flower.

The cone-shaped bud quivered and moved away from Sepp.

"See? It's afraid of me."

Or didn't like his scent. I moved closer, but he held his hands out. "Stop there or you'll be dinner."

A low rustle sounded. I halted.

"Let's go before it tries to get you." Sepp headed west.

I tripped when I stepped to follow. The Death Lily's vines had curled around both my boots, which explained the rustling. Unable to break the Lily's hold on my legs, I pulled my stiletto as it reeled me in. Sepp kept walking. I considered yelling for him, but didn't. When I reached the base of the flower, the petals parted and covered me.

A thorn jabbed into my neck. I grunted. Last time the Lily had been gentle. This felt like impatience. As my mind and body separated, I relaxed. Instead of flowing along its roots and seeing beyond its petals, Tohon's image loomed. Unpleasant feelings of fear, revulsion and loathing rolled through me followed by the urge to stop Tohon. To pull his roots from the earth. To fix the wrong.

When the Death Lily released me onto the ground, I held two small liquid-filled sacks. Orange in color, the outer hide didn't break when I squeezed it. I had no idea what they were, or what they were for, but I knew it was important.

Storing them in my knapsack, I mulled over the encounter as I searched for Sepp.

I caught up to him a short time later.

His gaze flickered to me. "What was the holdup?"

"My strap...I had to adjust it."

"Next time let me know. Kerrick would be mad if something happened to you before we reached Tohon's."

I noted his use of the word *before*. "If I were you, I'd be more worried about Belen."

"Belen doesn't have any magic."

"True, but he's very protective and will tear your arms off if he thinks you're responsible for hurting me." I smiled at the vision.

Sepp pished. "One touch and he'd be frozen."

As if Belen would let Sepp touch him. "If it makes you feel better, keep thinking that." I wasn't the only one in denial.

Even though we camped in the thickest section of the forest that night, we didn't risk a fire. After eating a cold meal of jerky, we discussed Sepp's hiding place. He needed to be close to Tohon's castle so I could reach him, but not too close or else he would risk being caught.

"Speaking of being apprehended," Sepp said, "you'll have to be captured. You can't just walk up to the front door. Tohon will suspect you had help getting through all his defenses."

He was right. I had been thinking the same thing, but it irked me to no end that he had such a low opinion of my intelligence.

Two mornings later, we crested a small hill. A fair-size town filled the valley below us.

"I don't relish camping out in woods filled with unfriendlies or hiding in some cave. That town is close to the castle. I'm thinking it would be a perfect place to blend in."

"It would depend on the residents," I said.

"What are you talking about?"

"In Estrid's occupied Realms, the citizens who hadn't embraced her religious beliefs and donned the red robes were scared of her. A stranger in town would attract attention and he would be reported to her priests."

"This isn't an occupied Realm. It's a Sogran city. They celebrated when Tohon was named king after his father died."

"If you're sure—"

"Of course I'm sure. *I've* gotten you this far, haven't I?"

I fisted my hands, but kept them pressed against my thighs as I wrestled the desire to punch him.

"You shouldn't be seen in town," Sepp said. "In fact, head away from this area before you surrender."

We parted company at dawn. Sepp seemed relieved, and almost gave me a cheerful goodbye. He had made his opinion clear. He believed I wouldn't succeed. Even though he detailed where I could find him in town, I suspected he would bolt if he heard any rumors about me.

As instructed, I headed in the opposite direction. After a few hours, I realized this was the first time I had been truly alone in more than four months. I stopped as a notion occurred to me. I could disappear. Go back into hiding. Except the dead and the bounty hunters would be after me. Plus I couldn't let Belen and the others down or go back to those dark days of being in hiding. I pushed on.

I listened for one of Tohon's living patrols. Around midday, I heard the unmistakable tread of a squad. Heading toward an intercept point, I hid a few of my throwing knives in unusual places.

Should I appear furtive or confident as I strode among

the soldiers? Tohon was expecting me. No need for me to hide. Although he would wonder why I didn't approach one of his border patrols sooner. I'd claim my pride wished to get as far as possible. From what I'd learned about him, he'd understand that.

The hardest part was altering my gait as I walked through the woods. After spending the entire winter blending in with the forest's song, I had to concentrate in order to make enough noise that would alert the soldiers.

Finally, I produced enough sound. They halted to listen, then hunkered down to ambush me. A small part of me was amused by their obvious actions, but fear dominated the rest. Once they brought me to Tohon, there would be no return.

I clutched Belen's and Flea's stones in my pockets, thinking about my keepers. All that I would face and endure, I would do for them. I needed to stop dwelling on the what-ifs, and focus on what I could do and would do, which was everything possible to heal Ryne.

When the ambush "surprised" me, I gathered my nerve as I stared at fourteen armed soldiers. Then the sergeant shouted standard questions at me: Who are you? Where are you going? Who sent you?

Easy enough to answer. "I'm Avry of Kazan. I'm planning to go to the castle. Tohon of Sogra invited me."

Despite the name dropping, the soldiers confiscated my knapsack, the weapons they found and secured my wrists behind my back. They marched me to the castle. On the way through a shallow valley, I spotted the Sogra castle on the opposite ridge.

It was a beautiful white structure with a black roof, six turrets and surrounded by a thick black stone wall. Behind it were a number of other smaller buildings. As we neared, I noticed a few other details of the main building. Black gargoyles hung over the edges of the roofs. Instead of one big building, the castle looked as if the different kings and queens who'd lived there had added additions to the original castle.

The squad dragged me in through the front gates and into a spacious courtyard. There, they made a big deal over my capture. Tohon and a number of bodyguards arrived. I was presented to the king with a great deal of fanfare. One cold look from Tohon stopped the celebration in a heartbeat. He ordered my release and my things returned.

I rubbed my raw wrists and wondered what game he played now.

"She is our guest. You are to treat her as such, until *I* say otherwise," Tohon said. He approached me with a swagger in his step. "My dear, so nice to see you again."

Before I could reply, he swept me into his arms and kissed me hard. His touch zipped right through me, igniting every single nerve ending. My body responded. Desire flared. I leaned against him and kissed him back.

So much for my plan.

CHAPTER 21

I was in big trouble. The logical side of my brain staged a coup, wrestling control from my emotional side. With much effort, I broke away from Tohon's delicious kiss. But he held me tight.

"Let go." My voice cracked since Emotional Avry was ready to rip her and Tohon's clothes off right here in the courtyard in front of the soldiers.

Amusement sparked in his gorgeous blue eyes. "How was your first *real* kiss, my dear?"

Unbelievable. I desired a second, third, fourth…. Logical Avry said, "Let go, now."

"No. I'm king—I give the orders, not take them."

"You're not *my* king. If you want my cooperation, you'll release me."

"It'll only take a few more kisses, my dear, and you'll be more than happy to do what I say."

"Won't work." And who was I trying to convince?

"It has with others." Tohon's playful tone held a warning note.

"Not with everyone," Logical Avry guessed. Emotional Avry was still reeling from the kiss.

Tohon's arms around my back stiffened. I'd hit a nerve.

"You don't want to manipulate me," I said. "Trust me on that. You need a healer. Do you want her scatterbrained and swooning over your every kiss? Or do you want me clear-headed and able to do my job?"

His grip relaxed a bit. "You do swoon so well. And it's so exciting to know *my* Avry is untouched by man."

"Because of you," I said. "Three years on the run from bounty hunters doesn't give a girl much time to have a love life."

"And Nasty Kerrick keeps such a tight lid on his emotions." He tsked. "My apologies about the bounty. I will lift it, my dear."

"Good. Now let go."

"Clearheaded and cooperative?"

"Let go and we can discuss conditions and terms."

Tohon wilted. "Spoken like a legal adviser. All right, my dear. We'll try it your way first."

He released me. Emotional Avry fought to return to his arms, but Logical Avry kept a tight grip until the other settled.

"Come inside. We'll talk terms." Tohon held his hand out.

I ignored it. "There has to be witnesses before I agree to anything."

"Why bother? They're all loyal to me."

"Humor me."

"You've no idea how agreeable I'm being, my dear."

Which worried me more than if he refused my request. He and four of his bodyguards strode toward the main entrance of the castle. I noted that only living guards were inside the complex as I followed him. The two-story-high stone doors parted for us without a squeak. I marveled at the skill needed to carve the intricate floral designs into the black obsidian.

Tohon noticed my stare. "Beautiful, aren't they?"

"Yes."

"My father had them commissioned from the craftsmen in Bavly. A decent battering ram will smash them into pieces, but my father preferred beauty over strength." He glanced at me. "He didn't realize he could have both." Tohon swept a hand out, indicating the large receiving room. Arched columns supported the ceiling. Gold-framed paintings hung on the walls. Vases and other sculptures sat on pedestals.

"This place is filled with my father's treasures. He spent an inordinate amount of time buying and collecting them. Inanimate objects that remain where he placed them years ago, collecting dust. Still here even though he is gone. Useless except they remind me that my father cared more for treasure than me."

Surprised by his honesty, I glanced at him.

"A harsh thing to say," he acknowledged. "And a harsh reality to admit, but once I admitted it to myself, it was quite liberating."

"Why tell me?"

"I'm sure Kerrick has brainwashed you into thinking I'm a monster. I'm not. Not only do I seek your cooperation, but your loyalty, as well."

In my mind, dead army equaled monster. Nothing would convince me otherwise. But I was smart enough to keep my opinion to myself.

Tohon led me into another room. Rich red curtains hung over stained-glass windows. Thick carpets covered the floor. And a huge throne sat on a dais.

"Come see this." Tohon jumped up on the dais. "My

father designed it. Look at the gemstones along the arms and headrest."

The throne could easily fit Belen and the monkeys. I moved closer, inspecting the jewels. Emeralds, rubies and sapphires had been used in the decoration. The seat of the throne was covered with diamonds. I reached out to touch them, but stopped.

"Go ahead," Tohon said. "They're smooth. My father sat on them every day. Visiting dignitaries had no idea King Zavier's ass rested on a fortune in diamonds. Probably made him feel powerful."

"Was your father a mage?" I asked.

"No. Both my grandmothers had strong magic, but the gift skipped a generation. When my powers woke at a very young age, I was a constant reminder of his inability to wield magic. And therefore became the perpetual target of his jealousy and hatred."

"I'm sorry to hear that."

Tohon shrugged as if the events of the past hadn't affected him at all. "Made it easier to kill him."

And just when I thought he might not be pure evil, but closer to *touched* by evil, he proved me wrong.

"I never use this room," Tohon said. "My father needed *things* to believe he was powerful." He gestured to the throne. "I've no need of worldly possessions. I command life itself and I decide who lives and dies. I've more power in my pinky than my father *ever* had."

Yet he kept the room intact.

"Come see where I spend most of my time," he said.

I hesitated.

"You have a dirty mind, my dear. It's not what you think."

Ducking my head to hide the blush of heat spreading across my cheeks, I followed him from the throne room. Tohon navigated the complex maze of hallways with ease. He cut through ballrooms, sitting rooms and drawing rooms without a glance at the lavish furnishings, crystal chandeliers and priceless artwork.

Then we climbed the stairs. They spiraled around and around until I felt dizzy. Each turn, I glimpsed the surrounding countryside. A thick forest covered in light green fuzz spread across the lands to the south. In a few weeks, the southern landscape would resemble an emerald carpet. I wondered if Kerrick's eye color would change as it had from autumn to winter. The gray color matched his coldness. Would a vibrant green help soften his face? Perhaps. Would it soften his personality? Probably not.

I pulled my thoughts from Kerrick to my situation. The huge castle would take weeks to search if I didn't get lost or wasn't locked in a cell. Both were possibilities.

"Here we are," Tohon said.

We had finally reached the top of the stairs. Two of his guards took up positions next to the door, while the other two remained a few steps below me. The plain stone door reminded me of the prison back in Jaxton. Unease rippled. Was this where Tohon tortured his prisoners? Or where he animated the dead? Icy goose bumps coated my skin.

He opened the door. I braced for an assault of horrors. Instead, bright light and humid air rushed out. The heady mix of living green, moist earth and fresh flowers filled my nose. Tohon disappeared into the sunshine. I stepped into the... What to call it?

Stunned, I gaped at the greenery. Trees, bushes, flowers, hanging vines, pools of water and birds all contained in a rectangular glass room.

"Gorgeous, isn't it?" Tohon asked. "This is my forever garden. The only nice thing my father did for me. Of course,

I had to convince him of the benefits of having medicinal plants and herbs close by. It's heated in the winter. And because it's up here it gets sunlight all day. What do you think?"

"It's...lovely. You spend most of your time here?"

"As much as I can. Wouldn't you?"

"Yes, I would." I walked around the garden. Containers full of soil held the plants and trees. Others held water. Moisture dripped from the clear glass walls. Even the ceiling had been constructed of glass. The view was unobstructed on three sides and as breathtaking as the garden.

"Did you plant this room?" I asked.

"Yes. Living things do well under my care." He gave me a wry smile, acknowledging the irony. "As long as I care about them." Then he sobered. "People, on the other hand, are not worth caring for."

Sounded like something his father might have said.

"Even your loyal subjects?" I asked, glancing at the bodyguards standing by the single entrance.

"My subjects don't lack for the basic necessities and are well protected. They are taken care of."

"Including your magicians?"

"Are you worried, my dear?" Tohon moved to take my hand.

I stepped out of his reach. "Of course. I'd be stupid not to be."

"You have nothing to fear as long as you don't cause trouble."

"And if I do?"

"Do you really want me to spell it out for you? Give you the details? There are cells below—"

"No." I did another loop around the garden. Kerrick would love this. Touching the leaves, I half expected to feel the tingle of his magic. Nothing. Disappointment panged for a moment.

"Is your forever garden the only thing you care for?" I asked.

"Oh, no. I care for the fate of the Fifteen Realms. We've lost so many leaders and the actions of certain survivors have been horrific. I'm sure you've encountered some of them. But one single leader will be able to unite those who wish to return to civility and don't wish to be forced to worship a nonexistent entity. The creator. Pah!" He waved a dismissive hand. "Has this divine being created an army from the dead? No." He stepped closer. His fiery conviction smoldered in his gaze. "I care for you, my dear. I plan to cherish you."

I stared at him. "Why?"

"You possess a number of qualities I admire. Intelligence, beauty and your powerful healing magic." He sidled closer. "One of a kind."

"Only because *you* killed all the other healers." And Belen's sister, and a whole long list of others. Logical Avry needed to remind Emotional Avry of this often.

"I wasn't referring to your magic, my dear. I meant you're the only one Kerrick has fallen in love with since Jael. And I tried to take Jael from him. Tried for years. I didn't tempt her, but that bastard Stanslov did."

Tohon stood inches from me. How did he manage that? He took my hands in his just like Kerrick had done before I left for this mission.

I knew I should pull away, yet I remained in place. "You're mistaken about Kerrick. He only cared for Ryne. Once his prince was no longer savable, he had no problem parting ways with me."

Cold calculation sharpened his gaze. "I've heard the rumors about Sepp. Is he truly dead?"

Could I lie to him while he held my hands? I focused on the image of the carnage in the cave. It had burned deep into my memory. Revulsion and horror flowed through me and I met his gaze. "Yes. No one survived the attack."

His body relaxed a trifle. "Good to know. As for Kerrick letting you go, he would have to admit his feelings for you to stay, and that he won't do."

Maybe the Kerrick Tohon knew in school would fall for me, but the man I'd traveled with was not capable of any warmth, let alone affection. "What do you have against him?"

"Prince Kerrick is handsome, rich and a powerful mage."

"Have you looked in a mirror recently? And I'd bet you could sell a few of those diamonds in your father's throne as long as you don't tell anyone where they came from."

Tohon laughed. His good humor shot right through me. I bit my lip to keep from giggling along with him. "I don't know," Tohon said. "'King Zavier's ass diamonds' has a certain ring to it. The moniker could make them more valuable."

"Good luck with that. However, my point is you possess all those qualities, as well."

"Thank you, my dear. But Kerrick had what I never did."

"A puppy?"

This time Tohon didn't crack a smile. "No. A father who loved him. For six years, I had to hear all about King Neil and how smart and funny and wonderful he was. No doubt Kerrick loved his father. King Neil visited the school often. They were almost as close as Kerrick and Belen." His grip on my hands tightened. "When Kerrick and Jael fell in love, I couldn't stand it anymore. It was unfair. Kerrick couldn't have it all. No. Bad enough he had a doting father *and* a best friend. I couldn't let him have a gorgeous, powerful wife, too. And I can't let him have you."

I yanked my hands from his. "No one has me."

Tohon's gaze went to his guards by the door. A silent reminder of my situation.

"I'm here, but I'm not yours." I crossed my arms. "State your terms, Tohon."

"Not here. This place is for…peace." He led me back down the corkscrew staircase and into an office.

The furnishings had a simple elegance. The desk was mid-size and organized. Tohon spoke with one of his guards before settling behind it. The paintings in the room were stark, capturing subjects like a single winter tree, a solitary horse and one chair in an otherwise empty kitchen.

A large map of the Fifteen Realms covered the right wall. Symbols and arrows had been drawn on it as well as troop information. I stood before it, examining it.

I pointed to Tohon's occupied Realms—Lyady, Zainsk and half of Vyg, with Sogra in the center. "Are you invading the other Realms just to spite Kerrick?"

He laughed. "I'll admit to being petty and jealous, my dear, but my invasion, as you so quaintly put it, is not due to him. We need a leader, and frankly, I already command life and death, so who better to rule?"

He gestured for me to sit in a soft, burgundy-colored armchair that had been pulled up to the side. Tohon shuffled a few papers on his desk, ignoring me until a knock sounded. The door opened without Tohon's permission and a tall woman around Tohon's age entered. With a sword hanging from her waist and her athletic build, she reminded me of Jael. She even had blond hair and blue eyes. The resemblance ended there. Her features were plain and her pudgy nose looked as if someone had sat on it.

"Cellina, this is Avry of Kazan," Tohon said.

Her name sounded familiar, but I couldn't place her.

Instant dislike flashed in her gaze. "The healer?"

"Yes. We're going to write up a contract and need you to bear witness to the terms and conditions."

"You've never needed a contract before, Tohon."

"Avry is different."

"Really?" Cellina peered at me with a shrewd calculation.

"Stay away from her, Cellina." Tohon's tone held a clear warning.

Cellina failed to be intimidated. She flopped into another armchair. "Go on, write your contract. I've things to do."

Tohon drew a clean sheet of parchment from a pile. He wrote a few lines. Anxiety swelled and I clutched my hands together. This was probably an exercise in futility. I couldn't trust him. His moods swung from perfect gentleman to perfect maniac.

He sensed my apprehension. "Basic introductory language." Setting the stylus down, he leaned back. "Time for the terms. I need you to heal my subjects as needed—not that it matters to me if they die, but they're easier to train while alive—to assist with an experiment I'm working on and to promise not to run away. In exchange, you will be well cared for and you won't be confined. Except for a few areas, you can roam the castle complex when you're not needed."

Other than the experiment, his terms matched what I had been expecting. I addressed them in order. "I'll heal the sick and injured, but *I* decide who is healed and who can be treated by herbs or time. I want to be in charge of the infirmary. You can't force me to heal anyone."

"Agreed." Tohon wrote down the conditions.

Too easy? I continued. "What type of experiment? I won't work with your dead soldiers."

"It's with Death Lilys."

Intrigued despite myself, I asked, "What are you trying to do with them?"

"I'll explain later."

"Not if you want me to agree. I won't hurt anyone."

"How about you'll help me with my research as long as *your* tasks don't harm anyone?"

I found a loophole. "But what about you? What if the research results in something you can use to harm another?"

"I can't agree to that. I'm going to be at war with Estrid." Tohon waited.

Realizing Tohon would negotiate only on my actions, I conceded the point.

"And I'll add that you will not sabotage any parts of the experiments, the research and the results." Ink flowed over the paper.

Last issue. "What do you consider running away?"

"Leaving the castle complex without *my* permission. I don't wish to lock you up every night or chain you to a chair in the lab. It would become tiresome. You kept your word with Kerrick, and he didn't deserve it. All I ask is the same thing."

Interesting and scary. "How did you know I gave Kerrick my word?"

"Please, Avry, don't insult my intelligence. I'd be a poor leader if I didn't know what's going on in the enemy's camp."

He had spies in Estrid's army.

Tohon smiled at my expression. "One robed acolyte looks much like another, don't you think?"

"What if Estrid storms the castle?"

Cellina huffed in amusement.

Tohon shot her a sour look. "In the highly unlikely event that I'm defeated or dead, you're free to go. How's that?"

"How long do I have to stay here?"

"As long as I say. I will be king of all the Realms soon, which will make me *your* king. Then I don't need a contract."

More incentive to find a way to stop him.

"You already have the clause in case my plans do not pan out. And you will be well cared for in exchange. *That* I promise."

Giving my word not to leave the complex, I would have a difficult time contacting Sepp, but it wouldn't be impossible. I hoped. Besides, I really didn't relish the idea of being confined. "Agreed."

He had the decency not to smile or gloat. "I'd like to add one more...request."

Uh-oh. I glanced at Cellina. Her amusement was gone. She stared at Tohon as if daring him to continue.

"What is it?" I asked.

"On occasion, I have formal events, parties and meals that I have to attend. I'd like you to accompany me to them."

"And in exchange?"

His grip on the stylus tightened, but he kept his ire from his expression. I guess I was supposed to be grateful for the opportunity to spend an evening with him.

"For each event you attend, you can make a small request like a trip into town or new clothes or a day off."

Those small favors might give me some wiggle room. "Agreed."

Tohon finished the document. He signed his name with a flourish, then passed it to me. I read every single word twice, seeking loopholes and wording issues. He had stated the terms and conditions in plain language. Nothing jumped out at me.

When I'd arrived here, I'd expected to be locked in a

cell. At least this had the illusion of being a better situation. Although I'd had no delusions that he would keep his word.

Tohon handed me the stylus. Signing this, I would once again surrender my freedom. Last time it had saved Melina and two others from a horrible life. This time it would save so many more. I had to believe that as I wrote my name. The alternative was too horrible to contemplate.

Cellina signed the contract last. She shoved the paper and stylus over to Tohon. "Can I go now?"

"You're dismissed."

She glared at us both and stormed from the room.

"Don't worry about her, my dear."

Hard not to. Although compared to what I just agreed to, Cellina's...anger or jealousy was a minor concern.

"You must be exhausted, my dear. Bashin, has Winter arrived?"

The guard poked his head out the door, then widened it to let a servant in. The young lady curtsied.

"Winter, this is Miss Avry. You will be her lady's maid for the duration of her stay. Show her to her rooms, and assist her with anything she needs."

"Yes, my lord." Winter curtsied. "Miss, please follow me."

"Go on," Tohon said to me. "Get settled and I'll stop by later to make sure you're comfortable."

My heart did flips in my chest as I followed Winter through the castle. The day had not gone as expected. Not at all.

My rooms consisted of a receiving area with a couch, armchairs, tables and a rug all arranged in a semicircle in front of a stone hearth built into the back wall. Lanterns lit the room, revealing the deep purple, blue and green colors of the fabrics and tapestries. The colors blended well together. A small wooden table with a few chairs occupied the left corner, and a desk, chair and bookcase had been placed in the right corner.

Next to the hearth was an entrance to a bedroom that shared the hearth. I bent down and spotted Winter building a fire to push back the chill. The huge canopy bed used up most of the floor space. I walked around it, thinking Kerrick and his gang could all fit on it. The room also contained an armoire, bedside table and a lantern. I removed my cloak and tossed it onto the bed.

Heavy curtains blocked the three windows on the far wall. I pulled them aside and peered out into the semidarkness of twilight. A few torches bobbed below. My rooms looked like they were on the third or fourth floor. I let the fabric drop. The swish-thud matched the leaden feeling inside me.

My mood lightened a bit when I found the washroom adjoining the bedroom. The marble walls, floor tile and pedestal washing basin were nice, but the tub had captured my full attention.

Winter appeared in the doorway. She held my knapsack. Blond wisps of hair had sprung from her bun and her blue-eyed gaze held apprehension. She wore a long white apron over a light blue linen shirt and a navy skirt that reached the floor.

"Shall I put your effects away now, miss?"

"No, thank you."

"But—"

"You were told to see to my every need?" I asked.

"Of course, miss." The girl's petite nose crinkled in confusion.

Winter had pretty alabaster skin and appeared to be around fifteen or sixteen years old.

"Relax, Winter. I'm not going to throw a tantrum or run

to Tohon if you don't see to my every need. I appreciate your help and hope we can work together."

Winter stared at me as if I was a hissing Death Lily. Scared and curious at the same time.

I took my knapsack from her. "I would love a hot bath."

"Yes, miss." She hurried over to the tub. Plugging the drain, she reached for a lever and yanked it. Nothing happened. Then the distinctive rush of water sounded from a round hole in the wall just above the lip of the tub.

Now it was my turn to be confused.

Winter noticed. "Water pipes, miss. King Zavier had them installed throughout the castle. They carry hot water from big heated tanks and, when you're done, just pull the plug. More pipes will allow the water to drain outside the castle. They're fabulous."

And expensive, I'd bet. Sure enough, steaming water gushed from the hole and poured into the tub. When the water level neared the top, Winter pushed the lever back up. "Your bath, miss."

"Thank you."

She smiled and laid out towels and a robe for me. Then waited.

"I can handle it from here," I said, escorting her to the main door of my rooms. "I won't need you again until the morning."

"But your bed—"

"I can turn down the sheets. I'll be fine. Good night, Winter." I closed the door and discovered it had a lock. I drew in a breath. A lock, a hot bath and a soft bed. A few unexpected perks that I planned to take full advantage of. Locking the door, I hurried to the washroom as I pulled off my smelly travel clothes. My necklace remained where it had been since Kerrick hooked it around my neck. The pendant rested at the base of my throat.

I soaked off about fifty days of road grime. Between the cold weather, the fast pace and being in the company of men, I hadn't been able to get as clean as I wished. I drained and refilled the tub a second time.

Finally clean, I dried and wrapped the white cotton robe around me. I couldn't bear to put on my other equally rank set of clothes or the skirt and shirt Kerrick had bought me—a reminder of…him. Instead, I kept the robe on. Not like I would have to escape or fight in the middle of the night.

I unpacked my knapsack, piling my meager possessions on the table, which included my weapons, bedroll, blanket, the herb pouch the monkeys had given me, the gloves from Belen, a few papers recovered from the Guild, the two sacks of liquid from the Death Lily and my apprenticeship journal. All that I owned in one pathetic pile. At least they had been easy to carry.

Picking up the journal, I curled on the couch and read through the pages. I noted a few interesting tidbits, and found an entry about Allie, my roommate at Tara's. She had talked in her sleep and had frequent nightmares. One night, I had to shake her awake as she screamed for her mother. Allie had been apologetic and told me she had been caught by a Death Lily when she was young. Her mother nursed her through the hard recovery.

I sat up straight. Except Allie hadn't been attacked. The Death Lilys sensed potential in people and snatched them. Potential for what, I didn't know. I scanned my notes, looking for a page that mentioned Tara's lecture about Death Lily toxin. My notes were incomplete, but I'd marked that when Tara described the symptoms she'd sounded like she knew about them from experience. There was a question mark next to my speculation. I never had the chance to ask her if she had been grabbed.

"Read anything of interest, my dear?" Tohon asked.

I jumped to my feet, dropping my journal. Tohon leaned against the bedroom's threshold.

"What... How did you get in here?" I asked as my heart thumped back down to its proper place.

"Secret passage between our rooms." Tohon's gaze scanned my robe. "I see you made yourself comfortable."

I tightened the sash. "I won't be ever again if you can pop in here without warning."

"I did knock, but no one answered. Not to worry, my dear. I'll show you the panel and how to secure it on your side. My side locks, as well." A slow hungry smile matched the desire in his gaze. "However, if you're ever lonely, please don't hesitate to visit me at any time."

"Don't wait up. Ever."

"Nasty." He tsked. "You've been with Kerrick too long. No matter, you will soon find I'm much better company." Tohon settled on the couch and patted the cushion next to him.

I remained on my feet.

He leaned back. "Tomorrow, Cellina will collect you and show you around the compound. I'd like you to start working in the infirmary. There are a number of cases that need your immediate attention."

I gestured to my clothes on the floor. "They're dirty and I'll need clothes that can be stained with blood."

"Didn't Winter show you what's in the armoire?"

"I'm sure she wanted to, but I desired privacy."

He stood, strode to my bedroom and pulled the doors open. Clothes filled the armoire.

"There are clothes for every occasion in here. And they're

all in your size. Medical tunics, everyday clothes and a few gowns."

"How did you know I'd come?"

He gave me a don't-be-daft look.

I pulled out a yellow skirt. "How did you know my size?"

"From your coffin."

Shocked, I gaped at him. "What—?"

"When my soldiers arrived in Jaxton after you had escaped with Nasty Kerrick, the authorities were not happy. They had built a coffin to your size—they had written your measurements on the boards, but had no body and therefore no bounty. My men paid for the coffin. They also donated quite a bit of gold to the town for all the trouble."

"Oh." I had known they measured me for a coffin, but never really thought that they had actually built one. I returned the skirt.

"It wasn't all a waste," Tohon said. "I learned a lot about you from your neighbors. They told my men you were a nice, quiet young woman. They were just appalled that you had the gall to live and work with them. That they never suspected the truth. I was—still am—impressed you survived so long. After that, I decided to change the bounty. I wanted to meet you."

What could I say to that? Other than wow. That single decision, to heal Fawn, had set so much in motion. Instead, I asked, "What did they do with…the coffin?"

"It's here at the castle."

CHAPTER 22

A coffin built for me was in Tohon's castle. "Why did—?"

"Oh, I think you know why, my dear."

"But we have a contract."

"We do. And I trust your word to the conditions we included."

Confused, I tried to reason it out, but failed. "What are you afraid I'd do?"

"Return to Kerrick. I'd rather see you make use of that coffin than return to his arms."

I relaxed. Of the multiple possibilities of how this mission will end, that one didn't even make the list. However, a far scarier scenario hit me. "Can you promise you would use my coffin, and not turn me into one of your dead soldiers?"

"And in exchange?"

"If you bury me in the coffin, then I promise not to return to Kerrick."

He laughed. "All right, my dear, you have a deal." Tohon held out his hand.

I stepped back.

"It's not binding unless we shake."

Clasping his hand, I shook it once and let go. He didn't. Heat raced along my skin as he pulled me close. Before I could protest, his lips were on mine. My magic responded, filling me with a hyperawareness, amplifying my senses. He pushed the robe off my shoulders and pressed his hands on my back. His touch sent burning waves through my muscles. The sensation bordered between pain and pleasure. I gasped and Tohon deepened the kiss.

A combination of desire and fury flared, yet my fingers laced in his short hair as I pressed my body against his. The room spun and we wound up lying on the bed.

Tohon broke off the kiss. "Good night, my dear." He stood and opened a panel near the headboard. Pointing to a small knob, he said, "The latch is here. Although I expect you to answer my knock."

"What if I can't?"

He waited.

"If I'm healing, I may be unconscious or having fever delusions."

"In that case, make sure Winter stays with you."

"I don't need—"

"I don't care. I don't want you to be alone." His stern expression softened. "I worked side by side with healers at the Guild for close to a year. When you wake in the middle of the night and need water or a change of clothes, Winter will be there to help you. It's not a request."

He disappeared into the passageway, pulling the panel closed behind him. Once my heart calmed, I realized my robe had slipped down to my elbows. Embarrassed, I yanked it up, secured the sash and then locked the panel.

I rummaged in the armoire for a set of nightclothes. Tohon's kiss had thrown me. If Tohon hadn't stopped... Why did he stop? Probably playing more games.

And I suspected it was my magic that betrayed me. When we touched, his life force acted like an elixir. It felt almost as if I had drank too much wine. I needed to figure out how to keep the touching to a minimum or I would do something I'd regret.

A small voice in my head asked, *What is there to regret? What is wrong with enjoying yourself with a gorgeous man who treats you like a queen? Do you want to die without experiencing one of life's pleasures?*

No, I didn't. But I had imagined it would be with someone I loved. Not a monster who woke the dead. And I needed to keep reminding myself of his misdeeds. Of the abominations he created. Because when he touched me…all logic and fear fled.

After I dressed for bed, I slid under the covers, luxuriating on the soft mattress. The white bedspread reminded me of Mom's inn. Waking up surrounded by such comfort, I had thought I'd reached the peaceful afterlife. Except Kerrick had anchored me to this world. He had held on and refused to let go. Memories of him sleeping beside me at the inn filled my mind along with the vision of his bare back when he'd sat up.

I jerked my thoughts to the present, focusing on how I would find Ryne. That night I didn't dream of Tohon's dead soldiers, which was a relief. Instead, dreams of Kerrick swirled.

Winter brought a breakfast tray in the morning. After I ate, I changed into a black medical tunic and pants. Comfortable and plain, they would be suitable to working with the sick and injured.

Cellina arrived soon after Winter left. She scanned my clothes and grunted. "At least you're practical. Well, come on. I don't have all day." Turning on her heels, she strode through the doorway, setting a quick pace.

If she'd hoped she'd lose me, she was in for a surprise. After all those months of walking, she'd have to run full-out to shake me. I stayed a step behind her as we hurried along hallways, down stairs and through various rooms.

She wore a pale lavender silk tunic and deep purple skirt. Her long blond hair had been twisted into a knot and held in place with a comb that flashed with amethysts. Her regal bearing and fine clothing contrasted with the sword hanging from her waist.

As we traveled, Cellina would stop on occasion. Each time, she pointed out a door or set of stairs that I was forbidden to enter or use. "See that symbol?" Cellina gestured to a circle with three crossed keys inside it. "That means keep out. No one who lives and works in the castle or the buildings in the compound is allowed in those rooms and areas. Understand?"

"Even you?"

"No. As Tohon's top adviser, I have full access."

Top adviser? She appeared to be around twenty-five or -six. Close to Tohon's age. "Your name is familiar. Are you a friend of his?"

"No. I'm another of his...collected. I met Tohon in school."

"Cellina of Lyady! Kerrick mentioned you had been one of the people trying to be king."

Her mouth twisted in disgust. "A foolish kid's game. At the time, I thought it would be fun to be crowned king. In Lyady we didn't have a monarchy. The people voted for my father to be the president. That game...was just a whole nasty experience. The others took it far too seriously."

Lyady shared a border with Sogra to the east, Alga to the

north and the Endless Sea lapped on its western and southern edges. "Tohon invaded Lyady."

"Last year. Nothing we could do. The plague had wiped us out."

"But you're helping him?"

She shrugged. "So are you."

Point.

"And it's better than being locked in some dank prison, rotting."

True. Although I sensed there was more between them besides school friends. Strange that so many of them should survive the plague. I almost tripped as an evil notion occurred to me. What if Tohon was still playing the king game? But then how would he have protected his classmates from the plague? No one could have predicted the outbreak.

Cellina continued with the tour, showing me the kitchen, dining room and the offices for the advisers. She led me outside. The chilly morning fog lingered in small pockets of white, but the day promised to be warm. The air smelled of spring, reminding me of Kerrick. I cursed under my breath. When I was finally free of him, he still haunted me. This would be a long season.

Behind the castle, the other buildings spread out in an arc. A stable, a couple of barracks for the soldiers, an armory, a kennel and finally the infirmary. Before we entered, Cellina headed toward the thick wall that surrounded the compound. Except, on this side, it wasn't black, but more of a green with patches of white. As we drew closer, I realized there were huge plants growing next to the wall. Their topmost stalks reaching the top of the wall.

Cellina halted twenty feet away. "I wouldn't try climbing over if you decide to escape. The only way out is through the front gate."

"Are they—?"

"Yep. They cover the interior of the entire wall. Tohon can be brilliant at times. Too bad he also has no conscience. At least he's consistent."

I stared at the row of Death Lilys guarding the wall. No one could sneak in or leave. It was genius. A memory tugged of Belen in the Guild's record room and the desiccated corpse protecting the broken crate of Death Lily seeds. Did Tohon murder that man for the seeds?

"Are there any more?" I asked.

"He has a whole garden full of the wicked things back in the northwest corner of the compound."

As we returned to the infirmary, I considered the abundance of Death Lilys. Sepp could move through them without worry. And I might be able to keep Ryne safe from them. The seed of an idea started to grow.

I stopped in the doorway. The smell of excrement and unwashed bodies polluted the air.

"This is where I leave you. Good luck," Cellina said, backing away.

"Wait." I chased after her. "Are there any of Tohon's… dead in there?"

"No, just Tohon's injured soldiers. He keeps the dead ones in a barrack."

Relief flowed through me. I returned to the infirmary. Pausing at the threshold, I scanned the big room. Rows of cots packed tight together were filled with patients, and only a few people walked among them. The workers had covered their noses and mouths with kerchiefs. Closed windows lined two walls. On the opposite side, I spotted an entrance.

Tohon forced me to be here, but these people needed me. This was my responsibility, regardless of a contract. I drew in a deep breath of clean air before plunging into the mess. Obviously, Tohon didn't care too much about his injured.

I strode to the first worker I encountered, and asked, "Who's in charge here?"

She pointed to the back room. Trying not to look at the patients just yet, I entered. The space had been divided into two sections. An office and an examination area. The office was the only clean thing in the entire building. Five people lounged on chairs, talking.

"Who's in charge here?" I asked.

A man behind the desk eyed me with a lazy insolence. "Who's asking?"

"My name is Avry of Kazan. I'm here at Tohon's request. Answer my question."

Tohon's name produced the desired effect. The man straightened. "I'm in charge of patient care."

"Wrong answer. You're in charge of a cesspit. The right answer is Healer Avry is in charge of patient care from now on."

The man shot to his feet. "You can't just barge in here and—"

"I can. If you have a problem with it, please feel free to take it up with Tohon."

He fisted his hands and stared at me. "That's *King* Tohon."

I met his fierce gaze and held it until he looked away.

"King Tohon will hear about this," he said as he stormed from the room.

The other four—three women and one man—gaped at me.

I frowned at them. "Do you work here?"

They nodded.

"No you don't. If you did, this place wouldn't reek. But we're going to correct that right now."

Along with the two in the main room, I sent them to fetch buckets of clean water, find clean cloths, clean linens, soaps and alcohol. While they were gone, I started checking the patients. Infections, fevers, broken bones, dehydration... The list continued. The man who had been in charge returned with a smirk and Tohon right behind him.

Tohon crinkled his nose in distaste, but didn't remark on the smell. "I sent you here to help, my dear. Not cause problems."

"My mistake. Is there another healer here?" I turned my head as if seeking another person.

"Quit the act, Avry. What's going on?"

"Look around, Tohon. Take a deep breath. This place is filthy. Your soldiers are dying, not from their injuries but from infection and poor care." I stabbed a finger at the man. "He's causing more harm than good."

Tohon considered. "It doesn't seem that bad to me."

I suppressed a growl. "Come back here in five days. I guarantee half these patients will be on their feet and have returned to work by then."

"You're rather confident for someone who doesn't have any experience," Tohon said.

"First thing an apprentice learns is the importance of cleanliness. Basic stuff, Tohon. Your guy and his crew are either too lazy, too stupid or don't care."

The man protested, but Tohon stopped him with a look.

"All right, my dear. You have five days."

The five days were exhausting, but gratifying to see the patients respond to my care. I had also found a way to avoid Tohon's touch. Since the dire cases all involved infected wounds, I spent every night in my bed, fighting fever and delusions as Winter stayed with me. Another unexpected bonus during that time, I'd found a set of keys inside a captain's uniform's pocket. I had been collecting soiled garments to send to the laundry and heard the rattle.

When Tohon arrived on the fifth day, he quickly quelled his surprise. A fresh breeze blew in through the open windows. The patients had plenty of room between them. They sat up, propped on pillows and talked. Care workers moved among them, filling water glasses and checking bandages. The place smelled of soap and alcohol.

"Nice work, my dear. If I assign you a few more helpers, will you have time to assist me with my project?"

"Even with the extra help, I'll need about ten days to finish implementing and training everyone on how to provide the standard care."

"Ten days, then." He left.

I really didn't need that much time, but I hoped, by then, Estrid's army would be keeping Tohon busy and distracted. Plus I could use the extra days and the stolen keys to search for Ryne.

I found Ryne a week later. Tucked in a corner of the castle, in an abandoned and off-limits wing, the room felt like a museum. I held up the lantern I carried, illuminating the contents. The light reflected off shiny boxes resting on top of black velvet-covered tables. Upon closer inspection, I realized the boxes were glass coffins. A knot of cold horror twisted in my chest.

Ryne occupied one of them, but he wasn't the only one on display. Two others had been encased. An older man, wearing formal robes and a gold crown must be King Zavier. The other was a much younger man—close to Kerrick's age. He had broad shoulders, short blond hair and familiar features. Did Tohon have a brother?

There was one empty glass coffin. To think it waited for an occupant was creepier than the occupied ones. I shuddered, then inspected the bodies.

Ryne actually looked many years younger than when he had visited Tara. He had shaved his full beard and bushy mustache. His dark brown hair had been cut short and, with his expression smoothed, he had a pleasant face.

While Ryne appeared to be asleep, King Zavier's skin had death's pallor and the other man was also dead. From his comments when he showed me the castle, I knew Tohon enjoyed using his power to take a life. But he hadn't taken Ryne's. At least, not yet. I wondered if the stasis prevented Tohon from finishing the prince.

Who was next? I suspected Tohon would enjoy seeing Kerrick inside the empty coffin. A strange feeling touched me, almost as if I felt protective of Kerrick. I dismissed it and searched under the tables.

A cheap pine coffin had been shoved underneath the empty coffin's table. I didn't need to open it to know I would fit inside.

I left the morbid room, setting a quick pace. The early-morning hours before dawn had been the best time for me to search the castle. Most of the inhabitants worked late, and remained in bed until midmorning. I'd been here long enough to know those were the hours Tohon kept, as well.

After I returned the lantern to my rooms, I walked to the infirmary in the gray half-light, mulling over various ways I could send a message to Sepp about Ryne. None of them seemed possible at this time. Half distracted, I almost missed a furtive movement to my left. Curious, I slipped between the stable and armory. Pressing against the armory's wall, I peeked around the building.

A lone figure moved along the pasture's fence and toward

the northwest corner of the compound. My memory tugged. Cellina had mentioned a garden...of Death Lilys! I sprinted after the person, cutting through the pasture. Was she or he a complete idiot?

In the weak light, the northwest corner appeared to be a copse of trees and bushes. The person had disappeared into the greenery, and I hoped a Lily hadn't attacked. As I approached the garden, the individual stalks and Lilys came into focus. The petals were bent in strange angles. At first I thought the Death Lilys had all caught someone, but then I realized the petals had been pulled wide open, exposing the inside of the flower.

I walked up to the closest one. It didn't move. The plant had been wired to a metal frame to prevent it from closing the petals. Whoever had come here didn't need to fear being eaten. Even the Lily's infamous vines had been wrapped and knotted tight around a metal lattice. My emotions tugged between fascinated and repulsed. Who could tie up a Death Lily like this?

Tohon. Why? No idea.

I turned to leave, but a rustle sounded behind me.

"Good morning, my dear," Tohon said, stepping between two Lilys. He carried a bag. "Are you finished with your snooping already or is this part of the compound on your agenda today?"

I shouldn't be surprised Tohon knew about my searches. "You don't seem upset."

He shrugged. "Look all you want. The only person who can wake Ryne is dead. Besides, you're stuck here and can't run off to Estrid or Kerrick and tell them all my secrets. And don't think you can send a message, either. My people are loyal and will report you. You don't want to anger me, my dear."

A chill rolled though me, pricking the hairs along my skin. Changing the subject, I gestured to the Death Lilys. "Why are they…spread apart? What are you doing with them?"

"Keeping the flowers open makes it easier for me to extract their toxin."

Horrified, I gaped at him. "Why?"

He smiled at my reaction. "Did you know the Healer's Guild tried a number of ways to obtain the Lily's toxin? The substance breaks down as soon as the Lily dies. But if it is taken from the living plant, the toxin retains its properties." Tohon reached into his bag and pulled out an orange-colored ball. "Working with the Guild, I discovered that I alone can remove these sacks of toxin. I'm immune to the poison. But if anyone else reaches inside, the Lily will sting him."

The sack in Tohon's hand matched the two I had hidden in my rooms. Why would the Death Lily give me them? "I know why the Guild wanted the toxin, but what do you need it for?"

"My dear, I can't believe you'd be that innocent. Think devious thoughts."

There were easier ways to kill, but the toxin caused a slow and painful death. A crazy connection occurred to me. The toxin's symptoms matched the first two stages of plague. Both ended in death except for those few who survived the Lily's poison. Since I doubted Tohon cared about the similarities or wished to find a cure for either, I concentrated on what he would find useful. He had called his people loyal, but from what I'd seen, they acted more terrified than devoted.

"You use the toxin to threaten people."

"I knew you had a dark side." Tohon beamed with pride. "It's amazing how effective the threat of injecting the toxin into a person is. They'll do anything I say or tell me what I need to know. Remember that, my dear."

He'd just confirmed I would find no allies here.

"Since you seem to have enough time to wander around each morning, I don't think you need another three full days in the infirmary. You can start helping me now." Tohon gestured for me to accompany him.

As we walked to the castle, he asked, "Have you discovered my lab yet?"

"No." I had hoped not to find it during my explorations. I could only imagine the horrors that awaited.

Tohon led me through the castle and into the base of one of the towers. Another corkscrew stairway had been built inside. Instead of descending as I had expected, Tohon climbed the stairs. We looped around and around until he stopped a few floors up. He unlocked a door.

"Why did you think I could find your lab when you locked the door?" I asked.

"I figured Nasty Kerrick taught you how to pick locks."

I huffed in amusement.

"What's so funny?"

"He wouldn't teach me. I think he was afraid I'd break my word, and he'd need to cuff me to the trees again."

Tohon tsked. "No surprise. He has such ill manners."

He pushed the door open. Sunlight spilled out, and it reminded me of his forever garden. But tables and equipment filled the long narrow space. Windows high up on the walls let the light in. The lab smelled of vanilla and anise.

Happy that my low expectations hadn't been met, I walked around. I recognized a few devices like the distiller, which extracted oils and other medicinal liquids from plants. The Guild had a whole building dedicated to research. It appeared as if Tohon had duplicated it on a much smaller scale.

He grabbed a bowl from a stack and set it on a table. Dumping the toxin sacks, he spread them out. I counted ten.

"Is there a limited supply?" I asked.

"Each Death Lily has two sacks. If they're removed, they will grow another set, but it takes a few months." He pointed to a ledger. "I keep track of when I harvest the sacks." Tohon opened a drawer full of syringes. Taking one, he pushed the needle into the sack, then filled the reservoir with the toxin.

Sickened by his macabre task, I asked, "What do you need me to do? I have patients to check."

Tohon gestured to a chair. "Have a seat, my dear. This won't take long."

Unease roiled as I sat. He tapped on the syringe to ensure no air bubbles were stuck.

Turning to me with the syringe in hand, he said, "Tonight I have one of those dreaded royal parties. You will accompany me. Wear the green gown."

My mind registered party and gown, but I couldn't tear my gaze from that syringe. When he set it on the counter, I relaxed.

He smiled. "Your emotions are such a delight, my dear. You can go from hating me, to fascinated, to repulsed, then to desiring me and back again. How am I to tell which is genuine, when you don't know yourself?"

"At least I'm not predictable."

"True." He crouched down before my chair so we were eye level. "The one thing I do know is you're getting satisfaction from your work in the infirmary, healing patients. You are finally doing what you're supposed to be doing. It's gratifying, isn't it?"

"Yes."

"And you have me to thank. If Nasty Kerrick had his way, you would have healed Prince Ryne and died." He rested his hands on my chair arms as he studied my expression. "Yes, I know the truth. I was helping at the Guild headquarters when the first plague victims arrived." With a slight smirk, he asked, "Did Nasty Kerrick convince you to heal the prince?"

"No. You did."

"Oh? Do tell, my dear."

"Do you want a list or should I just sum it up?"

"Not nice. Well, consider this. Ryne has been defeated. Even if you somehow managed to wake and cure him, he doesn't have the manpower or the resources to stop my army. Your sacrifice would have been for nothing. You're infinitely more valuable than Ryne." He paused and scrunched up his nose. "Which makes this harder to do, but it must be done."

"Makes what harder?"

He grabbed my right wrist and strapped it to the chair's arm. I squawked in protest, pushing at him with my left hand. Quicker than expected, he had trapped my left wrist, as well. I struggled against the bonds and kicked, but he stepped out of reach. How could I not notice the leather ties hanging from the arms?

"What…?" The question died in my throat as Tohon picked up the syringe and approached. I opened my mouth to protest, but he thrust the needle into my upper arm and depressed the plunger, sending the toxin into my body.

Logically there was no reason to be scared. I was immune to the toxin. But would the immunity still work if Tohon and not the Death Lily injected it into me?

CHAPTER 23

"Why did you do that?" I asked with a steady voice despite my fluttering stomach.

"You don't seem too upset," he said.

The toxin spread throughout my body. I leaned back and closed my eyes as my thoughts disconnected from my body. Except there wasn't a Death Lily to connect to. Only Tohon, but there was no way into him. As if he sensed my plight, he touched my cheek. And we linked consciousnesses.

Interesting reaction, my dear. This isn't your first experience with the Death Lily's toxin, is it?

Hard to lie when he heard my thoughts at the same time that I did.

No. My childhood encounter played, then the one where I had pushed Flea out of the way.

I suspected as much. They won't communicate with me.

You abuse them, steal their sacks.

They kill people, Avry.

So do you.

His amusement flowed through me. *Are you going to defend me, too?*

No. Stop you.

Another wave of mirth. *I doubt it.*

Why did you inject me?

To prove a theory. Too bad the Healer's Guild is no more. I would have liked to gloat. Tohon dropped his hand from my cheek. He returned to the table with the sacks and wrote in his ledger.

Disconnected from him and my body, my awareness hovered. Could I send it to another place? Too bad Tohon released my wrists and grabbed my hand before I could try. Our consciousness joined as he pulled me to my feet.

You'll feel better in a few hours, my dear.

How do you know?

I'm guessing.

We left the lab and he locked the door. As we spiraled down to the ground floor, I asked, *What theory did you just prove?* But the answer popped in my mind. *That all healers have survived an encounter with a Death Lily.*

Impressive, my dear. If you weren't already mine, I'd be worried.

I'm not yours.

So you say.

I suppressed the desire to argue with him. As my mother had often said, Pick your battles. Instead, I concentrated on the experiment. *Does surviving the toxin make us healers? Is our magic a gift from the Death Lilys?* I asked Tohon.

I believe so, but I haven't been able to prove it yet.

If I had control of my body, I would have skidded to a stop. Images of him injecting people just to see if he could turn them into healers flowed through my mind. However, Tohon kept a firm grip as he guided me back to my rooms.

You haven't been—

That's none of your concern, my dear. His tone warned me to drop the subject.

I mulled over what I'd learned. *If you're immune to the toxin, does that mean you can heal, as well?*

No, my life magic prevents me from getting sick. I've never had a cold, the flu or stomach problems. Even poison has no effect. Ah, here we are. He laid me on my bed and released me.

I hovered over my body, still able to see despite my closed eyes.

Tohon sorted through the clothes in the armoire. He held up a green gown. Sequins glinted from the low-cut bodice. "Wear this one tonight. I'll send Winter in a few hours to help you get dressed." He draped it over a chair before leaving.

Disembodied, I tried to move, remembering how I had flowed through the roots of the Death Lily. But then a vine had connected me to the Lily. I had also needed Tohon's touch. My body lay on a mattress; perhaps I could move through the bed.

Imagining traveling into the softness, I projected my awareness toward the bed. Nothing happened. I guessed I would remain an intangible being until the toxin's effects wore off. Yippee.

Winter arrived a few hours later. She called my name, but my body didn't stir. Perhaps I wouldn't have to go to the party, after all. The young lady touched my hand and I flowed into her consciousness.

Worry for me dominated her thoughts. Nice to know she genuinely liked me. Concern over King Tohon's reaction if she didn't have me ready in time pulsed at the back of her mind. She debated if she should report my condition to the king.

Can you hear me, Winter?

No reaction.

I didn't feel right hearing her thoughts when she couldn't

hear mine. However, I did learn a few things. One, she was terrified of Tohon. Two, she had been ordered to tell Tohon everything I did. Three, Winter would never deliver a message to Sepp for me.

She removed her hand and I floated up like a bubble released underwater. I stayed an invisible ghost for ages; at least, it seemed as if time had stopped. When I had been inside the plant, my body and soul had reconnected as soon as I'd been spat out, but Tohon's injection lasted much longer. At least it didn't kill me.

Without warning, I snapped back into my body. I kept my eyes closed until the strange feeling of weighing a thousand pounds dissipated. Then I sat up and stretched.

Winter returned while I soaked in the tub.

"Thank the maker you're awake!" She bustled around, gathering brushes and combs. "The king was getting impatient. Come on, miss. We have lots to do."

The desire to drag my feet and make Tohon wait surged. But I knew he would direct his ire at Winter so I cooperated with the girl, letting her arrange my hair and apply makeup. But when it came time to dress, I balked.

The plunging neckline aside, the silk gown's straps tied behind my neck so no material covered my back or my sides until my waist. I felt almost naked. Instead of putting the green one on, I found a yellow gown with layers of silk that wasn't as revealing.

Winter fretted over my decision, but she finished with my hair without saying a word. She had pulled it back with two combs and then curled the ends. It had grown past my shoulders.

As Winter was applying the finishing touches of my makeup, Tohon barged in.

"What's taking so—?" He stared at me. "Why aren't you

wearing the gown I picked?" he demanded. A crazed fury filled his eyes.

I stepped back automatically. "It didn't fit."

"Don't lie." He closed the distance between us. "You will change now."

"No. I was uncomfortable."

"I don't care. Change now."

"I—"

He grabbed my forearms. Intense pain shot up them and spread all over as if I had caught on fire. I yelped, yanking my arms in an attempt to dislodge his grip. Stronger than me, Tohon held tight. Waves and waves of fire boiled my blood. He stared at me as I yelled.

The attack stopped as quick as it started. With his fingers still clamped on me, Tohon leaned close to my ear. "The green gown. And if you give me trouble again, you'll be thrown into a cell below the castle for three weeks. Understand?"

Unable to control my ragged breathing, I nodded. He released me and watched as I fumbled to change. I turned my back on him to finish. Winter helped me tie the straps. When she moved away, Tohon came up behind me.

He touched one of the scars crisscrossing my skin. I stiffened.

"Is this why you didn't want to wear this gown?"

"Yes."

"Who did this to you? Kerrick?" Anger spiked his words.

"No one. I healed a man who had been whipped."

"Then you should be proud of them. The healers I worked with were always showing me their scars. The women especially enjoyed revealing *all* of them. They appreciated the intoxicating link between us."

Unlike me. I stepped away.

"Come on, then. We're late." His clipped tone warned that he remained unhappy.

I followed him to a carriage that had been brought to the main courtyard. The cold air sent goose bumps along my skin. Tohon helped me into the carriage and I flinched as he draped a blanket around my shoulders.

As the horses pulled us through the gates and toward the city, Tohon chatted as if he hadn't just attacked or threatened me. His mood swings made Kerrick's seem tame in comparison. If something as minor as a gown set him off, what would he do if he discovered the real reason I was here? I swallowed as fear bubbled up my throat. At least that incident provided me with more incentive to find a way to send a message to Sepp. My time here was limited.

The sun had set by the time we reached town. We stopped outside an impressive mansion that had been built with thick wooden beams and river stones. Gardens surrounded the structure and one side wall was covered in ivy. Bright firelight flickered behind the windows and music drifted through the open doors.

Tohon made a grand entrance. A room full of well-dressed people bowed before him and fawned over him. Their piercing gazes raked over me. I stifled the desire to hide within the folds of the heavy drapes. At least the house was warm.

Three rooms had been decorated for the event. A string quartet played in a corner of the ballroom. Food and wine filled the dining room. Laughter echoed and couples danced. Despite his claims of another dreaded party, Tohon enjoyed the attention. He introduced me as Avry of Kazan to a number of lords and ladies. They nodded politely, then ignored me while Tohon was with me. Which was fine until they aimed snide comments at me when he wasn't close enough to hear.

At one point in the evening Tohon abandoned me. I found an empty seat in a dark corner, glad to no longer be eyed as if I were dessert.

My peace didn't last long. Tohon sought me out. And for the first time he didn't have a group of admirers surrounding him.

"You have them all atwitter, my dear. The theories and rumors about you are quite amusing. Because of the scars on your back, some believe you're a prisoner of war, others say you're a lady for hire who likes it rough." He huffed. "As if *I'd* need to hire someone. And I've heard a few speculate that you're a bastard child of Sultan Kazan."

"What would they do if you told them the truth about me? Would they turn into a lynch mob?"

"No. They would smile politely."

"So, no change. Why didn't you tell them?"

"I like to keep them guessing. But I do want them to know you're special to me." He held out his hand. "Come dance with me." He wasn't asking.

"I don't know how."

"It's easy. Just follow my lead."

I wouldn't touch him until we were in the ballroom. With one hand on my hip and the other holding my hand, we joined the flow of dancers. At first, I couldn't match his steps and it felt as if everyone stared at me as I stumbled along. I ignored the people around me and concentrated on the moves. After a few turns around the floor, I caught on.

Once I found the rhythm, I relaxed. Big mistake. The heat of his touch ignited my magic and other things left unmentioned. He smiled. Moving his hand from my hip to my bare back, he pulled me close.

"I knew you'd look fabulous in that gown, my dear."

Intent on changing the direction of the conversation, I said, "As per our contract, this counts as an event. Correct?"

His good humor faded. "Asking for a favor already?"

"A small request."

He gave me a wry smile. "Go on."

"I'd like a shopping trip to town."

"Really? You don't seem the type."

"I need a few personal things."

"Winter will fetch anything you need, my dear."

"Yes, she will. She's wonderful, but I need a day away from the castle."

"And from me?"

A rush of desire flooded my senses. I closed my eyes for a moment, pushing the sensation away. "Stop."

He chuckled. "I'm just encouraging your own emotions. Besides, you'll give in eventually, my dear."

Probably, but not tonight. "The trip—"

"You can go, but Winter and half a dozen bodyguards will go with you."

Not good. "I don't want to attract attention," I tried.

"After tonight, there may be a few people who will try to get to me through you."

Wonderful. "Then I'll take Winter and Cellina. She can use that sword, right?"

"She learned at school with the rest of us." His gaze grew distant. "She considers you a threat. Do you really want to spend time with her?"

"Why would I be a threat to her?"

"Because, you're here with me instead of her."

"Oh." That explained a number of things.

"Growing up, I was a prince in name only. Once my father learned of my magic, he appointed my cousin as his heir. These young noble ladies had no interest in me then. Now that I'm king, they're tripping over themselves to get my attention. I knew Cellina in school. We became very close and I know I can trust her."

"Why am I here? You can't trust me."

"Such honesty, my dear. You're here because you're a challenge."

"When I'm no longer a challenge, will you be here with another lady?"

"Worried?"

"No. Hopeful."

His grip tightened. I gasped as every inch of my skin tingled. Light-headed, I swayed. He supported me. "Those comments try my patience, and you know what I'm capable of." We danced for a while in silence. Instead of clearing, my head felt fuzzy, as if I'd had too much wine to drink. Overheated, I glanced at the doors to the garden with longing.

"Something wrong?" Tohon asked.

"I need some fresh air."

He pulled us from the dance. Releasing his grip, he kept his hand on my back as we headed toward the exit. Right before the open doors, he swung around in front of me and kissed me.

Overwhelmed with sensations, I wrapped my arms around him to keep from falling. His hands stroked my bare arms and back. I was soon lost and the music and ballroom full of dancers faded to nothing.

"Er, excuse me, Your Highness." A voice pierced the haze. "Hate to bother you…but it's an urgent matter."

Logic returned to me when Tohon pulled away. "It better be an emergency, Dewan." Tohon's tone held a dangerous edge.

The man cleared his throat. "We've gotten some intelligence on Estrid that we need to discuss."

Tohon still didn't look happy, but he nodded. "I'll be right there." He gazed at me. "Sorry, my dear. Business. Should I return you to your corner?"

"No. I still need that fresh air."

"Stay in the gardens. And just in case you get any ideas, there are guards all around the perimeter."

"Too bad 'cause I'd probably get really far in this gown."

"Sarcasm is another one of those things that try my patience."

I bit down on my next comment, equally sarcastic. Satisfied, he followed Dewan and I hurried into the garden.

I pulled in deep lung-filling breaths of the night air. My head cleared as my body cooled. A few more of Tohon's kisses and I would be a drooling mess and unable to help anyone. Walking around the garden, I planned a way to contact Sepp during my shopping trip with Winter and Cellina. I hoped he'd be waiting in a public place so I could give him the signal. He'd been in town for two weeks and should know about the Death Lilys around the wall. Maybe he would arrange a distraction so I could talk to him. Not the best plan, and I was at a loss if I didn't see him at all, but it was all I had.

Torches blazed, casting a warm glow on early-spring blooms that swayed in the slight breeze. I marveled at the delicate plants nestled between evergreen bushes, ornamental trees and willows fuzzy with velvet catkins. Memories of my childhood flooded. Collecting the willow branches for my mother had been a rite of spring for my siblings. I touched one of the soft white buds. A little zip of magic tingled along my fingers. Odd. I glanced behind me, searching for Tohon. No one.

Then a hand clamped over my mouth as an arm wrapped

around my waist. Yanked off the path and into a dense clump of greenery, I didn't have time to resist.

A familiar voice whispered in my ear. "Easy."

Various emotions swirled around my heart. From relief to anger to annoyance to fear, to…delight and back. I settled on annoyance as he released me.

I spun around. "Kerrick, what…?" The rest of my question fizzled in my throat as I looked at him. Anger hardened his expression. He must have seen Tohon kissing me. "I can't avoid his touch altogether. A couple of kisses in two weeks is pretty damn good."

Kerrick studied me, taking in my green gown in the weak moonlight. I crossed my arms in front of my chest, feeling very exposed.

"Have you been following me since the Nine Mountains?" I asked.

"Yes."

It explained a few things. "That's why Belen settled down. Are the guys—?"

"With Estrid. Or they should be by now. They *follow* my orders."

I ignored the comment. "You shouldn't be here. It's too dangerous. Tohon hates you. He even has a glass coffin ready for you."

Kerrick failed to show the proper concern over his own welfare. "Have you found Ryne?"

"Yes. He's in one of those coffins. Along with King Zavier and another man."

"Who is he?"

"I don't know. Big blond guy. Young. Dead. Has a scar on his forehead."

"Stanslov?"

"Could be. He hated him, too."

"But he's quite taken with *you*," Kerrick said.

"Only because of *you*." Ha. I'd surprised him.

His anger slipped a bit.

I told him why Tohon had attempted to lure Jael away. "He's under the mistaken impression that luring me away from you would hurt you. Which works for now. Once Ryne is healed and this is over, he won't consider me a challenge and hopefully leave me alone." I suppressed a shiver and rubbed my hands along my arms. The night air had turned cold. Or was it due to Kerrick's gaze?

Kerrick didn't respond so I asked, "Have you seen Sepp?"

"Yes."

Relief puddled in my stomach. Finally something going right. "I heard one of Tohon's men talking about Estrid. Hopefully in the next week, Tohon will leave the castle to deal with the attack. Tell Sepp to come after midnight the first night Tohon is gone."

"What if Tohon doesn't leave?"

"Then tell him to come one week from tonight. Sepp can climb over the outer east wall at the midpoint—the Death Lilys won't bother him. And if he heads straight west, he'll see the infirmary. I'll be waiting there."

"All right. Do you need me inside?"

"No. Stay near the wall. We should be able to get Ryne past the Lilys." I explained as fast as I could about the Lilys and Tohon's experiments. Ryne would need to know. "And his dead soldiers are located in the barracks—"

"Avry," Tohon called from a distance.

I jerked. "You need to disappear. If he finds you..." I shooed him away, then turned to find the path.

"Avry," Kerrick said.

I stopped. He stepped behind me. I felt his warmth on my bare back and I resisted the urge to lean against him.

"Tohon isn't mistaken." Kerrick traced one of the scars along my shoulder blade. "I would be…upset if he succeeded in luring you away."

CHAPTER 24

Kerrick had lousy timing. And what exactly had he meant by being upset? Upset as in, too bad I've lost another soldier for our side? Or upset as in, I've lost someone I care for?

"Avry," Tohon called, louder this time and more annoyed.

I turned to Kerrick to ask him, but he had disappeared. Typical. "Keep out of Tohon's sight," I said to the bushes, then hurried to the path. Maybe it was better I didn't know what he'd meant. I couldn't allow myself to fall in love with him or with anyone else since I had no future if I healed Ryne. A little voice in the back of my mind said, Too late. I squashed it.

When I reached the path, I tripped over the edge on purpose. Hitting the stones hard with my hands and knees, I grunted as the sharp edges cut into skin.

"Over here," I yelled to Tohon. I sat on the ground and yanked off my left shoe, breaking the heel.

When Tohon strode into view, his scowled transformed into concern. "My dear, what happened?" He crouched down.

"I caught my heel. I think I twisted my ankle."

He helped me to stand. I wobbled.

Tohon cupped my elbow to support me. "Can you walk?"

"Yes." I limped beside him.

"I'll call for the carriage."

"You don't have to leave for me. I'll be better in a couple hours."

"Nonsense."

Within fifteen minutes the horses and carriage pulled up to the entrance. Tohon helped me up the steps, but before I entered, I glanced back at the garden. Was Kerrick still there?

"Something wrong?" Tohon asked.

Yes. Damn Kerrick. "Just a twinge." I sucked in a breath and settled into the seat.

Once again he wrapped a blanket around me. "Looks like you'll have to postpone your shopping trip a few days."

"My ankle will be healed by morning."

"But I'm going to need Cellina. Unless you'd rather take the bodyguards?"

"No. I'll wait." I sagged back against the cushion. Exhaustion settled over me like a heavy gown, sapping my strength.

Kerrick had given me no sign he cared for me before. Unless I missed it. Or was in denial. No. I'd heard it from Tohon, and he was either a master manipulator or a sociopath—probably both. Tonight was a perfect example. He'd thrown a fit over the dress, then acted like a gentleman the rest of the evening.

It would be best to concentrate on freeing, healing and delivering Ryne to Kerrick. And *not* dwell on an impossibility.

In the days following the party, Tohon spent all his time in meetings with his generals and Cellina. Taking advantage of his distraction, I continued my early-morning snooping to collect as much information about Tohon as possible. With a lit lantern in hand, I headed for his lab. The stolen key worked.

I entered and relocked the door behind me. Tohon's ledger remained on the counter. Flipping through the pages, I read his notes on the Death Lilys' harvest schedule, but nothing indicated what he did with all those sacks of toxin. I rummaged through the drawers and cabinets. They were filled with lab supplies, syringes and clippings from plants. I couldn't find any other books or notes.

Taking a last look around, I noticed a door behind the chair Tohon had strapped me into. Guess I had been too focused on the syringe full of toxin to see it before. I unlocked it and pushed it open.

The lantern light illuminated two rows of beds, one on each side of a long room. As I walked down the aisle, my stomach churned with nausea. Ten- to twelve-year-old children occupied the beds. Most were unconscious, but a few tossed and turned, caught by fever dreams. One girl moaned in pain. Another had curled into a ball and rocked on her bed.

Although my heart swelled with the desire to heal them, my magic didn't stir. Which confirmed my fear that Tohon had been injecting Death Lily toxin into these children in the hopes of creating more healers. Horror rose like bile in my throat.

I checked on each child, working my way down one side. At least they were being cared for. Glasses of water sat on tables next to each bed. The room smelled clean. No bed sores marked their skin, and the unconscious patients wore diapers. Tohon must care more for them than his soldiers.

When I reached the end of the left side, I paused to gather my strength. Three of them would soon die. Rage burned.

How could Tohon do this to children! Where were the people who cared for these kids? The thought *Probably killed by the plague* doused a little of my fury, but not the part directed at Tohon.

Resuming my inspection, I examined the children on the right side. The second-to-last patient stirred at my touch. He woke, squinting in the lantern light.

"Are you a new nurse?" he asked.

Mindful that this boy could tell Tohon or his nurse about my visit, I chose my words with care. "No, I'm just stopping in to check on everyone. How do you feel?"

"Much better now." He sat up in bed. His black hair stuck straight up on one side. He glanced around the room with a sad resignation. "I'd thought I was going to die, too."

Hope touched my heart. Maybe he'd survived the toxin. "How long have you been here?"

He shrugged. "Don't know. Awhile. Why?"

"Just curious. So you were very sick?"

He nodded. "Everyone here is very sick. This is the dying room."

I stared at him for a moment. It was all I could do as waves of dismay swept through me.

He stared right back. Suspicion lurked in his golden-brown eyes. "Shouldn't you know all this?"

The boy acted older than he looked. I crouched down next to his bed so we were eye level. "You're half right. I am new here so I don't know everything. But I want to."

"Why?"

"Because I don't like it when kids are sick."

"I don't, either, but no one can stop it."

"Why not?" I asked.

"We've been chosen by King Tohon for an important job.

He says we're helping him learn what medicines are good for his soldiers. And no one disobeys the king."

The boy reminded me of Flea—wise beyond his years. "How many rooms are there?"

"Three."

It was difficult to keep my expression neutral. Tohon must have a room for each stage of the toxin. "All filled with kids your age helping the king?"

"Yep."

"Is there a room for those who have survived?"

Another shrug. "Don't know." Then he smiled. "Guess I'll find out."

"What's your name?" I asked.

A guarded look replaced his grin. "Who wants to know?"

"I'm Avry. I'm working for King Tohon, too, but it's like you said, I can't refuse the king."

"I'm Danny."

I shook his hand. "Danny, can you do me a favor and not tell anyone I was here?"

"Why not?"

"It would get me into trouble with the king. I doubt anyone will ask you, but just in case."

"Okay."

"Thanks." I stood to leave.

"Will you come back and visit me?" Danny asked.

"If I can, I will. However, I have a feeling the king might bring you to me at some point."

"Why?"

"To help care for his soldiers."

He hugged his thin arms around his chest and shivered.

I rushed to assure him. "But not as a test subject. As a... nurse."

"Oh. That would be fun. I hope he does."

Smiling, I pulled his blankets up as he lay back on his pillow, tucking him in. If he considered being a nurse fun, then he would make a great healer.

My thoughts swirled as I left the room and Tohon's lab, locking the doors behind me. How many more children would die because of his experiments? How could I stop Tohon? Cutting off his supply of toxin would mean killing all the Death Lilys in the compound. And what would keep him from planting more? Assassination was the only solution I managed to produce. My contract with him hadn't included a clause for attacking or harming him. But could I? One-on-one, my magic wasn't strong enough. But with Kerrick's? Maybe, and only if we fought him in the woods.

I arrived at the infirmary without any memory of the trip. My workers moved around the main room, snuffing the lanterns and attending to the morning chores. Once they understood that the new procedures improved a patient's health, they were quick to adopt them. Those who refused had been replaced.

Starting near the door, I checked on each patient. A few slept, but most woke with the activity and brightening sunshine. Sweat beaded on the forehead of one soldier, who didn't stir when I placed a hand on his cheek. His skin burned.

"Emre, when did you last check on Gantin?" I asked.

"Before bed. He was sitting up and making jokes with Lieutenant Fox."

In the bed next to Gantin, Fox pushed up on an elbow. "He didn't complain of anything."

I glanced at the lieutenant. "Gantin wouldn't. Don't you remember how he kept quiet the whole time I stitched him up?"

Fox grinned. "No, ma'am, I believe I passed out after the first sight of blood."

"And you call yourself a soldier," I teased.

His humor faded. "I call myself a farmer, but King Tohon called me a soldier."

"We have something in common. He called me, as well. And he's a hard man to refuse."

"We could resist," Fox said. "But then we'd be dead and *still* working for him."

I shared a sympathetic look with Fox before I turned to my helper. "Emre, fetch me a tablespoon of fever powder, please." I inspected Gantin's stomach wound. It had been stitched closed five days ago, and the sutures would be removed in the next couple of days. No puss or red streaked his skin, therefore no infection. Which meant the cut had gone deeper than it looked, causing internal bleeding or it could be another problem altogether.

Emre returned with the medicine.

I mixed the white powder in a glass of water and handed it to Emre. "Dribble a little of this into his mouth at a time, letting him swallow between them. It should reduce his fever."

"What if it doesn't?" Lieutenant Fox's face creased with concern.

"Then I'll take care of him personally. Don't worry." I moved over to the lieutenant's bed to let Emre finish the job. "How's the leg?" I asked him.

"Better."

"Ready to put weight on it?"

He gave me a queasy look. "No."

I pulled back his covers and pressed my hands to his right leg. The thigh bone had been broken in three places and I'd had to heal him. His shin bone had also been fractured, but I allowed that one to heal on its own. The leg felt strong.

"I know you're enjoying being spoiled, but you have to work your muscles. Come on, up on your feet." I pulled his legs off the bed.

He groaned, but not in pain. "You're a hard lady to refuse."

I put his arm around my shoulder and helped him stand. Fox wobbled on one foot, leaning on me.

"Put the other foot down. Your leg will hold. Trust me."

He cringed in anticipation, but blinked with surprise. Distributing his weight, he straightened.

I beamed at him. "See? I wouldn't lie to you." I called another one of my workers over. "Please take the lieutenant for a walk. Once around the room."

As she led Fox down the aisle, I checked on the next patient. "How's the arm, Henson?"

He didn't get a chance to reply. A bang sounded as a group of bloody soldiers pushed through the door. They carried six wounded men. I rushed to them, calling for a few helpers. The injured men were all unconscious, which, considering the severity of their wounds, was a kindness.

It was times like this that I wished for another five healers. All the men needed extreme measures. One died as I inspected the gaping hole in his stomach. Three others wouldn't make it another hour. The remaining two had the best chance. But which one should I take first? I chose the weaker of the two. Before assuming his injuries, I instructed my helpers on how to keep the other alive. And how to assist with the walking wounded who had carried their buddies here.

My magic felt as if it jumped when I placed my hands on the first soldier. He had broken five ribs and one had pierced his lung. Breathing became difficult as pain ringed my chest; I collapsed on an empty bed. The commotion in the infirmary faded.

Darkness had fallen by the time I woke. Voices muttered, but no one in the infirmary was awake. In fact, it appeared as if everyone had been tucked in for the night. I reached over to the man lying in the bed next to me. The second man had survived the day and his pulse felt strong. Emre dozed in a chair next to him.

Before healing the soldier, I woke Emre.

"What's the status on Gantin?" I asked.

"Better. No fever and resting quietly."

"Good. Go to bed, Emre. I've got this one." Plus the night nurses would be doing their rounds soon.

The voices outside stopped when Emre left. I would have ignored them except I heard Estrid's name. The injured man would last a few more minutes. My ribs ached as I stood and searched for the source of the voices. They came from behind the infirmary. I crept back to my office. Glad the high window had been opened and no lanterns had been lit in here, I climbed up on my desk to peek outside.

Two men talked in low tones. My eyes needed a minute to adjust to the darkness. A weak yellow glow from the infirmary's windows shone on them and the four dead bodies. The bodies had been covered with linen sheets and laid in the large stone basin, waiting to be prepared for a proper burial. Since I started here, we hadn't had to use the prep area.

I recognized the one man as the captain of the injured unit. Tohon was the other.

"...sure, Captain?" Tohon asked.

"Yes, sire. No one matching that description was among

the attackers. All wore Estrid's red uniforms except for those three I described."

I wondered if the three were Belen, Loren and Quain. That would mean Tohon had been asking about Kerrick.

"Explain to me again how their smaller force overwhelmed yours?" Tohon didn't sound happy.

"We had no warning, sire. It was the middle of the night, in the middle of a town in Vyg that we had secured months ago. It was a small group who attacked. They came in quick, and left just as fast. We gave chase, but lost them in the woods."

Tohon appeared to consider the information. "Doesn't your unit have special forces?"

"No, sire. Captain Young's unit works with them."

"All right, Captain. Return to your men." Tohon remained standing next to the dead as the captain walked away.

He waited until the captain rounded the corner before lifting the sheet on the nearest body. Tohon pulled a syringe from his pocket. Shoving the needle into the dead man's arm, he pushed the plunger. Then he rested his hand on the dead man's forehead before letting the sheet fall. He did the same thing for the other three, injecting, then touching them. Odd. Was he doing an experiment?

I pressed both my hands to my mouth, muffling a very girlie scream when the first body moved. Tohon yanked the sheet off and helped the formerly dead and naked man stand. Soon the three others joined their comrade. Tohon pushed them and they walked in a line, heading toward the other side of the compound. A tiny macabre parade. He guided the dead men by touch. I watched until the darkness swallowed them.

Sinking down to my desk, I sat there in shock. Tohon had just reanimated the dead. What was in the syringes? Did he use magic? Probably when he touched their foreheads. I had known his special soldiers were dead—without souls—but their bodies hadn't decayed so I hadn't been entirely convinced the bodies had ceased to function.

Those four had been dead. No doubt about that. I mulled over the horror, but I couldn't think of an explanation for what had transpired outside.

"Miss Avry?" The captain stood in the doorway of my office. "My sergeant doesn't look good. He's coughing up blood."

Spurred into action, I slid off the desk. "Sorry, I needed a glass of water." I followed him back to the sergeant.

The man's body convulsed as he sputtered. His ribs had been broken as well, but his spleen had also been damaged.

"How did they get hurt?" I asked.

"A man the size of a bear came up from behind, picked him up and squeezed. He did it to both of them." The captain shook his head. "I'd take a sword to the gut rather than be hugged to death."

Only Belen had the strength. "Neither of these men will die from their injuries."

"They might die of embarrassment."

I laughed. "I won't tell if you don't."

"Deal." The captain shook my hand, but then he sobered. "Thanks for saving them."

"I wish I could have saved them all."

"It took us too long to bring them here. You should be in the field with us."

"I should. Talk to Tohon."

"My superior officer has already tried. His request was denied."

"Perhaps next time you could send a runner and I could meet you halfway."

"I'd like to be optimistic and say there won't be a next time, but Estrid has gone on the offensive and I think it'll just be a matter of time." He sighed. "In case we need you again, I'll remember to send word."

"Then I hope I don't hear from you." I meant what I said. If Ryne stopped Tohon, then the war would be over. Until Estrid decided she didn't like sharing power with Ryne.

The captain nodded. I assumed the sergeant's injuries and returned to my bed. For now, one problem at a time was all I could handle.

More midnight attacks harried Tohon's troops, which meant more soldiers for me to heal. On the fourth evening since I'd seen Kerrick in the garden, Tohon visited the infirmary. He walked around the main room, talking with the patients. When he finished, he gestured for me to follow him into my office.

He closed the door, then sat on the edge of my desk. "I'm leaving tomorrow morning for a few days. Estrid's holy army is getting feisty and needs to be taught a lesson."

Not sure why he confided in me, I asked, "Should I prep for more wounded?"

"Not too many more. I'm taking my special soldiers. They should upset Estrid's sensibilities."

I waited for him to get to the point.

He slid off the desk and stood close to me. "I debated taking you with me."

Not good. I kept my expression neutral. "And?"

"You're more useful to me here." He reached to touch my face.

I stepped back. "Do you know when you'll return?"

"Why? Are you going to miss me?"

"I'm assuming when you return, there will be fewer

wounded. I just wanted to gauge how much longer to expect casualties."

"I should be back within the week." He moved toward me again.

Retreating, I bumped into the wall.

Tohon pressed his hands on the wall on either side of me. He leaned in. "We've been so busy. I've missed you."

His lips brushed mine and a spark of heat shot through me.

"You're exhausted, my dear. Please don't overexert yourself for my men. You're more valuable than they are. Even if they're dead, they continue to serve me."

I opened my mouth to ask a question, but he cut me off with a deeper kiss. This time Tohon's magic buzzed through my body, turning my willpower into goo. Without thought or any control on my part, my arms wrapped around his torso as I pressed against him. Still locked in a kiss, the room spun...or was that me? The next thing I knew, I lay on top of the desk completely at his mercy.

The logical part of me had retreated to a small corner of my mind. It commented on the direness of the situation out of habit. Unfortunately, nothing could be done at this point. His life magic had overloaded my senses.

Tohon broke off the kiss. And I think I whimpered in protest.

"I'm getting tired of chasing you, my dear. Perhaps this little reminder of what I'm capable of will make you more willing to meet me halfway."

My senses returned. I clutched his arms before he could pull back. "Is this what you really want, Tohon? A lover forced by magic to be with you? Why not find someone who loves you without using your magic?"

A dangerous glint shone in his eyes. "Where's the challenge in that?" He pulled away.

"How is using your magic a challenge? I'd call that cheating. The true challenge would be to not use your magic at all."

"What are you suggesting?"

He used the same phrase as Kerrick had. I wondered if they had learned that technique in school. "I'm suggesting you find a woman who will love you. A lady who hasn't been influenced by your magic."

"And that's not you?" His voice stayed flat.

I stood on very thin ground. "You just used your magic on me."

"What if I hadn't?"

The ground crumbled beneath my feet. "There are... things about you I can't accept."

"Kerrick has killed people, as well."

"I know, but he doesn't turn them into dead soldiers."

"Anything else?"

"The Death Lilys. I can guess the next logical step in your experiments with the toxin." No sense letting him know I found the children.

"We need more healers."

"We do, but your methods are immoral."

He considered. "Do you realize your honesty could make your situation worse?"

"Yes."

"Then why are telling me all this?"

Good question. "I don't know."

"Perhaps you're scared."

"Of course I'm scared. It's bad enough that my own magic sends my heart reeling when you touch me. But when you use *your* magic, all my self-control is gone."

"I was thinking you're more scared that the things you

can't accept about me won't matter to you once you get to know me better."

Wow. This man was seriously deluded. I thought it best to stop with the honesty before I dug myself in deeper.

He took my silence as acceptance. "The heart is a strange beast and not ruled by logic, Avry. I think you've already figured that out."

Tohon left the next morning. I checked my patients and discharged a few. Both Gantin and Fox were strong enough to return to the barracks. Keeping busy all day, I tried not to dwell on what might happen this evening. All the soldiers in the compound were used to seeing me go between the infirmary and castle at all hours of the night. I had swiped and hidden a uniform close to Sepp's size in my office.

I debated about Danny. The boy shouldn't remain with Tohon, but after I healed Ryne, I wouldn't be able to teach him if he developed healing powers. If not, he still shouldn't be here. If there was time, I decided to send Danny with Ryne and Sepp. Kerrick and Sepp could teach him about magic, and I would give him my journal of notes. If there wasn't, I would help him escape before the plague symptoms incapacitated me. And if I wasn't locked in the dungeon.

The day seemed to drag. I practiced with my throwing knives, but it was more to burn off my anxiety. When I healed another person, a connection was forged. An emotional attachment like a sense of ownership that was impossible to ignore. They were *my* patients. My scars all had names and the thought of injuring a soldier I had healed—even if it was one of Tohon's—made me queasy.

Finally, the sun set and I tried to sleep for a few hours on an empty bed in the infirmary. My thoughts churned, making it impossible to relax, so I retreated to my office and waited for Sepp.

When he arrived, I almost jumped out of my skin.

"Any trouble?" I asked him.

He looked the same. "No. No one's insane enough to scale the outer wall. Your note said the Lilys won't harm Ryne. Are you sure?"

Note? "Didn't...?" Kerrick's name hovered on my lips, but I swallowed it back instinctively. "Yes, I'm sure. As long as he's with you."

If Sepp noticed my stumble, he didn't react. I handed him the uniform and turned around. He fussed about changing. I really didn't miss Sepp these past three weeks. In fact, I'd take Kerrick in a bad mood over Sepp any day.

When he was ready, we crossed to the castle. Only a few soldiers lingered outdoors. We entered without any problems. Lighting a lantern, I led him to the coffin room. Nothing had changed.

Sepp tsked over the display of death. "Typical of Tohon to be so showy." He tapped on the glass. "What keeps the other two from decaying?"

I glanced at Ryne, then the others. The difference between them and Ryne showed in the pallor of their skin. Sepp had said his powers were the exact opposite of Tohon's. I considered Sepp's death magic and how he froze life in a fake death. Perhaps Tohon froze death in a fake life.

"Could their bodies be in a stasis similar to the one you used for Ryne?" I asked. "That would explain why they haven't decomposed."

Sepp shot me a surprised look. "That's possible." Then he turned to a dark corner of the room. "Did she get it right, Tohon?"

CHAPTER 25

"She has it half right," Tohon said. He stepped from the dark corner.

The shock left me breathless and gasping, as if I'd fallen into an icy river.

"Surprised to see me, my dear?" He gestured to Sepp. "Have you ever heard the term *opposites attract?*"

"When...?"

"We first met at the Healer's Guild before the plague," Sepp said. "We got along rather well except we disagreed about helping the Guild."

Frozen, I chipped at my confusion. "Is that how you found Ryne? Through Sepp?" I asked Tohon.

"No. Kerrick is so predictable with his caves. Eventually, my men discovered the area where Ryne's guards had been taking their sunlight breaks. Then it was just a matter of time."

"He ambushed me," Sepp said. "But he spared my life and convinced me he is right. Tohon's going to unite all the Realms and bring peace to everyone. Think about it, Avry. It took Kerrick *two years* to find you. During that time, Estrid has moved west and Tohon built his army. Two years lost. I wasn't going to waste my gifts for the losing team. Bad enough you didn't arrive at the cave when you should have. I almost died from the infection." His tone was peevish.

"I'm regretting that already," I said. But his words *when you should have* clanked. Tohon had been the one to delay me. Was that on purpose?

"Oh, you'll be regretting much more, my dear."

Just when I thought that wasn't possible, Sepp asked, "You have an empty coffin. Do you want me to put her into a stasis?"

I clamped down on a cry of dismay.

"What are you thinking, Sepp?" Tohon asked.

"I'll go to Estrid's camp, find Kerrick, tell him Avry's plan failed and that she's in here. He'll come rescue her, and we'll set another trap for him."

"Rather time-consuming," Tohon said. Before Sepp could protest, he continued. "Kerrick's already here."

Pain crushed my chest.

"Here? In the castle?" Sepp seemed surprised.

"No. But he's around. Probably sulking in the woods nearby."

"But—"

"He probably watched you climb the wall. When you don't return and there's no sign of Ryne or Avry, he'll come."

"How can you be so sure?" Sepp asked.

"My people are loyal. There is no way Avry could have sent you a note. And I know Kerrick. He would *never* let her out of his sight. He talked to you in the garden the night of the party, didn't he?"

No sense lying now. "Yes."

"He's predictable, Sepp. Don't worry. We'll have him by this time tomorrow." Tohon turned to me. "You're a smart girl, Avry. How can you believe this one man can make a difference?" He swept a hand toward Ryne. "I've won. You would have sacrificed your life for nothing. I can see you still don't believe me. Kerrick has you brainwashed. Sepp, wake Prince Ryne."

"What?"

"Wake him so we can all watch him die. Once he's gone, he can join my special forces and I need not bother with him again. Avry can move past this nonsense and try to win back *my* favor."

Sepp stared at Tohon for a full minute. I suspected he wasn't accustomed to being ordered by Tohon. Then he moved to Ryne's coffin.

"The top pane slides back," Tohon said.

The death magician pushed on the sheet of glass, uncovering Ryne.

Tohon grabbed my wrist. "Don't get any ideas, my dear. If you heal him, I'll just take his life and then bury you."

Sepp touched Ryne's face. In less than a heartbeat, Ryne opened his eyes. He smiled at Sepp, but the mage kept his gaze on Tohon. The prince caught on quick. Sitting up in alarm, he scanned the room.

"Welcome to my castle, Ryne." Tohon switched his grip to my upper arm, yanking me close. "Kerrick found you a healer. Too bad—like you, she's mine."

I tried to jerk away, but he sent a wave of pain that turned my muscles to jelly. I sagged to my knees.

"Where's Kerrick?" Ryne asked. His voice was rough, but steady.

"He'll be along shortly. Then we'll have a nice little re-union before you die." Tohon called for his guards.

Six soldiers appeared from the dark corner. There must be

a hidden passageway like the one that connected my room and Tohon's.

"Escort the prince to an underground suite," Tohon ordered four of them.

The soldiers surrounded Ryne. The prince climbed from the coffin with dignity and grace. Impressive. He met my gaze and nodded before being led away.

Tohon's fingers dug into my skin. "What should I do with you, my dear?"

"I—"

"It was a rhetorical question. I know exactly what happens next."

He pulled me to my feet and leaned close.

"All the comforts and freedoms you've enjoyed are gone. You will have to earn your way back into my good graces." He threw a pair of gloves onto the floor. "Put those on."

When I didn't move, his magic blasted through me, sending me back to my knees. Even if I could break away from Tohon, my odds of getting far were slim to none. I slipped on the gloves. He yanked me to my feet, spun me around and held my arms behind my back while one of the guards snapped a pair of manacles on me, cranking them tight around the gloves and my wrists.

"Take her to a cell close to Prince Ryne's. Make sure her hands remain secured. I don't trust her."

The soldiers grabbed my upper arms—one on each side. They led me down so many steps, I lost track of the number. Better to count than to consider the future. Metal doors swung open and clanged shut. Rank odors fouled the air. Metal bars and sickly yellow torches blurred past. I glimpsed Ryne sitting on a big metal shelf that served as a bed in a cell two down from the one they shoved me into. They left, banging the door closed behind them. An empty cell separated us.

My accommodations included the same hard bed as Ryne's, and a slop pot. I sat on the edge. Wiggling, I tried to slide my body through my arms. It didn't work. Ryne watched my useless efforts through the bars. And so did the two who took up positions at the end of the hallway. The design of the prison made Ryne and I quite visible to anyone guarding this wing.

"Sorry the rescue failed," I said.

"What's your name?" he asked.

"Avry of Kazan."

"I remember you. You were one of Tara's apprentices. How is she doing?"

"Not good. She's dead."

He let out a slow breath. "What else have I missed?"

"Make yourself comfortable. This is going to take what's left of the night."

I told him about Kerrick's two-year search and everything that happened since. He didn't interrupt, but a few of the more alarming incidences caused him to cringe.

"Sepp's working with Tohon. If it wasn't for that little surprise, my plan might have worked." My throat was raw by the time I finished.

"You planned to heal me?" Ryne asked.

"Yes."

He stared at me as if trying to decide if my answer was genuine or not. "Even knowing you'll die?"

"Yes."

He flinched and glanced away. After a few silent moments, he said, "I can't believe Tohon's still experimenting with the Death Lily toxin. Even when he knows the danger."

"Besides the obvious, what danger?"

"He could start another plague."

Not the answer I'd been expecting. "Did he start the first one?"

"Not directly. He was helping the healers develop an antidote to the toxin. What they thought was an antidote turned into the plague."

"How do you know?"

"I stole their notes after my sister died."

"And you added to it," I said.

"I was furious. The Guild had been doing research without taking the proper precautions. They were playing with dangerous substances. I always worried something like that would happen."

He confirmed my suspicions about the Guild. "You should be happy that the Guild is gone, then."

"I'm… It's not like that. I wanted the handful of researchers in the Guild to be held accountable, not executed. I didn't know the people would kill healers." He rested his head in his hands. "I regret my actions. How could you even consider healing me when you knew about my involvement?" Ryne gazed at me as if in awe. "Can you even forgive me?"

"I already have." Saying the words confirmed my decision in my heart and soul.

"How could you?"

"Two reasons. Kerrick and Belen. I trust them. It's that simple." I smiled, remembering Flea had said the exact same thing to me long ago.

"You said Belen is safe with Estrid. But Tohon said Kerrick will be here soon. Has he been captured, as well?"

I explained. "Tohon's pretty confident Kerrick'll try to free us."

"Tohon's confidence is one of his weaknesses. Although

in this case, I'm with Tohon. I hope Kerrick finds a way to outsmart him."

"Kerrick suspected Sepp wasn't trustworthy." I told him about the note. "If he'd known Sepp would double-cross us, he'd never let him come…unless he planned for Sepp to show his hand. But did Kerrick guess Tohon would wake you?"

"Tohon hasn't changed since school. He likes to gloat. He likes to flaunt it when he has the upper hand—more weaknesses. I'm positive he meant to wake me at some point."

"But now we have…seven days at most." Until he died. "How do you feel?" I asked.

"Rotten. Everything aches and I'm sweating." He lay down.

Stage-two symptoms. "At least you're not throwing up."

"Small mercies," he muttered. "I'm not going to waste my time moping. Right now there's not much we can do—unless you have a set of lock picks on you?"

He seemed so hopeful, I hated to disappoint him.

Ryne glanced at the guards and lowered his voice. "Aside from the guards doing something stupid, we're stuck for now. Best thing I can do is learn everything I can about what Tohon is planning. Avry, can you tell me about his dead soldiers?"

I told him what I remembered. Thankfully, I hadn't seen them since being in Tohon's castle.

"You believe Tohon is putting them into a stasis right after they die. But he's injecting them with a medicine or chemical to animate them. Right?" Ryne asked.

"Yes."

"If we can figure out what substance he's using, we can stop him from making more. Any ideas?"

I thought of my journal back in my office in the infirmary.

It was possible, although unlikely, I had jotted down some useful information. "The Guild had lists of hundreds of different medicines from plants alone. My mentor knew all of them, but I only remember a few."

"You've been with Tohon long enough to learn about his experiments. Has he mentioned anything else?"

"No. All he talked about was the Death Lily…" A memory snagged. When Tohon had injected me with the toxin, my essence had detached from my body. I had no control, but Tohon walked me back to my room and laid me down on the bed. My body had obeyed him. What would happen if he injected the toxin into a body without a soul? Would it do the same?

"Avry?"

I told him about the toxin. "It almost seems too coincidental."

"It makes sense. The body has already died so the toxin won't kill it."

"But the body's been frozen in a stasis. Wouldn't that freeze the toxin, as well?"

"Good point. Don't give up. Keep thinking, Avry, you have a fine mind."

"And look where it's landed us."

"This is temporary."

I laughed. "I'm glad you can stay positive." And I was beginning to like Ryne.

"Positive thoughts lead to positive results."

"Did you learn that in school?" I asked.

"Yes. One thing the school excelled in was preparing us for the intricacies of politics and the harsh reality of intrigue and deception."

"That school certainly had an impact on the students.

Kerrick's still grieving over Jael. Tohon still wants to be king of all the Realms."

"It was life changing for all of us."

In the morning, guards woke me from a light doze. Yanking me to my feet, they marched me to the infirmary. One removed my manacles and gloves while the other gave me strict instructions. I could work with the patients, but I must not leave the infirmary without them. They would guard the doors and would bring me back to my cell in the evening.

I rubbed my wrists, drank a huge glass of water, visited the privy and sent my helpers out for more food. After I finished my rounds, I sat in my office and read through my apprentice journal. Although I made a list of useful plants, I found no mention of any substance that could animate the dead. No note of a substance that would render a man unconscious, either. Something I could blow in their faces or they could smell.

The guards had been smart enough to keep their distance from me until I put on the gloves. A new set of guards came for me after the sun set. With my hands manacled behind me again, they escorted me below the castle. Still lying on the bed, Ryne looked as if he hadn't moved since this morning. However, a tray of half-eaten food rested near the door.

When the guards left, he sat up and asked with concern, "Are you all right?"

"Shouldn't I be asking you that?"

"I'm not the one who pissed off Tohon. He can be quite cruel."

"I'm fine. I worked in the infirmary all day."

"Tohon's no fool. Your healing powers are a valuable resource."

I glanced at the empty cells around us. "He could also be trying to draw Kerrick out."

"That, too." After a few minutes, he chuckled.

"What's so funny?" I asked.

"You must have driven Kerrick crazy."

"What's that supposed to mean?"

"Kerrick's all about following orders and giving orders, there is no in between. However, I doubt you're the type to just follow."

"We did have our…disagreements."

"I'd bet. Can you tell me about them?"

"It all seems so stupid now."

"Consider it a dying man's last request."

"That's not—"

"I know, but I'm bored, in pain and wouldn't mind the distraction."

"When you put it that way, how can I refuse?" I regaled him with a few stories of our rocky relationship. Looking back, I couldn't see how my behavior would endear me to Kerrick. I'd been difficult and a pain in the ass.

Ryne enjoyed the tales. He certainly didn't act like a dying man in pain. I think that whole positive attitude was the way to go. Worrying and moping won't change his situation; he might as well enjoy his last days.

The next two days matched the first. Working in the infirmary all day, I stayed in my cell overnight, telling Ryne stories or brainstorming ideas on how to counter Tohon's defenses. His intelligence was obvious, and I knew he would do great things if he lived. However, his symptoms increased each day. In a few days, he would enter the final stage and nothing I could say would ease his torment.

Time was against us. And, so far, we hadn't found a way to

outsmart the guards. Frustration welled as I stood within ten feet of him, yet couldn't reach him. Tohon knew what he was doing when he picked our underground accommodations.

Trying to follow Ryne's example, I focused on the one good thing. Tohon hadn't caught Kerrick. But I wondered why Tohon hadn't been down here to gloat. Perhaps Estrid's forces had made inroads and he was preoccupied. No sign of Kerrick, either. Which was good. Nothing he could do if he was caught, as well—unless they let him keep his lock picks, which I'd learned the guards were too smart to do. Perhaps I could trick them into coming closer to me.

After I'd finished my rounds on that third morning, I read through my journal from cover to cover again, determined to find a way to escape. I also brainstormed ideas in my office. Perhaps there was a way I could trick them into coming closer to me—a fake swoon or direct attack?

A loud commotion interrupted me late in the afternoon. My infirmary helpers had all gone to fetch the dinner trays, so I hurried to the main room as two soldiers entered, each carrying an injured colleague. I gestured to the empty beds and they dumped them on the mattresses.

I turned to chastise the soldiers for their rough treatment. The taller one stood right next to me. I stepped back in alarm.

He said, "Easy there, miss."

My heart flipped over. I glanced at the other. He tried to act innocent.

"Can you heal our colleagues?" Kerrick asked.

I played along, examining the patients. They both had concussions and multiple bruises. "They'll be fine." I pointed to a gash on Kerrick's forearm. "You need sutures. Come to the exam room." Turning around, I walked to the back room.

A few of my other patients were awake. They watched as we passed them. Would they recognize Kerrick? Would they sound the alarm? My heart urged me to hurry, but I kept my pace even.

I shut the door after both men were inside. Then I sagged against it. Loren smiled at me and I suppressed the desire to hug him.

"You were smart to wait a few days," I said.

Loren glanced at Kerrick. "Told you. He wanted to rush in here right away."

"What's going on?" Kerrick asked.

He was business as usual. No sign of the other Kerrick—the one in the garden. I explained about Sepp and Ryne. When I had mentioned Sepp's name, Kerrick scowled as a flash of pain crossed his face. Yet another betrayal for him.

"Did you know about Sepp?" I asked him.

"I suspected. And I don't buy that Tohon's men found them. Sepp had to tip him off."

"They met at the Healer's Guild before the plague, so it's possible," I said. Then I looked at Loren. "Have you been here all this time, too?"

"No, we came after the first round of attacks on Tohon's defenses."

"We?"

"Quain's waiting on the other side of the wall. We'd thought it best to have a man on the outside."

"Where's Belen?"

"He's still leading the sneak attacks." Loren grinned. "Poppa Bear's quite devious when he wants to be."

Plus he'd be too noticeable. I studied the two of them. Kerrick had pulled back his brown hair and his face was unshaven. His eyes were now a vibrant green, matching the color of the forest exactly. Both of them wore Tohon's army's uniform, but their clothes had been stained with dirt and blood, and ripped as if they just returned from a battle.

"What's next?" Loren asked.

"You don't have a plan?" I tried not to let my voice squeak.

"This was it. Getting inside. We'd hoped you'd know all Tohon's weaknesses by now," Loren said.

"I do have an idea, but I was hoping with your experience in these things you had something...better."

"What's your plan?" Kerrick asked.

So much for my hope. I gave them a brief rundown.

"It could work," Loren said.

"We'll make it work," Kerrick said.

A man shouted on the other side of my door. Then a loud knock sounded. I moved away from the entrance.

"Time to go, Healer Avry," one of my guards said as he turned the knob.

Kerrick didn't wait. He yanked the door open, surprising the man. Without hesitating, Kerrick pulled the guard into the room and held him tight.

"Avry."

I pressed my fingers on the back of the man's neck and zapped him. Kerrick dropped him and sprinted for his partner, who backed toward the outer door. In two strides, Kerrick tackled him. I ran to them and zapped the struggling man.

Realizing we were in the main room with recovering soldiers all around us, I stood. Loren had drawn his sword.

"No, Loren. These men are *not* to be hurt," I said.

"We won't get far if they raise the alarm," Kerrick said.

"I know. But they're *mine*. I won't let them be hurt again."

My patients stared at me. No one said a word for a very long minute. Then, one by one, my patients lay down in their beds, pretending to be asleep. Touched by their silent support, I almost cried. But I didn't have the time. My infirmary workers would be returning soon.

"Thank you," I said.

Kerrick and Loren stripped the guards of their uniforms before dumping them in two empty beds. Their dirty uniforms had worked for getting them into the castle complex, but wouldn't do for escorting me to my cell. They changed.

I pulled on those horrid gloves, and Kerrick manacled my wrists behind my back.

Unable to resist, I said, "Just like old times."

Kerrick's smile reached his eyes. He placed his hands on my shoulders. "Except this time, they're loose enough to slide your hands through."

I walked between Loren and Kerrick as we headed toward the castle. Once inside, I led the way until we reached the stairs, then paused.

"At the bottom are solid double doors guarded by two men," I explained. "Beyond those doors is a large room for the guards to relax and play cards or dice between checks. There's always been at least four, maybe five in there with two or three in the cell area. The doors between the cells and room have bars so any noise will be heard by all six of them." I bit my lip. My plan wasn't going to work. There were too many guards. "Can you handle that many?" I asked.

"Think positive," Kerrick said. "Stage an escape attempt when we reach the inner room. Make lots of noise, too. Okay?"

"Yes."

We descended. When we reached the outer door, one of the guards grumbled, "'Bout time, I—"

Kerrick and Loren moved. I slipped the manacles off, but didn't let them clang on the stone floor. Both guards were soon immobilized. I zapped them.

Kerrick placed the manacles back on my wrists. Loren removed the keys from a prone form. He inserted it into the lock. "Ready?" he asked.

No. If anything happened to them...

Kerrick nodded.

He opened the door and we entered as if they escorted me. Two of the four guards playing cards glanced up, but didn't really see us as the game had their full attention. Kerrick squeezed my arm. My cue.

I yanked my left hand out and grabbed the manacles with my right. Yelling, I ran at the guards playing cards. Zapping one of them before they could react, I dove out of the way as Kerrick and Loren chased me. I screamed and carried on, swinging the manacles around.

"Stop her," Kerrick called as he slammed the hilt of his sword on a guard's head, knocking him out. He fought with a single-minded intensity.

"She's free! Watch for her hands!" Loren shouted. He picked up a guy and rammed his head into the stone wall.

My metal cuff connected on a temple and I grabbed a wrist. Sending my magic into the guard, I held on as he cried out in pain. Then I touched the back of his neck, sending him to the floor.

More voices sounded. Bars rattled.

"Get in here," Kerrick ordered. "We need help."

The door squealed as two more joined the fray. Another few seconds of chaos ensued. I darted in and zapped the men Kerrick and Loren held before dodging out of the way. Within a minute, we had incapacitated them all.

We stood amid the prone forms, panting from the effort.

Loren grinned. "That was fun. Damn, Avry, you have a healthy set of lungs. Did I hear some girlie screams in there?"

"That was from one of the guards."

"Ah."

Our good humor died when we approached Ryne's cell. The noise hadn't roused him. Covered with a sheen of sweat, he lay still. Loren unlocked his door and I rushed to his side. Fear lumped in my throat. It was time.

Before I could touch him, Ryne held up a hand. "No. Wait until we're free."

"Will you be strong enough to escape?" I asked.

"I just need water."

Loren went to fetch a glass. I helped Ryne sit up.

The prince smiled at Kerrick. "I knew you'd come. Avry had her doubts."

"Well, without Loren's good sense, he'd have been caught right away," I said.

"Hey, I'm standing right here," Kerrick said.

"Loren?" Ryne asked.

"At your service." Loren returned with the water.

"Thank you." Ryne gulped it down.

"We still have to get out of the castle complex," Kerrick said. "The sooner, the better. Like now."

Ryne wobbled at first, but steadied. Determined to walk on his own, Ryne led the way from the cells.

When we passed the guards, Kerrick asked me, "How long will they be out?"

"A few more hours."

On the stairs, I leaned close to Kerrick. "What's the plan once we leave the castle?"

"We head for the front entrance. Without Sepp, we can't go through the Death Lilys around the wall."

I hoped no one at the infirmary raised the alarm. Darkness had fallen by the time we slipped out the back entrance, which helped. Keeping to the shadows around the base of the castle, we headed toward the main gate. Once we reached the front, we would have to cross the courtyard before exiting. If we didn't run or act like fugitives, we might make it.

Too bad about thirty soldiers guarded the front gate.

CHAPTER 26

"Were they here when you came in?" I asked Kerrick.

"No."

"Flee or fight?" Loren whispered.

The torchlight illuminated the soldiers. Too many for the three of us. One of the guards we knocked out in the infirmary must have tipped Tohon off. I leaned against the wall. It seemed my life resembled a never-ending game of capture the flag, with me being the one player who is always getting caught in enemy territory.

"Flee," I said.

"There's nowhere to hide," Kerrick said. "We'll be captured. At least this way we die fighting."

"We'll go over the back wall."

"I'd rather be skewered than eaten," Loren said, sounding more like Quain.

"The Death Lilys won't attack you. Trust me."

Ryne looked at me as if I had lost my mind. But Kerrick and Loren had been through this with me with Flea.

"Take the lead," Kerrick said to me.

Ryne stifled his surprise and shot me a measuring glance.

I retraced our steps. When we reached the open area behind the castle, I stepped out as if going to the infirmary like
I had done dozens of times before. Kerrick and Loren stayed
close to my side with Ryne following us.

About halfway there, a shout broke the silence. Another
group of soldiers had been hiding in the shadows of the infirmary.

"Run for the back wall," I said.

Kerrick bent, picked up Ryne and draped him over his
shoulder. We bolted. The ground almost shook from the
pounding of boots behind us.

As we drew near, I shouted, "Don't get too close to the
Lilys. Let me go first." I rushed up to the closest Lily. Stop-
ping right under the petals, I waved my arms. "Come on!
Eat me!"

The Death Lily didn't move. Kerrick and Loren came up
beside me. Nothing happened.

I glanced at Kerrick in confusion.

He grinned. "Peace Lilys! Grab my hands."

Loren and I clamped onto Kerrick. His magic zipped along
my skin as he pulled us into the Peace Lilys. Enough of them
for Kerrick to use his power, covering us with a camouflage
so we blended in. We reached the wall, turned left for two
dozen paces before stopping at a good spot where we could
see through the leaves. Kerrick set Ryne down, but the prince
kept his hand on Kerrick's arm.

The number of soldiers increased, but they wouldn't come
near the Lilys. Voices shouted. No one had seen where we
had gone. Most claimed we were Lily food.

Tohon strode into the middle of the chaos. Everyone fell
silent at his command. He conferred with a few soldiers. I
wondered if he would tell his men about the Lilys.

What was more important to him? The illusion of Death

Lilys protecting his castle or finding us? I had to admit, it was an effective defense as long as no one knew they were Peace Lilys. Only we had been desperate enough to approach them.

"One problem," Kerrick whispered. "When we climb over, we'll be exposed. Is there another spot that's hidden?"

"Yes. There's a garden of Death Lilys in the back corner."

"Death? Are you sure?"

"Yes, but they've been neutralized."

We inched our way to the corner.

Tohon decided not to send his soldiers into the Lilys. Instead, he sent them to run outside through the front gate and position themselves around the walls to block our escape. We picked up our pace.

Tohon shouted, "I know you can survive the Death Lilys, Avry. I know what you're doing. It's temporary. You know I have my dead soldiers. You've signed a contract. You gave me your word. Don't do anything rash. Come out with your friends and all is forgiven, my dear."

We kept moving, but Kerrick's grip on my hand tightened. Cold fear knotted in my throat and clutched my heart in its icy grip. I knew what I had to do. When we reached the corner, Kerrick ordered Loren over the wall first so he could help Ryne.

When Kerrick's attention was focused on Loren, I touched Ryne's hand. My magic exploded from my chest and he rocked back in surprise. Then I collected the oily blackness that sickened him and transferred it into me.

Ryne squeezed my hand. "Thank you," he whispered.

"Stop Tohon and take care of my boys," I said in his ear.

"I promise."

Kerrick peered at us in suspicion.

"Ryne's turn," I said.

With Kerrick's help, Ryne climbed the Lilys to the top of the wall. When he was out of sight, Kerrick said, "Your turn."

"I can't. I gave my word. Don't worry, I've healed Ryne. Go and make sure he stops Tohon."

"You gave your word to a madman under duress. You don't have to honor it." He pulled me close. "Come with me. Please."

This was harder than deciding to heal Ryne. After all our bickering, he still wished to spend my last days with me. Leaning on him, I closed my eyes and breathed in his scent. Living green and spring sunshine. I opened my eyes. Tipping my head back, I met his gaze. Raw emotion shone on his face. He held nothing back.

Kerrick dipped his head. His lips met mine. A wonderful explosion of sensations started in the pit of my stomach and radiated out. His kiss was nothing like Tohon's. It wasn't manipulative or a show of dominance. It was his heart and soul. A gift.

And I wasn't about to let him watch me die a slow and painful death. I pulled back. "I've a bit of...unfinished business with Tohon." I couldn't leave without making sure Danny was taken care of.

Kerrick stared at me with a confused pain. "But he'll kill you."

Now it was my turn to be confused. "I'm going to die, anyway. You know that."

Kerrick shook his head, scowling.

Damn. A few little clues clicked into place. No wonder he didn't seem that upset when I'd agreed to save Ryne. "Go. Get Ryne far away from here. He'll explain it."

"Avry, if this is because I've hurt—"

I covered his mouth with my own, kissing him one last

time. "This isn't because of anything *you* did. If the circumstances were different, I would go with you in a heartbeat. Talk to Ryne."

Tohon's voice grew louder as he shouted for me to surrender.

He dropped his arms. "Why can't *you* tell me?"

"Go. Or all this is for nothing." I pushed him.

He wouldn't budge and his jaw settled into that stubborn line. Time for drastic action. Before he could grab me, I dashed between the Lilys and out to where Tohon could see me.

Kerrick's hoarse cry would haunt me for the rest of my days.

"Where are your friends?" Tohon asked with a deadly tone.

"Gone."

"Kerrick, too?"

"Yes."

"Come here." He held out a hand.

Bracing for the worst, I strode to him, but I balked at touching him. He snatched my hand, holding it with both of his. His magic vibrated through my bones.

He closed his eyes for a moment before meeting my gaze. "You're a fool." Dropping my hand, he shook his head in disgust. "You're not worth my time." Tohon pulled his sword. He pressed the tip to my chest.

Pain burned, but I stood my ground as I waited for the cold steel to plunge into my equally cold heart.

Tohon sheathed his weapon. "Killing you would be a kindness. And I'm not inclined to show you any. But what to do with you?" He tapped a finger on his lips. "How long do you have?"

"Ten to fifteen days. Twenty at most."

"Will you be able to function?"

Function? What an odd word. "After the initial bout of stomach problems, I'll be lucid and able to work for about ten days."

"Our contract stands until you're incapacitated. Make sure you teach your helpers everything they need to know to care for my soldiers before that point."

Not what I had been expecting. At all.

"Surprised?" he asked.

"Yes."

"Expected me to throw your sick ass in a cell?"

"Yes."

"It's tempting, but unnecessary. Nothing I can do will be worse than what you did to yourself. When you're in your final days, I'll be close by so you can beg me to kill you."

Nausea swirled. Plague symptom or fear? Hard to tell. "Will you?"

"No. You're going to suffer until the very end."

Except for the bouts of vomiting, diarrhea and nausea, my days resumed the pattern I'd established before Ryne's rescue. I worked in the infirmary all day and returned to my rooms at night. Other things had changed, though. Winter no longer helped me. Tohon no longer tapped on the secret panel. And he didn't ask me to help him with his Death Lily experiments. His absence was an unexpected bonus.

It took seven days for the stomach symptoms to cease. Then the bone-deep aches and shooting pains started. Knowing my time was limited, I sorted my meager belongings. I had placed the juggling rocks in my pockets. When a round of sickness overcame me, I clutched them in my hands. It helped.

I put my necklace in an envelope with a letter to my sister, Noelle. I apologized and explained everything to her, but couldn't even guess if she'd receive it, let alone read my words. Besides hurting Kerrick, she was my biggest regret. Maybe one of my patients would find a way to get the envelope to her.

As for Kerrick, I hoped Ryne explained. I had told Ryne everything about Tohon and what he'd been doing with the toxin.

I considered Danny's situation. The boy would be well cared for if he stayed here, but the thought of Tohon raising him horrified me. I would need to help him escape. Too bad, Tohon wouldn't stop injecting the toxin unless the Death Lilys stopped producing them.

Healing Ryne had been my main goal, and I'd achieved it. Yet, I would love to strike one blow to Tohon before I died. That night, I snuck up to the room behind Tohon's lab. More children had been brought in, and others were gone. I crossed to the outer door. A hallway stretched to either side, I turned left and found the other sickrooms Danny had mentioned. Then I went right, searching for him. He slept in a small room on the bottom of a bunk bed.

Relieved, I sat next to him, calling his name.

"Hello, Avry," he said when he woke. "What are you doing here?"

"Remember when I said I don't like to see kids getting sick?"

"Yeah."

"And you said we couldn't stop it?"

"Yeah."

"What if I told you I thought of a way to stop it. At least for a while. Would you be interested in helping me?"

He considered. "But what about the soldiers? That's important."

"Do you think it's right to kill children to test medicines?"

"No, but—"

"There are many other ways to test medicine and none of it involves harming kids."

His eyebrows drew together.

"I know because I'm a healer. I would never risk anyone for experiments."

Danny shrank back. "But healers are bad. They started the plague."

"Those healers are gone. I'm the last one and soon I'll be gone." I considered how much to tell him. "Danny, did King Tohon explain how you might develop healing powers in the future?"

He clutched the blanket to his chest. "No."

"It's not a bad thing if you do. This world needs healers and I think people are becoming more accepting." I told him about the toxin. "King Tohon's methods are too horrific, Danny. I want to take you someplace safe."

"Me, too?" a girl's voice said from above.

I glanced up in surprise. An angelic face surrounded by a mane of messy brown hair peered down at me from the upper bunk.

"That's Zila. She's eight," Danny said.

"I survived, too," she said. "I want to go. King Tohon's mean."

"Anyone else?" I asked.

"No. Just us," Danny said.

"We're special. King Tohon said so," she said. "Two from dozens."

"Dozens?" Danny frowned at her. "Are you sure he said dozens?"

"Yep."

He was old enough to realize what that meant. Danny's face paled, but he swallowed and met my gaze with determination. "We'll help you."

I filled them in on my plan. "Can you be ready to go tomorrow night around this time?"

"Yes," they both said.

"Don't tell anyone," I added.

"Do I look like I'm eight?" Danny asked.

"Hey." Zila threw her pillow at him.

He ducked it easily and tossed it back.

Curious, I asked, "How old are you?"

He straightened. "I'm twelve and three-quarters."

I kept to my normal routine the next day. When I returned to my rooms from the infirmary, I brought my journal, food and a few first-aid supplies, packing them in my knapsack along with the envelope for Noelle. We'd need money, but I'd planned to sell my throwing knives.

Danny had told me the nurses only came during the day, so it should go smoothly. When it was well after midnight, I collected the kids. Dressed and ready, they both had small packs slung over their backs.

Hurrying through the castle, we slipped outside without incident. The moon was brighter than I'd wished, but we crossed to the outer buildings without raising an alarm. I paused in the stable's shadows to listen for sounds of pursuit. After a few minutes of silence, we headed to the Death Lily garden.

Once there, I stopped next to the first one. Even though the petals were held open, I stuck my hand inside. A thorn pricked my palm. My awareness floated along the Lilys consciousness. Its misery consumed me.

How can we help? I thought.

Images of the orange toxin sacks filled my mind. I still had them in my pack. Then it showed me squeezing the liquid onto the ground around the plants. Its own toxin would kill the Death Lily. It wanted to die. Except I had the impression killing these plants was more like cutting off a limb than ending the Death Lily's consciousness.

It released my hand and I held another two sacks. I quickly explained to Danny and Zila what we needed to do. Giving them each one of my throwing knives along with a stern warning to be careful with the sharp weapons, I sent them to the other Death Lilys. After they started, I grabbed my stiletto and cut a toxin sack open. I poured the poison around the base of the plant, then moved to the next one.

We worked as fast as possible. While the kids went deeper into the garden, I stayed on the outer rows. Because of the plague symptoms, I moved slower than the kids. I hoped I would get them to safety before I entered stage three.

Dawn was only a couple of hours away when we finished. At least I succeeded in one more thing. Tohon would have to plant a whole new garden of Death Lilys and wait for the Lilys to mature before he could start again. Perhaps by then Ryne and Estrid would be victorious.

The three of us cut through the dying garden to the back wall. Danny and Zila hesitated when they spotted the Peace Lilys. I assured them they wouldn't be snatched. We pushed through to the wall.

Danny climbed over first, then Zila and I followed. As I crested the top, I felt no guilt in breaking my word to Tohon. Kerrick had been right. Tohon was a madman and there was no way I'd leave Danny and Zila in his care.

A surprised cry sounded as I dropped to the ground. I straightened and spun. Standing at the edge of the forest,

Tohon held Zila, and Sepp had Danny's arm twisted behind his back. I almost wilted in defeat right there. Damn.

"So predictable, Avry," Tohon said. "I puzzled over why you would stay behind once Ryne had been rescued. Then I figured you had discovered my experimental children. Once I understood, all I had to do was assign a nurse to watch and wait. You didn't disappoint."

I glanced around, counting the soldiers. He'd brought six guards.

"You don't think we needed an army to handle a couple of kids and a dying healer?" Sepp's sneering tone bordered on incredulity.

"A healer who saved your life. As I recall, you almost died because Tohon had his dead soldiers capture me on my way to the cave. If it wasn't for Kerrick's timely rescue, you would not have survived your injuries."

Sepp glanced at Tohon with anger and horror creasing his brow. I used the distraction to pull a couple throwing knives.

"Don't listen to her," Tohon said. "I *allowed* Kerrick to rescue her. I needed to touch her before they discovered Ryne was missing to ensure she'd return to me." He studied me. "Is that all you have?"

It might not have helped me now, but I had planted a seed of doubt in Sepp's twisted mind. "I have this." I brandished my weapons.

"And if you move, I'll hurt this little girl. So I suggest you drop all your knives on the ground," Tohon said.

When I didn't, Zila cried out in pain. I tossed my weapons down.

"Now, lead the way back to the castle. If you try anything stupid, I'll hurt her again."

I noticed movement along the ground in my peripheral vision, but I kept my gaze on Tohon. "How could I do anything, Tohon? All I have left are these." I reached into my pocket slowly and withdrew my stones.

"What are they?" Sepp asked.

"Juggling stones. See?" I juggled the three rocks. Belen was right. They were the perfect size and weight. I did a bunch of tricks, reversing direction, throwing them high, then low, using one hand and doing a spin-throw combination.

Tohon and Sepp looked at me as if I'd lost my mind, but the guards and the kids watched fascinated. Good. No one noticed the vines creeping around their legs. And Kerrick had called *me* stubborn. The man was supposed to be long gone by now.

At the first shout of alarm, I threw my rocks as hard and fast as I could. One hit Tohon square on the forehead. The second cracked Sepp in his temple. Both men let go of their hostages when hit.

"Run," I yelled to Danny and Zila.

They bolted into the woods as Kerrick, Ryne, Quain and Loren took advantage of the surprised guards whose feet were entangled in the vines. I dove for my knives.

But Tohon had already read the situation. Knowing his guards wouldn't last long, he took off with Sepp close on his heels, heading back to the safety of his castle. And a lot more than six guards. I moved to give chase, but Kerrick clamped his hand on my shoulder, stopping me.

"We're in enemy territory. Don't worry, we'll take care of Tohon another day," he said. "Find the kids, we need to go. It's not safe here."

"No, it isn't. You should be long gone by now."

"Frustrating when someone doesn't follow logic and common sense. Isn't it?"

I opened my mouth, but he said, "We can argue about it later."

I nodded and searched the woods for Danny and Zila. They hid under a bush. I coaxed them from their hiding spot and held their hands as we followed Kerrick to the north.

It was the longest, hardest, most exhausting trek in my entire life. Every inch of my body ached. Chills followed flashes of heat. Sweat gushed from my skin only to freeze a few minutes later.

The forest blurred into a green-hued watercolor painting. I lost track of time. When my body reached its limit, I tripped over my own feet and fell flat on my face. Content to remain there, I waved the others on. They wouldn't leave me. Picked up and cradled like a baby, I nestled against Kerrick's chest and fell asleep.

I woke…later. A bright campfire burned. Shadows danced on stone walls. Another one of Kerrick's caves. I almost groaned aloud.

"Avry? How do you feel?" Ryne asked.

"Like I've been squashed by Belen."

He laughed. "At least you still have your sense of humor."

I sat up. The cave spun and I put my head in my hands to keep from passing out.

"Here, eat." Ryne held out a bowl of meat. "It's fresh venison."

My stomach churned at the smell. "Save it for the kids." I glanced around. "Where are they?"

"They're with Kerrick. He's giving them a tour of the caves. They were quite fascinated by them. And Loren and Quain are on watch." Ryne filled a spoon with meat. He aimed it at me. "Are you going to eat or do I need to force-feed you?"

I growled.

"You'll feel better. I know."

"Fine." I snatched the spoon and bowl. Once I started eating, my stomach settled. When I finished every last morsel, I asked Ryne why they hadn't left for safer ground days ago. Once Tohon returned to his castle, I was sure he'd send out squads of his soldiers, both living and dead, after us.

"You know the answer."

Because Kerrick wouldn't abandon me. "Well, you're all going to leave tomorrow. I don't want anyone to stay and watch me die."

"You're going to need care."

"No. I don't want it."

"I don't think you'll have the choice," Ryne said.

"Then I'll run away."

He smiled. "Has that worked for you in the past?"

I huffed. "I saved your life—aren't you supposed to be nice to me?"

"I don't cater to whiners."

Checking my pockets, I searched for something to throw at him.

Ryne opened my bag and pulled out my juggling rocks. "Looking for these?" He dropped them into my hand.

My ire instantly dissipated. He had taken the time to find them for me. I rubbed my fingers along the names. Belen, Kerrick, Quain, Loren and Flea. My keepers. "Can you read minds?" I asked.

"No. I'm good at reading people."

Giggles echoed. Kerrick's deep voice vibrated in my chest. I met Ryne's gaze. "You'll take good care of them?"

"I will." He stood and waved Kerrick and the kids over. "The meat's done and it's delicious."

The kids ran to Ryne. They wolfed their food down. Between bites they chattered nonstop about the caves, the stalagmites and milky deposits. Kerrick ate in silence, seeming content to listen to the kids.

After they finished eating, Ryne took them out to surprise the monkeys. "I'll bet they fell asleep on duty. Who wants to bet me?"

"I'll bet you they didn't," Zila said.

"Loser washes the dishes?" Ryne asked.

"Deal." She shook his hand.

I smiled. She was going to be trouble. My grin faltered when I caught Kerrick staring at me.

He moved closer. "Why didn't you tell me?"

This was the conversation I wanted to avoid. "I thought you knew."

He sputtered. "How could you think...? You're smarter than... No wonder you hated..."

It was fun watching him be so...flabbergasted—a whole new side of him. I suppressed a smile. "You did tell Belen that Ryne was all you cared about. That was after you hit me. Not your best moment."

Sad acknowledgment smoothed Kerrick's face. "No, it wasn't."

"What would you have done if you knew?" I waited even though his conflicted emotions shone clear.

"I wouldn't have pushed you so hard," he said.

"And if I'd decided to heal Ryne and you knew the consequences, you'd feel guilty. I'm right and you know it."

"I still feel guilty," he said.

"You shouldn't. I told you from the beginning that it was *my* decision. And as I recall, you couldn't threaten, bully, coerce, bribe or otherwise make me decide in Ryne's favor."

"I remember. It's etched in my brain."

"Good to know I made a lasting impression."

"Oh, you made an impression. Like a stone caught in my boot."

"Gee, Kerrick, don't get all mushy on me."

He appeared chagrined. "Sorry. It's been over four years since… I'm a little rusty."

"Just be yourself. No. Wait," I said in mock panic. "Don't be yourself. Be like Belen. A sweet, lovable type." I grinned.

"And what do you consider Belen?" he asked.

"A good friend. Why?"

"I don't want to be your friend, Avry." Kerrick stroked my cheek, then leaned in and kissed me.

It was a wonderfully sweet kiss at first. But he soon let me know sweet and lovable wasn't his style at all. Intense and passionate would be a more accurate description. As desire swept over me, I didn't want to be his friend, either.

We broke apart when Zila rushed up to us to inform us that Prince Ryne would be doing the dishes tonight.

"Good," Kerrick said. "If you had found the monkeys asleep, then they would be doing the dishes for the rest of the trip."

She giggled. It took a while to settle both kids down, but soon their exhaustion caught up to them and they passed out.

"Here's the plan for tomorrow," Kerrick said. "Ryne, Quain and Loren will take the kids over the Nine Mountains to Ivdel. I'll meet up with you after—"

"You should go with them," I said. "With Tohon's patrols, they'll need your magic—"

"Not happening. Unless you're coming with us?"

I had depleted my strength getting here, and I wouldn't let Kerrick carry me again. "I can't."

"Then I stay with you."

"Can't I at least—"

"No."

Biting my lip, I kept quiet as Kerrick and Ryne discussed routes and strategy. Relieved to have company for my final days, I still worried over the unnecessary risk of sending the others on without Kerrick. Since changing Kerrick's mind was impossible, I decided to stop fretting over everyone else. It was time for me to be selfish for once.

In the morning, I pulled Danny and Zila aside. I gave Danny my journal, explaining as much about healing and a healer's powers as I could.

"I'm sorry, but I won't be here to teach you, but when you feel that tug, that desire to help another, to heal him, just let it go." I described the sensation.

Danny didn't like the idea of leaving me.

"Don't worry," I said. "These men are good. They're going to heal the world."

"But no one likes healers," Zila said. She was unusually subdued.

"If you develop the power, they'll accept you both. You're not tainted by the past. You'll be considered miracles." I hugged them. "You are miracles." Then I said goodbye to Ryne, Quain and Loren and shooed them all on their way before I cried.

Kerrick accompanied them for a bit, showing them the path. When he returned it seemed as if the cavern warmed. Or it could be due to the plague. Stage one had lasted seven days, and I was three days into stage two. I estimated I had another five days until stage three. Five days with Kerrick and then...

"Finally, I have you all to myself," he said, sitting next to me.

"So what do you want to do? Play cards, plot how you can defeat Tohon, or reminisce?"

Instead of answering, he drew me down with him onto my bedroll and kissed me. Passion and desire flared, igniting a fever within me. A good fever that prompted me to tug at his clothes with impatience.

He broke off the kiss and grinned. "Easy."

"Not this time." My hands sought skin.

Once I pulled his shirt off, I ran my fingers over his smooth back. He yanked off my tunic and distracted me from my explorations by kissing my neck. Soon there was nothing between us. Kerrick took the lead as I had no experience.

But I caught on quick. Every part of my body hummed and sang with his every movement. Waves of delightful heat pounded through me. When he whispered my name, shivers raced along my skin.

Afterward we lay together, still entwined. My aches and pains forgotten and replaced by a contented tingle.

Half-asleep, I protested when he moved, turning so he was behind me. Tucking me close, he pulled a blanket over us.

"Better?" he asked, draping an arm over my shoulder.

I snuggled against him. "Yes."

Unable to remain still for long, he swept my hair from my face and smoothed it. "After all that has happened, I can't believe you're here with me."

"I'm having a hard time believing it, as well."

"You were with Tohon for twenty-seven days. He could have done anything to you. And when I saw you kissing him, I feared the worst."

"All he managed was a couple of kisses."

"I know now. But that wasn't it. I feared I had lost you without ever telling you how I felt."

"Is that why you risked your life to talk to me in the garden?"

"Yes, and then you didn't say a word."

"You surprised me. Plus I wanted to keep everyone at a distance. I'd already decided to heal Ryne. Being close to someone would make it that much more difficult for me to give up my life for Ryne."

"Yet, you didn't hesitate to heal him. Does that mean—?"

I rolled over to face him. "No, it doesn't. Despite my best intentions, I spent those twenty-seven days thinking of you. Every day I smelled spring sunshine and living green. Drove me crazy."

He looked confused.

"That's your scent. It's imprinted on me and I can't get enough of it."

"I thought you said I stunk?"

"I lied."

A slow smile curled his lips. "Prove it."

I did. In fact, I proved it multiple times over the next four days. It was the best four days of my entire life. I thought it a perfect way to spend the time.

Reality hit me in the form of a sudden convulsion early on the fifth morning. I had entered the third and final stage of the plague.

When Kerrick returned from washing up, I worked on one of my juggling stones. Using a rock and a throwing knife, I chiseled my name into the opposite side of Flea's. I thought it fitting that we would share the stone.

"What are you doing?" he asked.

I finished and blew the dust from the grooves. "Here." Handing him the three rocks, I said, "Please give them to Belen. Tell him he was right. They're keepers."

"Avry—"

"And if you can find my sister, please give this to her. I'd ask you to sit on her until she reads it, but I fear she's stubborn like me. Oh, and give my gloves, boots and cloak to Danny. They should fit him next winter."

"Avry—"

"My pouch is filled with Loren and Quain's favorite herbs and spices, so make sure they get it back. I don't have anything for Zila, but when you get to a safe place, please buy her a bunch of hair ribbons for me."

"Avry—"

"You can have my stiletto and throwing knives. I—"

Kerrick pulled me into hug. "What's going on?"

Another convulsion hit. My muscles trembled as I gasped for air. Pain twisted deep inside me. I held on to Kerrick until it stopped.

"Oh, no." His voice broke. "I'd hoped we'd have another good day."

"Can you do one last thing for me?" I asked.

Instantly wary, he peered at me. "I'm not hurting you."

"Not that. Can you find a Death Lily close by?"

"For after?"

"No. For now. This afternoon. You know how bad it gets in the third stage. I don't want to suffer and I don't want you to watch me suffer."

"And if I don't do it?" He didn't wait for my answer. "Then you'll go out and search on your own." His shoulders drooped in defeat. "All right. I'll be back."

While he was gone, I had four more convulsions. Each one stronger than the last. I focused on the peaceful detachment waiting for me inside the Death Lily in order to keep from screaming.

I noted with a sick interest how excruciating pain could take the fear right out of dying.

When Kerrick returned, I grabbed his hand, tugging him outside. "Come on before the next—" I doubled over.

By the time the convulsion dissipated, my legs would no longer support my full weight. Kerrick carried me. I had two convulsions before we reached the Lilys. He set me down. Leaning on Kerrick, I peered at the huge white flowers. There were three of them. I smelled a hint of anise. At least one was a Death Lily.

I hugged Kerrick and kissed him goodbye. "Please don't shut down for another four years. You'll find another pain-in-the-ass girl to drive you crazy. Just don't manacle her to a tree, okay?"

He smiled despite the tears streaking his face.

"And listen to Belen. Poppa Bear knows what's he's talking about." I kissed him again. A salty long one, before I pulled back.

Wobbling on unsteady legs, I limped to the Lilys. The scent of anise grew stronger, coming from the middle one. I approached the one in the middle. A hiss sounded as its petals parted. I turned and met Kerrick's gaze before being engulfed in the comforting darkness.

Two pricks stabbed my arms, and I floated free of my pain-filled body. I relaxed, drifting. The Death Lily shifted. *Taste bad.* The thorns retreated. It spat me out.

Now I cried. I huddled on the ground and sobbed.

Kerrick crouched next to me in concern. "What happened?" he asked.

I wiped my eyes, trying to get my emotions under control. Above Kerrick, the Lily on the right hissed. Its petals opened. Without thought, I pushed him out of the way. It snatched me instead. There were two Death Lilys in this small patch. I waited to be expelled.

But this one was...odd. Instead of blackness, there was a fuzzy white light as if the petals were translucent. It smelled of vanilla. Two thin tendrils wrapped around my upper arms, then dug in with what felt like a hundred little barbs. I yelped in surprise and pain. My consciousness didn't float but I sensed another's presence with me.

Feelings of pride and ownership overwhelmed me as if the Lily thought of me as its child. *Our healer.* Then it injected a cold liquid into my arms. The icy toxin numbed at first, then burned like acid. I jerked. The convulsions were mild in comparison to this agony.

I writhed and screamed and yelled until I lost my voice. It felt as if the Lily was digesting me from the inside of my body to the outside. No matter which way I twisted, I couldn't get away from the burning torture. Finally, I curled into a tight ball.

Like a quick puff of air blowing out a candle's flame, my world ended.

I woke in Kerrick's arms. Head bowed, his eyes were closed. Had he stopped me from going to the peaceful after-life again? All my muscles ached. A rank cottony taste filled my mouth. My throat burned. Pins and needles swarmed over my hands, arms, feet and legs as if all my limbs had fallen asleep.

"Wh—?" My voice croaked.

Kerrick's eyes snapped open. He stared at me in astonishment.

Not able to talk, I raised my eyebrows, inviting him to explain.

He pressed two fingers to my neck, feeling my pulse.

"Ke—" I squeaked.

"A Peace Lily grabbed you. A Peace Lily!" He blinked.

Unheard of, but it explained the white light and soothing scent. But not the excruciating pain. I waved for him to continue.

"You cried out in such misery…but I couldn't free you. We should make body armor out of their petals. My knife didn't make a dent."

I tapped his chest.

"Oh…sorry." He smiled and stared at me again.

This time I punched him on the shoulder.

"The Lily eventually spat you out like the other had. Except…" His grin faded. "You were dead." He shuddered at the memory. "But now you're…not."

I considered. Peace Lilys must also contain a toxin. So I died from the Peace Lily's toxin, but still haven't died from the plague. Which meant I'd soon be dead again. And my attempt to cheat the plague had completely and utterly failed.

I struggled to stand, but Kerrick wouldn't let me. He carried me back to the cave and tucked me under the blanket. I fell asleep waiting for the convulsions to begin anew.

Except a funny thing happened. My health improved. I worried the symptoms would return, but after a few days without pain, I stopped panicking over every twinge and cramp.

"The Peace Lily cured you," Kerrick said.

His mood during the past couple days had been positively buoyant. I'd never seen him this way before. "But why didn't it help the thousands who suffered and died from the plague? Plus I was around all those Lilys by Tohon's castle walls when I was sick. None of them had moved. Why now? Why me? No one has survived the plague. It isn't possible."

Kerrick considered. "You didn't survive. I wasn't imagining it. You had no heartbeat, no signs of life at all. The way you described the agony from the flower's poison, it seems as if the Lily accelerated the plague inside you until you died."

It had certainly felt that way. "Then how did I come back to life?"

He shrugged. "Don't know. Don't care. I consider it a gift." He leaned close, kissed me and proceeded to unwrap his gift, distracting me from my churning thoughts.

Much later, as we sat around the fire, Kerrick handed me my things that I had given to him. "Looks like you're going to have to deliver Noelle's letter yourself."

And I'd promised Estrid I would return—I'd return for Noelle regardless, but still. However, all the rest of those problems I'd been happy to leave behind remained. I thought my job was done after I'd healed Ryne. He was supposed to fix everything, returning the survivors' lives to normal.

We had to find a way to stop Tohon and his army of living and dead soldiers. He had Sepp on his side now, which would make it harder. Jael tried to kill me and Kerrick. I'd injured her, so I was pretty sure she would be seeking revenge. Danny and Zila would need to learn how to be healers. The list went on.

At least I'd struck Tohon a major blow. He'd lost Ryne, Danny, Zila, a healer and his Death Lily patch. All because of me. Pride and a sense of accomplishment filled me until I remembered about the Peace Lily. More research into both the Death and Peace Lilys was needed. I felt I'd just scratched the surface of what these Lilys meant to the survival of our world. At least my pride remained.

As if sensing my thoughts, Kerrick pulled me close. "There's still a long way to go to put things right."

"I sense a *but* coming."

"However…" He quirked a smile. "You promised Danny we were going to heal our world. We can't do it without our healer."

"One healer might not be enough for what needs to be done," I said.

"Take it one task at a time. You've already checked off quite a number of them. Ryne." He mentioned the impact my actions had on slowing down Tohon's plans. "And you broke through the ice around my heart. Belen will be ecstatic. He'd thought it impossible. I did, too. And I won't miss him calling me a cold heartless bastard about my behavior toward you."

I laughed. "I don't remember that last task on my to-do list. Do I get extra credit for it?"

"Most certainly. I plan to atone for all my boorish behavior." He wrapped his arms around me and nuzzled my neck. "Starting now."

★ ★ ★ ★ ★

Look out for more of Avry's adventures,
coming in 2013!

Acknowledgments

Novel number nine has a nice ring to it. Don't you think? For the longest time, this book was either called the healer story, by my publisher/editor, or novel number nine by me. And yes, that's why the mountain chain is called the Nine Mountains. I can also think of nine people who I need to thank for helping turn this idea I had into a story.

My daughter, Jenna, for asking every night, "What's next?"

My agent, Bob Mecoy, for his help in sharpening the idea and selling it to MIRA.

My editor, Mary-Theresa Hussey, for her feedback and for the title of this and the next two books.

Assistant editor, Elizabeth Mazer, for all she does in getting the manuscript ready.

To my critique partner, Kim J. Howe, for all the comments and suggestions to improve this story.

My assistant, Becky Greenly, for helping with organizing the increasing number of reader emails and for getting the mail out so I have more time to write.

My niece and researcher, Amy Snyder, for finding cool little-known facts about the Black Death.

My husband, Rodney, for holding down the fort while

I'm out and about promoting books and for finding those misplaced commas and gaps in logic.

My son, Luke, for learning how to juggle and inspiring the character Flea.

Thanks so much!

I also need to thank the following nine groups of people who also work hard on my books and who have supported me and my books.

The art department for, once again, creating the perfect cover.

The public relations, marketing and sales departments for continuing to get the word out about my books.

Those who worked on the copy edits and line edits.

The digital team for ensuring all my books are available as ebooks and audio books.

Dianne Moggy and Reka Rubin for coordinating and selling my foreign rights.

To my local community for all the support and kudos.

To Seton Hill University's MFA program students and staff for the support, motivation and inspiration—every residency is a shot in the arm.

To my Book Commandos for their continuing loyalty and for recommending my books to everyone you meet.

To my extended family for the love and support as I continue to write books. Amazing, I know! And a shout-out to my father—who reads every book despite not being a reader and who tells everyone he knows about me whether they want to know or not. Thanks, Dad!

Thank you all!

CHOOSE:
A QUICK DEATH...
OR A SLOW POISON...

About to be executed for murder, Yelena is offered the chance to become a food taster. She'll eat the best meals, have rooms in the palace – and risk assassination by anyone trying to kill the Commander of Ixia.

But disasters keep mounting as rebels plot to seize Ixia and Yelena develops magical powers she can't control. Her life is threatened again and choices must be made. But this time the outcomes aren't so clear...

www.mirabooks.co.uk

MIRA

CONFRONTING THE PAST, CONTROLLING THE FUTURE

With an execution order on her head, Yelena must escape to Sitia, the land of her birth. She has only a year to master her magic – or face death.

But nothing in Sitia is familiar. As she struggles to understand where she belongs and how to control her rare powers, a rogue magician emerges – and Yelena catches his eye.

Suddenly she is embroiled in a battle between good and evil. And once again it will be her magical abilities that will either save her life…or be her downfall.

www.mirabooks.co.uk

MIRA

THE APPRENTICESHIP IS OVER – NOW THE REAL TEST HAS BEGUN

When word spreads that Yelena is a Soulfinder – able to capture and release souls – people grow uneasy. Then she receives news of a plot rising against her homeland, led by a murderous sorcerer she has defeated before.

Honour sets Yelena on a path that will test the limits of her skills, and the hope of reuniting with her beloved spurs her onward. Yelena will have but one chance to prove herself – and save the land she holds dear.

www.mirabooks.co.uk

MIRA

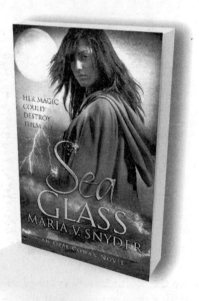

UNTRAINED. UNTESTED. UNLEASHED.

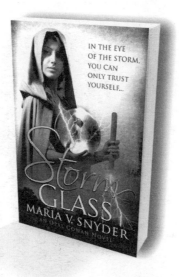

When the Stormdancer clan needs help, Opal's
knowledge and unique magical abilities make her
the perfect choice – until the mission goes awry.

Now Opal must deal with plotters out to
destroy the Stormdancer clan, as well as
a traitor in their midst.

With danger and deception rising around her,
will Opal's untested abilities destroy her –
or save them all?

www.mirabooks.co.uk